'TIS THE SEASON

For an instant family

for laughter and love, and sometimes…

miracles

Join

Judith Arnold

and

Pamela Browning

for two feel-good Christmas romances

Judith Arnold started telling stories before she could write. Since her first romance novel's publication in 1983, Judith has written more than seventy novels, with eight million copies in print worldwide. Throughout her career, she has received several awards from *Romantic Times Magazine*, including a Lifetime Achievement Certificate of Merit for Innovative Series Romance. She has also been a finalist for the Golden Medallion Award and the RITA Award from Romance Writers of America. She has written several plays that have been professionally staged at regional theaters in San Francisco, Washington, D.C., Connecticut and off-off-Broadway. Judith lives in Massachusetts with her husband, two teenage sons and a guinea pig named Wilbur.

Pamela Browning has written more than forty romance novels, and is also the author of award-winning novels and stories for children. She began her professional life as a newspaper columnist and reporter, and also teaches courses at writers' conferences. This winner of several national awards for her writing makes her home in North Carolina with her husband, and they are the parents of two grown children. In her spare time, she practices yoga, travels widely and volunteers as docent at a local art museum.

All They Want for

Christmas

Judith Arnold
Pamela Browning

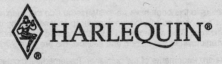

HARLEQUIN®

TORONTO • NEW YORK • LONDON
AMSTERDAM • PARIS • SYDNEY • HAMBURG
STOCKHOLM • ATHENS • TOKYO • MILAN • MADRID
PRAGUE • WARSAW • BUDAPEST • AUCKLAND

HARLEQUIN BOOKS

by Request—ALL THEY WANT FOR CHRISTMAS

Copyright © 2001 by Harlequin Books S.A.

ISBN 0-373-21725-0

The publisher acknowledges the copyright holders of the original works as follows:
COMFORT AND JOY
Copyright © 1987 by Barbara Keiler
MERRY CHRISTMAS, BABY
Copyright © 1993 by Pamela Browning

This edition published by arrangement with Harlequin Books S.A.

Visit us at www.eHarlequin.com

Printed in U.S.A.

CONTENTS

COMFORT AND JOY   9
by Judith Arnold

MERRY CHRISTMAS, BABY   265
by Pamela Browning

COMFORT AND JOY

Judith Arnold

Chapter One

Robin tore her eyes from the paper turkeys tacked to the bulletin board along the side wall and faced the front of the room again. She felt like a restless schoolchild—which wasn't surprising, given that she had spent nearly half an hour squeezed into an undersized chair attached to an undersized desk in Room 128 of the Brushy Plain Elementary School, listening to Ms. Becker describe, in an offensively chipper voice, what she had been doing with her seven- and eight-year-old charges for the past three months, and what she was planning to do with them for the rest of the term. The classroom's overhead fluorescent lights buzzed, the bright yellow walls cloyed and the green chalkboards gave off an aroma of dust. Every time Robin tried to squirm into a more comfortable position at the tiny desk, the soft soles of her loafers squeaked against the drab gray and beige linoleum floor tiles.

She forced herself to pay attention to what Ms. Becker was saying. "So, as you can see," the young woman at the front of the room chattered, "we did a great deal to commemorate Thanksgiving." Robin found the teacher's sunshiny smile and her singsong vocal quality oddly irritating. "But kids will be kids," Ms. Becker continued. "They're already badgering me about Christmas. So I've begun making plans for our class to celebrate that holiday, too. The turkeys were such a hit, I've prepared some lovely dittos of Christmas trees for the children to color in." She lifted from her desk a ditto stencil featuring an outline of a pine tree and displayed it for the parents.

Robin turned back to the side wall to study the turkeys. Twenty-four of them, each a blue ditto-ink outline decorated with individual touches by the children, each labeled with a student's name in the upper left-hand corner. Searching the row of drawings, Robin located the one with Philip's name printed on it. Bless him, she mused with a private smile. Not only had he crayoned most of his bird a garish orange, but in place of wings, he had drawn big purple hands.

Ms. Becker was less than inspiring. Robin should have given more weight to Philip's constant griping about his teacher. "She's *boring*," he frequently carped in his distinctive seven-year-old whine. "You know me, Mom, I can put up with a lot, but she's *boring*."

Robin had to agree. Her heart brimmed with sympathy for her son. The Branford, Connecticut school system wasn't the best in the world, but even here, teachers ought to know better than to stifle the creativity of their students by making them color already outlined pictures.

"In addition to decorating the trees, we'll be performing a classroom skit," Ms. Becker went on. "I've found a marvelous dramatization of Dickens's *A Christmas Carol* for the children to perform. I haven't cast any of the parts yet, but the children adore dramatic play. And, of course, it's a good learning experience for them. Dramatic play teaches co-operation..."

And it teaches how to take orders from a director,

Robin added silently. She tried to catch Joanna's eye, but Joanna was sitting sideways in the neighboring desk, her legs extended to her left and her back to Robin, her head angled over her right shoulder in order to see the teacher. Joanna was a good three inches taller than Robin; she was wise not to have bothered trying to fold her lanky limbs beneath the minuscule desk. Even so, Robin preferred banging her knees on the underside of the built-in book tray to courting a stiff neck. She was sure that Joanna would be in dire need of a chiropractor by the time they got home.

Robin reproached herself for dreaming about returning home. Open School Night was too important; she owed it to Philip to learn everything she could about what was going on in his class.

"We're also going to have a grab-bag gift party," Ms. Becker announced. The perfect circles of her auburn curls bounced around her face as she spoke. Robin stared at the teacher's hair, attempting to guess whether it had been artificially permed. "If any of your children want to exchange presents on their own, I'd recommend that you make arrangements for that outside of class, so other children won't feel left out. But the grab-bag idea—about which you'll be receiving more details in a handout I'll be sending home with the kids—seems to me to epitomize the concept of Christmas as a time of giving. That's why I think it's so important that we celebrate these traditional rituals in class."

"Excuse me, Ms. Becker, but don't you think that celebrating Christmas in a public school might be riding roughshod over the Constitution?"

The voice came from the doorway, and, slamming her knees on the polished wood of the desk, Robin shifted in her chair to locate its source. A man was lounging

against the doorjamb, clad in blue jeans and a suede
bomber-style jacket unzipped to reveal a ribbed white
turtleneck sweater that hugged his chest in a supremely
attractive way. His body appeared hard and lean and
magnificently proportioned. Robin twisted deeper in her
seat to catch a glimpse of the face that accompanied
such a terrific male body.

She wasn't disappointed. The man was gorgeous.

"Whose daddy is that?" Joanna whispered.

The same thought crossed Robin's mind, but she
brushed it off with the irrational notion that anyone who
was so utterly good-looking couldn't possibly be a
daddy. The man had a thick mane of coal-black hair
that fell about his face in long windswept waves. His
eyes were nearly as dark as his hair, and they were set
deep beneath a high, fierce brow. He had a hawklike
nose, thin lips and a square jaw. Robin didn't know that
men so strikingly handsome actually lived in a town as
sleepy and predictable as Branford.

If they did, she surmised, they were already married,
the doting fathers of second-graders. Only a handful of
fathers had chosen to come to this Open School Night,
and even if the man in the doorway hadn't bothered to
take a seat inside the room, the fact that he was present
informed Robin that he cared more about his child than
most fathers did.

Robin didn't condemn the other fathers for their absence. Some, like Joanna's husband Glenn, were undoubtedly at home baby-sitting for their children so their
wives could attend Open School Night. Others, like
Robin's ex-husband, were no longer in Branford, and
therefore were unable to fulfill their parental obligations.
Robin had parked Philip at Joanna's and Glenn's house
for the evening. Their son Jeff was Philip's best friend,

and Robin was grateful to Glenn for forgoing the Open School Night so Joanna and Robin could be there.

Although she would rather have continued her admiring inspection of the stranger in the doorway, Robin directed her gaze back to Ms. Becker, who seemed rather flustered by the man's question. "Hello, Jesse," she said, managing a smile. Robin was surprised by the informality of Ms. Becker's greeting; the teacher always referred to parents by their last names.

He must be a friend of Ms. Becker's, Robin concluded. If not a student's daddy, he must be the teacher's boyfriend. Any man that handsome had to be already taken. Robin couldn't smother a spiteful twinge of envy that a teacher as mediocre as Ms. Becker could have snagged a hunk like the fellow standing at the classroom door.

If they were friends, though, or lovers, why was Ms. Becker looking so defensive? "I don't think there's any need to worry about the Constitution," she rationalized, partly to the man she'd called Jesse and partly to the assembled parents contorted in their tiny desk chairs. "We discuss Chanukah in class, too, of course. We discuss the history of this special Jewish holiday. It isn't as if we deal with Christmas to the exclusion of all other religious holidays."

"You discuss Chanukah," echoed the man. His voice was low and smooth, a rich, lustrous baritone that might belong to a disc jockey. He quirked one black eyebrow skeptically as he regarded the curly-haired teacher at the front of the room. "Do you also discuss the Eastern Orthodox Christmas? Tet? Native American seasonal rites? And let's not forget the winter solstice. Perhaps there are one or two druids in your class."

"Well…" Ms. Becker moistened her lips anxiously

and grinned. "The fact is, the children are the ones who want to discuss Christmas. I mean, it's all around them. Even before Thanksgiving, the stores were already starting to put up their Christmas decorations. And, let's face it, Christmas is a school vacation. I'm sure that makes it even more significant to them."

The man shrugged. Observing the graceful motion of his broad shoulders as they shifted inside his jacket, Robin sighed. She really ought to do something about socializing more, she chided herself. For all she knew, Branford was filled with plenty of equally stunning specimens of masculinity who weren't dating boring elementary school teachers. Being a divorced mother with a demanding job didn't leave Robin much time for meeting men, but...she ought to do something about reviving her social life. Maybe if she did, the man in the doorway wouldn't look quite so enchanting to her.

He made no move to enter the room, even though he had willfully intruded on the teacher's presentation. Robin wondered whether it was easier to attack Ms. Becker's methods when one wasn't doubled up on oneself inside a student-size desk and chair. She herself had a few critical remarks for Ms. Becker, but she preferred to wait until they could confer privately. Unlike the man in the doorway, Robin didn't want to embarrass her son's teacher in front of an attentive audience.

"Well," Ms. Becker said, tossing the man an edgy smile and then beaming at the roomful of parents. "I'd like the opportunity to meet each of you individually. So why don't you stand and stretch your legs and have a look at our displays, and I'll circulate among you."

Joanna immediately pried herself out of her seat and made a great show of unkinking her joints. Robin took longer to climb out of her chair, probably because she had been more deeply imbedded in it, and Joanna helpfully gripped Robin's arm to prevent her from falling while she wriggled her right leg out from under the book tray. "One more minute in that chair and I'd be crippled for life," Robin moaned.

Joanna laughed and tossed back the overgrown bangs of her shaggy brown hair with a flick of her head. "What do you think of Ms. Becker?" she asked Robin.

Robin rolled her eyes, then lifted her wool blazer from the back of her chair. "Not much, if you want to know the truth," she admitted quietly. "I'd like to think she's competent, but she certainly lacks pizzazz."

Joanna concurred with a nod. "Last August, when Dot Hasselhopf found out Joey was assigned to Becker's class, she made such a fuss that they reassigned Joey to Mrs. Greenblatt's class. Greenblatt's supposed to be the best of the second-grade teachers at Brushy Plain. Now I feel guilty that I didn't throw a tantrum, too."

"Don't feel guilty," Robin consoled her. Mothers had more than enough to feel guilty about these days without shouldering the blame for their children's fate in teacher assignments. "As soon as I get Becker alone for a minute," she warned Joanna, "I'm going to throw a very discreet tantrum. She probably isn't such a bad teacher—she's just young and relatively inexperienced. You and I know more about seven-year-olds than she could ever learn in her education courses."

"I'd like to join you in that tantrum," Joanna said wistfully. "But I've got to save my strength to face off with the snake. Jeff told me that if I didn't acquaint myself with the class's pet reptile, he'd never speak to me again." Shoring up her courage, Joanna stalked to the windowsill, which held a variety of science projects:

incubating eggs, grapes drying into raisins, slices of Wonder Bread sprouting turquoise mold, and, inside a large glass tank, a corn snake that, according to Philip, was named Cookie Monster because the children liked to feed him cookies from their lunch boxes. Fortunately, Philip hadn't issued any ultimatums about Robin's developing a personal relationship with Cookie Monster, and she kept her distance from the tank.

Scanning the room, she noticed Ms. Becker standing to one side of her desk, surrounded by a throng of jabbering parents. Robin slipped her blazer on, smoothed her hair back and refastened the barrette holding it in a limp ponytail. Her hair was as fine and blond as it had been when she was a toddler, but she no longer had the time to set it and condition it. It was so much easier just to pin it at the back of her head and be done with it.

On the other hand, she ruminated, thrusting her hands into the pockets of her blazer and ambling to the periphery of the mob surrounding Ms. Becker, maybe a permanent wouldn't take much effort to maintain. A few springy curls—nothing as tight and foamy as Ms. Becker's, but maybe a body wave...

"You're Philip Greer's mother, aren't you?" Ms. Becker picked Robin out of the crowd and extended her hand. "I'm so glad you came tonight. There's something I wish to discuss with you. Excuse me," she said to the other parents, gripping Robin's elbow and steering her toward the bulletin board.

A subtle but sickening sense of dread curled through Robin's gut. Was Philip in trouble at school? Was he failing his lessons or acting incorrigible? Why else would the teacher haul Robin off, sidestepping all the other parents, for a one-to-one chat?

Inhaling to steady her nerves, she asked, "Is there a problem with Philip?"

"I'm not exactly sure, Ms. Greer," Ms. Becker confided. "He's such a bright boy, his reading and arithmetic skills are way above grade level and he seems popular with his classmates. But...well, look at this." She pointed at the bright orange turkey with the purple hands. "He drew this," Ms. Becker declared.

Robin gave the drawing a closer perusal. All right, so his orange scribbles had strayed across the dittoed outline in a few places. So he'd added nearly invisible blue antennae to the turkey's head. So what?

She turned to the teacher and awaited an explanation. *"Hands,"* Ms. Becker murmured ominously. "He drew *hands* on his turkey. Doesn't that strike you as...as somehow perverse?"

Robin suppressed a grin. If Ms. Becker hadn't already figured out that ninety-nine percent of all seven-year-olds were perverse, she ought to tear up her teaching certificate and try another line of work. "Did you question him about it?" Robin asked. "I'm sure he had a perfectly sound reason for giving his turkey hands instead of wings."

"Well, yes, I did question him," Ms. Becker conceded. "He told me that his turkey came from another planet—Geek or Bleep or something—"

"Gleek," Robin supplied. Gleek was a make-believe universe Philip had invented a few months ago. Whenever Robin ordered him to do something he didn't want to do, he would argue that on Gleek, the kids never had to make their beds or pick up their dirty clothes or do their homework when "Masters of the Universe" was on TV.

"That's right. Gleek," said Ms. Becker with a vigorous nod. "He told me that on Gleek the turkeys always have hands because turkeys can't fly anyway, so their wings don't serve any purpose, and because nobody likes to eat the wings at Thanksgiving. He told me that Gleekians—or whatever he called them—decided to breed their turkeys to have something useful, like hands, instead of wings."

The explanation struck Robin as brilliant; she had yet to meet anyone who liked to eat turkey wings. But she didn't want to come across as a gushing mama, so she only smiled. "Philip has an active imagination," she granted, "and I like to encourage him. Ms. Becker—it's only a suggestion, but instead of making the children color in your pictures, why don't you let them draw their own? Why not have them cut trees out of construction paper, any shape they want—and any color, for that matter—and then they can cut out decorations and glue them on. I know it's not my business to tell you how to run your class, but I think the children would enjoy the project a whole lot more if they got to design their own trees."

"Construction paper..." Ms. Becker gave the idea solemn consideration. "I'm afraid that's the art teacher's domain."

"Then let them make their trees during the art period," Robin advised, hoping she didn't sound too presumptuous. "I think it would be more challenging for them to make their own trees. And instead of having them enact *A Christmas Carol*, why not let them write their own skit? They might come up with a story closer to home, something they can identify with. Dickens is wonderful, but if you really want the kids to enjoy dramatic play, why not let them write their own dramas?"

Apparently she *was* coming across as presumptuous.

Ms. Becker pursed her glossy pink lips and her eyes narrowed on Robin. "Ms. Greer, these are second-graders. If there's a budding Shakespeare among them, that's just fine. But really, they need direction, they need guidance—"

"And they need a little freedom to use their imaginations," Robin asserted. It was too late to back off; her only concern was that Ms. Becker shouldn't take out on Philip her resentment of Robin's attack. "They don't have to be Shakespeare. They just have to have the opportunity to invent their own worlds every now and then. Like Gleek. I'd be willing to bet at least half the kids in the class escape to an imaginary place like Gleek every now and then."

"Well," Ms. Becker said with a dubious huff. "I'll...I'll think about it."

"Good." Realizing the need to appease the teacher, Robin added, "I think you're doing a terrific job, and Philip's learning a great deal." The part about the terrific job Ms. Becker was doing was an overstatement, but Philip *had* learned a great deal in the class so far, and Robin felt that a compliment was in order. Thirty-three years of living had taught her the benefits of diplomacy.

Ms. Becker's face brightened. "Thank you, Ms. Greer. I confess, this has been an extremely rough autumn for me, but I'm glad to know I'm reaching the children."

Robin nodded and bade the teacher a polite farewell. *An extremely rough autumn,* she pondered, watching as Ms. Becker was engulfed by another swarm of avid parents. Although Robin's primary concern was for her son, she felt a pang of sympathy for the young woman. Obviously she was coping with problems that had noth-

ing to do with her pupils. She was only human, a fact
that seven-year-old boys generally didn't take into account when crabbing about their teachers.

"You told her off, didn't you."

The voice floated over Robin's shoulders from behind, deep and mellifluous. It seemed to enter her mind
not through her ears but through some other, secret
route. It was low, seductive, insinuating, and it made
her scalp tingle. She spun around and found herself staring into the dark, luminous eyes of the man Ms. Becker
had called Jesse.

Close up, he was even better looking than he'd been
from afar—as if that were possible. He towered six or
seven inches over Robin, his eyes were adorned with
the thickest lashes she had ever seen on a man, he
smelled of leather and spice, his denim-clad hips appeared slim and firm... She felt inundated by a disor-
derly barrage of perceptions of the man. His smooth,
bronze-tinged cheeks. His laugh lines. His Adam's apple. His long legs.

And that honey-sweet voice. "Jesse Lawson," he introduced himself, reaching out to shake her hand. Jolting
herself from her daze, Robin pulled her hand from her
pocket to accept his. "And you're...?"

"Philip Greer's mother," she said automatically, then
bit her tongue. With so many people—particularly in
the context of school—she identified herself not as an
individual but as a parent. It had been that way ever
since Philip was born; she had gotten to know other
parents in terms of their children. "Hi, you're Becky's
mom, aren't you?" she'd greet a familiar woman at the
supermarket. Or, "I remember you—Eddie Romano's
folks," when a couple wandered into Woodleigh's and
accosted Robin at work.

Introducing herself as Philip's mother seemed natural to Robin not only because it was Open School Night but because she was busy racking her brain to recall if Philip had ever mentioned a classmate named Lawson. Maybe Jesse was someone's stepfather, and the child had a different surname. Like Philip, many children came from broken families, and some of those families entailed remarriages or mothers keeping their maiden names or whatever. It was hard to keep track.

The sound of Jesse's sonorous laughter brought her attention back to him. "Philip Greer's mother," he repeated. "That's an awfully long name. What do people call you when they're in a hurry?"

She laughed as well. "Robin. Robin Greer." Jesse's smile was cool but pleasant in an undefinable way, and she felt herself relaxing. "Which kid is yours?"

His smile remained. "I haven't got a kid. I'm here as a favor to Eileen. She asked me to drop off some documents she's been waiting for."

It didn't take Robin much effort to remember that Ms. Becker's first name was Eileen. Little more effort was required to conclude that Jesse Lawson's relationship with Eileen Becker was of a personal nature. Oh, well, she consoled herself. If a man with Jesse Lawson's physical attributes could exist, there must be others similarly endowed, somewhere. Three years of celibacy was enough. It was definitely time for Robin to start exerting herself to meet men.

Even knowing that Jesse was unavailable, she couldn't smother a vague insecurity about her appearance. At one time she had been totally confident about her beauty. Back then, however, during her teens and twenties, she had taken pains to make sure she always looked her best. Besides curling and fussing with her

hair, she had lavished hours on her face, learning how
to use the most stylish cosmetics in the most effective
manner. She had dressed in chic apparel, and although
there was nothing inherently wrong about the bulky
crew-neck sweater and corduroy slacks she had put on
before leaving the house that evening, there was nothing
inherently right about them, either. The clothes just
hung there, serving a function, concealing a body that
might weigh one or two pounds less than it had during
Robin's adolescence but lacked the nubile lusciousness
of youth. Robin's breasts were flaccid, her skin was beginning to crinkle at the corners of her hazel eyes, her
hands were perennially chapped and manicures were a
distant memory. Divorced working mothers simply
didn't have the time to pamper themselves.

Ordinarily, Robin didn't waste her energy worrying
about the toll the years had taken on her. She was doing
splendidly, considering. The divorce had been amicable,
and Ray was as much a part of Philip's life as he could
be, given his constant traveling. Robin's career was
flourishing; a year and a half ago, she had been named
manager of the Branford outlet of Woodleigh's. She had
even had the good fortune to secure the services of Kate
O'Leary, a widow who lived down the street from
Robin and who welcomed the income Robin paid her
to watch Philip every weekday from three o'clock until
closing time at Woodleigh's. Robin couldn't complain.

Except that, standing barely three inches from Jesse
Lawson, she felt peculiarly inadequate. Not that Eileen
Becker was fashion-model pretty, not that the woman
had revealed outstanding intellect or dazzling talent, but
Robin suddenly found herself wishing that she wasn't
just another suburban single mother trying to keep the

scad of balls she was juggling from tumbling down around her head.

"I only caught part of her speech," he was saying, "but it sounded dull to me."

"Ms. Becker's speech?" Robin eyed the teacher, who was prattling to a rapt couple about their daughter's academic progress. "She's...a decent teacher," Robin allowed, figuring that it would be in poor taste to belittle the man's girlfriend to his face, even if he himself had just referred to her as dull. "I only wish that she spent a little more time encouraging the kids to be independent, instead of turning them into conformists. They're going to be regimented enough in the upper grades. But when they're this young..." Realizing that she was rambling, she cut herself off and smiled sheepishly.

"I agree," said Jesse. "Not that I'm an expert when it comes to children, but, sure, they ought to be independent. Independence is too important to squelch, no matter what the age."

Robin assessed his statement. Despite his charming smile, he sounded awfully solemn. Then she remembered his interruption during Ms. Becker's presentation, when he had alluded to the constitutional separation of church and state. He must be a fanatical patriot, she deduced, enamored of independence as an American birthright. "Did you really mean that, about how celebrating Christmas in class is riding roughshod over the Constitution?"

His eyes darkened briefly, and then he shrugged again, moving his shoulders in that delightfully languorous fashion of his. "I think there's too much emphasis on Christmas."

"Too much? How can there be too much emphasis on something so wonderful?" As far as Robin was concerned, there could never be too much Christmas. Woodleigh's was one of those stores that had put up Christmas decorations before Thanksgiving, and Robin was all in favor of that. She loved the baubles and evergreen sprigs, the crystal snowflakes she and her staff had hung from the ceiling. She had already arranged for a delivery of a half cord of split logs to her house; she had considered and discarded at least three menus for Christmas dinner, and she was praying for snow. The holiday couldn't come soon enough—and it would be gone much too soon, she knew.

Jesse's attention had turned to the bulletin board. "Philip," he reflected, locating the bizarre orange-and-purple turkey. "Your son drew this?"

"Yes."

Studying the picture, Jesse frowned slightly. "Are the hands supposed to signify something?"

Robin laughed. "I guess they're supposed to signify that Philip has a mother who encourages independence rather than conformity."

Jesse's smile returned as he rotated back to her. "And what does Philip's father say about that?"

"Not much," Robin answered. "Philip's father and I are divorced."

"Ah." Something sparked in Jesse's eyes as they roamed across her small, hollow-cheeked face, and one corner of his mouth skewed upward in a lopsided smile. Then his gaze drifted past Robin and snagged on Ms. Becker. "If you'll excuse me for a minute, I think Eileen is temporarily free."

Robin watched him stride down the side of the room to the teacher, who had extricated herself from yet another cluster of parents. The babble of voices in the room remained at a steady, raucous pitch, and Robin sidled along the rows of desks to get closer to Jesse. Eavesdropping wasn't the most polite thing to do, but she was curious to know why her mention of her divorce had caused Jesse to abandon her. Besides, he had eavesdropped on her conversation with Ms. Becker. Fair was fair.

He reached into his hip pocket and pulled out a legal-size envelope. "Here you go," he said, handing it to Ms. Becker. "Signed, sealed, delivered. I imagine congratulations are in order."

Ms. Becker appeared flustered again, and then suddenly grateful. Her eyes glistened slightly as she accepted the envelope from Jesse. "I really appreciate your coming down to the school just to bring this to me, but since I'm going out with some of the other teachers afterward, and I probably won't be getting home till late—"

"I saw your note, Eileen. And I assure you, it was no problem."

"It's just—I wanted it in my hands, tonight. Just to get it over with, to have it with me—"

"I understand."

Ms. Becker's teary eyes met Jesse's for a moment. "Are you sure I can't pay you for this?"

"Positive," he said gently. "All it entailed was a couple of telephone calls."

"Perhaps you'd let me treat you to dinner or something?"

He shook his head. "No thanks, Eileen. Really. It wasn't any trouble. I'm glad I could help."

If he refused an invitation for dinner with Ms. Becker, Robin analyzed, then they couldn't be lovers. That understanding shouldn't have made any difference to her, but an unjustifiable sense of elation filled her. Not that a rusty, dowdy, out-of-practice divorced mother like her could ever instill more than a passing interest in a man like Jesse Lawson. But if he wasn't taken, then there must be others who weren't, either. Robin instantly began her mental list of New Year's resolutions with a promise to start putting forth an earnest effort to meet men.

She hadn't expected Jesse to turn around so suddenly. He found her standing indefensibly close to him, and her abashed expression informed him that she had overheard his conversation with Ms. Becker. Yet instead of appearing angry, he smiled. "That's my good deed for the day," he said. "I think I deserve extra credit for doing it in front of a witness."

"Your good deed?" she mumbled, trying unsuccessfully to hide her chagrin.

"Eileen's a neighbor of mine." He didn't owe Robin an explanation, and she considered pointing that out to him, but he didn't give her a chance. "She needed some minor legal assistance, and I was able to help her out with it."

Legal assistance. The man was a lawyer. That would explain the luxurious suede jacket.

That Jesse Lawson was rich as well as handsome struck Robin as almost unreasonable. No man deserved to have that much going for him. "Your assistance couldn't have been all that minor if you raced all the way here on Open School Night just to make a delivery."

Jesse shrugged. "I was going to drop the papers off at her house this evening, but by the time I got home she had already left for school. She had taped a note to her front door, asking if I wouldn't mind bringing the papers here. She didn't want to have to wait until to-morrow.''

The only legal paper Robin had ever been that anx-ious to have in her possession was her divorce decree. The divorce had been so long in coming, and the ne-gotiations, although devoid of bitterness, had seemed to take forever. Robin's attorney had offered to mail her the decree, but she had insisted on driving over to his office on her lunch hour the day it was ready, just to have it in her possession.

An extremely rough autumn. Ms. Becker's words re-sounded inside Robin. "You handled her divorce," she blurted out, her exasperation with the teacher abruptly replaced by a tide of sisterly compassion. No wonder Robin's mention of her own divorce had spurred Jesse to perform his good deed.

He appeared surprised by the accuracy of Robin's guess. He glimpsed the teacher, whose smile as she con-ferred with another student's mother seemed more gen-uine than it had appeared when she'd been lecturing the parents en masse. Then his gaze returned to Robin. "I don't think she wants the news broadcast in a big way," he said.

"I won't breathe a hint of it," Robin promised, her-self surprised that she'd guessed right. Then another sur-prise jolted her—Ms. Becker had offered him payment, and he'd refused. What sort of lawyer didn't take money for his services? Although Robin's and Ray's divorce had been completely free of acrimony, although they had worked out all the details without a quibble, al-though Ray had willingly left her the house, given her custody of Philip, and volunteered both generous child support and a small monthly stipend until she had been promoted at work and insisted that the alimony was no longer needed—in spite of all that, their lawyers had pocketed hefty retainers for doing little more than filling out the proper forms.

"Why won't you let her pay you?" she asked Jesse, assuming that if he minded her probing he would have walked away from her by now.

He shrugged. "I didn't do much. She had her own lawyer negotiate the settlement, but he's away on vacation now, and the other side was sitting on the papers too long. I just called them for her and gave them a nudge."

Despite his modest claim, Robin was impressed by his refusal to accept money from Ms. Becker. Most lawyers would charge hundreds of dollars for making a single telephone call. Inspecting the fine suede of his jacket, she realized that Jesse must be so wealthy that a few hundred dollars more or less didn't matter to him. Even so, his gesture in helping out his neighbor was generous.

She turned away, following Ms. Becker with her eyes for a moment. Then she shook her head. "I'm sorry for her," she commiserated.

"Are you? You don't seem sorry for yourself."

Her head snapped back to Jesse. His face was impassive, and she recognized that he had simply stated the truth. "I'm not. It's hard at the beginning, but after a while, you become so involved in other things that it doesn't hurt anymore."

"If you're lucky," Jesse noted. "What other things are you involved in?"

"Philip," she said, then grinned. "Of course, Philip. And I've got the house, my job—"

"Where do you work?"

"Woodleigh's," she told him. "On the Post Road."

"Woodleigh's," he repeated uncertainly. "Is that a store of some sort?"

His ignorance startled her. Woodleigh's served an affluent clientele. Her store specialized in hand-blown crystal and hand-painted Ironstone, fine linens, Danish modern flatware, butcher-block computer desks, ceramic napkin rings, and all sorts of elegant knickknacks. There were currently four Woodleigh's outlets, all located in shoreline Connecticut towns, all catering to the upwardly mobile, the yuppies, lawyers who were likely to wear expensive leather jackets.

"Yes," she remembered to answer him. "It's a store. I'm the manager. And—especially at this time of year— I'm much too busy to sit around moping—"

"Green!" a familiar voice squawked shrilly into her ear. "Oh my God, it's green!"

Spinning around, Robin found Joanna glaring at one of the crayoned turkeys on the bulletin board, her hands on her hips and her face contorted in a grimace. "Hi, Joanna," Robin hailed her. "How was the snake?"

"Either he was sleeping or he was dead. I didn't bother to ask. But look at this, Robin! Jeff colored his turkey green!"

"What's wrong with green?" Robin asked, laughing. "At least his turkey has wings."

"Robin," Joanna said sternly. "I happen to make the best roast turkey this side of Chicago. You know that— you've had Thanksgiving dinner at our house two years running. Now, what do you think Jeff is trying to tell me when he colors his turkey green?"

"I think he's trying to tell you that green was the first crayon he pulled out of the box. Don't take it so personally," Robin comforted her.

Joanna started to laugh, too. Then her eyes wandered

past Robin and she fell momentarily silent. "Oh," she said contritely. "I'm sorry, I didn't mean to interrupt."

Robin bailed her out with a smile and a courteous introduction. "Joanna, this is Jesse Lawson. Jesse, Joanna Calloway."

Joanna shook Jesse's hand, then shot Robin a quizzical glance. "Lawson? I didn't know there was someone named Lawson in the class."

"There isn't," Jesse smoothly corrected her. His gaze shuttled between Robin and her friend, and he nodded. "It was a pleasure meeting you both," he said by way of parting. "Green is great, but—" his eyes lingered on Robin for a split-second longer "—purple hands are exceptional. You must be quite a mother, Robin Greer."

With an economy of motion Robin found strangely hypnotic, he pivoted on his heel and strolled out the door.

Robin and Joanna stared for a wordless minute at the empty doorway through which he'd vanished. Then they simultaneously turned to each other. "So?" Joanna prodded Robin, obviously brimming with curiosity. "I'm all ears."

"There's nothing to tell," Robin declared truthfully. "We talked for a few minutes, that's all."

"If he isn't someone's daddy, what was he doing here?"

"He's a neighbor of Ms. Becker's," Robin informed her. "He had to bring her some…some documents she wanted." Sworn to secrecy about the teacher's divorce, she wasn't about to say anything more, not even to her close friend.

"Is he single?" Joanna asked.

"How should I know?" The question irked Robin, mostly because she had failed to find out that vital piece of information. "All we did was talk about the hands on Philip's turkey."

Joanna assessed Robin dubiously. "He approached you," she pointed out. "I was watching."

"You were supposed to be looking at the snake," Robin scolded.

"Which would you rather look at, a comatose snake or that spectacular man? I hope for your sake he *is* single," Joanna said, zipping her jacket. "I'm all done here if you are. Let's go home and rescue Glenn."

Rummaging in her purse for her car keys, Robin followed Joanna from the classroom. As they walked through the building to the parking lot out front, she listened with half her brain to Joanna's report on what Matthew Florio's mother had said about the gym teacher and on the gossip about Emily Gelb's father's transfer to Dallas. With the other half of her brain, Robin mulled over Joanna's remark about how she hoped Jesse Lawson was single.

Why should Robin care whether he was? They'd passed the time for a few minutes, that was all. She wasn't apt to see him again. If she ever started dating—*when* she started dating, she silently amended—she would be smart to stick with safe men for her first few outings. Her definition of "safe" was not too affluent, not too good-looking, not too suave. Not possessed of a voice that could tame wild lions and croon colicky babies to sleep, that could cause a woman to suffer heart palpitations merely by saying, "You must be quite a mother, Robin Greer."

His voice had sounded so sweet when he'd uttered her name. Sweet, velvety, seductive, as if those two bland words contained intimate secrets. Robin fleetingly wondered what Jesse Lawson would sound like murmuring *real* intimacies, whispering erotic incantations, caressing Robin's soul with flattery, with vows...

Starting the station wagon's engine, she clicked on the radio. The car filled with a buoyant rendition of "Deck the Halls," its rousing melody effectively erasing the memory of the man's mesmerizing voice. Indeed, Robin concluded with a wry smile, someone like Jesse would sound absolutely foolish singing "Fa-la-la-la-la."

Chapter Two

Loosening the knot of the navy-blue scarf at his throat, Jesse climbed the stairs to Mrs. Selby's third-floor apartment. The elevator still hadn't been fixed, which was both good and bad. Good, because the broken elevator was a major item on the list of grievances that Jesse had filed with the court on the tenants' behalf. Bad, because women like Mrs. Selby shouldn't have to trudge up and down several flights of stairs every time they wanted to run an errand or visit a friend.

The elevator was broken, and bags of garbage were heaped along the curb outside. The corridors were strewn with more garbage, and the front door lock had been broken for nearly a year. A couple of the windows were laced with cracks. Most of the tenants had already moved away, but Mrs. Selby and a few others were staying on because they had no place else to go.

The exposed lightbulb on the ceiling of the third floor hallway had burned out, Jesse observed. He pulled a pad and pen from an inner pocket of his tweed blazer and made a note of it. One more grievance. He hoped that there wouldn't be too many more before the landlord felt compelled to rehabilitate the building. It was too close to being condemned—and if it was, Mrs. Selby and the others would have no choice but to move. Mr. Cabot was probably hoping for condemnation. He had made little secret of his desire to remove the rest of the tenants, raze the building, and sell the land. Even in the rundown New Haven neighborhood of Newhallville, a person could turn a tidy profit on the sale of a double-size lot like the one on which the tenement sat.

Jesse knocked on Mrs. Selby's door—the doorbell had stopped functioning ages ago—and listened to her plodding footsteps approaching the door from the other side. He heard the click of the peephole lid opening, and then the slip of the bolt being released. "Mr. Lawson," she greeted him, smiling and stepping aside so he could enter the apartment. "You're early. I was just making some lunch. You hungry?"

"No, thank you," he declined, closing the door behind him. His polite smile faded as soon as he heard the orchestrated melody emerging from the television set in the living room. *Blessings at Noon,* he identified the show from its familiar theme music. He walked briskly into the living room, where he found Mrs. Selby's one-year-old grandson asleep on the floor in front of the television set, a blanket covering him and a pacifier protruding from his mouth. *I don't blame you for wanting to sleep through this,* Jesse muttered silently, stepping over the baby to shut off the television.

"I was just watching that," said Mrs. Selby, squatting down to tuck the blanket more snugly around the baby. "I just love *Blessings at Noon.*"

"It's a stupid show," Jesse snapped, then berated himself for responding so sharply. Lots of people loved *Blessings at Noon.* According to last year's Neilsen ratings—

"Well, the choir, they sing so nice," Mrs. Selby explained. "And today, well, the Reverend Robert Shepherd had on this amazing girl. You wouldn't believe it, Mr. Lawson. Paralyzed from the neck down in a ski accident, and then she prayed and prayed and the Lord saw fit to let her regain the use of her hands. It was a miracle, Mr. Lawson, and I saw it with my own eyes, right there on the show. I saw that girl write her name and throw a baseball from her wheelchair."

"It wasn't a miracle," Jesse argued, unable to modulate his scathing tone. "Chances are, the girl's spinal damage wasn't as severe as originally thought. When people recover like that, it isn't because of divine intervention. It's because of excellent medical care and physical therapy. And hard work."

"I don't know," Mrs. Selby debated him. "She and the Reverend said, right there on the show, they said they prayed together and the Lord saw fit to make this girl's hands work again. And right now I'm just praying and praying that the Lord see fit to fix up this apartment before it falls down on our heads."

Jesse permitted himself a dry laugh. Prayer wasn't going to fix the apartment building. Even if the Reverend Robert Shepherd, his enormous staff and the entire Grace Cathedral Choir prayed for the tenement's redemption, it wouldn't do any good. The only way to save Mrs. Selby's home was through legal maneuvers, the class-action civil suit Jesse had just initiated, and a lot of pressure on the recalcitrant landlord. In other words, hard work.

"Come on," Mrs. Selby said, urging him into the tiny kitchen where a couple of frankfurters were boiling in a pot on the dilapidated gas stove. She waved Jesse to one of the vinyl chairs by the table, then busied herself pulling two hot dog buns from a plastic bag. "You sure

I can't feed you one of these?" she asked as he took a seat.

"I'm sure," he insisted.

"Some coffee, then," she decided, filling a kettle with water and setting it on another burner. "You must be hungry, a big man like you. I know my boy Gerald, when he's home on leave, he'd as soon clean out the refrigerator with his bare hands."

Gerald was Mrs. Selby's oldest child, and he was in the Navy. Lucky for him, Jesse thought, surveying the cramped kitchen. As it was, Mrs. Selby lived in the three-bedroom apartment with her four other children and the baby one of her daughters had given birth to, out of wedlock, at the age of fifteen. At least that daughter had returned to high school.

The weight of Mrs. Selby's life seemed to rest heavily on her shoulders. In her mid-forties, she looked at least ten years older. Her hair was more gray than black, and her posture was hunched, as if she were too fatigued to stand up straight. Not that Jesse could blame her. Her husband had died eight years ago, leaving her a minute widow's pension on which she was trying to raise her huge family. And she was desperately close to joining the ranks of the homeless, thanks to the mendacity of Mr. Cabot. It was no wonder she watched trash like *Blessings at Noon* and looked to the Lord for help. Until Jesse and the staff of New Haven Legal Assistance had entered her life two months ago, nobody else had bothered to lend a hand to Mrs. Selby and the other few stubborn tenants.

She handed him a cup of instant coffee and sat facing him at the table, her frankfurters rolling about on a chipped plate. Jesse took a dutiful sip of the coffee. It was weak but hot, and it thawed his chilled bones. His shirt, V-neck sweater, tweed blazer and scarf hadn't succeeded in keeping out the midday chill. Jesse never wore a suit and tie when he visited his clients. If he did, they wouldn't trust him. They'd think he was "The Man."

"Still having problems with the heat?" he asked Mrs. Selby.

She chewed, then swallowed and shrugged. "It comes and goes," she said. "Mostly comes, these days."

"That's good." He set his cup on the table and wrapped his hands around it to warm them. "I spent an hour this morning at the building inspector's office, and so far I've managed to persuade them not to condemn the building."

"Praise God," Mrs. Selby said with a sigh, and Jesse pressed his lips together to prevent himself from rebuking her about her useless faith. "They condemn this place, and we'll be on the streets. Or they'll put us in one of them hotels. You know as well as I do, there's no room in any of the projects."

"I've put you and the other tenants on the waiting list for public housing," Jesse informed her. "Just in case. But you're right—the list is long. We can't have this building condemned. Most of the building code infractions here are inconveniences, but they don't really constitute a risk to life or health. The light is out in the hall, by the way."

"Been out for four days," Mrs. Selby lamented. "I figure, Gerald's got leave for Christmas, I can get him to fix it."

"Don't," Jesse instructed her. "By the time he gets home, maybe we'll have prodded Mr. Cabot into action. I've begun formal proceedings against him. I filed the civil suit this morning."

"You did?" Her round brown eyes met Jesse's, glimmering expectantly. "How much you asking for?"

"A hundred and fifty thousand dollars per tenant," Jesse told her.

Mrs. Selby dropped her hot dog. "A hundred fifty thousand? Are you kidding?"

"No, but—"

"A hundred and fifty thousand dollars!" She clasped her hands to her breast, evidently transported. "I can't hardly think that big! What we could do with money like that—"

"Mrs. Selby, you're not going to wind up with that much money," he cautioned her.

"Well, I know, you take your cut, Mr. Lawson, but—"

"I don't take a cut," he explained patiently. "I'm on a salary from Legal Assistance. However, you should understand that the amount we're asking for is only a starting point. We want to shock the landlord into action. By asking for a large amount, we hope we can drag him to the negotiating table. We'd be willing to settle for much less."

"How much less?" Mrs. Selby asked suspiciously.

"If we can arrange to have all the infractions taken care of—plus a settlement of, say, two years' back rent plus interest…"

"Two years back rent." Mrs. Selby closed her eyes and calculated the amount. Her face fell. "That's less than five thousand dollars."

"Plus interest," Jesse reminded her. "Maybe more, maybe ten thousand per unit. And the repairs. It's better than living in a hotel, Mrs. Selby."

"I suppose it is," she allowed, nibbling on her frankfurter. "Better than we got now, too. 'Tween you and me, Mr. Lawson, I'd settle for a working elevator."

"You'll get that and more," he said. "At least, I hope you will. Now, as far as December's rent, did you write it out to the escrow account, like I told you?"

She scowled. "I don't see why I got to pay it at all, the way this place is falling to pieces."

"I understand your feelings. But you've got to keep paying the rent until this matter is resolved."

"I know you'll resolve it," Mrs. Selby said confidently. "I got faith in you, Mr. Lawson."

That's better than having faith in God and the Reverend Robert Shepherd, he grunted to himself as, a few minutes later, he took his leave of Mrs. Selby. She was typical of the sort who wasted their time with junk like *Blessings at Noon* and Shepherd's Sunday morning show, *Holy Hour.* His audience comprised the poor, the benighted, people struggling under a burden they were unable to comprehend. How much easier it was to send a check to the Reverend Shepherd's Grace Cathedral and send their prayers skyward than to raise arms against their self-serving landlords, to roll up their sleeves and exert themselves to improve their lot.

It had taken Jesse a long time to reach this level of cynicism, to break away from the powers that had once dominated his world. He, too, had believed, at first. Like the child he had been, he hadn't known any better, and so he'd tried his hardest to believe. Then he'd grown up and discovered the truth about outfits like the Grace Cathedral and its television empire. The money that flowed in was obscene in its quantity, and where did it go? Into the coffers of Shepherd and his henchmen, into the grotesque enormity of the cathedral, into the TV studio. "The more people we reach," Shepherd liked to preach, "the better we can do the Lord's work. So dig deep, brothers and sisters, and send us whatever you can. Let us extend our network into every home, into every heart, so we can bring our good work to all people."

"Hah," Jesse snorted out loud at his memory of Shepherd's sermons.

He had already visited the other tenants to update them on his legal action at the court and his success in stalling a condemnation of the building. Settling himself inside the Volkswagen Rabbit he'd bought second-hand when he moved to Branford last June, he remembered the Mercedes he'd left behind in Los Angeles. It didn't take a fleet of extravagant automobiles to do good work, any more than it took a religious broadcasting network or a flashy cathedral. It didn't take millions upon millions of dollars subtracted from the skimpy savings of impoverished believers. All it took to do good work was a humane attitude and a willingness to skip lunch every now and then.

Newhallville was dressed for Christmas, Jesse noted with another surge of cynicism. Some of the tenements were adorned with strings of colorful lights, and a number of windows had electric candles or silver stars displayed in them. The people who lived in those tenements could barely afford to live from one paycheck— or welfare check—to the next, yet they wasted money on inane decorations instead of buying themselves food, clothing, things that would truly make their lives better.

Jesse didn't consider himself a Scrooge—Scrooge was a miser, after all, and Jesse believed in giving. On the other hand, the hoopla attached to Christmas, the gaudiness and commercialism, set his teeth on edge. People called themselves Christians, yet they gave of themselves only one day a year. The whole thing was hypocritical, overdone, superficial. Doing good that one day freed people to be selfish and thoughtless the other three hundred and sixty-four days. The emphasis was wrong.

Something so wonderful... For not the first time that day, Jesse heard a soft, gentle voice echoing inside his skull, counteracting his irritation about the holiday. *How can there be too much emphasis on something so wonderful?*

Robin Greer. More than her voice had haunted him after he had departed from the elementary school the previous evening. At least a dozen times—hell, at least a hundred times—since he'd walked out of Eileen Becker's classroom, an image of the petite blond woman with the bright hazel eyes and even brighter smile had floated across his mind. Something in the intensity of her defense of Christmas struck Jesse as almost childlike in its exuberance, childlike and innocent and immensely appealing.

Not that Robin Greer was an innocent child. The woman managed a store, she raised a son, she was divorced...

That was part of it, too, he acknowledged as he started up the engine and waited for it to warm up so he could turn on the heat. Most of the divorced women Jesse knew were like his neighbor Eileen, infused with bitterness or brittle with rancor. Women like Eileen, or like that hard-bitten lady to whom Bill and Sally Hammond had introduced Jesse at their Thanksgiving party last week. Still something of a newcomer to the New Haven area, with absolutely no desire to fly back to Los Angeles to spend the holiday with his parents, Jesse had been delighted by the Hammonds' invitation. He hadn't known that within minutes of entering their house, he would be dragged across the living room to meet Tracy LaPorte. "She's a knockout, eh?" Bill had whispered to Jesse some time later, when Jesse had escaped from the woman's clutches long enough to flee to the kitchen for a drink of water.

Tracy LaPorte was a knockout—except for the rage seething just below her pretty surface, the resentment emanating from her. Less than ten minutes after they were introduced, Tracy had been enumerating for Jesse all the sins of her ex-husband. Her gripes differed from Eileen Becker's in the particulars, but in tone they were no less petulant than those of Eileen, or of any other divorcée's.

But Robin Greer—if she hadn't told him, he never would have guessed that she was divorced. She seemed so happy, so lively, so much at peace with herself.

He admired her feistiness in criticizing Eileen's teaching methods. He admired the fact that she had produced a son who drew hands on a turkey. When Jesse was seven, he would never have dared to commit such a bizarre act. He might have considered it, but he would have lacked the gumption to go through with it. Years of training, discipline and force-fed piety had driven his independence out of him. No wonder it had taken him this long to find the courage to leave that whole scene and forge a new life, faithful to his own ideals and nothing else.

He was still thinking about Robin Greer a few hours later when he'd finished up at his office and begun the short commute from New Haven to Branford, eight miles east of the city. He was still thinking of Robin's silky yellow hair and her delicate cheeks, her stunningly bright eyes. What he wasn't thinking about was the route he was taking until he found himself coasting off the turnpike several exits before the one he usually took. He would be able to get home from this exit; the Post Road paralleled the turnpike throughout most of southern Connecticut.

With an amazed smile, he understood why he'd taken the wrong exit onto the Post Road. If he traveled home this way, he'd pass Robin's store. Woodson's, he thought it was called. Woodson's, or Woodmont's, or Woodsomething. Crossing the town line into Branford, he slowed enough to read the signs marking the numerous stores that bordered the road. Woodson's could be anywhere along the route; it could be any one of those countless stores trimmed with blinking lights and electrified Santa Clauses, plastic wreaths and tinsel garlands.

Woodleigh's. That was it, Woodleigh's. Applying the brakes, Jesse navigated into the parking lot and coasted to the first parking space he found. Then he locked the car, strode to the building and shaded his eyes as he peered through the broad panes of the glass front wall. The displays lining the windows featured attractive modern stained-wood tables festooned with holly and poinsettias, red and green tapers protruding from silver candlesticks, decanters wrapped in red ribbons and delicate, hand-crafted Christmas tree ornaments. Beyond the window display, he saw more of the same—elegant housewares, table settings and carved wooden train sets, all sprayed with tiny flecks of rainbow created by the light from the overhead fixtures passing through the crystal stars dangling from the ceiling. A dwarf Christmas tree stood on one end of the polished wood sales counter at the center of the store.

The sight of so much seasonal detritus almost caused

Jesse to leave the shop without entering. Stores like Woodleigh's lived for Christmas—he assumed that they raked in unconscionable profits at this time of year.

And yet…and yet he couldn't shake the image of a lovely blond woman somewhere within that room full of holiday merchandise, a cheerful woman with penetrating eyes and a son who gave his turkey hands. Jesse drew in a deep breath and entered.

GLANCING UP from the cash register, Robin saw him standing beneath the mistletoe.

The mistletoe had been hung above the front door by the salesclerks as a gag. It was hardly noticeable to unwary customers, and the clerks had strung it up with the notion that if a foxy-looking man happened to venture into the store, they'd have a perfect excuse to fling themselves upon him and bury him in kisses. Not that they would actually do anything that forward—they'd have to answer to Jack Woodleigh himself if they did. But since they were supposed to approach any customer who remained loitering too long near the front door, the mistletoe gave them an added incentive to do their jobs.

The man unknowingly standing beneath the mistletoe right now went beyond foxy, however. In his well-tailored blazer, pale gray sweater and open-collared oxford shirt, his scarf draped untied around his neck, his long legs flattered by his slate-gray corduroy slacks and his hair, adorably unruly and so black it put Robin in mind of such concepts as midnight and infinity… Jesse Lawson was easily the best-looking man ever to plant himself under that wicked sprig of green leaves and white berries.

Not surprisingly, Kirsten was the first of the clerks to spot him. A tall, well-groomed woman with ash-blond hair and discerning eyes, Kirsten was easily the prettiest member of Robin's sales force, and the most overtly man-hungry. Robin spied on her employee, who managed to look seductive even when she was wearing a plain white sweater and tan flannel slacks beneath her starchy brown Woodleigh's pinafore, as she wandered over to Jesse and offered him her most winning smile. *If she kisses him, Jack Woodleigh's going to have a conniption,* Robin mused, watching and wondering just how brazenly Kirsten would behave.

A customer jarred Robin by plunking seventy dollars' worth of Christmas linens—napkins, place mats, and hand towels—onto the counter and demanding gift boxes. Robin reluctantly turned her back on the door and began to punch numbers into the computerized register. "Lisa, could you put these things in boxes?" she called to her assistant, who had just finished bagging another order.

"Do you think she's going to kiss him?" Lisa murmured, her eyes glued to the doorway as she reached for the stack of unfolded white boxes on the shelf below the counter.

"If there's anything Kirsten likes more than men, it's money," Robin answered with a chuckle, accepting the customer's credit card and fitting it into the charge machine. "I doubt she'd risk her job, even for him."

"I'd risk mine," Lisa said with an exaggerated sigh. She joined Robin's laughter for a moment, then caught herself. "He's coming over here," she whispered, dropping the box she had been assembling in order to preen and fuss with her hair.

If Robin had wanted to run her hands through her own hair, she wouldn't have been able to. As usual, it was pinned back into a ponytail. Even so, as Kirsten led

Jesse among the display tables to the counter, Robin dropped her gaze to her pinafore, hoping her skirt and blouse hung straight beneath it. She knew she looked better now than she had last night at the Brushy Plain School, but better didn't seem good enough.

"Hello, Robin," Jesse said in that delicious voice of his.

She raised her eyes and presented him with a surprisingly relaxed smile. "Hello, Jesse. I see you've finally decided to find out what Woodleigh's is."

Lisa and Kirsten exchanged a glance at this proof that their boss, good old Robin, for whom no man had ever come to call at the store, was actually on a first-name basis with such a fantastic-looking gentleman. Robin's smile widened at the comprehension that her acquaintanceship with Jesse might win her a bit more respect from her underlings.

"I've got to finish this order," she said, excusing herself to fill out the charge slip.

"Take your time," said Jesse.

Needless to say, she completed the charge slip in record time. As soon as the customer signed it, Robin abandoned her to Lisa, who had resumed assembling boxes for the linens, and glided around the counter to Jesse. "Are you looking for something special?" she asked.

He opened his mouth, then shut it and gazed around the shop. "Just curious," he said. "What is all this stuff?"

Robin laughed. "All what stuff?" She surveyed the bustling store. "It's what we sell here. Housewares, decorator items—"

"Stationery," he mumbled, lifting a box of note cards featuring a silkscreened winter scene on the front. He turned the box over, saw the price tag and winced. "Expensive stationery."

"High-priced, but worth it," she justified. "These note cards feature one-of-a-kind designs on recycled paper, and..." She trailed off. Somehow she knew that Jesse hadn't come into the store to listen to a sales pitch.

His gaze circled the room again, pausing at one of the butcher-block tables with its matching cane-and-Haitian-cotton chairs, pausing again at the colorful array of place mats and tablecloths exhibited against one birch-paneled wall, and again at the hand-painted toy-soldier nutcrackers lined up in formation on a shelf covered with green felt and bedecked with holly. When he turned back to Robin, his eyes seemed darker, shadowed by an undefinable sadness. "What's wrong?" she asked instinctively.

He shook his head and grinned. "I was just thinking about some people I visited today, through work. I was thinking about their apartments, and how out of place these things would be inside them."

Visiting some people through work? "I thought you were a lawyer," she said.

"I am."

"Do lawyers make house calls?"

"Legal aid lawyers do, sometimes."

A legal aid lawyer? Since when could legal aid lawyers afford extravagant suede jackets? Or, for that matter, Harris Tweed blazers? Jesse's clothing fit him too well to have been purchased off the rack at Sears. That sweater had to be angora, and his loafers appeared hand-stitched. The scarf looked like cashmere.

"Would this stuff be out of place in your home?" she asked. It was admittedly a nosy question, but she couldn't imagine a man like Jesse Lawson living in the sort of house a legal aid lawyer might be able to afford.

He shrugged. "At the moment, anything would look out of place in it," he confessed. "I moved here from Los Angeles six months ago, and except for a few pieces of necessary furniture, I haven't done much with my place."

"Do you live in Branford?"

"In one of the condominiums off Brush Plain Road," he replied with a nod.

"Mondo Condo," Robin let slip. That was the derogatory name she and Joanna had given to the sprawl of condominium developments north of the elementary school. The developments had proliferated in the last few years like toadstools after a downpour. When Robin and Ray had first bought their modest Cape Cod house in Branford, the town had been little more than a quiet, underdeveloped bedroom community for people who worked in New Haven. In the nine years since then, however, the town had been built up beyond recognition. Robin had signed petitions and attended town meetings calling for a halt to the development, but the condos kept sprouting.

Jesse apparently wasn't offended by the epithet. "Mondo Condo," he repeated. "That about sums it up."

She didn't really have to make amends for having slighted his residence, but she felt she ought to, anyway. "Some of those condominiums are pretty classy. Your home would probably look nice with a few fancy items in it. A wine rack, maybe, or some of these crystal tree ornaments from Denmark—"

"I don't plan to have a tree," he said curtly. "What

would I want with ornaments?'' Then he relented, his smile returning. ''But I do drink wine on occasion.''

No tree? The notion seemed incomprehensible to Robin, but she refrained from blurting out any more impolitic remarks. She was lucky that he hadn't been insulted by her comment about his condominium-infested neighborhood. Even if not having a Christmas tree was, to her mind, a lapse bordering on inexcusable, she didn't dare to question him about it.

Instead she ushered him through the store to a display of wine racks. Some were constructed of varnished wood, others of brass. He appraised their price tags first, then their designs. ''I'd probably do better at K-Mart,'' he muttered.

''In terms of price, maybe,'' she said loftily. ''Not in terms of quality.''

Abruptly he turned to her. He dug his hands into the pockets of his trousers and gazed down at her, his eyes unnerving in their resonant force, in their vividness. ''I didn't come here to shop,'' he admitted quietly. ''I came here to see you.''

Robin laughed. She often laughed when she was shocked, and Jesse's announcement shocked her. A series of emotions clamored through her—that she was immeasurably flattered, that she wished she were as beautiful as Kirsten, that she didn't have to be as beautiful as Kirsten because Jesse was here to see her and not the statuesque salesclerk. That she truly wanted to start dating again, and that Jesse seemed much too attractive, much too perilously intriguing, to become her first boyfriend in thirteen years.

''What did you want to see me about?'' she asked guilelessly.

A tender smile danced across Jesse's thin, strong lips. "About your son, I think."

"Philip?" Had Eileen Becker confided in Jesse about her concerns regarding Philip? Had the teacher told her neighbor she thought Philip Greer was perverse? And why had Jesse added, "I think"? Wasn't he sure why he had come to see Robin?

"I'd—I'd like to meet him," Jesse said.

"Why?"

"Because…" He hesitated, taking time to sort his thoughts. "Because any boy who's got the guts to draw hands on a turkey must be pretty special."

A wave of maternal pride flooded through Robin. Philip was special—he was the most special, darling, brilliant, magnificent little boy in the world. "He also drew antennae on his turkey," she reminded Jesse.

"More power to him." He reflected for a minute, shoving his hands deeper into his pockets and striking an almost diffident pose. As diffident as it was, however, the motion of his arms pulled back the flaps of his blazer, revealing the fine, soft wool of his sweater and, beneath it, the fine, hard shape of his torso. "Am I out of line?" he asked. "Asking to meet your son, I mean."

"No, of course not," Robin said quickly. She wondered what Philip would say if she brought Jesse home—she wondered what he would say if she brought *any* man home. That particular situation had never occurred before, although Robin assumed that if she started dating, it was bound to crop up sooner or later.

Not that she was dating Jesse. It was Philip he was interested in, not Robin.

And yet the idea of bringing Jesse home had an undeniable appeal to it. "We close up in half an hour," she told him. "If you want to stick around until then, sure, you can meet my gutsy son."

"I'll stick around," Jesse promised.

Her gaze locked with his for an instant. Despite his affable smile, there was something somber in his dark, piercing eyes, something earnest and oddly wistful. Before Robin had a chance to interpret it, Lisa raced over to her and jabbed her arm. "Robin? Are we out of the Swedish votive candles?" she asked. "Ginny went downstairs to the stock room, but she couldn't find any there."

"We just got a delivery of them yesterday," Robin said, snapping into her professional mind-set. "If I know Kevin, he misplaced them." She grinned apologetically at Jesse. "Crisis time," she explained. "Heavy is the head that wears the crown, or however the saying goes."

"Don't let me interrupt your work," Jesse said swiftly, taking a step backward and then bending down to examine one of the wine racks more closely. "I'm not going anywhere."

Chapter Three

Forty-five minutes later, he *was* going somewhere. He was following the red taillights of Robin's compact station wagon off the Post Road and onto a winding back lane that lacked adequate lighting. He hadn't bothered to purchase a wine rack—for a thirty-four-year-old man, he knew pitifully little about wines, and he tended to buy bottles singly, on impulse. He had browsed through Woodleigh's, engaged in silent debate about whether the toy-soldier nutcrackers were cute or tacky, whether food tasted better when eaten off expensive dishes than when eaten off cheap ones, whether someone like Mrs. Selby, unexpectedly bestowed with a hundred fifty thousand dollars in an out-of-court settlement with her landlord, would choose to spend any of it in a place like Woodleigh's.

At six o'clock, he had stood by while Robin locked the shop's front door, reminded her salesclerks to double-check the pre-Christmas schedule of store hours, which had been extended to accommodate the holiday shoppers, removed her brown apron and shut off the lights. Her car was parked in back, and he had waited until she'd driven around to the front parking lot and flashed her station wagon's lights at him before he started his engine.

Now he was going to meet Philip.

He wanted to meet the boy. He wanted to see for himself this child who had been raised to give his imagination free rein, to invent a make-believe universe— Jesse had overheard Robin and Eileen discussing the alien planet from which Philip's turkey had allegedly descended. He wanted to befriend a child who was allowed to believe whatever he wanted and to create whatever he wanted. Although Jesse didn't know much about children, he wanted to meet the son Robin Greer had produced.

That was the other reason he was trailing those beacon-like red taillights through the darkness: Robin herself. There was something so alive about her, something so vibrant, so warm. From a distance, he had observed her banter with her clerks at the store, her competence in solving the mystery of the temporarily missing votive candles, her sedate control over her domain. Jesse didn't particularly care for the items Woodleigh's sold, but he liked the way Robin ran the store. She seemed capable and strong and...at peace. Again it occurred to him— she was at peace with herself.

They entered a quiet area of modest but lovingly tended Cape Cod houses that backed on a dense forest. Their front lawns were neatly mowed and their walks lit. Many of them were trimmed with Christmas lights. The driveway up which Robin turned led to a blue house with a woven willow wreath hanging on the front door.

Jesse's car trailed hers onto the long driveway, and he killed the engine and climbed out. Robin had parked inside the garage and was pulling down the garage door when Jesse reached her. "Let me give you a hand," he said. She seemed much too delicate to be able to yank the massive door into place.

She waved off his assistance with a simple "I've got it," and sure enough, the door slid into position. Then she accompanied Jesse up the walk. "You're welcome to stay for dinner if you'd like," she invited him matter-of-factly. "Philip is always starving by the time I get home, and the roast is probably ready. It's too big for two people, anyway."

"Roast? Your son cooked a roast?"

She laughed and jiggled her key ring to select the right key for the front door. "No. Kate O'Leary put it in the oven. She's Philip's baby-sitter." The door swung open, and Robin hollered, "Phil? I'm home!"

A wiry tow-haired youngster bounded into the living room from a hallway behind the staircase. "Hey, Mommy!" he shouted, springing into her arms and giving her an exuberant hug. "I did all my homework and I watched *Masters of the Universe* and I fed all my cookies to Cookie Monster at school so that means I can have more cookies for dessert tonight, okay? Hey, who's this?" he asked, releasing his mother and fixing his gaze on Jesse.

Jesse was only subliminally aware of the redolence of cooking meat that filled the air, the homey furnishings in the living room, the broad brick fireplace on the far wall and the sturdy maple occasional tables scattered about the room. The bulk of his attention was focused on the boy.

Philip looked exactly like Robin—or at least, exactly like a seven-year-old male version of Robin. His hair was the same flaxen shade, the same flyaway texture. His eyes were as bright and multicolored as hers, his cheeks as cleanly defined, his jaw as pointy. His build, like hers, was slim yet strong, exuding energy. And his greeting was just as down-to-earth and accepting as Robin's "Hello, Jesse" had been when he'd entered her store.

"This is Jesse Lawson," Robin said. Jesse had wondered how she would explain his presence to her son, whether she would introduce him as a friend or an acquaintance, or, perhaps, as a cheapskate who didn't give a hoot for one-of-a-kind silkscreened notecards. But she avoided labels and simply provided his name. Jesse liked that. "Jesse, my son Philip, on leave from the planet Gleek. Hi, Kate," she greeted the plump silverhaired woman who had entered the room behind Philip. "How did it go today?"

"No problems," Kate O'Leary reported, eyeing Jesse curiously as she moved past Robin to the entry closet for her coat. "Philip just gave you the whole story—except he pestered me for cookies. I thought it best to leave that up to you."

"Thanks," Robin said with a laugh. "Phil knows I'm more of a pushover than you are when it comes to sweets. By the way, Kate, I'm going to have to work late a couple of nights this week—"

"No problem," Kate assured her, slinging on her coat and reaching for the front doorknob. "Just let me know your schedule when you've got it."

"'Tis the season," Robin reminded her with a contrite smile. "Our hours are going to be crazy for the next few weeks."

"I don't mind, I really don't," Kate insisted. "I could use the extra money—lots of presents to buy."

"You gonna buy me a present?" Philip asked, climbing up to the second step of the staircase and then jumping down dramatically. "I ask only on account of I'm gonna buy you one."

"You are?" Kate feigned utter astonishment. "In that case, I'd better revise my shopping list. I'd be mortified if you gave me a present and I didn't have one to give you!" She winked at Robin, gave Jesse another interested glance, and said, "So long, everybody. See you tomorrow."

"Thanks, Kate." Robin left the porch light on for Kate, then locked the door and removed her jacket. "Give me five minutes to change my clothes," she requested, "and then we'll have some dinner."

"You staying for dinner, Jesse?" Philip asked, climbing up the stairs again and leaping down with death-defying courage. "I think maybe we'll have cookies for dessert. What's your favorite kind of cookie?"

"Chocolate chip," Jesse answered the child, though his gaze remained on Robin, watching the playful bounce of her shiny blond hair, the graceful motion of her hips, the slender curves of her calves and her small, dainty feet carrying her up the stairs and out of sight.

BY THE TIME Robin returned to the living room, Jesse and Philip were gone.

She had taken longer than the promised five minutes to change her clothes. Ordinarily when she got home from work, she threw on her old jeans and a sweat shirt, washed off what little makeup she was wearing, and bounded down the stairs to spend the evening with her son. But tonight she had taken an unreasonable amount of time combing through the double closet in her bedroom, searching for an outfit that would look both casual and flattering. The jeans and sweat shirt met the first of those conditions, but definitely not the second.

After donning a pair of wool slacks and a patterned blouse, Robin headed for the bathroom, not to scrub off her makeup but to freshen it. She pulled the barrette from her hair, brushed it out, and then decided to leave it loose. Hurrying down to the living room, she hoped that Philip wouldn't be a big-mouth and question her about her uncharacteristic dinnertime appearance.

She gazed about the empty living room for a moment, spotting Jesse's blazer draped over the back of a chair, and wondered where Philip had dragged him off to. Then she heard her son's piping voice floating out of the den.

She strode to the doorway and found Jesse seated on the sofa and Philip kneeling on the coffee table facing him, holding the poor man captive as he displayed for him various stamps, papers and envelopes, which he pulled from an old shoe box. "This one, it's from Mexico," Philip announced. "See? It's got Spanish words on it. That's what they speak in Mexico," he explained with great self-assurance. "This one's from Brazil. And you know what, Jesse? It looks like Spanish, but it's not. Guess what it is."

Jesse labored to appear ignorant. "I don't know, Philip. What is it?"

"Portuguese!" Philip crowed, obviously thrilled to have shown up an adult with his superior knowledge. "They speak Portuguese there. Did you know that? My dad doesn't really understand Portuguese, but he speaks Spanish real good. I'll show you—he wrote me this message in Spanish..." Philip rummaged through the shoe box and withdrew a sheet of white note paper. "Here, he wrote, *'Hasta la vista, Filipo.'* Do you know what that means?"

"What does it mean?" Jesse asked politely.

"It means, Goodbye, Philip. Mostly my dad goes to Spanish places, like in South America and the West Indies and stuff, so he can talk to the people. Sometimes he gets stuck going to Brazil or something, though. Then he needs a translator."

Clearly, Philip and Robin were novices at this business of entertaining a strange man in their home. If she had been more savvy about such situations, she would have trained her son not to besiege a male guest—a potential boyfriend, at that—with the collection of letters and exotic postage stamps Philip had received from his father. Robin was glad that Ray corresponded regularly with Philip, but she didn't think that having the boy chatter nonstop about his father was exactly the proper way to make Jesse feel welcome.

"Philip?" she said, trying not to sound disapproving as she entered the den. Not only had Philip been sharing his father's letters with Jesse, but he'd brought Jesse into the messiest room in the house—not counting Philip's bedroom, of course. With Kate O'Leary's help, Robin managed to keep the living room and kitchen relatively tidy, and the dining room was practically immaculate since it was used so rarely. The den, however, was a place for unwinding, kicking back, overlooking the rubble of scattered toys and games, half-read books and magazines, two-month-old issues of *TV Guide*s and piles of sewing projects yet to be completed.

At the moment the den seemed even more cluttered than usual because Robin and Philip had recently lugged the cartons of Christmas decorations down from the attic storage area. Robin had insisted that it was too early to start decking the house with holiday adornments, but Philip was so eager for Christmas to arrive that he'd cajoled his mother into bringing the cartons downstairs.

He had also begun badgering her about buying a tree, but she had maintained that if they bought one too early in December, it would be all dried out by Christmas Day.

"Please put the letters away," she firmly ordered her son. "And what's the rule about climbing on the tables?"

At the sound of her voice Philip jumped off the table and spun around. Collecting a few scattered postage stamps into his box, he grinned. "Did you know that on Gleek, kids are allowed to climb on tables all the time?"

"Then I'm glad I don't live there," she said succinctly. "Speaking of tables, Philip, perhaps you could give me a hand setting the one in the dining room. We're going to eat there tonight."

"Yeah? How come?"

"Because Jesse is here, and we use the dining room when we've got company."

"We don't use it when Mrs. O'Leary stays for supper," Philip reminded Robin as he set the lid on the box and returned it to a shelf.

Were all children of divorced mothers this difficult the first time a new man entered their home? "Mrs. O'Leary," Robin said as evenly as she could, "spends more time in this house than I do. She's practically one of the family."

Philip shrugged. "Okay. The dining room, huh. I guess I gotta wash my hands, then." He pranced out of the den and vanished into the downstairs bathroom.

Robin risked a glance at Jesse, who was rising from the sofa. If Philip had made him uncomfortable by discussing Ray, Jesse didn't show it. He had shoved up the sleeves of his sweater and rolled up his shirt sleeves beneath it, exposing his slender, sinewy forearms. He had bony wrists and long, tapered fingers, and his skin was a gold-tinged color just a shade lighter than the skin of his face. Robin wondered what he would look like in the summer, his entire body shimmering with a rich, toasty tan, and then she swallowed a shocked laugh. That she should be thinking of viewing Jesse's unclothed body startled her, and she swiftly chased away the image by concentrating on the subject he and Philip had just been discussing—her ex-husband. Surely fifteen minutes listening to Philip sing the praises of his peripatetic father was enough to smother any romantic inclinations on Jesse's part.

He offered her an amiable smile and crossed the room to join her at the doorway. "Gleek—that's Philip's make-believe planet, right?"

She nodded. "Among other things, Gleek is a place where seven-year-old boys do everything they aren't supposed to do on earth, and don't do anything they are supposed to do on earth. Ten'll get you twenty that during dinner Philip's going to announce that on Gleek kids don't have to eat their vegetables." With that, she marched down the hall to the kitchen, removed the bag of already washed green beans from the refrigerator, and dumped them into the steamer to cook.

In spite of the fact that they ate in the dining room instead of the kitchen, Philip was as rambunctious as usual. He monopolized the mealtime conversation with a long-winded description of his day in school. "Cookie Monster is such a pig," he informed Jesse. "He eats grapes, lettuce leaves, bugs and cookies. He gobbled up all my cookies and all of Adam Worblin's. Did you know that Adam Worblin is the worst speller in class? We're having a spelling test on Friday. Spelling is dumb, don't you think, Jesse? When I grow up, I'm gonna have a secretary and she'll check my spelling for me."

"When you grow up," Robin asserted, "maybe you'll be a secretary."

"Uh-uh." Philip soberly shook his head. "I wanna be a scientist. I wanna have lots and lots of snakes."

Robin didn't bother to hide her grimace. Jesse chuckled. "What you want to be is a herpetologist," he told Philip. "That's the name for a scientist who specializes in snakes."

"Yeah?" Philip's eyes grew round. Clearly he considered Jesse a genius for knowing such an arcane fact, even if the man had to be instructed by a mere second-grader that people in Brazil spoke Portuguese. "That's what I want to be, then. What's the word again?"

"Herpetologist."

"Herpetologist," Philip murmured, cementing the term in his memory. "I think Jeff Calloway wants to be one, too. We could have a snake farm together, and then we could spend all day catching bugs to feed our snakes. And buying cookies for them, too. Can I have some cookies now, Mom?"

Robin eyed her son's plate. He had distributed his uneaten green beans around the dish, as if by dispersing them he would give the impression of having consumed most of them. She considered nagging him to finish his vegetables before he requested dessert, then decided not to. It was a special night; Jesse was present. She didn't want to have a face-off with her son about something as trivial as beans.

"I tell you what," she negotiated. "Why don't you help me clear the table, and then you can have some cookies and milk in the den."

Philip let out a hoot. This was a double treat—Robin rarely permitted him to bring food into the den. He bolted from the table, gathering his plate and silverware, and charged into the kitchen.

Robin smiled at Jesse. "We can have some coffee in the living room, if you'd like," she offered. Then she remembered that he had asked to come to her house specifically to meet her son, and she added, "Or you can have cookies and milk with Philip."

"Coffee sounds great," he said, standing and lifting a few more dishes.

It didn't take long to clean up the dishes and cram the leftovers into the refrigerator. After preparing a pot of coffee to brew, Robin arranged a few cookies on a plate, filled a tumbler with milk, and carried the snack into the den. "Can I watch TV, too?" Philip asked hopefully.

"All right," she said. "You can watch reruns of *WKRP*. No news, though." Turning to Jesse, she explained, "Whenever he watches the news, he wants to ask me a thousand questions about each story. Not that I mind—I'm glad he has an interest in the world—but it would be nice to have our coffee without interruptions."

Philip switched on the television, then flopped onto the couch and balanced the plate of cookies on his knees. Pivoting to leave the room, Robin noticed that Jesse was gazing at the shoe box in which Philip stored his mail from his father. She cringed, then forced a faint smile and left the room. Jesse followed.

A vision of his intense stare fastened to the shoe box remained with her while she filled two cups with coffee, asked him whether he took cream or sugar, and carried the cups to the living room. Although Jesse didn't mention the letters Philip had shown him, Robin couldn't keep herself from contemplating his reaction to them. Had he felt uncomfortable listening to Philip go on and on about his father? In Jesse's place, she would have felt uncomfortable.

Her smile still felt forced as she sat on the chintz-covered sofa and gestured for Jesse to take a seat beside her. She watched him as he lifted his cup, sipped, and lowered it. "I'm sorry about that stuff with my ex-husband's letters," she said finally, to alleviate her own awkwardness if not Jesse's.

Jesse eyed her steadily. His lips shaped a hesitant smile. "Don't be." He took another sip of coffee, then leaned back against the cushions, stretching his long legs out under the table. "I take it your son and your ex-husband are close."

"As close as they can be, given that Ray travels so much."

"I think that's terrific," he said. He sounded as if he meant it, and Robin felt her tension abate. "It's probably one reason Philip is such a well-adjusted child. So many kids of divorce aren't."

Robin nodded.

"Does he get to see much of his father?"

"They get together about twice a year," she answered. "Whenever Ray is stateside, he spends as much of the furlough as possible with Philip."

"Furlough?" Jesse questioned her. "Is he in the armed forces?"

Robin laughed and shook her head. "Just a habit of speech," she explained. "I spent my youth as an army brat. I've gotten most of the military jargon out of my system, but every now and then a word slips in."

Jesse mused for a moment. "Can I get personal, Robin?"

A frisson of anxiety rippled through her. Was he going to kiss her? Proposition her? With her child in the next room? As Jesse's dark, piercing eyes met hers and his sensual lips curved in an enigmatic smile, she found herself almost wishing that he would make a pass at her. She would have to reject him if he did, but still... How heavenly it would be to have a man like him getting personal with her.

Mustering her courage, she said, "Go right ahead."

Jesse continued to study her, mulling over his thoughts before he verbalized them. "Why did you get a divorce?" he asked.

Personal, granted—but hardly what Robin had been bracing herself for. She felt the muscles along her spine go slack and her heartbeat slow. She wasn't really ready for him to make a pass at her anyway, she consoled herself. "What do you mean, why?" she countered.

His smile widened, growing warmer. "It's more than just that Philip seems well-adjusted. You seem well-adjusted, too. Most divorced women I know are so bitter and vindictive about it."

"Do you know many divorced women?" she asked.

He chuckled. "Enough to make totally unsupportable generalizations," he conceded. "Seriously, Robin. You seem so sweet and open. You invited me to dinner on the spur of the moment, without making a big deal about it—"

"Around here, eating in the dining room *is* a big deal," she joked. Then she accepted his question in the spirit in which it had been posed. "When I was growing up, we moved around a lot. Every two or three years, my father would be reposted, and we'd ship off to a

new base. We never had roots, we never had a real
home. And I was always being thrust into a new community where I didn't know anybody, where I had to
start all over again making friends. To make it easier
for me, my mother had what she called her 'Open Door
Policy.' Whenever I met anyone I thought might become a friend, I could bring her home with me for dinner, without advance notice. My mother often dragged
acquaintances home, too—army wives and their kids.
You had to work fast making friends in that kind of
environment.'' She shrugged. ''It amazes me that Philip
and Jeffrey—you met his mother, Joanna, at the Open
School Night—it amazes me that the boys have known
each other practically since their conception. Until I
moved to Branford, I had never lived in any one place
for so long.''

''And now your ex-husband travels all over the
world,'' Jesse noted.

Robin grinned. ''Bingo. You figured it out.''

''I did?'' He appeared perplexed.

''You asked me why I was divorced.'' She drank
some coffee, then nestled deeper into the couch's plush
upholstery and folded her legs underneath her. ''Ray
had traveled a lot as a child, too. He wasn't an army
brat, but his father was an executive with one of the
airlines, and they were always moving. When we met,
I told Ray that my dream in life was to have a real
home, to settle down someplace and know that this was
my house, *my* place, my little corner of the world. He
understood and he agreed with me, at first. He took a
job teaching economics at Yale, and we bought this
house, and I dug in my roots. And then...'' She sighed
wistfully. ''He began to get restless. Neither of us was
used to living in one place for so long, but I loved it.

He never got used to it. So he took a job with the Agency for International Development. The next thing I knew, he was being shipped off to Honduras for on-site observation. And..." She sighed again. "I stayed here."

"Your choice?" Jesse half asked.

"My choice. Ray knew how I felt about moving. A good wife would have gritted her teeth and packed up and followed her husband wherever he went, but..."

The tiny lines framing Jesse's eyes deepened as he laughed. "Is that what good wives do?"

Robin smiled reluctantly. "It's what my mother did. I always assumed that she loved the transfers and the life of an army wife. But then Ray and I were facing this crisis, and I called my mother for advice, and she admitted that she had despised the constant moving, that she had always resented my father for denying her a home, and that if I refused myself what meant the most to me, I'd wind up resenting Ray, too. I didn't want that to happen. So, yes, I made my choice."

Jesse took a minute to digest what she'd told him. "Your ex-husband's the bitter one, then?"

"No, he's not bitter, either. He knew that gallivanting about Central and South America wouldn't necessarily be the healthiest thing for Philip, and that I had a right to live the kind of life I wanted to live. We just grew apart—literally, I guess. His career meant more to him than I did. And my desire to have a home meant more to me than he did."

"And now you have your home," Jesse concluded.

"A home, a job, a son...a place where I can plant perennials and get to watch them bloom, year in and year out. And Philip can grow up secure, belonging to a neighborhood and knowing that his friends are here

where he is. He isn't going to have to spend his childhood memorizing dozens of different addresses and
guessing which drawer the silverware is in, and being a
chameleon at school, trying to fit in with a new crowd
of kids every couple of years.''

Her gaze journeyed around the cozy living room,
which was furnished with pieces she'd selected specifically for this room. Growing up, she had lived in so
many strange houses where the furniture that had been
bought three houses earlier never quite fit and the wall
colors and carpet never quite suited her family. Those
temporary residences had never represented home to
Robin. This unassuming Cape Cod house did.

"The tree is going to go in that corner," she murmured, pointing to a nook beside the fireplace. "It always goes there. And we'll wrap holly and red ribbons
around the balustrade, and put red candles in the windows. That's why having a tree is so important to me,"
she said, justifying her affection for Christmas. "It's a
part of home. Christmas means being with Philip and
having our tree in that corner.''

Robin hadn't consciously intended to introduce the
subject of Christmas trees. Yet it was all part of a whole
to her. The house, the tree, her son and the spirit of the
season. Christmas equaled home in Robin's mind.

Jesse's expression changed as soon as she mentioned
the holiday, however. A shadow flickered within his
eyes, and he shifted slightly on the couch. Then he
smiled crookedly. "I don't condemn other people for
having trees," he remarked, apparently sensing the need
to reassure Robin.

She had already told Jesse a great deal about herself,
and she found talking to him surprisingly easy. Hoping
that he would find it as easy to talk to her, she twisted

on the cushions to face him fully and inquired, "Why don't you want to have one?"

He glanced at his coffee cup, which was empty. Robin was about to ask him if he wanted a refill, thoughtfully giving him a chance to avoid responding to her blunt question. But before she could speak, he answered, "I don't believe in it."

"In what? In Christmas trees?"

"In Christmas."

She gaped at him. There was nothing defensive in his claim; he'd stated it as bluntly as she'd stated her question. And since Jesse was already to blame for having directed their conversation into the personal, she felt free to grill him as he'd grilled her. "Are you Jewish?" she asked.

"No."

"Druid?" She recalled his having commented in Ms. Becker's classroom that some of the students might be druids. Robin had little understanding of what druids were all about, other than what Jesse had said at Open School Night about the winter solstice.

He chuckled, apparently amused that she remembered his remark. "No," he said. "I'm an atheist."

"An agnostic, you mean?" She'd met a few people who admitted to having their doubts, which made them agnostics. But she'd never met anyone who declared himself an actual atheist, refusing to hedge his bets on the possibility of God's existence.

"I mean I'm an atheist," Jesse insisted.

"Just like that?" she pressed him, fascinated. "You don't believe in anything?"

"Oh, I believe in some things, Robin," he claimed. "I believe that every person has the inherent ability to do good in this world, and that it's his or her choice whether or not to do good. I believe that strength comes from knowledge, not faith, and that it comes from within, not without. What I don't believe is that there's some old geezer in a white beard who lives in the clouds and pulls the strings."

Surely that was as absurd a definition of God as any Robin had ever heard. "Then you don't believe in Santa Claus, either, do you?" she said, unable to stifle a laugh.

"Other than the guys who stand on corners in funny costumes and ask for handouts, no, I don't."

"Please don't tell Philip," she whispered conspiratorily.

Jesse nodded in understanding. "It'll be our secret."

She settled against the throw pillows, pondering what Jesse had revealed. Because of her childhood on army bases, Robin hadn't had much formalized religious instruction. The chapels on most army bases offered non-denominational Christian services—when they weren't being used for Jewish services. She couldn't quite say that she was a Methodist, as her father had been, or a Lutheran like her mother. But she did believe in God. It seemed much too depressing *not* to believe.

She peered curiously at the man beside her: an atheist, without any sense of a guiding power larger than himself, without any faith, without any belief in a greater being to whom he could turn in times of stress or despair. Jesse appeared unconcerned about what he'd just confessed to, although he looked as if he was willing to answer more questions from Robin. "Don't you believe in heaven?" she asked.

"As a place where people go after they've died? No."

"Then what do you think happens when they die?"

She noticed another shadow hovering over his sharply

chiseled features, a pensiveness tugging at the corners of his mouth. Then he shrugged resolutely. "I think that when people die, they get buried—or cremated—and their remains are absorbed by the earth."

"What about their souls?"

That shadow again, that brooding sadness darkening his eyes. He turned to gaze out the window, staring into the darkness beyond the glass. "I don't think of the soul as something separate from the body," he explained haltingly, addressing the cold night outdoors. "I think of it as a person's mind, his personality, the capacity for goodness inside him. When he dies, it's gone."

"Jesse." It was such a bleak thought, Robin felt compelled to refute it. "If there's nothing beyond that, then why do people bother to be good at all?"

He turned back to her and snorted. "Most people bother because they *do* believe in heaven. It's a bargain they're cutting: 'I'll be a decent human being now, and I'll get my payback later.' I do my best to be decent, too, Robin, but I'm not expecting a payback. I just do it because it's nicer and fairer to live my life that way." He stood and ambled to the window, gazing past the swagged curtains into the moonlit front yard. Rotating, he leaned against the windowsill and shoved his hands into his pockets. "When I was thirteen years old, my sister died of leukemia."

"Oh, God," Robin groaned, not even thinking that, in the context of atheism, such a statement was meaningless. "That's terrible, Jesse. I'm sorry."

"It was terrible," he confirmed. "But...you see..." He grappled with his thoughts. "When I tried to comprehend Marybeth's death, everybody said, 'God loved Marybeth so much, He wanted her in heaven with Him.' That was the answer religion provided. And all I could

think was, if there *was* a God, how could He be so
selfish? If He really loved Marybeth, He would have let
her live a full, happy life. He could have waited fifty or
sixty years before snatching her away and flying her up
to heaven. What's fifty years to God, right? But no, He
was selfish. He must have hated the rest of us to have
taken her away from us. And He must have hated her,
too, to make her suffer so much before she died. If God
did exist, He seemed far too capricious and self-centered
and thoughtless to believe in.''

"But that was one thing, Jesse, one incident. I could
see where it might shake your faith. If anything ever
happened to Philip—'' Robin cut herself off, unwilling
to imagine such a horrible possibility. "Yes, it might
shake my faith, too. But—''

"And take war,'' Jesse posited. "Or famine, or earth-
quakes. Would a loving God let such things occur? If
He's truly in control of the world, why has He fouled
it up so much?''

"But then other things happen,'' Robin argued.
"Wonderful things. Miracles. And when the bad things
occur, many people turn to God to help them through.''

"Sure. Religion offers easy answers. It's a lot easier
to say 'God works in mysterious ways' than to say
Marybeth got unlucky, her blood cells got screwed up
and she died.''

"Did losing your sister turn your parents away from
God, too?'' Robin asked.

He issued a short, dry laugh. "Hardly. They're su-
perreligious. They've made a full-fledged career of their
devoutness. I tried it their way, Robin. I honestly tried.
But it never really made sense to me.''

"And *not* believing does make sense to you?''

"It allows me to be who I am and to do what I want,''

he explained cryptically. "It enables me to help someone simply because I want to see them smile, without
worrying about whether I'm scoring points for the here-
after."

Robin lapsed into a bewildered silence. She hadn't
expected that she would wind up describing the circumstances of her divorce to Jesse this evening—she discussed them only with people she had known close to
forever. She suspected that Jesse didn't explain his atheism to near strangers, either.

Yet she hadn't expected that he would enter her store
several hours ago and ask to meet her son, and she
hadn't expected that she would impetuously invite him
to join them for dinner. Nothing that had happened since
she'd noticed Jesse standing beneath the mistletoe at
Woodleigh's could have been predicted.

Even so, it seemed natural that she should be having
this conversation with him. Debating the existence of
God with Jesse seemed as reasonable as talking about
her childhood as the daughter of an army colonel, and
her decision to remain true to her ideal of home rather
than trying futilely to salvage a shaky marriage. Jesse
Lawson might indeed be a near stranger, but she felt
close to him.

She wasn't going to persuade him to rethink his view
of religion. She saw no need to. He was entitled to his
beliefs—or his non-beliefs—and he was a decent human
being. In his profession, he could be raking in hundreds
of thousands of dollars in fees, but instead he made
house calls to his indigent clients as a legal aid lawyer.
Whether the goodness came from within or without
didn't matter. Jesse was a good man.

"Maybe," she said, grinning whimsically, "the reason you don't like Christmas is because you haven't

experienced one of Philip's and mine. Some pine wreaths, a bit of tinsel, the smell of evergreens and wood smoke and baking cookies, and you'd be a believer, too.''

"Or maybe I'd turn into a snake," he quipped. "Depending on what kind of cookies they were, of course.''

His allusion to Philip's dinnertime discourse on Cookie Monster prompted Robin to check her wristwatch. A quarter to nine. "Yikes," she groaned. "It's past Philip's bedtime. God knows what he's been watching on TV all this time.''

"No," Jesse said with a laugh. "God doesn't know. Only Philip knows.''

Robin chuckled, too. "Well, his mother is about to find out." She sauntered into the den and found Philip seated on the floor, barely ten inches from the television, watching a shoot-em-up scene of mayhem on the screen. "Bedtime, pal," Robin announced, lifting the empty cookie plate and milk glass from the coffee table.

"Awww!" Philip automatically whined, although he obediently stood and turned off the set. "Is Jesse still here?''

"Yes. Now how about some pj's, pronto?''

"Can I say good-night to him first?''

"As long as you don't make a two-hour production out of it," Robin warned, carrying the dishes to the kitchen sink. Reentering the living room, she found Philip swinging on the newel post at the bottom of the staircase and squawking to Jesse about how he wanted to buy a remote-control Jeep for Mrs. O'Leary for Christmas. "They're really neat, Jesse," he went on. "They just showed an advertisement for them on television. They're four-wheel-drive, with big fat tires, so you can drive them on gravel and everything.''

"I'm sure that's exactly what your baby-sitter's been dreaming of owning," Jesse muttered wryly, though his eyes sparkled with humor. "Are you sure that's not what you want for yourself?"

"Uh-uh," Philip swore. "I want some new Masters of the Universe stuff, and another Transformer, and maybe a rocket ship. And I don't want anything with Smurfs on it. I'm too big for that," he added pointedly, glowering at Robin. He still hadn't forgiven her for her assertion that the Smurfs lunchbox he had pleaded for when he started first grade was in excellent shape and she wasn't about to buy a replacement. According to Philip, he was the only boy in the entire second grade who had to use a Smurfs lunchbox. Smurfs were strictly for girls and wimps.

"You know what I want for Christmas?" Robin declared sternly. "I want a certain seven-year-old boy to be in pj's and brushing his teeth by the time I count to twenty."

Philip pretended to be annoyed, but when he swung back to Jesse he was smiling. "Was your mother this mean, Jesse?"

"She was much, much meaner," Jesse said soberly. "If I were you, I'd count my blessings and put on my pajamas."

"Oh, all right," Philip relented, issuing an exaggerated sigh. "'Bye, Jesse."

"Goodnight, Philip."

Philip plodded up a few steps, then leaned over the railing and, in a stage whisper that was undoubtedly audible three houses away, commented, "Jesse's pretty nice for a grown-up, Mom."

Robin laughed. "We grown-ups do the best we can. Now git!" Philip scampered up the stairs.

"I guess I should be leaving," Jesse said, lifting his blazer from the chair where he'd left it. "I didn't mean to impose myself on you for half the evening—"

"Don't be ridiculous," she interrupted, silencing him. "It was my pleasure. Philip's pleasure, too. Anybody who can distract his mother for a few hours so he can watch blood and gore on television is tops in his scheme of things."

Jesse turned to the front door, then hesitated and spun back to Robin. "I'd like to see you again," he said.

She remembered the way he'd looked a few hours ago at the store when he'd asked if he could meet Philip—diffident, earnest, vaguely unsure of himself. He didn't seem at all unsure of himself now. His eyes pored over her face, and the hand that had reached for the doorknob instead alighted on her shoulder. "You're always welcome for dinner, Jesse," she assured him.

"That wasn't what I had in mind."

A date. He was asking her for a date. Her first date in over a decade, the first time in thirteen years that she was faced with the possibility of a date with a man other than Ray. She tried to recollect the apprehension she'd felt when she had first seen Jesse at the school—that he was too handsome, too debonair, too much for her to handle on her first social outing in eons. But that was before she'd gotten to know him, before he'd exposed his soul to her—if atheists were allowed to have souls.

Whether or not they were allowed, she knew that Jesse had one. And her reply came easily. "I'd like to see you again, too."

"What night's good for you?"

"Friday?" she suggested. "The store's open late, but I won't have to be there past six."

"Friday," Jesse confirmed. "I'll be here at seven.

Get a baby-sitter.'' Then, so swiftly Robin couldn't prepare herself for it, he bowed and kissed her. It was a light, friendly kiss, landing half on her lips and half on her cheek, but it was tantalizing in its promise.

Too handsome, perhaps. Too risky. But as she watched Jesse open the door and stride down the front walk to his car, she knew intuitively that she was right to trust him.

SHE DID HER BEST to conceal her nervousness at work on Friday. The only three people, other than Jesse and herself, who knew about the date were Mrs. O'Leary, who agreed to baby-sit for Philip, Philip himself, and Joanna. Joanna was beside herself with delight. ''That gorgeous guy from Open School Night? I knew it, Robin, I told you I saw him approach you. I could tell he was interested!''

Joanna's excitement about Robin's date only fed her own anxiety. She could trust Jesse, but could she trust herself? Not that she was worried about losing control around him, hurling herself at him and engaging in irresponsible orgiastic pleasures, but rather, could she trust herself not to botch things up? What if she dressed wrong? What if she spilled her soup? What if she accidentally smudged her mascara, or tripped on a step and wound up sprawled across a parking lot with her skirt around her waist? What if, when she got home from work today, she discovered a pimple on the tip of her nose?

Had dating been this frought with tension when she'd been a teenager? She supposed that it had been, but she'd been younger and more resilient in her youth. Everybody had pimples back then.

''Relax,'' Mrs. O'Leary ordered her when she finally

arrived home, ten minutes later than she'd hoped because one of the salesclerks had returned late from her supper break and because a sleety rain was falling, slowing the rush-hour traffic to a crawl. "Everything's going to go fine. He's a good-looking fellow. If he were thirty years older, I'd ask him out myself. Now go upstairs and get dressed. Philip and I will go ahead and have dinner."

Robin raced upstairs, took the quickest shower since indoor plumbing was invented, and then pawed through her closet in search of a suitable outfit. She put on her gray wool dress, decided that it made her look pale and flat-chested, and traded it for a bright red sweater and skirt ensemble. That looked too Christmasy, and she pulled it off and put on the gray dress again. Then she darted into the bathroom, fixed her makeup, brushed her hair back, brushed it up, brushed it down, and exhumed her curling iron from the back of the linen closet. She curled the droopy ends of her hair, jogged back to her bedroom to slip on her shoes and grab her purse, and discovered in the mirror above her dresser that the curling iron hadn't done its job. Her hair appeared just as limp and lackluster as usual.

Relax. Kate O'Leary's command echoed inside Robin's skull. This wasn't the high school prom, and if Jesse didn't already like her, he wouldn't have asked her out. If he didn't like her, he wouldn't have kissed her. Closing her eyes, she relived in her mind that brief, glancing kiss. She recalled the whisper-soft pressure of his lips on hers, the subtle flavor of him, his musky scent. Of course he liked her, and everything was going to go perfectly. Confidence washed through her, and she was smiling when she went downstairs to keep Kate and

Philip company while they devoured the chicken Kate had broiled for their supper.

By a quarter after seven, they were done eating and the kitchen was clean. That Jesse was fifteen minutes late wasn't unforgivable, Robin tried to convince herself. She joined Kate and Philip in the den, where Philip wolfed down an apple and three cookies and grilled Robin interminably about the stories presented on the network newscast. Where exactly was Nicaragua? he wanted to know. Had Daddy ever worked there? Which of the candidates did Robin support in the upcoming presidential primary?

Robin answered all of Philip's questions as calmly as she could. She didn't want him to know how overly conscious she was of the ticking of the clock, of the passing of the minutes. But soon it was seven-thirty, and then it was a quarter to eight, and Jesse didn't come.

Her first date, and she had been stood up. So this was the way atheists viewed their obligations, she fumed. Oh, Jesse might be noble when it came to his poor clients, but when it came to Robin, a woman he'd invited out for dinner, a divorcée who believed, just a little bit, in Santa Claus...

At nine o'clock she tucked Philip into bed. Then she changed out of her dress and into her sweat shirt and jeans. She told Kate she could go home, but Kate insisted on staying a little longer. Obviously she felt that Robin shouldn't be left alone when she was in such a foul mood.

After washing off her makeup, Robin stormed to the kitchen and helped herself to a leftover drumstick. Once she had nibbled it to the bone, she again requested that Kate go home. Sighing, shaking her head and mumbling about the disproportionate number of men who were cads, lice, and assorted other vermin, Kate pulled her coat from the closet and slipped it on.

And then the phone rang.

exclaimed, and swept into venting. Jane pulled her
coat open the closet and slipped... cloth
And pack the box in boxes.

Chapter Four

"I'm sorry," said Jesse.

Just those two words, delivered in a tired monotone, as if they'd dropped off his lips rather than risen from his heart. He had ruined Robin's evening, skewered her ego, and all he could say was "I'm sorry."

An inane memory visited her, of Philip when he was about three years old. Whenever he did something naughty back then, she used to remand him to the corner, where he had to stand until he said he was sorry. It didn't take him long to conclude that the sooner he said he was sorry, the sooner he'd be released from his sentence. So when she'd confine him to the corner, he would jam his little nose against the wall and, within a second, holler "I'm sorry!" and then romp out of the corner to resume playing. As if all he had to do was verbalize those two words and his transgression, no matter how severe, would be overlooked.

Did Jesse actually believe that uttering "I'm sorry" was enough to win him Robin's instant forgiveness? The way she was feeling, she'd like to send Jesse to the corner for a few years.

"Robin? Are you there?" he asked as her silence extended beyond a minute.

"Yes." She stared at the yellow kitchen wall to which the phone was attached, hoping that the daffodil color would soothe her bruised, bristling nerves and keep her from letting Jesse know how hurt and angry she was.

"I'm sorry about our date," he said. "I'm calling from Yale-New Haven Hospital. I was in an auto accident on my way home from work this evening."

Robin felt deluged with remorse. An accident! If ever a man had a valid excuse to break a date... "Are you all right?" she asked, frantic.

"I'm fine."

"Then why are you in the hospital?"

He emitted a short, humorless laugh. "I'm a lawyer, Robin. I know enough to plan ahead, in case there's a lawsuit. I feel all right now, but if I wake up six months from now and find myself paralyzed, I want it on record that I sought immediate medical attention."

"Jesse—"

"I'm fine, Robin," he insisted. "Really. I only wish I could say the same for my car." When she didn't speak, he added, "The doctors looked me over and released me. I'm free to leave."

"Maybe you should be spending the night there," she suggested, dubious. "For observation or something."

"There's nothing to observe. They've told me to go home."

"Then let me come and get you," she offered.

"No, that's all right. I think the policeman who brought me here can take me home. I don't want you driving when the roads are so bad."

"Don't be ridiculous," Robin argued. A little sleet was no big deal to someone who'd viewed nine New England winters through her windshield.

On the other hand, someone who hailed from Los
Angeles, as Jesse had, probably thought that ice was
something that came out of the freezer compartments of
refrigerators, never out of the sky. Immigrants like him
ought to be forced to take special driving courses the
minute they arrived in the northeast. "I'll be at the hospital as soon as I can," she told him, resolved. "Where
are you, in the emergency room?"

"That's right—but really, Robin, you don't have
to—"

"Stay put," she ordered him. "I'll be right there."
Before he could dispute her, she hung up.

Turning, she found Kate O'Leary unbuttoning her
coat in the doorway. "No problem," Kate assured her,
evidently having heard enough of the conversation to
recognize that Robin needed her baby-sitting services
for a while longer. Her round, generous face registered
dismay. "Is he hurt?"

Robin shook her head. "According to him, not as
badly as his car. I don't know how long I'll be, Kate,
but—"

Kate shooed her out of the kitchen with an impatient
wave of her hands. "Go and take care of him. And don't
you ever let him know I referred to him as vermin."

Robin donned her parka, grabbed her purse and keys,
and hurried through the front door. In the hours since
she'd left Woodleigh's, the temperature had risen a few
degrees, converting the sleet into fat drops of rain,
which quickly drenched her hair and face. Robin opened
the garage, climbed into her car, flicked on her lights
and windshield wipers and backed down the driveway.

She was no longer anxious. Jesse had insisted that he
was all right, and she believed him. Certainly no phy-
sician facing the current malpractice crunch would re-

lease a patient if there were the slimmest chance that he might not be in perfect health.

It took her twenty minutes to reach the hospital. She found a parking space not far from the emergency entrance, locked the car and went inside. The waiting area was well lit and crowded, an assortment of people occupying the vinyl chairs and hovering around the nurses' station. One dingy-looking elderly man appeared to be drunk; he swayed and mumbled to himself. A few family groups huddled here and there, some with sick-looking children. A uniformed police officer was conferring with one of the nurses at a desk.

Jesse sat alone near an end table covered with outdated magazines, a trench coat and a leather attaché case lying on the chair next to his. He had on a dark blue business suit, his tie gone and the collar button of his white shirt unfastened. His hair was rumpled, his jacket creased. Robin was unable to see his face because he was hunched over, perusing an official-looking form. "Jesse," she said, approaching him.

He peered up and smiled hesitantly at her. A large bluish welt marked his cheekbone below his left eye, and his lower lip looked puffy. The front of his shirt bore a splotch of dried blood.

"What's that from?" she asked, pointing at the small stain.

He glanced down, then lifted his face to hers again. "My lip," he said quietly. "I bit it."

She sighed, feeling the last of her tension ebb away. As composed as she'd felt during the drive to the hospital, she'd had to see him with her own eyes to make certain that he was truly safe and sound. One bruised cheek, one bitten lip. He hadn't lied; he was all right.

"I'm so sorry," she murmured, closing the distance between them.

He shrugged and reached for his attaché case. His actions were slow and deliberate, Robin noticed, and his left wrist was taped.

"Your arm?" she asked, requiring a full inventory of his injuries, no matter how minor they were.

"A slight sprain," he told her as he slid the papers into the briefcase and snapped it shut. Then he stood and slipped on his coat, moving woodenly. "From fighting the steering wheel. They x-rayed it, Robin. Nothing was broken. Seriously."

Her gaze roamed down his body, searching for further hints of physical damage. If he was bloodied or bandaged anywhere else, she found no evidence of it. Still, his stride lacked its usual grace. His limber legs carried him cautiously to her side, reminding her of the stiff way her mother sometimes moved when her arthritis acted up. "Are you sure you're free to leave?" Robin asked.

"Yes. And I'd love to. This place is beginning to get to me."

Nodding, Robin accompanied him outdoors. The pounding rain pasted her hair to her cheeks, and she thought wryly of her wasted effort with the curling iron earlier that evening. She also thought of her concern about her outfit, her exertion with her seldom used makeup applicators, her attempt to appear ravishingly beautiful for Jesse. Instead, here she was in her faded jeans, her University of Wisconsin sweat shirt, her loafers and parka, saturated and bedraggled.

Yet the way that Jesse gazed at her, the way his eyes glowed with gratitude and relief, made her feel as if she did look ravishingly beautiful.

She unlocked the passenger door of her station wagon, and Jesse gingerly lowered himself onto the seat, balancing the attaché case on the floor between his knees. She dashed around the car to the driver's side and climbed in, shaking the excess rainwater out of her hair and off her hands.

Jesse watched her for a moment as she started the engine and steered out of the parking lot. Then he turned to stare out the window. Robin respected his silence until they merged with the traffic on the turnpike. "Where did it happen?" she asked.

"On Brushy Plain Road," he answered, still facing forward. He sounded incredibly weary. "The vast majority of automobile accidents occur within ten minutes of home, isn't that right?"

She wasn't about to discuss statistical probabilities with him. "What happened? Did you forget to put snow tires on your car?"

"It wasn't my fault," he grunted.

She smiled gently. "I'm not blaming you, Jesse. This is your first winter in Connecticut, isn't it?"

"Just because I'm from Los Angeles doesn't mean I've never driven in bad weather before," he asserted. He sank into the seat, rolling his head back to the headrest and closing his eyes. "Some clown was tailgating me," he told her. "When I slowed down at a curve, he rear-ended me, and that put me into a spin. If it weren't for a strategically placed electrical pole, I'd probably still be spinning. The road was awfully slick."

A rear-end collision, a spin, a crash into an electrical pole. Robin shuddered. "It's a miracle you weren't hurt worse."

His eyes still closed, he issued a dry laugh. "I wasn't

saved by a miracle," he disputed her. "I was saved by my seat belt."

Of course. Atheists didn't believe in miracles. "How's the other driver?" she asked.

Another bitter laugh escaped him. "The poor guy—his bumper was dented."

She accepted his sarcasm without question. Wasn't that always the way it went—the person responsible was the person to suffer the least. "It must have been very frightening," she commiserated. She'd never been in an accident herself; she could only imagine how dreadful the experience must have been.

"It was," Jesse confirmed.

"I'm so sorry," she repeated, reaching across the seat to squeeze his hand.

Still leaning against the headrest, he turned to her and opened his eyes. Her attention was glued to the road ahead, but she could feel the intensity of his gaze as it coursed over her. "So am I," he admitted. "This wasn't the night I had planned for us."

"What I mean is—" She surrendered to a strong compulsion to confess. "I'm sorry that I was mad at you for standing me up. There you were, going through this terrible thing, and—"

"You were entitled to be angry. You didn't know."

"Where's your car now?" she asked, coasting onto the exit ramp in Branford.

"It was towed to that Mobil station on the corner," he said, gesturing with his arm. "They said I could leave it there overnight. The insurance adjuster has to have a look at it before it's salvaged for scrap metal."

Succumbing to curiosity, Robin turned right instead of left, heading for the Mobil station. "Can I see it?"

"Be my guest."

She turned into the dimly lit lot and cruised around the building to the back. Her headlights cut through the slanting rain to illuminate the mangled wreckage of Jesse's Volkswagen, which had been left at the edge of the asphalt lot. The rear end of the car was smashed in on one side, with the bumper and taillight missing. The entire front end of the car had accordioned inward from the impact of its skid into the electrical pole, and the windshield was a spiderweb of cracks.

Robin let out a cry at the gruesome sight. The image of Jesse's body trapped inside that heap of twisted metal and broken glass, the comprehension of what the car had undergone to have wound up so demolished… "I don't care what you say," she declared. "It *was* a miracle. Simply surviving would have been a miracle. But to have been able to walk away from a mess like that—"

"It was a seat belt," Jesse tersely refuted her.

Tension emanated from him as he stared through the downpour at the wreck. Robin suspected that looking at it was forcing him to relive the accident in his mind. She hastily shifted into gear and sped around the building, fleeing from the ghastly sight.

Neither of them spoke for a few minutes. Robin drove north toward her house, wondering exactly where on the road the accident had occurred. Would there be skid marks etched into the pavement? Shards of glass lying around? The missing Vokswagen bumper? She hoped that the scene had been cleaned up; she didn't want Jesse to have to view it. For that matter, she didn't want to view it herself.

Near the turnoff leading to her house, she slowed. "Come home with me," she suggested. "I'll fix you a

drink—some brandy, soup, whatever—and you can unwind.''

"No." His resolute gaze seemed to penetrate her,
seeping beneath her skin as he studied her from across
the front seat. "I appreciate the invitation, Robin, but...
I think I need some time alone."

"I understand," she said. She wasn't sure how wise
it was to leave him all by himself after what he'd just
been through, but he must know his own needs. She had
no right to question his decision.

Bypassing her turnoff, she continued up the road to
the neighborhood she and Joanna had dubbed Mondo
Condo. Eventually, Jesse directed her to turn left, and
at the bottom of a hill they entered his condominium
complex. "That's my house," he said, pointing to a
spacious-looking town house at the bottom of a rolling
hill of grass, and then to a staircase leading down the
hill from the road. "Park anywhere near the stairs."

Robin shut off the engine and scrutinized the stairs.
They appeared slippery with rainwater. Recalling how
stiffly Jesse had moved in the emergency room, she
climbed out of the car and around to his side. "I'm
walking you to the door," she announced before he
could ask what she was doing. "You're creaky and sore;
I don't want you taking a spill on those steps."

"Yes, ma'am," he complied, grinning reluctantly. He
refused to let her carry his attaché case, however. As
creaky and sore as he was, he clearly wasn't going to
let Robin treat him like an invalid.

The steps were as slippery as they looked, and Robin
gripped Jesse's elbow to steady herself as much as him.
When they reached the bottom, he led her along a winding walk to his front porch, which was protected from
the rain by an overhang. He set down his briefcase, dug

into his pocket for his keys, then paused and turned to Robin. "Thank you for bringing me home," he said.

"It was the least I could do."

"Sure. After I stood you up." He offered a lopsided smile, then cupped his hands over her shoulders. "I…" He seemed momentarily at a loss, and then his eyes came into focus on her upturned face, on the raindrops trapped in her eyelashes and skittering down her cheeks. "Thank you," he whispered, his tone freighted with a meaning Robin was unable to interpret.

She checked herself before protesting once more that she hadn't done anything particularly wonderful, that picking him up at the hospital hadn't been such an onerous task, that she cared about him and acted accordingly. Jesse's gaze seemed to impale her, numbing her ability to think, let alone speak.

His mouth descended to hers, and their lips met cautiously, tenderly. Remembering that he'd bitten his lip deeply enough to bleed from it, Robin didn't dare to lean toward him or press her mouth too eagerly to his. She didn't want to hurt him.

The pressure came from him. He seemed oblivious of his wound, his mouth moving with surprising force against hers, his arms winding tightly around her and his fingers digging possessively into her wet hair. His tongue thrust past her teeth and deep into her mouth, filling it, consuming, shocking her with the sudden throbbing desire it aroused within her.

It wasn't just that she hadn't been kissed like this since her divorce—since long before her divorce, if she wanted to be honest about it. Her response to Jesse's kiss defied logic, just as his kiss itself did. Reeling with sensations that had lain dormant inside her for so long she had all but forgotten about them, she slid her hands beneath the flaps of his trench coat, circling his waist and holding him close, absorbing the warmth and hardness of his body, feeling the shift of his muscles, his hips, the tension in his thighs as they met hers.

When he finally drew back, he was gasping for breath. "Oh, Robin…Robin." He cradled her head against him, combing his trembling fingers through her hair. "I don't know what I'm doing."

"You're kissing me," she breathed.

"Yes." His lips brushed over her forehead. "I'm kissing you." His arms pinned her to him for a moment longer, then relented. He drew his hands forward to frame her face, tilting it up so their eyes met. "I want to ask you in," he whispered. "But I can't."

"I know," she murmured. She knew that he wanted to ask her in, and that he couldn't, but she didn't know why. Nor did she know whether, if he had asked her in, she would have said yes or no. In fact, she wasn't sure what she knew, beyond the fact that Jesse was about to go inside by himself and she was about to get back into her car and drive home. His kiss had left her with the disturbing notion that she didn't know anything at all.

"Can I see you tomorrow?"

"Tomorrow," she echoed, scrambling to resurrect her sanity. "I've got to be at Woodleigh's till three, and I promised Phil I'd take him to the Milford Mall afterward to do some Christmas shopping."

"I could come with you."

"Christmas shopping?" She laughed. It was a delayed laugh; his kiss had shocked her, but she couldn't have laughed then. The possibility that Jesse would want to go Christmas shopping was nearly as shocking, however, and the familiar sound of her own laughter relaxed her.

"I've got to meet with the insurance adjuster tomorrow morning, and make arrangements for a rental car until I can buy a replacement," he explained. "But I should be done by three o'clock."

"Do you really want to go to a holiday-infested mall?" she questioned him. "With Philip?"

"I want..." He sighed, his fingers raveling through her hair again. "I want to be with you. It doesn't matter where."

The extravagance of his claim disconcerted her. She understood that he hadn't said it simply to compliment her. It had been an expression of need, and she wouldn't deny him what he needed. She didn't want to. "Come by around three-thirty," she said. "We'll be ready to storm the mall by then."

He nodded slightly, then bowed and touched his lips to hers one last time. Then he released her, unlocked the front door and stepped inside. "Tomorrow," he murmured. He remained in the open doorway, watching until she returned to her car, backed out of the parking space, drove down the road and away.

PEOPLE OFTEN SAID that, at such times, your life passed before your eyes. Jesse had never before had the opportunity to test that hypothesis, but he now knew that it was true.

It hadn't been what he might have expected, though. He would have guessed that a person viewed his life as if it were a chronological film, from birth to the present, running in fast-forward. In his case it had been quite different: a series of strobelike images, out of sequence, defying order or rationality. In those few agonizing seconds, from the first sickening thud and lurch of the car, through the nauseating spin and into the final, horrifying crunch of metal against solid wood, he'd seen instants, tasted memories, experienced split-second slices of personal history.

Mrs. Selby's face, that was the first. Her worn, demoralized expression as she'd sat across his desk that very afternoon, moaning, "You got to help me, Mr. Lawson! I want my boy home for Christmas!" Then his mother's face, her distant half smile as she benignly announced, "Marybeth's gone." His father's voice, floating to Jesse from another room, crowing, "It's mine, they've chosen me, but they want me to change my name." Anne, her lush auburn waves tumbling about her lovely face, muttering, "If you won't stay in line, then you don't belong here." A crystal star shooting rainbow lights into his eyes, temporarily blinding him. A towering palm tree casting a shadow across the swimming pool behind his parents' house. And then another swimming pool, a huge public one, seemingly miles below an eight-year-old Jesse as he stood on the high diving board. Mickey Santangelo had dared Jesse to jump off, and he'd been petrified. But he'd filled his lungs with air, bounced on the spring end of the board, and heard Mickey behind him, shouting, "Cross yourself, Jesse, cross yourself!"

And then the jump, the breathless, endless, shapeless fall, the deafening roar of water in his ears, water below him, above him, around him, the disorientation, the certainty that he was sinking, that he would never see the sky again...and then the triumphant burst to the surface, to light, to life.

To the sight of his car's front end molded around an electrical pole, to the sound of sleet drilling against the roof of the car, to the throbbing of his pulse in his temples, the fierce ache in his wrist and on his cheek.

To the melodic whisper of a woman's voice. *Something so wonderful. A home, a job, a son...* That sweet, mantric whisper, a vision of truth, stability, morality. A glorious woman with blond hair and steadfast eyes and the most genuine smile Jesse had ever viewed, whispering; *Other things happen, wonderful things. Miracles.*

Gradually he came to grips with what had occurred. He returned to full consciousness, to the fact that his car was demolished and he himself wasn't, that he was really alive, essentially unscathed. As his mind clarified itself, he realized that that whisper, that chant had been with him throughout, a counterpoint to all the other images, an affirming continuum, a guide to lead him out of the nightmare.

The time he had plunged off the high board at Mickey Santangelo's goading, Jesse had been certain he was going to die until the moment he opened his eyes and saw the rippling surface of the water just inches above him and, beyond the surface, the sun. This time, as he'd fought his way to that glittering surface separating death from life, it hadn't been the sun directing him upward to life. It had been Robin, her face, her voice, her strength, her golden hair and her smile.

"Guardian angel," he mumbled, trudging up the stairs to his bedroom. He dropped onto the bed and stared at the ceiling, utterly drained. He ought to remove his clothing, take a hot shower—or maybe a bath. He ought to soak his traumatized body until it felt whole again. Then he ought to fix himself a drink. He didn't have anything as strong as brandy in the house, but he supposed a glass of wine would do. Or a bowl of soup, wasn't that what Robin had offered him? A bowl of hot soup, a couple of aspirin, a night of uninterrupted sleep.

But he couldn't do that as long as the concept of a guardian angel was lodged inside his skull. Jesse didn't believe in angels, guardian or otherwise. He didn't believe in miracles. He believed in seat belts.

Then why was it that, when he reviewed the accident in his mind, he kept coming to the conclusion that what had saved him wasn't his seat belt but rather a small, beautiful woman with a halo of yellow hair, murmuring, *Something so wonderful...*

When he finally heaved himself up to sit, he discovered that he'd been lying on the bed for over an hour. He was exhausted. He barely had the energy to peel off his clothes. The suit could be dry-cleaned, and the shirt—maybe bloodstains were removable, but he wasn't going to bother. He tossed the shirt into the garbage pail and stepped into the bathroom to take a shower.

The hot water pounding down on his aching body felt excruciating at first, but eventually it began to affect his knotted muscles and joints, loosening them, restoring them to their former elasticity. He remained beneath the spray until the water began to cool off, then wrapped himself in his terry-cloth robe and went downstairs for a drink. He didn't have a bottle of wine open, and he opted for hot chocolate instead.

He carried his mug into the living room and sank onto the leather sofa, which was positioned across the room from a bentwood rocker, a pedestal table, a lamp and a blank wall. The room looked stark, lacking any of the intimate touches that would make it a real home. Jesse wasn't good at decorating. It hadn't mattered out in Los Angeles; once he and Anne had gotten together, he'd wound up spending more time at her place than at his. She knew how to fix a place up, how to select pictures for hanging, how to arrange objets d'art. Her apartment hadn't been nearly as warm and lived-in as Robin's house, but it had been nicer than Jesse's sterotypically characterless bachelor pad.

They both had been earning huge incomes, but one of the differences between Anne and Jesse was that she knew how to spend money on herself and Jesse didn't. Anne had helped him to pick out his leather sofa and his leather jacket. "Being rich and living well isn't a sin," she used to say.

To that, Jesse would silently reply, "Then why are we living in sin?"

Not that Anne wanted him to marry her. "It doesn't matter, as long as we're discreet," she would insist. "Let's face it, Jesse, you and your father have different last names. Nobody has to put two and two together. You aren't going to embarrass him. I like things the way they are now. If we decide to get married down the road, then we have that option."

What she hadn't predicted was that Jesse had another option: leaving. Turning his back on the hypocrisy of it all.

The cocoa felt good going down. Jesse wondered whether Robin ever made cocoa for Philip. Of course she did, he recognized. If Philip had a rough day, Jesse imagined that Robin would give him cocoa, cuddle him to her, sing him lullabies. Even if the kid protested that only girls and wimps enjoyed lullabies, Robin would continue to croon to him—and Philip would secretly love being crooned to.

Jesse hadn't meant to kiss her.

He hadn't even expected to see her that night—the policeman had been hanging around the emergency room for hours, taking Jesse's statement between sessions with an X-ray technician and then taking more statements from the doctors. Jesse was sure the officer would give him a lift back to Branford.

But even if Jesse had expected to see Robin, he hadn't meant to kiss her. Not like that.

Yet he hadn't been able to help himself. It had started as a kiss of thanks and then escalated, until he was drinking her in like a drug, savoring her sweetness, her womanly warmth and power. Until he'd felt all over again as if she were beckoning him back to life, to triumph, to the miracle of his own survival.

"It *wasn't* a miracle," he grumbled, setting down his empty mug. A physicist, a highway safety expert, anyone with a bit of knowledge about momentum and resistance, centrifugal force or whatever it was that had buffeted Jesse could provide a perfectly reasonable, unmiraculous explanation for his having been able to walk away from such an accident. If it had been a miracle, that would imply divine intervention. And God didn't exist.

After all, if God did exist, why would He be putting a religious woman like Mrs. Selby through the wringer? Why, on top of the threat of losing her home, had God decided to foul up her son Gerald's Christmas leave so the poor woman had to drag herself all the way to Jesse's office that afternoon, sobbing about how if Gerald couldn't be home for Christmas she might as well just die, and please, *please*, couldn't Jesse do anything to get the Navy to see its way clear to send Gerald home for Christmas, because he had nothing to do with the outbreak of violence on board his ship and he shouldn't have to be sequestered along with the rest of the crew for the term of the investigation.

Jesse had explained to Mrs. Selby that taking on the

United States Navy was a tall order, and he doubted that much would come of any effort he made on her behalf to get her son released in time for the holiday. But she'd been so plaintive, so desperate, that he'd yielded and promised to make some inquiries. And she, in turn, had promised that she'd go home and pray to God to bring Gerald home for Christmas.

If God existed, Jesse mused, He shouldn't have arranged to have Gerald and his shipmates sequestered in Newport for Christmas. And if God existed, He shouldn't have given drivers the ability to tailgate other drivers on sleety, dusklit evenings. For that matter, God should never have invented sleet.

But then...then there were other things. Wonderful things. Miracles. Sunshine, and air, and life.

And women like Robin Greer.

Chapter Five

Robin lay awake for hours, writhing beneath the comforter, punching her pillows, tangling her feet in the hem of her nightgown and listening to the rain hammering against the roof that sloped above her head. She lay awake, picturing Jesse as he'd hovered in his open doorway watching her departure. Then she pictured him before her departure, when they'd stood together on his porch. She could still feel his arms around her, his hands coursing through her hair, his body, despite its injuries, strong and firm against hers. She could still taste his lips on hers, his tongue, his breath filling her. Hours after she'd bade him good-night, his presence was still with her.

His kiss hadn't been romantic, she realized in retrospect. It had been passionate—no question about that—and her passionate reaction to it had been understandable. She could accept the possibility that Jesse desired her, but desire hadn't been his motivation when he'd kissed her so powerfully outside his door. What she'd sensed in Jesse's kiss was raw, desperate need.

He'd been straightforward about not wanting her to enter his house. Surely, after a nearly devastating automobile accident, only a sex-crazed animal would want to race home and bed down a woman he hardly knew. Admittedly, Robin was flattered that Jesse had bothered to mention the idea, that he'd confessed that he did want her—but she wasn't surprised that he'd chosen not to follow through.

Yet he'd needed her. For that one devastating moment when his mouth had taken hers, and his arms had clung to her, he'd needed her. Not the way he'd needed her to pick him up at the hospital and ferry him home, but some other way, some mysterious way.

And now he wanted to go Christmas shopping with her and Philip. She wondered whether he was still intrigued by her son, or whether he would have agreed to anything just for the opportunity to spend the following day with her. Oddly enough, she found herself hoping that the former, and not the latter, was the truth. She wanted Jesse to like Philip. As Philip's mother, she wanted the entire world to like him—but especially Jesse. And as moved as she was by his kiss, as fascinated as she was by him, she wasn't at all certain she was ready for an attachment to develop between them.

Even though she slept poorly that night, she didn't require her alarm clock to awaken her in the morning. Philip took care of that, rising at seven and engaging in a strident game of fire chief—complete with vocalized sirens—right outside her closed bedroom door. "It's about time you got up," he chastised her once she stumbled groggily from her room. "We're going to the mall today, remember?"

"After I get home from Woodleigh's," she reminded him. "I'm sending you to Jeff's house till I get home."

"Okay," Philip said agreeably. "Santa Claus is going to be at the mall, right?"

"I'm pretty sure he is," Robin answered. "Jesse's

going to be coming with us, too," she added, praying that Jesse wouldn't balk or make snide remarks when Philip demanded to sit on Santa's knee. He had promised that he wouldn't disillusion Philip about Santa Claus, but— "Jesse?" Philip squawked, trailing Robin to the bathroom and gaping at her as she brushed her teeth. "Did he ever come last night?"

"No," she replied after spitting out the toothpaste. "He was in a car accident. A very minor one," she fibbed, hoping not to frighten Philip. "But he's all right, and he's going to come to the mall with us this afternoon."

"I guess he's got to do his Christmas shopping, too," Philip commented.

Did he? Robin wondered as she returned to her bedroom to dress. Would a confirmed Christmas-tree-hater like Jesse bother to do Christmas shopping at all? Or was he so negative about the holiday that he didn't even exchange gifts with his family and friends? Did atheists refuse to believe in green-and-red foil wrapping paper, ribbons and bows, stockings stuffed with goodies? Did they refuse to believe in fruitcake and eggnog and rolled sugar cookies shaped like bells and stars? There was a whole lot more to Christmas than simply the religious aspects—they were important, of course, but the holiday entailed so much else. How could anyone, no matter what his faith, thumb his nose at such delights?

She probably should have refused Jesse's offer to join her and her son this afternoon. He might turn out be a grouch, bah-humbugging throughout the mall and transforming Philip's favorite annual outing into a miserable episode. But it was too late to disinvite Jesse. All she could do was hope that he behaved himself around the child.

Despite the hectic activity at the store, Robin was able to escape a few minutes before three. She drove directly to the Calloway house, around the corner from her own, to pick up Philip. Joanna answered her ring and hastened Robin inside. "Come on in," Joanna welcomed her. "I'm just fixing some coffee."

"I can't stay," Robin said, not bothering to open her jacket. "Philip and I are going to—"

"The Connecticut Post Mall," Joanna completed with a phony yawn. "He hasn't shut up about it all day. But you can spare a minute," she insisted, ushering Robin into the kitchen. "Glenn and the boys are downstairs, tearing up the rec room. I want to hear about what happened last night with Jesse."

"Nothing happened." As soon as the words were out, Robin acknowledged their falseness. Too much had happened last night—the accident, the drive to the emergency room, the pilgrimmage to view Jesse's crushed car. The kiss.

Joanna filled two cups with coffee and presented one to Robin. "What do you mean, nothing happened?"

"He had to cancel," Robin told her. "He was in a fender-bender on the way home from work."

"A fender-bender?" Joanna appeared indignant. "He canceled for that?"

"It was a little worse than a fender-bender," Robin conceded. "He sprained his wrist and got a black eye."

"Oh, no," Joanna moaned, now persuaded that he'd been justified in breaking his date with Robin. "That poor man. Did he make another date with you, at least?"

Robin took an obligatory sip of coffee, then set the cup down on a counter and sighed. Joanna was her closest friend, yet she didn't feel up to divulging what had happened when she'd taken Jesse home. She could scarcely make sense of it herself; she wasn't about to describe the moment to Joanna. "He's coming with us to the mall today," she answered carefully. "That's why I can't stay."

Joanna's face brightened. "He's going shopping with you? How romantic!"

"Shopping is hardly romantic," Robin argued.

Joanna shrugged. "Humor me," she said. "I'm an old married lady. I've got to get my thrills vicariously."

"Shopping isn't thrilling, either. The mall is going to be overcrowded and noisy. We're going to spend more time standing in lines than getting things accomplished. You know what a zoo that place is at this time of year." Robin knew she sounded surly, but she refused to allow herself too much optimism about how the remainder of the day would proceed. Jesse was definitely not the sort of man who would consider Christmas shopping either thrilling or romantic. "I'd better get Phil and go home," she resolved, jingling her key ring. "I've got to change my clothes before Jesse comes."

Descending to the finished basement, Robin found Philip, Jeff, and Jeff's younger brother Brian dueling with the bolster cushions from the couch while, oblivious of the circus around him, Glenn watched a college basketball game. As soon as he saw his mother, Philip threw down his cushion. "We're going to see Santa!" he shouted, practically knocking Robin over as he raced across the room. "Maybe we'll even get a tree tonight!"

"It's much too early for a tree," Robin objected, although Philip gave no indication of having heard her. In a trice, he was upstairs, buttoning his jacket and bounding out the front door to the station wagon. Robin quickly thanked Joanna for having watched Philip, then dashed down the walk to join him in the car.

As soon as she turned the corner, she spotted the small white automobile parked at the curb in front of her house. Her gaze shot to the door, where she saw Jesse seated on the porch step, clad in jeans, a crewneck sweater and his suede jacket. "There's Jesse," Philip announced unnecessarily. "We can leave right away."

"No, we can't," Robin cautioned him, coasting to a halt in the driveway and turning off the engine. "I'm not going shopping in my work clothes."

Jesse stood as Philip sprang from the car and scampered up the walk. Robin moved at a more leisurely gait, appraising Jesse's face as she neared him. The bruise was still visible below his eyes, but it had faded from a vivid purple to a subdued grayish-blue. His wrist was still taped. "Are you sure you're feeling well enough to do this?" she asked as she climbed the step to the porch.

Jesse smiled and grabbed Philip by the arm, halting him before he'd executed a complete circuit around the adults. "Hello to you, too," he greeted Robin before admonishing Philip, "slow down, pal. You'd better save your energy for the mall."

Relief swept through Robin. Jesse's remark assured her that he had the correct attitude about Christmas shopping. At least in front of Philip, he was willing to display the proper enthusiasm. "I'll be five minutes, guys," she said, unlocking the front door and leading them inside. "I've got to get out of this skirt."

"Five minutes is all you're getting," Philip warned her as she headed up the stairs. "Any longer and I'm gonna make Jesse take me without you."

It would serve you both right, Robin countered silently, although she was laughing as she hurried into her bedroom to exchange her skirt for a pair of slacks. Clearly, Jesse was fond of Philip, and sensitive to the youngster's need to believe. He wasn't going to spoil the day.

True to her word, she was downstairs before five minutes had elapsed. The three of them trooped out to the station wagon, and Jesse didn't quibble when Robin volunteered to drive. "I'm not crazy about that rental car," he admitted, glaring at the white automobile as Robin backed past it. "It's an automatic, and I'm used to a standard transmission. And it doesn't have enough leg room."

"Why didn't you rent something bigger?" she asked.

"My insurance wouldn't cover it," he explained. "Anyway, I don't plan to have it long. The adjuster said he'd process my claim today, which means I should be receiving a check by the end of the week. I'll get a replacement as soon as I can."

"Is Santa bringing you a new car?" Philip called from the back seat.

Jesse twisted to look at the boy. Robin held her breath, awaiting his reply. "Actually, I'm buying myself a new car," he told Philip. "December twenty-fifth is a long way off. I don't think I want to wait till then."

There was definitely no cause for concern, Robin mused, relaxing in her seat and steering toward the turnpike. Jesse couldn't have provided a better answer to Philip's question.

"How are you feeling?" Robin asked Jesse once Philip had subsided in the back seat.

"Pretty good."

"You aren't moving as stiffly as you were yesterday," she observed.

Jesse gazed thoughtfully at her. Her mention of the previous night evidently stirred his memory of what, besides the accident, had occurred the last time they were together. "Look, Robin," he murmured softly. "About last night—"

She cut him off with a brisk shake of her head, then angled it toward her son in the back seat. "Some other time," she whispered. In a louder voice, she asked, "I take it you had no problems with the insurance adjuster?"

"None at all. The whole thing took less than two hours." He turned to face the windshield, studying the smoothly flowing traffic on the highway. "I wound up spending most of the morning working."

"Really? On a Saturday?"

Jesse chuckled. "Lawyers who make house calls also work on weekends," he rationalized.

"It must be an important case if you'd work half of Saturday on it, right after totaling your car."

He shrugged. "It's an impossible case, actually. One of my clients found out that her son, who's in the Navy, had his Christmas leave revoked. She's asked me to take on the Pentagon and get him home for the holiday."

Robin groaned. She was naturally interested in tales about the hassles the armed forces regularly visited upon its personnel. How many times had her father's transfers been subjected to last-minute alterations? How many times had a transfer date been changed, so that her father had to ship off weeks ahead of Robin and her mother, stranding them to pack everything and empty the house without him? How many times were their belongings rerouted by mistake, leaving them living in a strange new residence without any clothing or furniture for days on end? "Don't tell me the Navy's as bad as the Army about these things. How come they revoked the kid's leave?"

"There was a violent incident on his ship," Jesse related. "Some sort of gang rivalry. A small fire was set, and a few seamen were injured. Once they dock in Newport, the whole crew is being held for questioning."

"At Christmastime?" Robin exclaimed. "That's terrible! Why can't they do their investigation at sea?"

"I may be a lawyer, but I don't pretend to understand military logic," Jesse countered with a dry laugh. "Nor do I expect to be able to help my client. But she's so heartbroken about it, I promised her I'd make some inquiries."

"Of course she's heartbroken," Robin concurred. "If I couldn't have Philip with me for Christmas, I'd die."

Jesse shot her a skeptical glance. "You wouldn't die, Robin. Christmas isn't worth dying over."

Robin glimpsed Philip, who was staring out the window, apparently not listening to the adult conversation. She turned her attention back to the road. "All right, so maybe I've overstated the case," she allowed. "But not by much. Christmas is the most important time of the year when it comes to family. Philip's my family. If I couldn't have him with me…what point would there be in celebrating the holiday?"

"I don't know," Jesse answered slowly. "I'm not sure there is a point, even in the best of circumstances."

Robin grimaced. This was not the proper attitude. "I take it you aren't going to celebrate Christmas with your family," she presumed, not caring if she sounded judgmental.

"No." His tone was lighter when he asked, "How do you want to work this shopping expedition, Robin?

Would you like me to keep Philip occupied while you buy his presents?"

The gloom that had momentarily settled around Robin lifted at his generous offer. "Would you? That would be great, Jesse. I'd really appreciate it. If you wouldn't mind—"

"If I minded, I wouldn't have suggested it."

"He's going to run you ragged," she warned.

Jesse laughed. "I'm bigger than he is. I can handle him."

The parking lot outside the mall was crammed with cars, and residual puddles and patches of ice from the previous day's storm marred the paved surface. Robin had to park at the far end of a row of cars. As soon as Philip climbed out of the car, he stepped on an ice patch and took a spill. His anguished roar resounded throughout the parking lot.

"Where did you hurt yourself?" Robin asked swiftly, kneeling down beside him and arching her arm around his heaving shoulders. He didn't appear to be seriously injured, and she wondered whether his overreaction was a result of embarrassment or simply of being so keyed up. Or maybe it was a prophecy of what the rest of the day had in store for them, she thought grimly.

He held up his hand. The palm was scraped, and a few pebbles of gravel stuck to the skin. She dusted them off and kissed his hand several times. "There. All better?"

"All better," he said, bravely sniffling away his tears and heaving himself to his feet.

As she trekked to the nearest entrance with Jesse and Philip, passing countless cars and dozens of scowling people burdened with packages, she cringed at the comprehension of how crowded the mall would be. Her expectations bore out. Massive swarms of shoppers milled around the mall's interior, blocking the store entrances and promenades, jamming their rear ends onto benches, littering the floor with food wrappers and cigarette butts. The throngs wouldn't have bothered Robin, except for Jesse. He must hate this sort of thing, she realized—thousands of people spending hundreds of thousands of dollars in honor of a holiday he didn't consider worth celebrating. And, to top it off, the mall was decorated to the limit with evergreen bowers, artificial snowmen, glitter and tinsel and electric candles with flashing flame-shaped lights. Overhead speakers boomed sprightly renditions of Christmas carols down to the shoppers.

At the center of the mall, across the fountain from an enormous spruce tree dripping with electric lights and painted balls, a fenced-off area covered with fake snow housed a cute little red-and-green hut bearing a sign reading Santa's Workshop. Plastic reindeer—including one with a glowing red nose—and red-garbed elves were positioned inside the fence. In front of the hut, a huge man in an impressive Santa Claus costume sat on a throne. A snaking line of children waited their turn to sit on Santa's lap, and a photographer was on hand to preserve on film each child's encounter with Santa.

"Santa Claus!" Philip shrieked, racing to the fence and gawking at the bearded, pot-bellied character. "Can I talk to Santa Claus before we go shopping?"

"It's a very long line," Robin pointed out. "Maybe later, when everybody goes home for dinner—"

"I'll wait in line with him," Jesse declared. "Why don't you take care of your shopping?"

Robin hesitated. She couldn't imagine Philip having the forebearance to wait in the line for more than fifteen minutes, and her shopping would take much longer than that. Still, if Jesse was willing...

"Better yet," he recommended, "why don't we arrange to meet somewhere in, say, an hour and a half?" He surveyed his noisy, teeming surroundings in search of a good meeting place. "The entry to the steak house," he decided. "By five-thirty we'll be ready for dinner."

Robin wavered. "Are you sure you don't mind?"

He gazed down at her, his eyes dark and constant, glittering with good-natured tolerance. "I wouldn't mind sitting on Santa's lap myself. I want to ask him for a Porsche, preferably silver, with a sunroof, delivered two weeks ahead of schedule."

Robin laughed. "Well, if you insist. The steak house at five-thirty." Before Jesse could change his mind, she kissed Philip's cheek, ordered him not to give Jesse a hard time, and slipped away.

"I'VE ALREADY TOLD Mom what I want for Christmas," Philip solemnly informed Jesse as they inched along the line. "But just to be safe, I think I ought to tell Santa, too."

"That sounds like a wise strategy," Jesse confirmed.

At another time he might have found all the seasonal hoopla repulsive. But his current mood left no room for disgruntlement. Ever since he'd awakened that morning, feeling well rested and not at all achy, his spirits had been high. He was glad to be alive, glad and grateful. All of this holiday nonsense—the mannequins spruced up in silver furs and red stocking caps, the silver-foil snowflakes dangling from the vaulted ceilings, the screaming children competing with the choral performance of "Little Drummer Boy" oozing from the overhead speakers, the tight grip of Philip's small hand within his—it was all a part of being alive.

Christmas was just the outer trapping. The inner truth of this frenzied environment was that these people, these frazzled parents and demanding children, were alive, too. They were all survivors. That was what they were here to celebrate.

"Are you really gonna ask him for a Porsche?" Philip questioned Jesse. "I used to have a Matchbox Porsche, but I don't know where it is. I think Jeff's kid brother Brian lost it. He loses everything. He's four years old."

"That's a rough age," Jesse noted, nudging Philip forward in the line. "Does your mom want a picture of this?" he asked, scanning the placard posted by the fence listing the prices the photographer charged for his snapshots and enlargements.

"Nah. Too expensive," Philip said rationally. "I've got to get a present for her, too. And for Mrs. O'Leary. I've got almost fifteen dollars. You know what? Adam Worblin, he's the worst speller in our class, he said he's gonna give Ms. Becker a Christmas present. Ms. Becker's my teacher."

Jesse nodded. "She's my neighbor."

"She is?" Philip confronted him with a saucer-eyed stare. "She lives near you?"

"She lives next door to me."

"Wow." Philip took a minute to absorb Jesse's astounding revelation. "Is she as boring at home as she is in class?"

Jesse laughed. One of the best things about children was that they weren't hypocrites. They said exactly what was on their minds. "She isn't that boring at home," he told Philip. "Maybe what's boring about your class isn't the teacher but the schoolwork."

Philip considered that possibility, then discarded it. "Nah. It's her. She's really boring. My turn's next!" He strained at Jesse's hand, leaning toward the gate. "What a wienie," Philip whispered to Jesse after listening to the wish list of the child on Santa's lap. "He wants books."

"What's wrong with books?" Jesse asked.

"You can get them for free at the library. It's my turn!" After practically colliding with the young bookworm leaving the fenced enclosure, Philip hopped onto Santa's knee. Jesse stood to one side of Santa's throne, signaling to the photographer that he wasn't interested in a photograph. "My name's Phil Greer," Philip announced, "and here's what I want: another Transformer, some more Masters of the Universe things, and a rocket ship. Maybe a battery-operated one, with lights that go on and off. Okay?"

Grinning, Santa glanced at Jesse to make sure he'd heard Philip's requests. He winked, then bowed to address the boy on his lap. "That's a lot of stuff, Phil. Have you been a good boy this year?"

"I've been so good it's disgusting," Philip asserted.

"Well, I'll see what my elves can do for you."

"Okay, but no clothes," Philip implored him. "My grandma's going to send me clothes. She always does."

"That's what grandmas are for," Santa allowed. He reached into a sack at his feet and pulled out two candy canes. "Here you go, Phil, one for you and one for your dad. Merry Christmas! Ho-ho-ho!" With that, he lifted Philip off his lap, eyed the line, and sighed wearily.

"Hey, did you hear that?" Philip asked Jesse, handing him one of the candy canes and tearing the wrapper off the other. "He thought you were my dad. Pretty funny, huh?"

Jesse was too nonplussed to find Santa's error funny. He liked Philip a lot, and he liked Philip's mother at least as much. But to be mistaken for Philip's father was a bit unnerving.

"You got any kids, Jesse?" Philip inquired, taking Jesse's hand and leading him toward the department store at the center of the mall. He playfully hooked the rounded end of his candy cane over his lower lip, smirked, and bit off an inch of minty candy.

Jesse pocketed his candy cane and tightened his hold on Philip, afraid of losing him in the surging throngs of customers. "No, I don't," he answered as nonchalantly as he could.

"Maybe you ought to have some," Philip advised him.

Jesse closed his eyes and tried to sort his thoughts. First Santa had taken him as Philip's father, and now Philip was counseling him on paternity. Was this what the Christmas spirit did to people?

"My mom told me where kids come from," Philip claimed. "It sounds pretty gross to me."

"It isn't gross," Jesse calmly corrected him. "It's the most beautiful thing in the world." He was surprised to hear himself make such a statement. The subject of birth and babies had never been particularly relevant to his life. Anne hadn't wanted children—if she had, she might have been keener on the idea of marriage—and Jesse had assumed that if children were ever to enter his world, it would be sometime in the distant future.

Yet what he'd said to Philip was the truth, and as soon as he'd said it, he understood how right he was. "I bet your mother looked beautiful when she was pregnant with you," he mused aloud. "I bet those were some of the happiest days of her life, Philip."

"Call me Phil," he said, effecting a mature tone. "Wow. Look at that necklace. Maybe I'll get that for Mom."

Jesse followed Philip's outstretched finger to the diamond-and-gold pendant on display inside a locked glass showcase. Grinning, he shook his head. "I think that might be beyond your means," he commented gently.

"Yeah? How about those gloves, then?" Philip asked, pointing to a pair of fur-lined leather gloves inside another showcase.

Jesse chuckled. "Rule of thumb, Phil—if it's locked up and doesn't have a price tag showing, you can't afford it."

Philip considered Jesse's observation and accepted the sensibility of it. "What are you gonna get my mom?" he asked.

Jesse swallowed. He hadn't planned to buy any Christmas gifts this year. But then, he hadn't planned to meet someone like Robin. Or like Philip. "I haven't given it much thought," he admitted.

"Maybe I ought to get Mrs. O'Leary's present first," Philip resolved. "Where do you suppose they've got those remote-control trucks?"

"I don't know that she'd really want one of those," Jesse remarked. Not that he was on intimate terms with Philip's baby-sitter, but he felt it safe to assume that an elderly woman like Mrs. O'Leary wouldn't be enamored of such a toy. "How about a book?" He recalled the boy Philip had called a wienie at Santa's Workshop. "That might be within your budget."

"Hey, that's a good idea," Philip agreed, masterfully

weaving among the crush of shoppers and dragging
Jesse out of the store. "She likes crossword puzzles.
Maybe I could get her one of those books of puzzles."

"She'd love that," Jesse heartily concurred. They
made their way across the mall in the direction of a book
emporium.

Philip paused near the workshop and studied Santa
for a moment. "You know what?" he whispered. "That
guy—he isn't really Santa Claus."

"Oh?" Jesse didn't bother to temper his smile. No
wonder he'd liked Philip right from the start—he must
have recognized the boy as a fellow cynic. "How do
you know that?"

"Two things," Philip explained. "Number one, the
real Santa doesn't have time to sit around shopping cen-
ters. He's too busy supervising the elves at the North
Pole right now. And number two, the real Santa
would've known that you weren't my dad. This guy's
a fake. But that's okay," he concluded with a shrug.
"Maybe he'll get my message to Santa, anyway."

"I'm sure he'll do his best," Jesse said solemnly as
he led Philip into the bookstore.

ROBIN JOGGED PAST the lengthy rows of cars and back
into the mall. It was five-thirty-five, and she'd just
locked her packages inside the station wagon. The
crowds had thinned slightly with the arrival of dinnertime, and she had little difficulty locating Jesse and
Philip near the entrance to the steak house. Jesse was
holding a large paper bag with a bookstore's logo
printed across it.

"Didn't you buy me anything?" Philip asked, his
face registering disappointment as he stared at her
empty hands.

"It's in the car," she told him before lifting her face to Jesse. "You seem to have survived," she observed.

"By the skin of my teeth," he complained, though he was smiling. "Can I interest you in some food? We menfolk are starving."

They entered the steak house. The restaurant was doing a brisk business, but they didn't have to wait long for a table. Jesse and Robin ordered steaks, Philip a hamburger. He scrutinized his mother while they waited for their food. "Did you get lots of stuff?" he asked.

"I got what I came for," she answered cryptically. Part of the fun of Christmas was to keep Philip fretting and guessing, even though he had to know that she wouldn't let him down on the big day.

"You didn't get me clothes, did you?"

Robin laughed. "I'm leaving that for your grandmothers. And don't worry—I've already sent them both linens from Woodleigh's. With your name on the cards."

Philip's relief was palpable. He twisted to Jesse. "Mom takes care of everything," he boasted. Then he turned back to Robin. "Did you get something for Jesse?"

Her cheeks colored slightly as she glanced across the table. Jesse leaned back in his seat, obviously amused by Philip's lack of discretion. While she'd been running from store to store, purchasing toys for Philip, a sweater for Kate O'Leary, yo-yos for Jeff and Brian Calloway and a box of chocolates for Joanna—Joanna loved chocolates but Glenn refused to buy them for her because he didn't want her to get fat—Robin had searched for something that would be right for Jesse. But other than a new car, she didn't know what he could use, what he might want. She had decided to wait until she knew him better. Maybe she could find something for him at Woodleigh's. Given what he'd told her about his condominium, she felt safe in assuming that he could use a household item of some sort. Maybe one of the brass wine racks.

She hadn't yet made up her mind, but she knew she was going to give Jesse something.

"So, listen, Mom," Philip ventured. Their food had arrived, and he was drowning his hamburger in ketchup. "I think we ought to get our tree tomorrow."

"Philip, we've already discussed this. It's too soon to get a tree."

"They've got a tree here," Philip argued. "And it isn't an artificial one, like the one you've got at Woodleigh's. Jesse and I checked. It's a live one."

"This is a huge mall," Robin pointed out. "If their tree dries out, they can afford to get a replacement for it. If ours dries out, all we'll have by Christmas morning is a carpet full of brown needles."

"Not if we water it a lot," Philip maintained. Then he glanced at Jesse, seeking an ally. "Tell her, Jesse. Tell her we should get a tree tomorrow."

"You should get a tree tomorrow," Jesse obliged.

Robin's eyes widened. She had concluded from his happy, exhilarated mood that Jesse hadn't had too terrible a time with Philip. But to hear him state that Robin ought to buy a Christmas tree—let alone that she ought to buy one tomorrow—astonished her. "Get serious," she chided him.

"I am serious," he insisted, carving his steak. "It won't dry out if you keep it watered."

"Jesse. I thought you didn't...well..." She refused to finish the sentence; she didn't want to reveal to Philip that Jesse cared little for the holiday rituals.

"It's for Phil, not for me," Jesse reminded her.

Phil. Apparently things had gone quite amicably between her son and Jesse, if Philip had given him permission to call him by that name. Yet, as amicably as they'd gone, she couldn't imagine why Jesse was exhorting her to buy a tree. "Jesse—"

"What's the point of having a tree for only a few days?" he posed, his eyes meeting hers above the table and twinkling enigmatically. "If you're going to have one, you may as well enjoy it for as long as you can."

"I can't believe this," she muttered, unable to disguise her pleasure. "I can't believe that you, of all people—"

"Having trouble with your beliefs?" he teased. "Perhaps it's time you revised your philosophy."

"There's nothing wrong with my philosophy."

"Then get the kid a tree."

"Two against one, Mom," Philip chimed in. "You lose."

Robin laughed. There *was* nothing wrong with her philosophy. She believed in miracles, and Philip had obviously worked a miracle on Jesse to get him excited about a Christmas tree, of all things.

And the truth was, two against one notwithstanding, Robin didn't feel the least bit as if she'd lost.

Chapter Six

It was one thing for Jesse to argue that Robin ought to buy a Christmas tree. It was another for him to insist on accompanying Philip and her when they went to get it.

In saner moments, she told herself that her relationship with Jesse—if "relationship" was the proper term—was downright peculiar. Weren't men and women supposed to get acquainted, go out on a few dates, explore their sexual attraction gradually, and, much later, attempt to build a friendship with each other's offspring? Once she had decided, during Open School Night, that she was going to reactivate her social life, she had assumed that this was the route she would take.

She had also decided that night that Jesse Lawson wasn't the man with whom she was going to embark on her new life as an available single woman. Perhaps she had sensed intuitively that he wasn't the sort of man with whom one could follow a predictable pattern in developing a relationship.

Everything about the times she'd spent with him seemed fragmented, backward, bewildering. And yet in her less sane moments—and she seemed to be having more and more of them—she was too delighted by whatever it was she had with Jesse to care about the route she was supposed to take.

Abandoning him to spend most of Saturday afternoon with Philip at the mall might have been incorrect, but it had worked out wonderfully. Driving to his condominium late Sunday morning to pick him up for their tree trip made just as much sense to her. The fact that Philip was as excited about seeing Jesse as Robin herself informed her that Jesse and her son had struck a fine friendship.

Maybe Philip needed a man in his life—a mentor, a role model, someone with whom he could act macho. Unlike so many children of divorce, he didn't have a father who neglected him. But Ray simply wasn't around most of the time. Twice a year might not be enough time for Philip to spend in a man's company. Maybe he saw Jesse as a substitute daddy.

Which was well and good, Robin supposed, except…except shouldn't she and Jesse be forging something, too? Or did Jesse merely view the Greers as a family that conveniently afforded him an opportunity to be a Big Brother without joining the national organization?

He had to view them as more than that. If that was all he wanted he wouldn't have kissed Robin the way he had Friday night. But was he ever going to kiss her again?

She turned onto his street and braked. "Which house is his?" Philip called from the back seat. He had courteously left the front passenger seat empty for Jesse.

"That one," she said, pointing to one of the town houses as she pulled into a parking space. The door to the adjacent town house swung open and a curly-haired woman in a stylish pink sweat suit emerged, lugging a huge evergreen wreath.

"Yucch!" Philip moaned, slinking down in his seat. "It's Ms. Becker!"

"Don't you want to say hello to her?" Robin asked as she opened her car door.

"Uh-uh." Philip slouched lower, covering his face with his arms. "I don't want her to see me. It's Sunday."

Robin shrugged. "Suit yourself. I'll get Jesse." She shut the door, strolled around the car to the steps, and started down them.

As soon as Eileen Becker spotted her, Robin suffered a twinge of apprehension. How would Philip's teacher view the fact that the mother of one of her students was involved with her neighbor? Ms. Becker might be privy to information about Jesse, knowledge about his affairs with women. Maybe Ms. Becker had seen him escorting numerous young lovelies into his house at odd hours. Maybe Ms. Becker herself was one of those young lovelies.

"Ms. Greer?" Ms. Becker called out, obviously startled. Drawing closer, Robin noticed that Ms. Becker had a hammer and a nail in her hand.

"That's a beautiful wreath," said Robin, figuring that the only way to handle this potentially awkward encounter was to behave as unruffled as possible.

"Isn't it? It used to be my husband's job to hang the wreath every year, but…" Ms. Becker bit her lip to cut herself off, and Robin felt a new swell of sympathy for the woman. Her own experiences the first few months after her divorce hadn't been too trying since Ray had been gone for long stretches of time during the preceding year, flying off to Bolivia and Honduras in his new job with the Agency for International Development. By the time they were legally divorced, Robin had grown accustomed to his absence. Yet certain jobs, chores that she'd always associated with Ray, had been difficult to tackle. It had taken her nearly a year to check the oil in her car, not because she didn't know how but because that had always been Ray's responsibility.

Evidently hanging the wreath had been Mr. Becker's responsibility. But since Robin wasn't supposed to know about Ms. Becker's divorce, she couldn't offer her condolences. "Do you need any help?" she said instead.

"No," the woman refused. "I've got to learn how to do these things for myself." She tapped the nail into her door, banged a couple of times on it, and then turned back to Robin. "Are you here to see me?"

"Actually, I'm, uh, I'm here to see Jesse Lawson."

Digesting this bit of news, Ms. Becker eyed her neighbor's front door with curiosity. "Legal business? I swear, he does more work at home than at his office."

"It's personal." Robin admitted, adding, "We're friends."

"You are?" Ms. Becker grinned broadly. "I didn't know that. I wonder why he didn't say anything that night he dropped by the school."

Because we weren't friends then, Robin answered silently.

"He's such a sweetie," Ms. Becker effused. "I have never in my life known anybody so eager to give of himself. The fact is, if I started to have trouble with this wreath, I would have asked him to help me. He's such a dear man, always lending a hand to everybody around here."

Robin wasn't sure whether she was surprised by Ms.

Becker's remark. Jesse was helpful; his willingness to watch Philip yesterday while she shopped was probably something he would have done for anyone. On the other hand, his obstinacy about rejecting God didn't seem particularly sweet or dear to Robin.

She wondered whether Ms. Becker expected confirmation of her opinion of Jesse. But, without waiting for Robin to speak, the schoolteacher once again busied herself with her hammer, pounding the nail into the door and then hanging the wreath on it. "There," she announced, taking a step back and beaming at her achievement. "Looks good, doesn't it?"

"It looks terrific," Robin agreed.

Ms. Becker opened her door. "Say hi to Philip for me," she requested before vanishing into her house.

Robin analyzed their exchange and decided that it hadn't gone badly at all. As a divorced woman, Ms. Becker must assume that other divorced women had male friends. Indeed, if she wasn't already one of Jesse's ladies, the recently divorced teacher might herself have designs on her good-looking neighbor. But that was between them, none of Robin's business. She resolved not to succumb to jealousy.

She rang Jesse's bell, and when he answered, he already had on his jacket. "Good morning," he greeted her. Then his gaze circled the porch and the sidewalk beyond. "Where's Philip?"

"Hiding in the car," Robin said. "Ms. Becker was out here when we drove up, and he didn't want to talk to her."

"Ah." Jesse glanced at the vacant porch abutting his and then at the station wagon parked beside his rental car in the lot. Finally his eyes returned to Robin. He ran his index finger down her cheek to the underside of her chin, then tilted her face up and bent to kiss her.

His lips felt delicious on hers, so warm and tender and inviting that she had to muster all her willpower not to give herself over to his kiss as she had a few nights ago. She allowed her mouth to revel in the feel of his for only a moment, then pulled away.

"Okay," Jesse whispered, clearly requiring no explanation for her reticence. "Let's go."

Maybe he required no explanation, Robin pondered as they walked together along the walk to the stairs, but she required one. She needed to know what was going on between them, what he thought of her, what he expected of her. She needed to know whether Jesse considered them something more than friends—and, if so, exactly how much more. She needed to know why he was so interested in joining her and Philip when they went to pick out their tree.

But these were questions that would have to wait. She and Jesse arrived at the station wagon, and Philip pulled himself up to his usual posture. "Hey, Jesse, we're getting our tree!" he hooted as soon as Jesse opened the door.

"That's right."

"Did you get your tree yet?" Philip asked Jesse as Robin started the engine.

"I'm not going to have one," he replied.

Robin winced, afraid of how Jesse would react to the inquisition she knew Philip had in store for him. Jesse had been so good with Philip yesterday. Was he going to ruin everything now?

"How come you aren't going to have a tree?" Philip demanded to know.

Robin cast Jesse a quick glance, but he ignored her,

twisting to look at Philip. "Not everybody gets trees, Phil."

"Why not?"

"Because it takes all kinds," Jesse answered. "Some people believe that having a Christmas tree is great, and some people don't."

"How come you don't?" Philip persisted.

"I think..." Jesse paused, shaping his words with care. "I think that the people who really want trees ought to have them. And that's why you're going to have one."

"Don't you like Christmas trees?"

"I'm going to like yours," Jesse promised. "I bet your tree is going to be the best one in the world."

That seemed to satisfy Philip, who smiled and settled contentedly in his seat. Robin cast Jesse another glance, this one filled with awe. She was impressed that he'd managed to parry all of Philip's questions without lying, and without burying the child in anti-Christmas claptrap. Yet Jesse didn't appear smug about his superlative performance under pressure. Nor did he seem uncomfortable. His smile reflected his pleasure at the bright sunshine, the crisp blue winter sky, and—she hoped—the company he was in. Nothing more.

She drove to the same tree vendor she patronized every year; buying a tree at the abandoned fruit stand on the Post Road was a tradition, and that particular vendor's trees were usually fresh, healthy and reasonably priced. Philip was the first out of the car. By the time Robin and Jesse climbed out, the boy had vanished between the tagged rows of cut pine trees. "Have you ever done this before?" Robin asked Jesse, her eyes sparkling with a mixture of humor and concern.

"Not in ages," he said. "When I was very young,

we lived in northern California, in the foothills of the Sierras, and we used to cut our own trees there. But once we moved to Los Angeles, an evergreen would have been as out of place as a blizzard. Everyone had artificial trees down there. My parents had a white one.''

Robin wrinkled her nose. A fake white Christmas tree would probably sour the whole holiday for her, too.

Philip ran to them, breathless. ''Come on, Mom! I found the perfect one!'' He grabbed Robin's hand and yanked her between two rows of cut trees to the biggest, fullest tree on the lot. Robin didn't even bother to check the price. ''It's too tall,'' she said, rejecting it. ''We'd have to saw it in half to fit it into the living room.''

''We could cut a hole in the ceiling,'' Philip recommended.

''Forget it, Phil.'' She guided her son back to a stand of smaller trees. ''Pick out one from here,'' she advised him. ''These aren't too tall.''

''They're puny,'' Philip complained, even though they weren't.

''We go through this every year,'' Robin muttered to Jesse. ''He always swears that the one we picked is puny until we get it home and untie it.''

Jesse gallantly came to the rescue. ''Check this one out, Phil,'' he suggested. ''It's nice and full all around.''

''It's puny,'' Philip sulked, although he held Jesse in enough esteem to give the tree a reluctant perusal.

Robin lifted the tag. Forty dollars. ''We'll take it,'' she told the vendor.

Once the limbs were tied, Jesse insisted on helping the vendor carry it to the car. ''Don't!'' Robin tried to stop him. ''Your wrist—''

Shrugging off her solicitude with a good-natured grin, he hoisted up the trunk with his right hand, using his

injured left one to balance it. Obviously he didn't want
to be pampered. The bruise on his cheek was still visible, and his wrist was still taped, yet he stubbornly carried the heavier end of the tree and assisted the vendor
in wedging it into the back of the station wagon.

He was just as stubborn about carrying the tree into
the house, once they'd driven home with it. Robin had
already spread an old waterproof tablecloth on the floor
in the corner of the living room to protect the carpet,
and she had dug the tree stand out of one of the Christmas boxes in the den. Philip eagerly played the boss
man as the two adults set up the tree, commanding
Robin to tilt the trunk slightly forward, slightly to the
left, slightly back again, while Jesse tightened the
screws around the base. Once they were all in agreement
that the tree was perfectly straight, they untied the limbs.

"Wow!" Philip whooped, darting to the den. "Let's
get the decorations."

"Not now, Phil." Robin attempted to halt him.
"We've got to let the branches settle for a day before
we start hanging things on them." In truth, her primary
concern was not the branches but Jesse. After yesterday's trip to the mall and this morning's purchase of
the tree, he might be dangerously close to overdosing
on the holiday.

To her astonishment, he pulled off his jacket, tossed
it onto a chair and gave the tree a comprehensive inspection. "I think you could decorate it now," he remarked. "The branches can settle with the decorations
on them."

Robin eyed him speculatively. Did he intend to help
hang the decorations? Was that why he had removed his
jacket? And why was he trailing Philip into the den to
fetch the boxes? "I'm going to like yours," he had said

when Philip had grilled him about why he wasn't going to have his own tree. "I bet it's going to be the best tree in the whole world." Perhaps, she mused as she hung the strewn jackets in the coat closet, decorating a tree didn't necessarily offend an atheist's sensibilities, as long as it was someone else's tree.

Jesse emerged from the den with a carton cradled in his arms and Philip at his heels. Jesse set the carton down near the tree with a thud and straightened up. "You sure have enough stuff in those boxes," he muttered, his dark eyes twinkling with amusement. "You could open your own store."

"I've already got a store," she countered, crossing to the box and pulling back the flaps. "There's only one more box with tree ornaments besides this one. The other boxes are filled with things for the rest of the house. We won't be unpacking those today."

Philip knelt by the box and began lifting items from it. "Remember this little rocking horse, Mom?" he shouted, displaying the wooden ornament for her. "Remember this felt Santa?"

Ignoring him, Robin studied Jesse. She gazed into his eyes; their powerful radiance offered her no hint of his thoughts. "You don't have to do this if you don't want to," she reminded him quietly.

"I know that," he responded. Then he gave her a reassuring grin, squatted down next to Philip, and helped him to unload the decorations.

It took the three of them nearly two hours to adorn the tree. There were strings of lights, garlands of tinsel, reflecting balls, and all the individual ornaments, each with a story attached to it. Philip took it upon himself to fill Jesse in on their significance. "This star, it came from Woodleigh's," he announced. "Mom's boss gave it to her. This little stocking, my Grandma Greer sewed it. The snowman came from the Calloways. Jeff Calloway's my very best friend, Jesse. See this little teddy bear? I got this when I was a baby. I don't remember it, but Mommy does.'' He turned to his mother for the full account.

She smiled apologetically at Jesse. "One of Ray's colleagues at Yale gave it to Phil," she explained. "I'm sure this can't be as interesting to you as it is to Phil."

Jesse laughed. "I'm hanging on his every word. How about this silver bell, Phil?" he asked, dangling another ornament in front of the boy's eyes.

"That's the 'Jingle Bell'," Philip informed him. "Shake it, Jesse—it really rings. Mom found it in the street a few days after Christmas one year, and she polished it up. It fell off Santa's sleigh, right?"

"That was my guess," Robin said, offering Jesse another sheepish smile. She refused to feel guilty about using a fortuitously placed prop to buttress the Santa myth for her son. But if Jesse condemned her for feeding Philip malarkey about St. Nick, he didn't show it. He shook the bell, producing a gentle tinkling sound, and mirrored Robin's smile.

By one-thirty, the tree was embellished with every item from the cartons. Philip and Jesse stood back to assess the result of their labor while Robin plugged in the lights. This year's tree looked essentially the same as last year's, but the moment the chains of bulbs were illuminated, Robin viewed the tree as something unique, a symbol of both continuity and newness. Every year it was like this: the lighting of the tree instilled a feeling of rebirth deep within her, a blossoming in her soul, softly glowing and magical. If only Jesse could feel it, too, if only he could allow himself to know the wonder of it...

"I'm starving," Philip declared, shattering her brief reverie. "I want lunch, Mom."

"Lunch. Of course." Forcing herself back to reality, she marched into the kitchen, followed by Philip and Jesse, who thoughtfully deposited the empty cartons in the den on his way.

"Peanut butter," Philip requested, flopping onto a chair. "Cut the sandwich in triangles, okay?"

"How about a 'please'?" Robin remonstrated as she pulled a jar of peanut butter and a loaf of bread from the refrigerator.

"Please," Philip obliged.

Spreading the peanut butter on the bread, Robin glanced at Jesse. "Would you like lunch, too?"

"I'd like dinner," he answered, leaning against the counter next to where she was working. "Just you and me. Tonight."

Jesse's decision to ask Robin for another date in front of Philip struck her as indiscreet, but it was too late for her to silence him. The boy at the table immediately piped up. "Yeah, Jesse—you owe her one, after standing her up Friday night. She was real sore about that."

"Philip!" Robin's cheeks burned with embarrassment.

Jesse indulged in a low, warm laugh. "She couldn't have been as sore as I was," he commented before turning to Robin. "How about it, Robin? Dinner tonight?"

Robin set down the knife and faced him. "You obviously don't know the first thing about baby-sitters," she lectured, her pleasure at his invitation tempering her discomfort about having this conversation in front of Philip. "They have to be booked days in advance.

Weeks, sometimes. I'll never be able to find anybody on such short notice."

"It can't hurt to try," Jesse noted, lifting the receiver from the wall phone and handing it to her, then delivering Philip his sandwich.

"Go ahead, Mom," Philip urged her. "Try Mrs. O'Leary."

Two against one, her son's voice echoed inside her. *You lose.* Grinning at the irrepressible team Philip and Jesse made, she pushed the buttons for Kate O'Leary's number. "Well, Jesse," she said a few minutes later, after bidding Kate goodbye, "if you don't already believe in miracles, you'd better start."

"Mrs. O'Leary's available?" he asked.

"Not exactly. She was planning to have a friend over for an evening of canasta, but when I told her she could bring her friend along, she said she'd come. That means you've got to be twice as well behaved tonight, Phil," she concluded, shooting her son a warning look.

"Canasta," he groaned, curling his lip. "Mrs. O'Leary once tried to teach me that game. It's really boring."

"She'll be playing canasta in the kitchen with Mrs. Lindblad," Robin explained. "And you'll be watching television in the den. Until eight-thirty, and then straight to bed. Do we understand each other?"

"Yeah," Philip said before slugging down a drink of milk. "I'm not allowed to call it boring in front of Mrs. O'Leary."

"You got it, pal." She pivoted to Jesse. "Satisfied?"

"I will be, tonight," he said. "Is seven o'clock all right?"

Robin nodded. "Do you want me to drive?"

Jesse shook his head. His eyes glittered mysteriously

as they met hers. In what way would he be satisfied tonight? she wondered. Had he found the activities of the past two days unsatisfying? Would a once-delayed dinner date be enough to satisfy him?

Much as it troubled her to admit it, she hoped that dinner wouldn't be enough to satisfy him. She wanted more than a meal from Jesse. And the way he was looking at her, the way his eyes seemed to overpower her and his mouth quirked into that dazzling smile of his, conveyed that he wanted more from her, too. "I'll see you at seven," he promised, giving her shoulder a light squeeze before he strode from the kitchen.

THIS TIME, HE CAME. Promptly at seven o'clock he arrived at her front door, dressed in a turtleneck, wool slacks, his tweed blazer and cashmere scarf. He was treated to the vision Robin had planned for him on Friday night: the gray sweater-dress—which, she decided after lengthy deliberation, didn't make her appear too wan or flat-chested—the artfully made-up eyes, the curled ends of her glistening blond hair. His reaction convinced Robin that her efforts had been worthwhile. "You look fantastic," he said as he entered the house.

Philip had already eaten dinner, and he and Kate were negotiating over dessert while Mrs. Lindblad stood by, peeking around the bend in the hallway to spy on Jesse and Robin. Feeling the need to settle the dispute between Kate and Philip before she left, Robin dashed to the kitchen and pronounced judgment. "One slice of apple pie, Phil, and you've got to eat it in the kitchen. It's too messy for the den. Be good, and don't forget to brush your teeth before bed."

Philip scowled at her maternal admonition. "Of course I'll brush my teeth. Toothpaste is the only sweet thing I ever get to eat around here,'' he grumbled. Perhaps Mrs. Lindblad was moved by his lament, but Robin and Kate knew better. Indeed it was hard to feel any pity for the boy while Kate was slicing him a hefty wedge of pie.

Robin joined Jesse by the front door, pulled her coat from the closet, and picked up her purse. ''Are you sure you don't want me to drive?'' she asked as they strolled down the walk to the driveway.

Jesse's answer was to unlock the passenger door of the small rental car. ''I'm not going to drive into any more electrical poles, if that's what you're worried about,'' he assured her before closing the door and moving around to the driver's side.

That wasn't what Robin was worried about. She was worried about whether he might be nervous about driving, given what he'd recently been through. She knew the old adage about climbing back on the horse after it threw you, but still, she was more than willing to drive if Jesse wanted her to.

Obviously, he didn't. He cruised to the corner, the steering wheel rubbing his knees whenever he turned it, and headed up the hill to the main road. ''I want to do it right this time,'' he answered her unformed question. ''That includes my doing the driving. In the words of Phil, I owe you one.''

Robin shifted uneasily in her seat. ''I wish you hadn't asked me out in front of him,'' she said. ''It kind of put me on the spot.''

''Oh?'' Jesse halted at a stop sign and turned to her. ''If he wasn't there, would you have said no?''

Robin returned his gaze. All afternoon she had been inhaling the tangy perfume of pine tree in the living room, but now that smell was replaced by the scent of

Jesse, a warm, musky, undeniably masculine fragrance. His eyes were piercing, his hair thick and velvety, his hands on the wheel strong and certain. No matter what the circumstances, Robin could never have said no to his dinner invitation.

"I just—I'd rather you had asked me in private," she explained. "I mean, so much of what we've done has been all three of us. If this was just going to be between the two of us, Jesse, then that's how you should have gone about it." As soon as she uttered the words, she realized how much she had divulged. Her confusion about whether Jesse liked her because she was Philip's mother or because she was herself had to be evident to him.

He contemplated her for a long moment, then nodded. "You're right. I've never been involved with a mother before, and I guess I've been a little clumsy. I'm sorry."

"Don't be," Robin said swiftly, elated by his admission that he was involved with her.

He drove to a Mexican restaurant on the eastern end of town. After hurrying inside to escape the evening chill, they were seated at a cozy, candle-lit booth. Robin removed her coat, Jesse his scarf and jacket. A classical guitarist stationed not far from them serenaded them with delicate arrangements of Bach fugues.

A waitress approached their table and asked if they wanted drinks. Robin meditated. What went with Mexican food? A tequilla sunrise, maybe, or a margarita, or— "Have you got any wine?" Jesse asked the waitress.

Robin's jaw dropped. Wine? With tacos and enchilladas?

"We've got a house burgundy, chablis and rosé," the

waitress informed him. "You can order it by the glass. We've also got sangria."

Jesse turned to Robin. "I think beer might go better with this food," she suggested. "Sangria's too sweet."

"I hate beer," Jesse declared.

Her astonishment increased. The man hated beer. Well, she wasn't going to drink alone, and she wasn't going to drink wine with Mexican food. "I think I'll skip," she said prudently.

Nodding, Jesse accepted two menus from the waitress and dismissed her. He handed one of the menus to Robin, but she didn't bother to open it. She was too busy gaping at him. "Is something wrong?" he asked.

"I don't think I've ever met a man who hated beer before."

"Then I'm your first," Jesse said, unperturbed. Sensing that she was awaiting an explanation, he informed her, "I tried beer in law school. Not only did it taste awful, but it gave me a whopping headache."

"Law school?" she blurted out. "What did you drink in college?"

"Nothing."

"Nothing?" Her gaze narrowed on him. "What were you, a teetotaler?"

"Yes. I'm not anymore, Robin. I do like wine."

She lowered her menu to the table and studied him in fascination. She had never met a teetotaler before. "Why didn't you drink?" she asked.

"I was raised very strictly," he said. "I've already told you my parents are very religious. They raised me to think consuming liquor was a sin."

"In excess, maybe," Robin granted. Then she refuted herself. "No—it's a problem, and sometimes a disease, but it isn't a sin. I've known a lot of heavy drinkers,

Jesse. My mother had some rough times with booze—
lots of army wives do. It's a lousy life, being uprooted
all the time, and they do whatever it takes to help them
feel like they fit in. But my mother's problem resolved
itself right after my father retired. And it *wasn't* a sin,"
she stressed.

"I know that now," Jesse granted. "I had my doubts
even as a child. But when drinking isn't a regular part
of your life, taking that first taste of liquor is a fearsome
experience." He shrugged. "I think I can survive the
rest of my life without beer being a part of it."

The waitress returned to take their orders. Once they
were alone again, Robin regarded the puzzling man
seated across the table from her. "I just can't picture
you as devoutly religious," she commented.

He chuckled. "I'm not sure I ever was. My parents
were. I always had too many questions. There's no room
for questions if you're buying into fundamentalism,
Robin. You either accept it or reject it. You swallow all
of it or none of it."

"And you couldn't swallow it."

"I tried," he admitted, his smile expanding. "But I
kept choking on it."

It dawned on Robin that her knowledge of Jesse Lawson was woefully slim. All she knew about fundamentalists was what she saw on television: militant preach-
ers spewing sermons of hellfire and brimstone, orating
against sex and the theory of evolution, alerting parents
to the perils of exposing their children to certain books
and ideas. She could scarcely believe that a man as ur-
bane as Jesse had been raised in such an environment.

You either accept it or reject it. Apparently he refused
to recognize any middle ground. Unable to accept any
part of it, he'd rejected all of it.

She had to learn more about him. She had to make sense of him. "How did you wind up in Branford?" she inquired.

"I was offered a job with New Haven Legal Assistance," he replied. "It was exactly what I was looking for, so I took it."

"Were you doing legal aid work in Los Angeles?"

He shook his head. "Far from it, Robin. I was raking in the bucks working for a big company."

Robin could imagine Jesse as a high-powered corporate attorney more easily than as a fundamentalist. But the pieces weren't falling together, and she plowed ahead, ignoring the waitress who came to deliver their dinners. "Why did you have to come all the way across the country just to switch jobs? I bet there were plenty of legal aid jobs in L.A."

"I was ready for a change of scenery as well as a change of jobs," Jesse admitted.

"So it seems." She tasted her quesadilla, smiled at its piquancy, and cooled her tongue of the fiery spiciness with a long sip of ice water. "I've lived in so many places," she said, "but never southern California. I know it's wrong to think of Los Angeles as a bunch of movie stars and television production companies and nothing else, but that's what I picture."

"Add a few palm trees and you wouldn't be far from the mark," Jesse joked.

"What big company did you work for?"

"G.C.E."

"Was that a show-biz company?"

Jesse grinned ironically. "In a sense." At her bemused stare, he clarified. "G.C.E. stands for Grace Cathedral Enterprises."

"Grace Cathedral? You mean—that big chapel on

television, with the Reverend Robert Shepherd and his famous choir?''

Jesse appeared irritated. "Don't tell me you watch *Blessings at Noon*, Robin.''

"I don't," she swore, surprised by the stinging bitterness in his words. "But it's hard not to know about Grace Cathedral. I'm sure everybody's caught a few minutes of Shepherd's shows at least once in their lives. You really worked there?''

"I did.''

Perhaps the Grace Cathedral broadcasts were a bit overdone, but Robin found it exciting to think that Jesse actually worked with a certified television star. "What's he like?" she asked. "What's Shepherd really like? Is he just as bombastic when the cameras aren't on him? Or is all that sanctimoniousness just an act?''

Jesse toyed with his fork for a minute, then placed it on the edge of his plate. "He's an actor," he said, laboring over his words. "He plays to his audience.''

"But when he's off the air—''

"He's an actor, just like any other TV performer. His concerns are the same—ratings, popularity, audience. He's never 'off'.''

The difficulty Jesse seemed to be having in describing his former boss indicated to Robin how uncomfortable he must have felt in his work for the man. "What do all those holy people need a lawyer for?" she asked.

Jesse let out a caustic laugh. "You're an innocent, aren't you. Don't you know what outfits like Grace Cathedral are all about?" He consumed some of his chicken, then elaborated. "Money, Robin. Contributions. Distribution rights, royalties, agency fees, air time and commercials. Money. Whenever you've got that much money pouring in, you'd better have a lawyer handy to protect your interests. And to oversee contracts, to avoid lawsuits. To make sure that the cured cripples Shepherd likes to parade across the screen aren't phonies.''

"So you admit that Shepherd does cure cripples," Robin said, pouncing on his words. "You admit that there are miracles, Jesse."

He shook his head. "I admit that people who are injured can sometimes defy their prognoses and get better. I admit that people facing seemingly insurmountable personal problems can sometimes overcome them. But that doesn't mean that miracles have occurred. It just means that prognoses are sometimes wrong, and that with enough fortitude, most people can overcome their personal problems. It isn't God, Robin. It's people working hard to improve their lives and reach their goals. But...yes, as a lawyer, I had to get affidavits from all of Shepherd's guests, from the doctors and witnesses and all, to avoid legal problems over false claims.''

"Why on earth did you ever take a job like that?"

Jesse ruminated for a while. He was obviously trying to work through his thoughts, to discover a precise response to Robin's reasonable question. "Let's just say it was part of my upbringing," he answered vaguely. "I may have started experimenting with liquor in law school, but there was still too much of the obedient son in me. I questioned a lot, but...there were some things I should have questioned that I didn't.''

Robin leaned back and examined the man facing her. Her badgering questions didn't seem to annoy him—if they did, he would have changed the subject. Instead he appeared open to her probing. His gaze was unwavering, his smile hesitant, his bandaged left hand resting palm up on the table, cupped slightly, as if shaped to hold whatever she might give him, to lift whatever might be weighing on her.

"I'm sorry," she mumbled, not sure why she was apologizing. "This is all a bit bewildering."

"It doesn't have to be." Jesse extended his arm across the table and captured her hand in his. "I'm pretty forthright about who I am and what I think," he commented. "I admire you for asking. That's my favorite yardstick for measuring others, Robin. I like people who are willing to ask questions."

"But still..." She tried to unravel her snarled thoughts. "For someone who choked on religion and rejected it, how come you got into our Christmas tree in such a big way today?"

Maybe Jesse liked people who asked questions, but this question held a genuine challenge. He didn't back away, though. Nor did he release her hand. He simply held it, curling his fingers loosely around her slender wrist. "I'm not quite sure," he said.

"And the shopping trip yesterday, and the visit with Santa Claus..."

"That has nothing to do with religion," he argued. "Visiting Santa made Phil happy, and keeping him entertained while you shopped made you happy. And the tree..." He hesitated, a wistful smile curving his lips. "The tree was beautiful because it means so much to you both. I was honored to be included in something that special to you and Phil. It was fun. And the mall was fun, too. After what happened Friday night, all I wanted was to enjoy life, to have fun."

That hadn't been all Jesse had wanted. Particularly not on Friday night. Jesse had wanted more from Robin, more than he was able to ask for. They both knew that.

Everything about Friday night was etched into her

soul. Every excruciating detail, every sensation, every inchoate thought that had flitted through her brain during those few heady moments when she had stood kissing Jesse on his porch—it was all still with her, perplexing her. Her confusion must have shown plainly in her face, because Jesse's hand tightened slightly on hers and his smile disappeared. "Robin, if there's more you need to know, ask."

She raised her eyes to his. "I don't even know what questions I'm supposed to be asking," she confessed with a nervous laugh.

He regarded her for a long, contemplative minute, interpreting her bewilderment, supplying the explanation she seemed to be seeking. "When I was in that accident," he murmured, "it wasn't just the seat belt that saved my life." He paused, his gaze holding hers, uncompromising. "You saved my life, too."

"Me?" she sputtered. "All I did was pick you up at the hospital—"

"You did much more than that, Robin. Or maybe…maybe we did it together." His thumb moved against her wrist, tracing the bones, dancing across her throbbing pulse. "I kept thinking of you throughout the accident, clinging to thoughts of you. And that's what pulled me through. I'm convinced of it."

Stunned, Robin fell back in her seat. She was incredibly flattered by what Jesse had said—flattered and frantic. How had she pulled him through? How had she come to mean that much to him?

The same way he had come to mean something to her, she concluded. Her shopping trip with Philip on Saturday had been one of the most enjoyable she'd ever had, not only because Jesse had kept Philip occupied for her but because Jesse was there. Her outing to purchase a tree that morning had been wonderful because Jesse was there. Decorating the tree had been joyous, because Jesse was there.

She had always believed that what made the holiday special was the tradition of it. Jesse wasn't a part of any tradition for her. Yet his presence had somehow made the traditional activities much more meaningful.

"You look scared," Jesse observed, withdrawing his hand and studying her, concerned.

"I don't think I am." Robin emitted a small, breathless laugh, and then, as she absorbed Jesse's affectionate smile, a more confident chuckle. "What I do think is that you're just too stuck on being an atheist to admit that it wasn't me who pulled you through. It was the Lord, watching over you."

"I think I know the difference between a beautiful blond woman and a bearded old geezer in the clouds."

"Your idea of God is ridiculous," Robin retorted, laughing even harder.

Jesse joined her laughter. "That's probably why I don't believe in Him. Do you want dessert?"

"No." What Robin wanted was time, time to shape all the questions she had for Jesse, time for him to provide all the answers. What she wanted was time alone with him, time to come to terms with the fact that he held her responsible for saving his life.

Time to figure out what it all meant, what Jesse meant, how much he was coming to mean to her.

Chapter Seven

"I'll drive you ladies home," Jesse chivalrously offered as Kate O'Leary and her friend reached for their coats.

"That's very nice of you," Kate disputed him, "but you don't have to. We're only going down the block."

"Then I'll walk you home," Jesse said with a finality that even Kate wouldn't dare to contradict.

The two women exchanged impressed glances behind Jesse's back before allowing him to escort them out of the house. Robin imagined that Kate would be doing penance for weeks to atone for having once implied that Jesse Lawson was no better than vermin. She watched as the trio strolled down the front walk, Jesse turning up the collar of his blazer and tightening his scarf against the frigid December night. Then she closed the door, leaving it unlocked for him, and removed her own coat. She stepped out of her shoes, tiptoed up the stairs to check on her sleeping son, and returned to the living room.

The tree nearly overwhelmed the room, towering regally in its corner. Robin bent down by the wall socket and plugged the lights in. The room filled with a multicolored glow from the tiny sparkling bulbs.

Her gaze wandered to the fireplace. Jesse would be

freezing by the time he got back from Kate's house. Her smile widening, she tugged open the mesh curtain protecting the hearth, balled up a few sheets of newspaper, piled on some kindling and applied a lit match to her construction. It caught instantly, lending the room a cozy warmth. Robin remained seated by the fireplace, admiring the yellow licks of flame as they flared upward. When she thought the fire was hot enough she added two seasoned logs. They crackled as the flames danced around them, and then finally caught fire. A feeling of contentment infused her as she inhaled the pungent scent of burning wood and let the heat wrap around her.

"You read my mind." The mellow sound of Jesse's voice startled her; she hadn't heard him enter the house. Flinching, she glanced over her shoulder and found him standing less than a foot behind her, unwinding his scarf. "It's cold out there," he announced, sliding off his blazer and tossing it onto a chair. Then he dropped onto the carpeted floor beside Robin and extended his hands palm forward to catch the fire's warmth.

"I'm going to sound like a mother for saying this," Robin muttered, "but why do you run around in nothing but a blazer when it's wintertime?"

He grinned. "I'm from southern California, remember? The only coat I own is an unlined raincoat."

"Then it's high time you bought yourself something warmer," she reproached him. "This is yankee country. Treat yourself to a coat for Christmas."

"I'll treat myself to a coat out of respect for Mother Nature," Jesse corrected her with a chuckle. He turned to face the fire, resting his left forearm across his bent knee and gazing into the blaze. It cast a golden glow across his face, delineating the harsh angles of it, em-

phasizing the dynamic lines of his nose and chin, the
planes of his cheeks and brow, and making his hair seem
impossibly blacker in contrast. His lingering smile grat-
ified Robin. She'd been smart to build a fire, to warm
this outlander who didn't know how to dress for a New
England winter.

She still harbored many questions about Jesse. She
had assailed him mercilessly with her questions over
dinner, and he'd answered them without hesitation, yet
he remained an enigma to her. She wanted to know
more; she needed to. She needed to know, among other
things, why he'd chosen to live in Connecticut, a part
of the country with a climate that required clothing he
didn't own and driving skills he'd had little chance to
master. He had said he was ready for a major change,
but a three-thousand-mile change? "There has to be
more to it," she pondered, surprised to hear herself giving voice to her bemusement.

Jesse eyed her, perplexed. "More to what? Mother
Nature?"

She laughed meekly and turned to stare at the fire.
When Jesse had enough of her questions, she supposed,
he'd let her know. But although he wasn't complaining
about her nosiness, she couldn't look directly at him
when she said, "There has to be more to your decision
to move to New Haven. It couldn't have just been the
job. There must be openings in every city in the country
for lawyers willing to do legal aid work. You didn't
have to move so far away from home."

She could feel his eyes upon her, studying her profile
as she continued to face the fireplace. He lapsed into
thought for a moment, then said, "I think I did have
to."

"Why?" she posed. "You lived in L.A. for so much

of your life. Your family was there, and your roots...
I'd give my eyeteeth for the chance to have lived in one
place for so long, to really become attached to it. I'm
beginning to feel attached to Branford, but it's taken me
nine years."

"Maybe I want to become attached to Branford,
too," Jesse remarked.

Robin laughed again, and Jesse joined her. Branford
was a nice enough town, with some beautiful neighbor-
hoods and a breathtaking coastline bordering the Long
Island Sound. But it was too modest to deserve the sort
of instant attachment Jesse alluded to. "It isn't Branford," she debated him, finding the courage to turn back
to him. "And it isn't New Haven. You weren't coming
here—you were only trying to get as far from L.A. as
possible."

Jesse conceded with a grin. "Is there anything wrong
with that?"

"Of course not," she hastened to assure him.
"Only...I can't believe your job was the only reason
you left."

His smile faded. This time it was he who turned to
the fire, staring at the hypnotic flickering of the flames
because it was easier than looking at Robin. "What are
you getting at?" he asked, his tone low and even. "Do
you want to know if I left a woman behind? I did."

That hadn't been what Robin was getting at, at least
not consciously. Without giving it much thought, she
had assumed that Jesse would have been seeing
women—or, for that matter, a specific woman—wherever he lived. But since he'd introduced the subject, she
wasn't about to let it drop. "You came here to recover
from a broken heart?" she asked, then felt her cheeks
darken with color at her relentless prying. "It's none of

my business, Jesse. I don't know why you've put up with so many questions from me—''

He touched her shoulder reassuringly. Ignoring her belated apology, he said, ''I didn't have a broken heart, Robin. Just like you and your ex-husband, we grew apart.''

''Were you married?'' she asked, although she felt safe in presuming that he hadn't been. If he had, he would have said so the evening she'd told him about her divorce.

He shook his head, confirming her guess. ''Anne and I were pretty serious, but it didn't get that far.''

''Was she in show biz?''

''She was a television producer.''

A television producer. Robin imagined someone rich and polished, ambitious and successful. Someone with a magnificent wardrobe, someone who didn't have to worry about clothes making her look flat-chested, someone whose hair didn't require a curling iron to make it appear thick and wavy and lustrous. All in all, Robin concluded, someone who was brainy and gorgeous and everything Robin wasn't.

She was so busy wrestling with her insecurities that she missed part of what Jesse was saying. ''…for G.C.E., too.''

''Hmm?''

''She was one of the producers of *Blessings at Noon*. We met through work. We were together, on and off, for about four years. But she bought into the whole scene and I didn't, and finally we were forced to admit that the differences between us were irreconcilable.'' He paused, then angled his face to view her. ''What's the matter, Robin? You wish I hadn't brought it up, don't you?''

"It isn't that," she said quickly. "It's just...I can't help wondering what you're doing here with me when you could be with some glamorous lady who produces television shows."

He gazed steadily at her, neither smiling nor frowning, simply looking, absorbing her with his eyes. "You know what I'm doing here with you," he said.

He was with her, she reminded herself, because he thought she had saved his life.

If she had, it hadn't been through any intentional action on her part, and she wasn't sure she was ready to accept the responsibility his statement implied. She had heard it said that when you saved another person's life, you owned that person's life, and it was yours to look after forever. The very idea made Robin uncomfortable.

Yet she didn't exactly want to shirk the responsibility Jesse was giving her. She wanted to keep him safe, to protect him, to build fires to warm him. Deep in her heart, she wanted to believe that, however inadvertently, she *had* helped him to survive the crash.

The fact of that crash was brought home to her as Jesse shoved up the sleeves of his turtleneck sweater and revealed the tan Ace bandage around his sprained wrist. "You shouldn't have been lugging around the tree today," she scolded. If she was going to accept responsibility for his life, then she had a right to chide him for taking unnecessary risks with it. "You ought to give your wrist a chance to heal."

His gaze traveled from her to his arm and back again. His smile reached his eyes, imbuing them with a captivating glitter. "If you're really so worried about making it better," he goaded her, "you can kiss it. I saw you heal Phil with a kiss after he took that tumble in the parking lot yesterday."

Seemingly an innocuous request. But Jesse's earlier words echoed inside her: *You know what I'm doing here with you.* Perhaps he was with her because she'd saved his life, and perhaps he was with her only because he wanted to seduce her. Asking her to kiss his sprained wrist sounded more like the latter, and she faltered for a moment, mulling over how best to deal with a seduction attempt. He'd taken her out for dinner and then returned with her to her house. Did he believe sex was next on the agenda?

"I think," she said, fighting against the waver in her voice, "that making an injury better with a kiss works only when you're related by blood."

"Let's try it and find out."

Despite Jesse's light tone, despite the laughter dancing in his eyes, Robin understood his intention. She might be rusty when it came to male-female games, she might be inexperienced, but she wasn't an idiot. She sensed in his attitude not the overpowering need that had compelled him to kiss her the last time they were alone, but rather a strong, healthy attraction, a masculine hunger, controlled but very real, very present.

"If I do try it..." She faltered again, unsure of how receptive she should be to his overture. She was just as attracted to him as he was to her, just as anxious to recapture the passion they'd shared on his porch a few nights back. But she was nervous, too, and she bought time by pointing out, "Making an injury better with a kiss is a miracle cure. You've got to admit you believe in miracle cures, Jesse, or it won't work."

His eyes met hers. Perhaps he understood her hesitancy; perhaps he thought she was testing him. His smile vanished but his gaze intensified, searching her face for a clue of how to proceed—if he should proceed. "I'll admit that I do believe in miracles," he said quietly. "Not divinely inspired ones, Robin, but—I believe that people can create their own miracles." He raised his wrist in front of her, daring her to create a miracle for them.

She shyly touched her lips to his exposed thumb. "There. All better?"

"Miraculously." He ran his thumb gently over her lower lip, tracing the full curve of it. "Should I say hallelujah now?" He moved closer, his face a mere breath away from hers. "Should I sing your praises before heaven and earth?"

"No," she answered on a sigh, her entire body attuned to him, yielding, welcoming the kiss she knew was coming. "You only have to believe."

"I believe," he murmured, molding his mouth to hers. His tongue traced the line his thumb had sketched over her lips, but didn't venture farther. Before she could relax fully in the heavenly sensations his kiss elicited, he drew back, patiently waiting for a cue from her to continue.

"I guess some things are allowed," she mumbled with a hazy smile.

"What?"

"Well, you weren't allowed to drink," she said. "But even ultra-religious people must be allowed to kiss. You didn't wait until law school to learn how to kiss did you?"

A soft laugh bubbled up from his chest. "I always assumed this was allowed. Where else would baby fundamentalists come from?" Refusing her a chance to reply, his lips covered hers again. This time his tongue penetrated her mouth, conquering her with an intimacy that was both shocking and tender. Her tongue eagerly

met his. Kissing Jesse this way, not in desperation but
in sheer pleasure, felt as natural as talking to him, ar-
guing philosophies with him, taunting him about his bizarre beliefs.

He had said he believed. As his kiss deepened, as her
flesh melted in the heat of it, she believed, too. She
believed that some things defied logic, and that, logical
or not, Jesse was the man with whom she wanted to
make love, now, tonight, the man with whom she
wanted to end her long years of solitude.

Her arms curled around his shoulders as he bowed to
her, urging her down onto the carpet beneath him. Her
hair splayed out about her head, and his fingers twined
through the silky blond tresses, reaching for her ear-
lobes, for the smooth skin of her throat, the nape of her
neck. Without breaking the kiss, he shifted above her,
his chest moving against hers, his hips settling provoc-
atively between her thighs. She reflexively arched her
back, pressing her breasts into the wall of rib and muscle, and he groaned.

Lifting his mouth, he slipped his hand between their
bodies and roamed downward to stroke the rounded
swell of her breast. Despite the layers of cloth separating
his palm from her skin, he easily located her nipple and
centered on it, causing it to stiffen against his fingers.
The heat roaring through her flesh and gathering below
her abdomen had nothing to do with the fire in the
hearth. It was a result of Jesse, the weight of him upon
her, his sensitive caresses igniting a blazing yearning
within her.

Her arms moved down to ring his waist. Through his
shirt, she explored the sleek, firm muscles of his lower
back, the tension in them as his hips shifted above hers

again. She felt his arousal, hard and unyielding as he moved against her, urging her legs to accommodate him.

"Where's your bed?" he whispered, the hoarse rumble of his voice burning against her ear as his lips grazed her hair.

Upstairs, her soul cried out in a silent answer. *Take him upstairs.* Yet the words wouldn't come. Twisting beneath him, she glimpsed the staircase across the room, the polished railing that would soon be draped in garlands, the steps rising up to her bedroom, to the bed in which she'd slept alone for three years. Once more she tried to speak, but her lips refused to shape the words, her lungs refused to support them.

Jesse nudged her face back to his. He peered down at her, his eyes smoky, his lips parted as he struggled with his erratic breath. He couldn't help but discern her irresolution. "Are you worried about Philip?" he asked.

Philip could sleep through a train wreck, Robin knew. Concern about disturbing his rest wasn't what was holding her back. She shook her head, afraid to trust herself to say anything until she knew precisely what it was she had to say.

"Tell me, Robin," Jesse prompted her, sensing her confusion. "Tell me what's bothering you."

"I'm not…" She swallowed, then forced herself to speak. "I'm not sure that I love you, Jesse. Not yet. And if I don't love you…we can't. I know that must sound ridiculously outdated, or infantile, or—"

He cut off the spate of words with a brush of his fingertips over her trembling lips. Then he leaned back, scrutinizing her, his expression revealing nothing. For a long time the only sounds in the room were his labored breathing and the crackle of the fire. "I guess that leaves me with two options," he granted.

"Oh?"

"Either I can say, yes, it's outdated and infantile, and we both want each other, so let's enjoy ourselves." He smiled crookedly. "Or else I can be a gentleman, respect your feelings and go home."

"There's a third option," Robin told him. "You could convince me that I do love you." And it wouldn't take much persuasion on his part to convince her of that, she acknowledged privately. He was such a good man, so thoughtful, so caring, considerate enough to suggest leaving when they were both feeling an imperative desire for each other. He was so generous, accepting her endless questions, providing answers for questions she hadn't even asked. How could she not love him?

It wasn't that she didn't; it was only that she wasn't sure. She'd been single for too long, and her experience so far with Jesse didn't fit any of her expectations about how love was supposed to develop. More than that, she felt ignorant, nervous, frightened by the prospect of making love with someone who wasn't Ray. She didn't love Ray anymore, she hadn't loved him for a long time, but she had never loved anybody else. She was too old to remember how one was supposed to go about falling in love. And she was much too old—or old-fashioned— to think that love didn't matter when it came to sex.

"I can't convince you that you love me, Robin," Jesse said gently. "It's something you'll have to decide for yourself." He rose languorously to a sitting position, his aroused body obviously reluctant to give hers up, and then helped her to sit as well. The flickering light from the fire played across his features, highlighting his eyes for an instant and then casting them in shadow.

"Are you angry?" she asked timidly.

"Angry?" He looped his arm around her shoulders

and cuddled her to him, then planted a kiss on the crown of her head. "No, I'm not angry."

"But you think I'm outdated and infantile—"

"I think you're a very wise woman," he said. "If you want to know the truth, Robin... I want your love as much as I want you."

Simply hearing him express such a sentiment was so touching that Robin nearly shouted "Yes! I love you!" How could she not love someone who wanted her love so much?

Love was more than being wanted, she reflected. For her, at least, it took time, commitment, knowledge and understanding. She was willing to invest the time and the commitment. She was willing to do whatever it took to know Jesse fully, to reach an understanding of the man at her side. But right now, as she nestled into his shoulder and shared the fire's beauty and warmth with him, she admitted that she didn't yet know everything she had to know about him—and she definitely didn't understand everything she had to understand. He was so complex, so strange, in many ways as alien to her as a creature from Gleek.

But in time, she vowed, in time she would know him. In time she would understand.

Chapter Eight

"Let me explain this one more time," Jesse said, his patience strained to the breaking point. "Gerald Selby had nothing to do with the outbreak of violence. His commanding officer knows that, you know it, and I know it. Selby has never been friendly with the sailors under investigation. He's a good kid, and it would mean the world to his mother if you could see your way clear to grant him his Christmas leave."

The captain on the other end of the telephone remained unmoved. "And I've outlined our position for you, Mr. Lawson. If we grant a leave for Gerald Selby, we've got to grant leaves for the entire crew."

"I don't care about the entire crew," Jesse snapped. "All I care about is one man."

"We have our rules, Mr. Lawson," Captain Stevenson recited. "This is the way the military operates. Without rules, it can't function. I'm very sorry for your client. But this is the way the investigation is going to proceed. We need the entire crew here for questioning."

"You know what's going to happen," Jesse argued, not bothering to disguise his caustic tone. "The damned investigators are going to go home for Christmas, and Selby and his crewmates are going to sit around twiddling their thumbs on the base in Newport for the day. There's no need for that. The investigators can question Selby some other time.''

"We have our rules, Mr. Lawson."

Jesse cursed under his breath. "Newport is three hours from New Haven, where Selby's family resides. All he needs is forty-eight hours. He isn't under suspicion. He understands his obligations. He'll be back on base by December twenty-sixth.''

"That would be contrary to rules, Mr. Lawson. If we allow one man his leave—''

"Yes, I know," Jesse interrupted. He didn't think he could stomach another repetition of the Naval Code. Just beyond his open office door, a hysterical client was ranting in Spanish to one of the paralegal volunteers. Outside his window, sleet drizzled against the pavement in a staccato rhythm, glazing everything below—including the cramped white rental car that Jesse had driven to work that morning. He needed a new car. And a coat.

And he needed to talk about Gerald Selby's Christmas leave to someone who didn't respond like an automaton. "Consider the holiday," he implored Captain Stevenson. "Consider the issue of morale. Depriving Gerald Selby of this one special day with his family—''

"If we grant him his leave, Mr. Lawson, then everybody's going to want their leaves.''

"So what?" Jesse retorted. "It's Christmas, for crying out loud. Even the Navy must believe in Santa Claus!''

What was he saying? What kind of fool argument was that? Jesse was a lawyer, and as a lawyer it was his duty to use any and every tactic at his command to turn an opponent around. But Santa Claus?

Captain Stevenson said nothing for a moment. *He's*

probably running me through his computer, Jesse thought morosely. *Checking to see if I've ever been committed to a mental hospital. Or else he's sending a telegram to Mrs. Selby, recommending that she seek new counsel...*

And then, suddenly, Captain Stevenson started to laugh. Authentic human laughter. The man wasn't an automaton, after all.

Jesse laughed, too. He didn't believe in Santa Claus, but if the Navy did—if this one desk-bound officer did—Gerald Selby might have a chance to spend the holiday with his mother. "I tell you what," Captain Stevenson suggested. "Send me something in writing. And for heaven's sake, ask for twenty-four hours, not forty-eight. I'm not making any promises, Mr. Lawson. I'm operating within a strict hierarchy here. I've got to answer to people."

"Anything you can do for my client will be greatly appreciated," Jesse swore. "I'll get something into the mail right away. With a copy to the North Pole. Thank you for your time, Captain Stevenson."

He hung up and surrendered to another laugh. What some people might call the Christmas spirit, Jesse called goodwill and human kindness. If more people exercised the spirit year-round, it would no longer be associated with one single day, and the world would be a much better place. But such a hope was fruitless; Jesse knew that the goodwill, human-kindness argument he'd just presented to Captain Stevenson would have been utterly ineffective in June or September. But then, if Gerald Selby's leave had been scheduled for June or September, Mrs. Selby wouldn't have been so crushed by its postponement.

She might still wind up crushed, Jesse reminded himself. Captain Stevenson might not be able to arrange Gerald's release for the holiday. And that was the least of Mrs. Selby's problems.

Jesse had been contacted that morning by the attorney representing Mr. Cabot, the man who owned the Newhallville tenement where Mrs. Selby lived. "We've received a copy of your class-action suit," the lawyer had announced, "and my client has instructed me to inform you that he has no interest in negotiating a settlement. We'll leave it up to the courts to decide whether he's been remiss in fulfilling the obligations of your clients' leases."

It was a ploy, of course. Any court in the country would find against Mr. Cabot, and his attorney had to know that. Their strategy clearly was to bide their time and hope the tenants gave up and moved out. The civil court wouldn't set a date for a hearing for months. By then Mrs. Selby and her neighbors might well be so sick of living in a building without any services that they'd evacuate on their own. Or else the building would be condemned, Cabot would pay a nominal fine, and the tenants would still have to move out.

Perhaps Jesse should have mentioned Santa Claus to Cabot's attorney.

The Spanish-speaking man had stopped hectoring the paralegal in the hallway, and the sleet stopped drumming against the window. Jesse stood and crossed the small room to peer outside. An impotent winter sun was fighting its way out from behind the broken ceiling of leaden clouds. Jesse rooted for the sun to win the tussle. But even if it did, he still needed a coat.

Buying a coat wouldn't be as difficult as buying a car, he assured himself. He'd spent his lunch break at a Nissan dealership, listening to a snappy-looking blow-dried kid tell him that a man like Jesse would truly appreciate the extra power of a 200-SX. The price the salesman had bandied about was less absurd than the stratospheric numbers Jesse had heard the last time he'd bought a new car, six years ago. But at least the Mercedes dealer hadn't treated him like a doddering old fogie.

It had been one of those days, Jesse meditated as he witnessed the ongoing battle between the sun and the clouds. The call from Cabot's lawyer, interviews with two new clients—a handicapped woman being hassled by the Social Security Administration and a distraught teenager who claimed his employer, a gas station owner, owed him back wages—the encounter with the car dealer, and a conversation with a Navy captain. And the sleet, the same treacherous precipitation that had nearly killed Jesse last Friday.

So why was he in such a good mood? "Robin," he said aloud.

He ought to be in a bad mood about her, too, but he wasn't. He ought to be frustrated and resentful of her refusal to make love with him. What they'd begun on her living room floor last night was sensational, and she shouldn't have been so prim and resistant about following through on it. It was obvious that they had both wanted what was happening, that they'd both desired each other.

Yet he wasn't resentful. Frustrated, maybe, but not resentful. He admired the courage it had taken her to put a stop to the situation before she was overwhelmed by it. He admired her willingness to trust her mind and her heart. He admired her decency and her principles. He didn't consider her outdated or infantile.

A woman who wouldn't sleep with a man she didn't

love... He didn't know such people still existed. Even the most pious of the folks he'd worked with at Grace Cathedral—sure, they'd claim that a couple ought to be married before they engaged in sex, but love didn't necessarily have anything to do with it. Men lusted, and they had to pay the price by marrying the women they lusted after. Women submitted—that was the price they paid for the security of marriage.

More sophisticated practitioners of the Grace theology, like Anne, didn't feel obliged to sanctify their relationships before allowing them to become intimate. But that made people like Anne even more hypocritical, in Jesse's opinion. "Nobody has to know we're having an affair," she had often said. "We're discreet about it. Nobody's watching."

"What about God?" he'd posed sarcastically. "Isn't He watching?"

"I'm sure God doesn't mind," Anne had maintained. "After all, we're doing His work."

Robin would never make such a ridiculous claim. Jesse didn't doubt that she believed in God, but she didn't cling to the superficial aspects of religion. She hadn't brought things to a halt last night because she was trying to extort a marriage proposal from Jesse. Nor had she brought things to a halt because she was afraid of bringing God's wrath upon her. She had acted in the interest of love. And for that alone, Jesse loved her.

He loved her for more than that, of course. He loved her for having known how cold he would be and building a fire in her fireplace. He loved her for buying her son a Christmas tree. Jesse loved her for listening, for wanting to know, for not condemning him for his beliefs.

He did have beliefs. They differed from most people's, but they were just as valid. He hadn't been exaggerating when he'd told Robin he believed; he believed in the inherent goodness within people, in human strength, in bravery and conviction. He believed in Robin.

And, as the clouds closed in front of the sun again, dark with foreboding, he believed in the practicality of buying a warm coat.

ONE HOUR and two hundred fifty dollars later, he left a men's clothing shop on the Post Road in Branford, wearing a brand-new coat of gray cashmere. The evening air was bitterly cold, and he didn't want to know what the wind chill factor computed to. But with the coat on, he felt snug and toasty. He would have to thank Robin for having talked some sense into him.

In fact, he could thank her now. Woodleigh's was just a few buildings away on the strip, and he was reasonably certain the store would still be open. He climbed into his car, grimaced at the faint rattle of the engine as he revved it, and cruised down the road to Woodleigh's.

Entering the store, he spotted Robin almost at once. She was hard to miss, standing on the top rung of a ladder and reaching for a boxed set of woven place mats on an upper shelf. In her brown pinafore and her buoyant ponytail, her pleated skirt and loafers, she looked surprisingly girlish. But the shapely calves visible between those loafers and the hem of her skirt were exceptionally sexy, and Jesse suffered a fresh twinge of disappointment as he recalled how close he'd come to ravishing her on the carpet of her living room.

He willfully directed his vision to the dwarf Christmas tree on the counter to distract his attention from Robin's sexy legs. By the time he risked glancing back

at her, she had descended the ladder and was handing
the box of place mats to a grateful customer. Bypassing
numerous other shoppers and clerks in a meandering
path through the store to the cash register with her customer, Robin noticed Jesse and hesitated. Then she
smiled, revealing her tiny white teeth. Another twinge
ripped through him as he remembered how marvelous
it had felt to kiss her.

"I'll be right with you," she said by way of greeting
before she glided around the counter to ring up the purchase. Jesse waited by the counter, gazing at her small
hands as they efficiently punched the buttons on her
computerized register, as they counted the customer's
change and gift-wrapped the box. Those slender fingers
that manipulated the wrapping paper and ribbon with
such finesse had run through his hair and down his back,
had dug into his muscles and compelled his body... No.
He'd come here to show her his new coat, not to pressure her into picking up where they'd left off Sunday
night.

The customer departed, and Robin slipped away from
the register to greet Jesse. "I love it!" she exclaimed,
circling him and examining the coat. "It looks so warm,
Jesse. And the color suits you perfectly."

"It cost a fortune," he complained half-heartedly.

"And worth every penny," she asserted, stroking the
sleeve and sighing at its soft texture. Abruptly she
pulled her hand away, as if embarrassed at having
touched him.

He wouldn't increase her embarrassment by com-
menting on it. "Do you have a minute?" was all he
asked.

She surveyed the bustling store and frowned. Apparently she didn't have a minute. "I'm sorry, Jesse, but

it's crazy here tonight. And I've got to work till nine. With the extended holiday hours—"

"One minute," he persevered.

She raised her eyes to his. He sensed doubt in them, and wondered whether it was doubt about her feelings for him or doubt about his claim that he'd take only a minute of her time. Either way, it didn't matter, he decided, because he also sensed humor in those glittering hazel irises, and joy at seeing him. "One minute," she capitulated, striding briskly to the rear of the store.

He followed her through a door and into a hallway. She stepped through another door, which led into a minuscule lounge, equipped with a coffeemaker, a water-bubbler and a compact refrigerator. A two-seat couch of orange vinyl was jammed against a wall of the windowless room, but she didn't bother to sit. She paced the brief length of the lounge, fidgeting with the tie of her pinafore.

Now that they were alone, Jesse acknowledged privately that he hadn't come here to thank her for pushing him into buying a coat. He came here to see her, to hold her, to reassure her that last night meant everything and nothing, that it meant whatever she wanted it to mean. When she reached the far end of the room and about-faced, he caught up to her and slipped his arms around her narrow waist. "Hello," he murmured, containing the urge to kiss her. Hugging her would have to do for now.

"Jesse." She sighed again, and rested her head against his shoulder. "I'm sorry about last night."

"You have no reason to be."

Evidently she disagreed. "It's just..." Her words were muffled by the thick fabric of the coat and she pulled away. Rotating, she eased out of his arms and began to pace again. "I'm—I'm new at all this, Jesse. I mean, I—I haven't dated much since my divorce. That's a lie. I haven't dated at all since my divorce."

"It's okay, Robin," he tried to console her.

She pivoted, facing him from across the lounge, her arms folded defensively over her chest. "It's more than that, Jesse. Ray—my ex-husband—he was the first... what I mean is, he was the *only* man I've ever...." Dropping her gaze to the floor, she drifted off.

"Robin." Jesse didn't want to laugh; she might be insulted if he did. But she appeared so ludicrously upset, so worked up over something he considered irrelevant. "I don't care about your past, Robin. All I care about is us."

"I care about us, too," she allowed, toying with the tie of her pinafore again.

Jesse couldn't bear to see her fidget. It indicated that she was nervous, and he couldn't bear the thought that he made her nervous. Closing the space between them, he enveloped her hands in his to immobilize them.

"And it's just—well, we haven't known each other very long, and you aren't like anyone I've ever met before, and—"

"Relax," he whispered, brushing his mouth against hers. He wasn't kissing her to pressure her, he told himself. He was only kissing her as a means of putting an end to her babbling.

She laughed anxiously and turned her head. "What can I say? I'm a dowdy old mother and—"

"And you don't have to say anything," he insisted. "How do I shut you up?"

She laughed again, a genuine, heartfelt laugh this time. "You must think I'm nuts," she mumbled.

"I think you're fantastic," he said. "When can we

see each other for longer than a minute? Are you going to have to work late all week?''

She shook her head. "Just tonight and Thursday. But I've got to save some time for Philip. I hate it when I work late and don't get to spend the evening with him. Especially now, at this time of year. I promised him that we'd decorate the rest of the house when I got home tomorrow, and he and I have a hot date at McDonald's lined up for Wednesday. And Joanna's hosting a Christmas party for some of the neighborhood kids after dinner on Friday, and I told her I'd help her out—''

"You're a busy lady," Jesse conceded. "How's Saturday?''

"I don't know yet. Can you call me a little later in the week?''

"I think I can manage that." He kissed her again, a light, lingering kiss on her lips. "My minute must be up," he whispered reluctantly.

"I forgot to time you," she confessed, touching her mouth to his once more and then breaking from him. "I'd better run. Drive carefully tonight, Jesse. It's slippery out there.''

"Yes, ma'am." He accompanied her out of the lounge, and the instant she reentered the store she was accosted by frantic clerks. Where were the extra boxes of star-shaped crystal tree ornaments? What should be done about the woman with the overdrawn credit card? Where did Kevin put that morning's shipment of sterling silver napkin rings? Could Robin please deal with the cantankerous old man who wanted to return the beach umbrella he'd bought at the store last July?

Tossing Jesse a beleaguered smile, Robin allowed her employees to sweep her away.

WHAT WAS SHE THINKING? How could she treat the man so shabbily? Sunday night, she'd pushed him away after blatantly encouraging him to seduce her, and today she'd declared that she was all but unavailable to see him for the next century. If he had any brains, he'd wash his hands of her.

By nine-fifteen, she'd waved off the last of her sales-clerks and locked up the store. Trudging through the back door to the employee parking lot, she let out an anguished breath and shook her head. She had essen-tially told Jesse that she didn't have time for him. He would have to be superhuman to put up with her. And he wasn't superhuman.

The truth was, she didn't have time for him, not now, not during the most important month for business at Woodleigh's. She didn't have time to build a friendship with a man when she scarcely had time for her own son. Whatever free moments she had belonged to Philip.

She hated these late-night schedules. Whenever she had to work past nine, she always gave Philip permis-sion to stay up until she got home. But he would be in his pajamas, and they'd get to spend at best ten minutes catching up on their day's activities before she'd have to send him to bed. If she let him stay up any later, he'd fall asleep in class the following day.

She wanted to make time for Jesse, too. She owed herself the opportunity to develop a relationship with a man. She couldn't let her life revolve entirely around work and Philip. She was a person, too, with her own needs.

Grunting, she unlocked her car and started the engine. "That's a swell thought," she muttered, wondering whether she'd read it in some magazine or book on self-actualization in the eighties. The people who preached that kind of drivel obviously didn't have to contend with the realities of day-to-day living. Robin was a mother first, a breadwinner second. Social butterfly ranked way down there at the bottom of the list, below car-washer and checkbook-balancer.

And yet...and yet, for a brief, mystifying moment Sunday night, lost in the awesome power of Jesse's lovemaking, she had forgotten about being a mother, a breadwinner, and all the rest of it. She had been only a woman, a mature, sensual woman reveling in the magic that mature, sensual women were supposed to experience with like-minded men. For those few minutes, nothing had been important but her own physical awakening, her longing...her needs.

All right, so she had needs. Big deal. Ever since she'd made a conscious decision to become a mother, she had voluntarily put her own needs on hold. Philip's needs came first. Right now, he needed his mother, his home, a magnificent Christmas. And that took precedence over anything Robin might want to discover with a man.

Except...except for those few damnably glorious minutes when she'd gazed up into Jesse's face, when she'd felt his body moving passionately against hers... "Don't even think about it," she cautioned herself. "If he's really interested in you, he'll accept your priorities."

Fat chance of that, too, she mourned. Any woman whose priorities had Christmas with her little boy coming before a love affair couldn't hope to hold an atheist's interest for long.

Philip was cavorting around the living room in his pajamas when Robin got home. "Hey, Mom!" he bellowed, racing to her and giving her a boisterous hug. "I got a hundred on my spelling test, and Ms. Becker wrote 'Good job' on it, with a big explanation point.''

"Exclamation point," Robin corrected him, returning his hug. "That's wonderful, Phil. I'm very proud of you."

"Yeah, well, she wasn't too boring today. And a bunch of us decided we've got to give Cookie Monster a Christmas present. Like, maybe, a big box of cookies. Will you bake some for him?"

"Philip!" Chuckling, Robin pulled off her coat and hung it in the closet. "If I'm going to go to all the trouble of baking cookies, I'm sure not going to let you feed them to a snake."

"On Gleek, mommies bake cookies for snakes all the time," Philip said.

"Then send Cookie Monster to Gleek."

"And—oh, yeah! We got a package in the mail from Grandma and Grandpa Greer," Philip continued. "Mrs. O'Leary said it was probably Christmas presents and I couldn't open it up."

"She's right," Robin confirmed. "I'll open it, and if it's presents, they'll go right under the tree and stay there until the big day."

"Aww!"

"It's way past your bedtime, fella," Robin said, giving Philip an affectionate swat on his backside. "How about heading up the stairs while I pay Mrs. O'Leary?"

Once Robin had written a check for Kate and sent her home, she climbed the stairs to Philip's room. He was seated on his bed, his blond hair tousled and his pajama bottoms drooping to expose his belly button. That was the way boys were, Robin reminded herself— they never grew gradually, but instead stayed the same height for months and months, and then shot up two inches in a week. She would have to buy him some new pajamas.

"Where's your spelling test?" she asked, skirting the bed to reach his desk. She found the paper lying on top of his arithmetic workbook. A big red 100 appeared at the top, along with Ms. Becker's glowing message at the bottom.

Beaming, Robin returned to Philip's bed and gave her son another hug. "I'm so proud of you."

He snorted modestly. "It was easy, Mom. I guess I'm just naturally smart."

"Just last week you were telling me that spelling was dumb," Robin teased, pulling back the blanket for him. As he lay down, she noticed the gap between his pajama top and bottoms again. He was growing up, both physically and intellectually. No matter how much Robin wanted to make room in her life for Jesse, she would never do it at the expense of missing out on Philip's daily growth. Go out on dates, become embroiled in an affair, blink, and your son would change on you overnight. Philip's development was simply too important to miss. "I love you, Phil," she whispered, momentarily overcome by sentiment.

"It was just a spelling test," he said nonchalantly. "Don't get carried away."

Laughing, Robin kissed him and shut off the light.

She stole to her bedroom to change into her jeans and sweat shirt, then headed downstairs. The parcel from her former in-laws was sitting on a counter in the kitchen, and she cut it open with a steak knife. Sure enough, it contained two gift-wrapped boxes, both tagged with Philip's name. Robin was happy that, in spite of the divorce, Philip's paternal grandparents kept in touch with him.

After placing the gifts under the tree, she returned to the kitchen to fix herself a light supper. Given how late it was, she didn't have much of an appetite, and the leftover macaroni and cheese Kate had prepared for Philip and herself hardly looked appealing. Robin wearily opened a can of soup, dumped it into a pot, and set it on the stove. Just as it started to bubble, the telephone rang.

She answered it at once, hoping the bell hadn't roused Philip. "Hello?"

"Hi, Robin." It was Jesse.

Whatever she'd told him, however inanely she'd blabbered in the staff lounge, she obviously hadn't scared him off—yet. A giddy smile shaped her lips as she murmured, "Hello, Jesse."

"There was so much I wanted to tell you today," he said. "A minute wasn't enough."

He *had* told her so much today—he had told her that her inexperience didn't bother him, that she had no reason to apologize for her behavior last night, that all he cared about was "us." Anything else he might say now would seem trivial in comparison.

But she wasn't about to stop him. Instead she shut off the stove, poured the soup into a bowl, and carried it to the table, the phone receiver wedged against her shoulder. "I'm listening," she prompted him.

"I gave the Navy a lecture on Santa Claus," he announced.

"What?" She dropped her spoon, splattering drops of soup across the table.

"I told you about my client whose son is in the Navy, didn't I?"

Robin retrieved her spoon and wiped the surface of the table with her napkin. "Something about how the

Navy was denying him his Christmas leave," she recalled.

"That's right. I called up a captain stationed at Newport today and told him that if the Navy believed in Santa Claus, they had to let the boy go home for Christmas."

"You didn't!"

"I did, Robin, and I think it's your fault."

If this was his way of remonstrating with her, he certainly didn't sound terribly angry. Indeed, he sounded quite amused. "In that case, have your client pay me instead of you," she quipped.

"This is legal aid, Robin. The clients don't pay."

"Oh. Right." She sipped her soup, inordinately pleased by this conversation—inordinately pleased that Jesse had felt he had to share his news with her. "What did the Navy say?"

"They asked me to send them a written brief on the matter," he told her. "What do you think, Robin? If I send them an affidavit on the existence of Santa, are they going to blackmail me with it?"

"I wouldn't lose sleep over it," she consoled him.

His laughter faded. "Seriously, Robin. You know more than I do about how the military functions. Do you think the Navy will bend its rules to accommodate Christmas for this one kid and his mother?"

Had he called her up for legal counsel? Astonished, she lowered her spoon and tucked the receiver more firmly against her chin. "I don't know, Jesse. The Navy does things differently from the Army. But there are a few officers here and there who've got hearts. It probably depends on whether the captain you spoke to is one of them."

"Hearts," Jesse echoed, his tone soft and sincere. "That's really what it's all about, isn't it?"

"What Christmas is about? Of course, Jesse," she said firmly. "That's exactly what it's about."

"*I* don't have to be converted," Jesse pointed out good-naturedly. "It's the Navy that has to be convinced."

Robin almost blurted out that, of all people, Jesse *did* have to be converted. But he didn't, really. He'd already gone Christmas shopping with her and Philip, and helped them to buy a tree, and participated in decorating it. If he hadn't gotten sick of the holiday by now, then he probably was half the distance to believing in it.

"Well," she said, "I wish you lots of luck. And your client, too. In her son's place, if the Navy refused me my leave, I'd go AWOL."

"Great," Jesse snorted. "And Mrs. Selby would be begging me to represent him at his court-martial. Something tells me I shouldn't have asked you for advice."

Advice wasn't why Jesse had called her. Nor had he called her to complain about his challenges at work. He had called her for no other reason than to talk, to include her in his day.

She remembered how she and Ray used to talk this way, back when things were good between them. He would arrive home from work, and she would arrive home from one of the various jobs she'd held before Philip was born, and they'd compare notes, describe moments, chatter about anything that crossed their minds, no matter how inconsequential. It had been for Robin one of the nicest aspects of being married.

And now Jesse was offering her that same companionship. He was presenting himself as a kindred soul with whom she could share a few thoughts at the end of her day. An unexpected sense of well-being flooded her, a warmth and contentment she hadn't experienced in years. "I'm close, Jesse," she admitted, startling herself.

"Close to what?" he asked, bewildered.

"Close to loving you."

He said nothing for a moment. And then, "I'm glad, Robin. Very glad."

Chapter Nine

He called again Tuesday evening. Robin and Philip
were in the kitchen, Philip pasting together a chain composed of red and green construction paper links, and
Robin arranging flexible sprigs of pine around the bases
of the red candles she planned to display in the living
room and dining room windows. She and Philip had
already replaced the willow wreath on the front door
with the fresh pine wreath, and spiraled a long rope of
holly and red velvet ribbon around the staircase railing.
The tree was lit up, and Robin had tuned the television
set to a rebroadcast of an old Bing Crosby Christmas
special so they could listen to carols while they worked.

"Is it just my imagination," Jesse asked when Robin
answered the phone, "or are Japanese cars small?"

When the phone had begun to ring, she'd hoped that
the call would be from Jesse, and she was delighted to
hear his voice on the other end. "Hello, Jesse," she
greeted him.

He regaled her for a few minutes with a tale of his
fruitless effort to find a suitable new car for himself.
"Either the cars they're making these days are over-
priced and underequipped, or I'm too demanding," he
concluded.

"A little of both, probably," Robin noted affectionately.

"So," he said. "About Saturday night—are you free?"

"Yes and no," she answered. "The problem is, I've got to work until five on Saturday, and from noon to five Sunday."

"That still leaves Saturday evening," Jesse noted.

Robin knew that she would be exhausted after a full day at the store on a Saturday. She also knew that she would want to spend the evening with Philip. But that didn't mean she had to deprive herself of Jesse's company, too. "Maybe you could come over for dinner," she said. "I won't be able to prepare anything too elegant, but—"

"Better yet, why don't you come here for dinner?" Jesse offered. "After working all day, you shouldn't have to prepare anything at all. Phil can come along, too, if he'd like."

Robin didn't doubt that Philip would like that just fine. "Are you sure that would be all right?" she asked.

"If he likes spaghetti and meatballs, he's my kind of guest," Jesse replied. "I'm not exactly a gourmet cook."

"Spaghetti and meatballs is one of his favorites."

"Great. Come over whenever you're ready after work."

"It'll probably be around five-thirty or six," Robin estimated. "We'll see you then." After hanging up, she went in search of Philip. She found him in the den, switching the TV channel to a police show. "Forget it, fella," she scolded, twisting the dial back to the Bing Crosby special. "I want to hear Bing and the whole

Crosby family sing, 'We wish you a Merry Christmas.'''

"He's dead," Philip pointed out. "Why should we watch a dead person?"

"We aren't watching, we're listening," Robin said. "And if you want to decorate this house with me, you'd better steer clear of all those violent shows."

Philip shaped his hand into a make-believe pistol and created an explosive *pow* sound through his lips. "Okay, Mom," he said, his imaginary assassination accomplished. "Let's decorate."

"THERE HE IS AGAIN," Kirsten whispered to Lisa as the two clerks spied on the handsome dark-haired man in the gray cashmere coat who had just entered Woodleigh's and was unknowingly standing beneath the mistletoe by the store's front door.

"Forget it," Lisa whispered back. "He's Robin's."

Robin suspected that she wasn't supposed to have overheard their exchange, but how could she help herself when the three of them were crowded behind the counter, bagging merchandise for customers? Not that Jesse was hers, but she knew instinctively that he'd come to Woodleigh's to see her. She straightened her pinafore, handed her customer a receipt and a bagged package of clove-scented candles, and scooted around the counter to greet Jesse.

"I won't ask for one minute," he said, grinning. "This might take two. Can you come outside?"

"Two minutes, huh," she muttered with pretended dismay, eyeing the frantic shoppers milling about the store. Her gaze alighted on Lisa and Kirsten, who were watching her and Jesse with inordinate curiosity, and she decided to let them think Jesse was hers. Slipping her hand through the bend in his elbow, she said, "Two minutes. I'm timing you."

Laughing, he ushered her out of the store. Parked at the curb, in a no-parking zone, was a sky-blue Volkswagen Rabbit. He gestured at it with his free arm, then grinned proudly at Robin.

For a minute she feared that she was hallucinating. The last time she'd seen this car, it had been smashed fore and aft, with a splintered windshield and a missing bumper. How had Jesse managed to get it repaired? Why had he bothered?

"I just bought it this afternoon," he boasted, guiding her around the car so she could view it from every angle. "It's an '80. What do you think?"

She shivered as a gust of freezing air assaulted her. Jesse opened the flap of his coat and wrapped it around her, snuggling her against himself. It wasn't the coat that warmed her, she acknowledged, but his body, his nearness. The delectable heat that infused her was nearly enough to eradicate her discomfort at the sight of his car.

Nearly enough, but not quite. "Why did you buy a car identical to the one you were driving when you had your accident?" she asked.

"I was looking at new VW's," he explained. "But the dealer had some used ones in the lot. I saw this car, and I thought—why not? I was lucky the last time I was in a car like this. I was so lucky I survived with barely a scratch. It's obviously the right car for me."

She tilted her head back to see his face. The thick collar of his coat rode up beneath her ponytail, soft against the nape of her neck. Jesse smiled down at her, such a sweet, wonderful smile that she couldn't help mirroring it. "So you believe in luck, is that it?" she teased. "What's the difference between luck and God, Jesse?"

"I..." He hesitated, sorting through his thoughts. Then his smile grew even more gentle. "I believe that my life was saved by a blue VW Rabbit and you. Now I've got another blue VW Rabbit."

And you've got me, Robin almost said. She curled her arms around his lean torso, trying to ward off the encroaching numbness in her hands. "If it's the car you want, then congratulations," she mumbled into his shoulder, hating herself for not declaring that she was willing to be part of the lucky package for him as well. If only he would admit that he did believe in luck, if only he would admit that Robin hadn't saved his life, if only he would bend that much...

Did she really need him to bend for her? Did she really need him to say, "Yes, I believe in luck. I believe in Santa Claus. I believe in family and the good Lord and all the things they represent, I believe my life was saved by divine intervention." Was that why she was holding back, refusing to give herself over to love?

She wasn't sure. All she knew was that whenever Jesse started talking about her having saved his life, she became edgy. Whenever she analyzed the differences in their outlooks on life, she held back. Whenever she remembered how much she had desired him last Sunday night, she felt scared. She wanted things simple; she wanted the expected routines and rituals. She didn't know how to deal with a man like Jesse.

"You're turning to ice out here," he commented quietly, tightening the coat around her and hurrying her back indoors. A blast of hot air from the heating vent by the door slammed into their huddled bodies, and she extricated herself from his coat and rubbed her fingers together to restore sensation to them. "You don't like the car," he inferred.

"I do, Jesse," she countered, forcing a smile. "I think it's great."

"But...?"

But I want to love you, and I'm frightened. I want you to make this easy for me. "I think the car's terrific," she said, "and I'm happy you won't have to drive the rental car anymore. Rabbits handle well in bad weather."

"Maybe I should have bought a new car," he mused, glancing through the front window at his illegally parked Rabbit. "But I kept thinking of what it would look like to my clients in Newhallville if I drove up in some flashy sixteen-thousand-dollar car. It would be like shoving their noses in their own poverty."

"And your radio would get ripped off," she observed. "A used car is probably a smart idea for someone in your line of work."

He nodded. "Well. I just wanted to show it to you. I'll let you get back to work." He kissed her cheek, then straightened up and buttoned his coat.

She touched his arm, holding him in place. She had failed to tell him she loved him, but she had to let him know in some way how pleased she was by his impromptu visit. "Jesse...I'm really glad you came by to show the car to me."

The corners of his mouth twitched upward. "One of these days, I'll take you for a spin in it."

"Heavens, no!" she cried, groaning at his unintended pun. "The last thing I want to do is sit next to you when you're spinning in a car."

His laughter mingled with hers. "No spins, Robin.

Scout's honor. I'll see you Saturday.'' With that, he left the store.

A heavy sense of loss overtook her as, gazing through the glass, she watched Jesse climb into the blue VW at the curb, fasten his seat belt, gun the engine and drive away. What was wrong with her? Why did she want so desperately to play it safe with him? Why was she so afraid to let go?

She wanted him, yes. But the thought of any man other than Ray loving her, knowing her so intimately...

She'd been afraid the first time with Ray, too. Even in high school she had been aware that some of her classmates slept with their boyfriends. But Robin never had, not because she was a prude, not because she didn't understand the facts of life or possess a healthy streak of curiosity, but because she didn't love those boys. She had dated Ray for a year and a half in college before she finally agreed to spend the night with him. And as excited as she'd been, she'd also been petrified.

Ray had been gentle with her, and she'd enjoyed the experience greatly. But her fear had never been based on the physical aspects of what was occurring. It had been a matter of emotions: did she love Ray enough to make the moment meaningful? Was it more than simply sex they were sharing? She believed that making love had to be spiritual to be right. It had to entail a joining of souls as well as bodies.

It had been right with Ray. They'd loved each other then, and they continued to love each other for nearly seven more years. After their relationship began to disintegrate, they still made love whenever he was home. Yet it was no longer as satisfying to Robin, no longer as fulfilling. Her love for him was on the wane, and their sexual relationship was no longer spiritual. Their souls were traveling in different directions.

She didn't doubt that she would enjoy making love with Jesse, but enjoyment wasn't the issue. The issue was, how could she make love with a man who claimed to have no soul at all? How could she ever find something spiritual with him?

ON SATURDAY EVENING, Robin and Philip drove to Jesse's condominium. Philip expressed great relief when Ms. Becker didn't appear on her porch. He galloped down the stairs to Jesse's door and rang the doorbell, causing it to sound incessantly until Robin shoved his hand away.

Jesse opened the door, dressed in jeans and a crisp white shirt. "Come on in," he welcomed them, stepping aside so they could enter the living room.

It was big. Robin could say that much for it. A swanky-looking leather couch stood against one wall, a rocking chair, a table and a lamp against another. An empty modern fireplace consumed a third wall. And that was it. No pictures, no plants, no knickknacks or clutter. Not a single personal touch, nary an idiosyncratic item to personalize the room.

"I like this place," Philip announced, pulling off his jacket and darting to the rocking chair. He sat on it and energetically pumped his legs, giving himself a ride. "I like it a lot better than my dad's apartment in Washington. His living room has books and newspapers lying all over the place, and he gets real mad whenever I touch them. Can I see the rest of it?"

"There's not much to see," Jesse warned, running to catch up with Philip as he raced into the dining room.

Robin followed, and tried to hide her shock. There

wasn't a stick of furniture in the room, not a table, not a chair, not a sideboard. A breakfast bar separated it from the kitchen, and four stools were positioned two on each side of the counter to provide an eating area. The kitchen looked like a real room only because it was filled with the cabinets and appliances that had come with the house. "Oh, wow!" Philip hooted, noticing the three neatly arranged place settings on the breakfast bar. "Are we gonna be eating here? It's almost like a restaurant, Mom!"

She laughed sheepishly. "That gives you an idea of the quality of the restaurants I take Philip to."

"Well," Jesse addressed the boy, "we're eating at the counter because we haven't got anyplace else to eat. I haven't bought a dining table yet." He took Robin's parka, scooped Philip's jacket off the floor, and hung them both in the coat closet. Then he returned to the kitchen and filled a pot with water.

"Can I help?" Robin asked.

Jesse shook his head. "The meatballs and sauce are already made, and so's the salad. All that's left is cooking the spaghetti."

"What's for dessert?" Philip asked.

"Ice cream," Jesse told him.

"All right!" Philip flopped onto one of the stools, discovered that the seat revolved, and busied himself with spinning in dizzying circles.

Robin scanned the vacant dining room one last time, then moved around the counter to the kitchen. "Why haven't you bought a dining table yet?" she asked, hoping she didn't sound disapproving. "You've lived here since June, Jesse."

He pulled a fistful of dry pasta from a box, estimated its volume, and dumped it into the boiling water. Then he shrugged. "I guess this place doesn't feel like home to me yet."

"Of course it doesn't," Robin said with a laugh. "How could it feel like a home when you haven't done anything to make it a home?"

Jesse glanced at her, grinning impishly. "You think I should spend a fortune at Woodleigh's?"

"Woodleigh's or K-Mart," Robin answered. "It doesn't have to be a fortune, Jesse. Just a few pictures on the walls, or something…"

He shrugged again, apparently not sharing her concern. "I'll get around to it one of these days," he said, "once I start settling in."

"Are you sure it's not that you're planning to return to California eventually?"

"Are you from California?" Philip interjected. "Wow, that's neat. I've been to California, sort of. Once, when we visited my grandma in Hawaii, we changed planes in Los Angeles. I never got out of the airport, though."

"L.A.X.," Jesse grunted. "What a tourist attraction. I bet Hawaii is much nicer than L.A. Do you visit your grandma often?"

"Uh-uh. It's too expensive. Mostly, she visits us, on account of she's just one person. She comes every summer. She won't come in the winter. She hates cold weather," he added with a disdainful sniff.

"It makes her sick." Robin defended her mother to Philip. "It aggravates her arthritis." She turned back to Jesse, who was vigorously stirring the spaghetti in the pot. "I can't imagine living in a place for six months and not settling in. My family spent only five months on a base in Wyoming, and you wouldn't believe how lived-in my mother made that house."

"It's obviously a knack you've inherited," Jesse praised her. "You know how to make a house a home."

"Because it's important," she asserted, then stifled herself. She wasn't going to torment Jesse with yet another sermon on her feelings about the necessity of having a real home. She had probably already bored him to death on the subject.

Jesse served the meal, including red wine for the adults and soda for Philip. Robin winced inwardly as she recalled her advice to Jesse about purchasing a wine rack. That was the least his condominium needed.

Maybe she could buy him something homey for Christmas. She wanted to get him something he'd like, something he would be able to use. Certainly not a dining table, but maybe a framed print, or some andirons for his fireplace, or a crystal fruit bowl for the table in the living room. A houseplant, perhaps, or...a tree. A full, towering Douglas fir, festooned with lights and tinsel and a huge silver star at its apex, would do wonders for his living room.

Philip's behavior at dinner was exemplary. He even ate half his salad, along with plenty of spaghetti. He sang one of his favorite songs, "On Top of Spaghetti," to the tune of "On Top of Old Smoky," and assessed with Jesse the odds that Ms. Becker could hear their voices through the wall dividing the two condominiums. After dinner, he wolfed down a generous portion of ice cream, and Robin didn't object when Jesse led him downstairs to watch television in the den.

"It was delicious," Robin complimented Jesse once they were alone in the kitchen. Over his protests, she insisted on helping him to rinse the dishes and stack them in the dishwasher. Once the pots were scrubbed and the counter wiped, Jesse refilled their glasses with wine and led her into the living room. No sooner were they seated on the couch when Philip appeared at the top of the stairs to ask, "This guy on the news said something about the deficit, Mom. I forget, which is worse? The deficit or the debt?"

"In twenty-five words or less?" Robin chuckled. "The deficit."

"That's what I thought," Philip muttered, vanishing down the stairs again.

Jesse leaned back into the leather-covered upholstery and arched his arm casually around Robin's shoulders. "You ought to go into politics," he joked. "You sure know how to cut right to the meat of the matter."

"I'll let Philip go into politics for me," Robin rejoined. "I'll explain things for him, and he can carry out the policies. He's got more energy than I do."

"He does have an abundance of energy, doesn't he," Jesse agreed.

Philip might have energy, but he lacked diplomatic skills. Gazing about the austere room, Robin remembered what her son had said as soon as he'd entered Jesse's house; that he liked it a lot better than he liked his father's apartment. "Does it bother you when Philip mentions his father?" she asked Jesse.

"Why should it bother me?"

Robin mulled over her answer. It shouldn't bother Jesse, but she had presumed that most men would feel uncomfortable about the ex-husbands of women in whom they were romantically interested. "You told me all about your ex-girlfriend in Los Angeles," she recollected. "But you never ask me about my ex-husband."

Jesse meditated on her words, then shrugged. "What should I ask? You grew apart, you broke up, he cares about Phil and you aren't bitter. Is there anything else I need to know?"

"You know more than that," Robin recalled, her eyes meeting Jesse's for an instant and then shifting away in embarrassment.

He studied her attentively, reminiscing. Then he nodded. "You mean, that he's the only man you've ever made love with? Robin, that's not important to me. *You're* what's important to me."

"Yes, but—"

"Robin." His fingers floated through her hair, stroking in a consoling rhythm. "The only thing that matters is that you're a woman with strong values. I admire that. I really do."

"Maybe you admire it," she said, smiling timidly, "but you'd rather have gotten me into bed last Sunday, wouldn't you?"

"Not if you were entertaining doubts."

"You weren't frustrated?"

"Of course I was frustrated," he admitted with a short laugh. His thumb reached her earlobe and traced its curve, causing a ripple of longing to twist through her. "I'm still frustrated, Robin, but frustration isn't fatal."

"I'm sorry, Jesse," she confessed. "I'm trying to work it out, I'm trying very hard—"

"Don't try," he urged her. "It's all inside you, and it'll come out when it's ready."

"And in the meantime, you'll get tired of waiting and—"

Jesse leaned toward her, brushing his lips along her temple. "I don't think I'll have to wait that long," he whispered.

The implication in his words was as arousing as the

tender caress of his thumb along her ear. She suffered another surge of longing, dark and demanding, and if it weren't for the intrusive patter of sneakered feet on the stairs, she might have been tempted to act on it.

But Philip rescued her from her rashness by barging into the living room. "The guy on the news said something about Koala Lumpy. Where's that, Mom?"

"Koala Lumpy?" she asked. "You mean, Kuala Lumpur. It's a city in Malaysia."

"Malaysia," Philip repeated. "That's in Asia. They rhyme, Jesse. Malaysia, Asia." With that astute observation, he disappeared down the stairs again.

"He's amazing," Jesse commented, staring at the staircase. "You've got yourself an incredible little boy."

"Any little boy could figure out that Malaysia rhymed with Asia," Robin argued, although she was thrilled that Jesse considered her son as amazing as she did. "And never call him a little boy to his face. He thinks he's a big boy."

"Ah, yes. Little boys play with Smurfs, isn't that right?" Jesse deliberated for a minute, his smile deepening. "I don't know much about kids, Robin, but Philip seems so...so free-wheeling, so eager to embrace the world. If I had ever asked my parents about Kuala Lumpur, they would have treated me to a ten-minute dissertation on the good works of the missionaries in Malaysia. And when they were through, they would have told me to spend more time studying the scripture and less time asking so many questions."

"Then you're the amazing one," Robin observed. "You turned out pretty well, under the circumstances."

Jesse chuckled modestly and drew Robin closer to himself, cushioning her head against his shoulder.

"Phil's turning out better," he said. "You're lucky to have a son like him. Or maybe he's the lucky one, having a mother like you."

If Robin challenged Jesse, he would swear that he didn't believe in luck. So she simply accepted his observation, letting its truth sink into her and settle comfortably inside her heart. Jesse did believe in luck. And so did Robin. Like Jesse, she believed, among other things, that she was immeasurably lucky to have a son like Philip.

BUT IF ONE BELIEVED in luck, one had to believe in bad luck as well as good. When Robin's phone rang early Sunday morning, her voice was thick with sleep and contentment when she answered it, expecting to hear Jesse's voice on the other end. Words of gratitude took shape on her tongue, gratitude about the lovely evening she and Philip had had with him, his kindness in making dinner for them, his generosity in choosing to respect rather than despise her. If pressed, she might even confess that he was the finest man she'd ever met, and that she did love him.

The voice she heard in response to her drowsy hello wasn't Jesse's, however. Cutting through the static in the long-distance connection, she heard her ex-husband say, "Robin? It's Ray. I'm going to be stateside for Christmas, and I want Philip with me."

Chapter Ten

She bolted upright in bed, struggling for lucidity. "Ray?" she mumbled. "Where are you?"

"I'm in Buenos Aires right now, but I'm going to be back in the States next week. It cropped up at the spur of the moment. I know you weren't expecting this, Robin, but...if I'm going to be in the country, I'd really like to see Philip."

"But—but you just saw him!" That wasn't exactly true. Ray had been stateside in October, and after a couple of days in his Washington, D.C., apartment, he'd flown up to Connecticut and spent a weekend with his son. Whenever Ray was in the country during the school term, he took a room at a motel in Branford so he would be able to see Philip without interrupting his son's class attendance. Usually, however, Ray timed his furloughs for February, when the school system shut down for a week-long vacation to coincide with Washington's birthday, and for August. That way, Philip could travel to the capital to visit his father.

"I know, I know," Ray said. "But, Robin, this is special. An Argentine businessman I've been working with was planning to take his children to Orlando for Christmas, but he suddenly found out that he couldn't take the time off from work. He's passed the reservations along to me, and I was able to wheedle some free time. Robin, it's Orlando.''

''Florida?'' What on earth did Ray want to do in Florida? She wished she wasn't so muddled, so absurdly drowsy.

''Disney World. I've got the room, I've got the tickets to Disney World, Epcot Center... Mickey Mouse, Robin,'' he explained. ''Phil's going to love it.''

Of course Philip would love it. No argument there. But... ''Not at Christmas, Ray. You can't take him away at Christmas.''

For several seconds all she heard was the scratchy sound of long-distance disturbances on the line. Then Ray spoke again, slowly and precisely. ''You have him every holiday, Robin. We've never fought about that. You have him for Thanksgiving, Easter, Halloween, his birthday. You've had him every Christmas since we split.''

She couldn't dispute Ray's claim. But the reason Robin had Philip for the holidays was that Ray had left. He had preferred to traipse around the world, living out of suitcases, instead of establishing a home and celebrating the rituals of each season with his family. Ray had never once quarreled with Robin over custody of their child. She willingly accepted the responsibility of raising their son, and one of her rewards was to have him with her for the holidays. Especially Christmas.

''Robin.'' Ray sounded cajoling. ''We're talking about Mickey Mouse. When is Phil going to have another opportunity like this? I'd like to fly him down to Florida and spend a few days with him here. What better Christmas present can we give him?''

''He doesn't want Mickey Mouse for Christmas,''

Robin retorted. "He wants a rocket ship, and some Masters of the Universe toys—"

"He can have them, too," Ray pointed out. "How can you even consider denying him this? It's a kid's dream come true."

It was Ray's dream come true, too, no doubt. But Christmas without Philip wasn't a dream for Robin. It was the worst nightmare she could imagine.

"Why don't you ask him?" Ray proposed. "Ask him if he'd rather spend Christmas in Connecticut or go to Disney World."

"That's not fair!" Robin raged. "You know damned well he'll choose Disney World."

"Then be Santa for him. Give him his wish."

"Ray." She squeezed her eyes shut, refusing to succumb to tears, trying to force her words past the lump in her throat. "I don't want to deny him Mickey Mouse. But at Christmastime? You know how I feel about Christmas."

"Yes, I know how you feel," Ray said soothingly. "But this was when my colleague had the reservations, and I can't do anything about it." In a firmer tone, he added, "Phil's my son, too."

"Who's on the phone?" Philip shouted through the closed bedroom door.

Robin shuddered. "Your father," she replied.

Philip hurled the door open and scrambled onto the bed beside his mother. He grabbed the phone from her and hollered, "Hi, Dad! Where are you?"

Robin kicked off the blanket, stood and stalked to the window. Pulling back the drapes, she gazed outside. The sky was overcast, gloomy with thick gray clouds hinting at snow. Who cared if it snowed, though? If Philip went to Florida, he'd have a hot, muggy Christmas. And without him here, Robin wouldn't want Christmas at all, let alone a white one.

She let the drapes fall across the window and turned to study her son. He looked small in the wide double bed, despite the fact that he was outgrowing his pajamas. His eyes were bright and round as he clung to the telephone, his high-pitched voice ebullient. "Yeah, school's okay. I got a hundred on my last spelling test.... Oh, guess what? We had dinner at Jesse's house last night. He made spaghetti and meatballs, and ice cream.... He's a friend of Mom's," Philip reported.

Great, Robin grunted inwardly. Now Ray was going to find out that Robin had a male friend. The next thing she knew, he'd be accusing her of moral turpitude, demanding a new custody hearing and taking her child away from her forever.

"Mickey Mouse!" Philip shrieked, and Robin felt her stomach twist into a knot. Ray must be telling Philip about Disney World. Her son's expression was ecstatic. She'd never be able to keep him home for Christmas now. "No kidding, Dad? Really? And I could come down to Florida? Oh, wow!"

The tears rose again, causing Robin's vision to blur. She hastily looked away. She wasn't going to let Philip see her cry.

"He wants to talk to you, Mom," Philip announced, extending the phone in her direction.

Nodding, she swallowed and crossed the room. She sat gingerly on the edge of the mattress, took the receiver from Philip and pressed it to her ear. "That was low, Ray," she muttered. "You shouldn't have mentioned it to him before we'd worked it all out."

"He wants to come," Ray told her—as if she hadn't already figured that out. "Who's Jesse, by the way?"

"You heard Philip," she said impassively. "Jesse's a friend of ours."

"Don't get me wrong," Ray hastened to placate her. "It's about time you started dating."

"I'm not dating," she said. "He's just a friend." Whether or not that was an honest response, she wasn't about to provide Ray with explanations he didn't deserve. Right now the man deserved nothing, nothing at all. "So, now that you've shot your mouth off to Phil about Disney World—"

"He wants to come," Ray repeated. "He'll hate you if you stand in his way."

And I'll hate you if you take him, she nearly screamed. But she couldn't verbalize such an ugly thought in front of Philip. She couldn't even allow herself to think it. Philip wanted to see Mickey Mouse, and Robin would never stand in his way. Ray was right about that.

A low, tortured breath escaped her as she resigned herself to the miserable promise of a Christmas without her son. "What's the plan?" she asked listlessly, trying unsuccessfully to ignore Philip, who was bouncing on the bed and chanting, "Mickey Mouse! Mickey Mouse!"

"Today's the thirteenth," Ray outlined. "My ticket will get me to Florida on the twenty-second. Phil can fly down the twenty-third, and I'll be here to meet him. I'll arrange for a ticket out of LaGuardia or Kennedy. Which is better for you?"

She sighed. "LaGuardia."

"Fine. I'll call you in a couple of days, after I've finalized things. I don't know whether it'll be warm enough to swim, but the hotel has a pool, so pack his bathing suit."

"Yeah."

"Robin." His tone was ameliorating. "I'm sorry it's happened now. I know you're sad. I know how you feel about the holiday. But think of how much fun Phil's going to have."

"Thanks for the counseling session," she snapped. "I've got to go."

"I'll be in touch," Ray said before hanging up.

Robin dropped the receiver into its cradle and sighed again. She attempted a smile for Philip's sake and twisted to face him. "Quite a surprise, isn't it," she murmured.

He jumped off the bed and performed a giddy dance. "Mickey Mouse! I'm gonna see Mickey Mouse for Christmas!"

"I guess you are," she conceded, wiping her hand across her damp eyelashes and reaching for her bathrobe.

She went downstairs and made Philip breakfast—a heaping bowl of Cheerios, a bagel, two glasses of orange juice and a cup filled half with coffee and half with milk. Exciting events always made him gluttonous. Robin herself barely managed to consume two bites of her own bagel and a cup of black coffee. Some exciting events stirred her appetite, too, but this one left her feeling distinctly nauseated.

After eating, Philip went to his room to get dressed. Robin poured herself a second cup of coffee, stared at it for ten minutes, and then dumped it down the drain. Then she wandered into the living room and glared at the magnificent tree, the ribbon-and-holly-trimmed balustrade, the decorated candles in the windows. She inhaled the tangy scent of pine. Christmas without Philip. She couldn't bear it.

Returning to the kitchen, she reached for the phone. Perhaps ten o'clock on a Sunday morning was too early to call Jesse, but in another half hour, she'd have to shower, get dressed, summon Kate O'Leary and leave for Woodleigh's. She pulled the new telephone book from the shelf, flipped through it until she located Jesse's number, and dialed.

He sounded reasonably awake when he answered; Robin found solace in that. "Hello, Jesse—it's Robin, and I..." A fresh lump of tears took up residence in her throat, and she was unable to continue.

"What happened?" he asked, worried.

"Disney World happened," she moaned, then related the details of Ray's call to Jesse. Maybe he thought her divorce hadn't left her bitter, but she didn't bother to disguise her bitterness now. "Of all the times, Jesse— of all the times, it had to be Christmas. Any other time of the year I wouldn't have minded. But to do this—to do this to me at Christmas—"

"It doesn't sound like he's doing anything to *you*," Jesse calmly pointed out. "It's something he's doing for Philip."

"Don't you think I know that? I hate myself for being so angry, Jesse. I want Philip to have this opportunity. But Christmas—" She stopped short. How could she expect Jesse to understand her anguish? He didn't care about Christmas at all.

"Oh, Robin." Maybe he couldn't understand, but he did seem sympathetic. "I wish there was something I could do. I don't suppose it would help to send another Navy captain a legal brief about Santa Claus."

Of course he understood. He had been going through a similiar crisis with the client of his who wanted her son home for the holiday. Just because Christmas signified nothing to Jesse didn't mean he couldn't commiserate with people for whom it signified everything.

"What am I going to do?" she asked, desperate for words of wisdom from him, a straw to grasp at.

He ruminated. "Maybe you could spend Christmas with your mother," he suggested. "Wouldn't she come to Connecticut for the holiday?"

"No, she'll never be able to tolerate the cold weather."

"You could go to Hawaii, then."

"No," Robin said decisively. "Christmas is a time for home, Jesse. I'm not going to leave home."

"Then you'll stay here," he said. "And I'll be here, and we'll make the best of it."

The tension in her gut slowly ebbed, replaced by a shimmering warmth. Christmas with Jesse. Christmas with a man she was only beginning to know, a man who rejected so many of the things she believed in, a man who claimed he had no soul. Christmas with a friend. "You'll celebrate with me?" she asked timidly.

"I'll do my best," he said. "But I'm not going to strap on a false beard and climb down your chimney."

For the first time since Ray's call, a smile teased her lips. It wasn't much of a smile, rather feeble and forlorn, but if Jesse was willing to do his best, she would have to do her best, too. "No false beard," she assured him. "But I make a gingerbread house for Philip every year, and—" she swallowed the catch in her throat "—somebody's got to eat it."

"That I'll do," Jesse volunteered.

"Hey, Mom!" Philip's shrill voice sliced through the air from upstairs. "You'd better shake a leg or you'll be late for work!"

"I've got to go," Robin said.

"I'll talk to you later," Jesse promised before hanging up.

Robin dropped the receiver into place. Although Jesse was less than a mile away, and Philip was separated from her only by a flight of stairs, she felt lonely. So profoundly, so oppressively lonely that picturing Jesse impersonating Santa Claus made her want to cry.

There would be time enough for weeping once Philip was truly gone. For now, she had little choice but to get herself to Woodleigh's and pretend to be full of holiday cheer.

IF I COULDN'T HAVE PHILIP WITH ME for Christmas, I'd die.

Jesse picked up the piece of toast he'd been in the middle of eating, then dropped it back onto his plate as Robin's words echoed inside his skull. She had ultimately admitted that equating Christmas without her son to death was an overstatement, but her sentiments had been obvious. For a woman like her, Christmas without Philip was life without a purpose.

Why was it that this one day meant so damned much to so many people? That was all it was—a day, a date on the calendar, one three-hundred-sixty-fifth of a year. In honor of that one single day, people became maniacs. They spent money they didn't have, drank more than they could stomach, partied until they were ready to drop. They filled their homes with trees and lights, littered their floors with dead twigs and ran up extraordinary electric bills. They made promises of love and bonhomie that were quickly forgotten.

All right, so there was also some religious import to the day. It commemorated the birth of Jesus Christ—but to accept that, you had to swallow a few myths: the myth that Jesus was the Messiah, the myth that He was actually born on the twenty-fifth day of December, the myth that snow could fall in the Middle East. Jesse was one of those people who believed that Jesus was merely a man, a preacher, possibly mystic and possibly misguided, and that December twenty-fifth was declared his birthday to satisfy a lot of pagans who preferred to celebrate the winter solstice. As for snow falling in Bethlehem—well, Jesse had never seen a shred of proof about that ostensible meteorological phenomenon.

But he *had* read the scriptures as a youth, and the one message that remained with him was that it was essential to give of oneself. Not in the hope of salvation—he hadn't bought that particular aspect of it—but because helping others was a decent, humane thing to do. If Robin was in agony, Jesse would help her any way he could.

He wished he knew what it was he could do for her. Bringing Gerald Selby home for Christmas seemed a cinch in comparison, and Jesse hadn't had much success there yet. He'd received an acknowledgment of his letter to Captain Stevenson, nothing more. And even if he could bring Gerald Selby home, what home could he bring him to? Mrs. Selby's landlord was sending out feelers, but days were slipping away and the elevator still didn't work. The trash was being picked up only sporadically, and the lightbulb in Mrs. Selby's corridor hadn't been replaced.

At least Jesse had the legal training to attempt to straighten out Mrs. Selby's various dilemmas. His legal training wouldn't do him any good with Robin, however. All he could offer her was his companionship, his support, his love.

He rested his head in his palms and gazed at the plate

of toast. If he offered her all he could, perhaps it would be enough. Simply thinking of her, thinking of the hope and confidence she exuded, had helped him to survive his accident. Now she was devoid of hope and confidence, and he wasn't sure how to go about giving them back to her.

Maybe Philip could help in some way; he owed Jesse a favor. Jesse had done a favor for him by stopping by the Greer house on Thursday evening, while Robin was still at work, and spiriting Philip's Christmas gift for his mother out of the house so she wouldn't find it. It was a peculiar gift, Jesse had to admit: a statue constructed of modeling clay and painted with a garish orange glaze, supposedly depicting a boy from the planet Gleek. Jesse wondered whether Robin would ever be able to guess what the stout object with the pointy feet, the wings protruding from its shoulders and the seashell-shaped ears was supposed to be. She'd recognize the halo Philip had shaped out of wire and propped up above the creature's head, though. Angels didn't dwell in heaven; evidently, they came from Gleek.

Jesse and Mrs. O'Leary had helped Philip to wrap the awkwardly shaped object in paper, taped a lopsided bow to the package, and fastened the home-made card Philip had written. Then, vowing secrecy, Jesse had brought the gift to his condominium for safekeeping.

How would she feel when she found Philip's gift under her tree Christmas morning? Jesse hoped she wouldn't resent her son for abandoning her. Philip was just a kid. He couldn't know the despair his trip to Florida was going to cause his mother. He shouldn't know.

Jesse would make sure he didn't. He would keep Robin from despairing, somehow.

HE WANTED TO TAKE HER out to dinner, but she kept refusing his invitations. It wasn't only that managing Woodleigh's through the final Christmas crush consumed a disproportionate amount of her time, but that, irrational as it was, she felt compelled to spend every spare second with Philip. She kept thinking that if she collected as many memories as possible of her son, she could seal them, store them in her brain, and then cheer herself up by breaking them open on Christmas morning and using them to get her through the day.

Such a wish was impossible, yet she couldn't seem to stop herself. She talked to Jesse often on the phone, and he came to the house for dinner a couple of times, but even when Philip wandered into the den to watch television after dinner, Robin insisted on being in the room with him. She and Jesse sat on the couch, and while Jesse gazed at the screen Robin gazed at her son. She memorized the cowlick at the rear of Philip's head, the sparkle in his eyes, the scuffs on his sneakers and the faded ovals on the knees of his jeans. She absorbed his every utterance, his every giggle.

Perhaps Christmas would be tolerable if she tape-recorded him, she contemplated. She could turn on the cassette at sunrise on December twenty-fifth, and listen to Philip's adorable voice plying her with questions: "What does Dan Rather mean when he says fifteen people are *presumed* dead? Are they dead or aren't they?" No, that wouldn't work.

"When am I going to see this gingerbread house you've promised me?" Jesse asked on Saturday evening. It was the third night he'd come for dinner, the third night he'd had to witness Robin obsessively shadowing her son around the house. But eight-thirty had arrived and they had just put Philip to bed. She couldn't very well hover for the next few hours in Philip's doorway, watching him sleep.

"I haven't made it," she confessed, descending the stairs to the living room with Jesse. She had accumulated all the ingredients required for the house: the molasses, the chocolate wafers she used for the roof, the gumdrops with which she trimmed the windows and door. She should have baked the damned thing by now; ordinarily she baked it a week before Christmas so she and Philip could admire it and pride themselves on their ability to resist temptation until Christmas afternoon, when they traditionally disassembled the house and gobbled it up.

But she hadn't been able to bring herself to make the confection this year. It seemed like so much effort to go through when Philip wasn't going to be around to eat it with her.

"Why don't we make it now?" Jesse proposed.

"It takes hours," Robin warned him, glancing at her watch. She had already put in a full day at Woodleigh's, and Jesse had told her over dinner that he'd spent half the day at his office in New Haven, reviewing a pile of depositions he'd taken from his Newhallville clients. Neither she nor Jesse had the energy to tackle a project like the gingerbread house at this hour.

"We can sleep late tomorrow," Jesse pointed out.

Robin glanced sharply at him. Where, exactly, was he planning to sleep late? Why had he said "we"?

She trudged into the kitchen and slumped on a chair. "Jesse, I'm a horrible person," she muttered, focusing on her clenched fists, which rested on the table before her. "You want to spend the night here, and the last thing I can think about right now is whether I want you to do that."

He glided behind her and began kneading the tense muscles along her shoulders. "I thought we were discussing baking gingerbread," he said quietly.

She closed her eyes to savor fully his comforting massage. "How can you stand being around me? I've been such a pill. All I think about is Philip, Philip, Philip."

"And maybe, every now and then, you think about yourself," Jesse reproached, his tone gentle. "You think about how sorry you are for yourself, and you wallow in self-pity. You go on and on about the importance of the Christmas spirit, but I haven't noticed much of it coming from you."

"I haven't got any," she agreed dolefully. "It's like the bottom's fallen out of my world. I don't expect you to understand it, Jesse. I only wonder why you haven't given up on me and moved on."

"Bottoms fall out of worlds all the time," he noted, ending his massage and circling the table. He took a seat across from her and gathered her hands in his. "If you haven't got the strength to make your world livable again, then I'm here to help you."

"Why?" she asked, genuinely curious. "Why me?"

"Because...because deep down inside you, you do have the strength," he replied, his eyes riveted to hers, a trusting glow emanating from their profound depths. "Because your world—more than any other world I've ever seen—deserves to be repaired."

Her fingers wove through his and curled tight, clinging to him. "I do love you, Jesse," she whispered, returning his unwavering gaze.

He nodded. "I know."

"Then why aren't you pushing things? Why aren't you making demands?"

"Is that what love means?" he shot back. "Pushing and making demands?"

"Is it that you don't want me anymore?"

"Oh, Robin…" He let out an incredulous laugh. "Of course I want you. Every time I talk to you, every time I hear your voice… Every time I leave your house alone, I feel like some sort of oversexed adolescent, half-crazy with fantasies."

"Then why…?"

"Because in my fantasies, you're ready for me. You're thinking only of me—of *us*. Not of Phil and not of some overdressed pine tree. Just us. That's what I want, Robin. That's the way I want it."

His candor touched her, and made her feel even more unworthy of him. "You could have that with someone else," she reminded him in a tremulous voice. The last thing she wanted was to drive Jesse away. She had scarcely survived the past week; without him, she wouldn't have survived at all. But she loved him. She loved him enough to want him happy. And she knew she wasn't doing a good job of making him happy.

He pulled her hands to his mouth and kissed her knuckles. "Don't you think I'm aware of that?" he asked, smiling crookedly. "The problem is, you're the lady in the fantasy."

Robin's eyes glistened with tears. For the first time since she'd come to terms with Philip's leaving, they weren't tears of sorrow and loss. "I don't deserve you," she murmured, sliding her hands from his and pushing away from the table. "But since you're here, I'll make you a gingerbread house."

"Make it right," Jesse urged her. "I don't want the bottom falling out of it, too."

IT WAS RAINING lightly when Robin and Philip left for the airport. The temperature hovered in the mid-thirties, and if anything, it would be warmer at the airport, so Robin wasn't worried about the possibility of ice on the runway.

Nor was she worried about Jesse's having to contend with foul weather during his drive to Newport. He had phoned her last night to inform her that the Navy had finally agreed to release Gerald Selby into Jesse's custody on a two-day pass. Selby would have to be back on base by Christmas night, but Jesse had assured Robin that he didn't mind making the long round-trip drive twice in three days. He was thrilled for his client and her family, delighted that their holiday would be brightened by the presence of their son. Most of all, he admitted, he was jubilant that he'd gotten the United States Navy to come around.

And he didn't believe in miracles?

"Now remember," Robin instructed her son, who was squirming on the seat beside her. "The only people you're going to talk to on the plane are the flight attendants and the officers. No strangers, nobody who isn't wearing a uniform. Right?"

"I've been on airplanes by myself before," Philip scoffed. "I know the rules."

"The only time you're to leave your seat is if you have to go to the bathroom," she continued, undeterred.

He rolled his eyes. Then he twisted to confront her. "You're not going to forget to leave milk and cookies for Santa, are you?" he asked, concerned.

"I won't forget."

"The star-shaped ones. Those are his favorite."

Robin pressed her lips together. She hadn't baked her rolled sugar cookies yet. Baking them was something she and Philip always did together the night before Christmas Eve. She had assumed that she would skip making them this year; the gingerbread house had been a pain in the neck to make, and Jesse had refused to take it home with him. "It belongs here," he had insisted when she'd tried to foist it upon him.

So now it was sitting at the center of the dining room table, growing stale. The cookies would grow stale, too. Why should she bother to make them?

"You listening to me, Mom?" Noticing the glassy look in her eyes, Philip nudged her. "Santa likes—"

"The star-shaped ones. Okay, I'll make them."

Temporarily satisfied, Philip settled into his seat. Then he suddenly looked concerned again. "It's on account of, if you don't leave them for Santa, he might not leave my presents under the tree."

"Of course he will," Robin assured her son.

"Yeah, but I won't be there. Like, what if he leaves them, and then when he finds out I'm not home to open them, he takes them away?"

"He won't do that," Robin insisted, wincing at the slight crack in her voice and hoping that Philip hadn't noticed. "You've been a good boy all year, and your presents will be waiting for you when you get home. I'll make sure of it."

"Because it's not like I don't want them," Philip asserted. "It's just that I won't be there."

Don't, she moaned silently. *Please don't say that again. I already know it.*

The drive to the airport took them less than two hours. Robin parked in one of the short-term lots and, holding Philip's hand in one of hers and his suitcase in the other, she strode stoically to the terminal. It was mobbed with holiday travelers, most of them lugging shopping bags overflowing with gift-wrapped boxes. Obtaining a ticket to Florida for Philip at this time of year, on such short notice, was yet more proof that miracles did happen. But this was one miracle Robin would gladly have done without.

The check-in line zigzagged within a roped-off area, and Robin and Philip took their place at the end. For the forty-five minutes it took until they reached the desk, Philip chattered nonstop about what he would say to Mickey Mouse and Donald Duck, which rides he expected to enjoy, what souvenirs he planned to bring home with him. "Would you like a Minnie Mouse watch, Mom?" he asked. "I could get one for you. I have some money left over from my Christmas shopping, and I could probably borrow the rest from Dad. Would you like that?"

"No, thanks," Robin declined, though moved by Philip's generosity. "I've got a perfectly good watch. I want you to spend your money on yourself, Phil."

"Should I get a Mickey watch? Or maybe a T-shirt. They're probably cheaper. Maybe I'll get an Epcot lunchbox or something. Then I can get rid of that Smurfs one."

And on and on, until they finally checked Philip's bag and he received his boarding pass. Robin accompanied him to a special lounge the airline set aside for children who were traveling without adult escorts, and an offensively cheery woman in an airline uniform promptly showered Philip with a plastic VIP badge, a coloring book and crayons, and a deck of playing cards. "Aren't you a lucky boy, taking a big trip like this at Christmastime," the woman babbled.

"Yeah! I'm going to see Disney World," Philip bellowed.

"And your father," Robin coached him in a brittle voice.

The airline employee offered Robin a rueful smile, then turned her attention back to Philip, filling him in on how long the flight would take and what would be served for lunch. This must be what most divorced parents endured at Christmas, Robin mused disconsolately: losing their children to their former spouses and putting up a brave front about it. For all she knew, Philip's departure today might be the start of a brand-new Greer Christmas tradition...but that thought was too horrible to dwell on.

Eventually, Philip and the other unescorted children were beckoned to board the plane. Doing an estimable job of hiding her depression, Robin kissed him good-bye and wished him a wonderful time in Florida. It pained her to watch him vanish down the connector to the jet, but she waved brightly and shouted another good-bye at his receding form. Then, feeling indescribably mournful, she left the airport.

She drove directly to Woodleigh's. The store was in a state of bedlam. Kevin seemed to have mislaid at least half the items in the stockroom; the customers were short-fused and the clerks were frazzled. None of it bothered Robin, however. She needed the distraction, and she was happy to be surrounded by people with worse tempers than hers.

At five o'clock she was free to leave, but she loitered for a while longer in the store, loath to return home. Meandering among the festive displays of merchandise did little to leaven her mood, not even when she calculated the dwindling supplies of many items and the profits the store was accruing. She was seized with the urge to buy something, but she didn't know what. Capitalizing on her in-house discount, she had already bought one of just about everything she'd ever wanted from Woodleigh's stocks.

Jesse. Robin had to buy something for Jesse. She ambled the length of the store again, considering numerous wares. Linens? No, he didn't even own a dining table—what would he do with a tablecloth and matching napkins? The absence of dining room furniture also precluded candlesticks or a hand-embroidered runner for a sideboard. Given his aversion to hard liquor, she couldn't buy him a bar set. A knickknack of some sort? She hadn't noticed any shelves in his condo. He'd laughed at the stationery. And what could be less appropriate than a Christmas tree ornament?

As it was, most of the ornaments had already been bought. Just a few remained on the green felt-covered table. They looked somehow sad to Robin, lonesome and neglected.

She lifted a tiny crystal angel from the table and studied it. Its face was sweet and cherubic, its wings almost gossamer in their delicacy, its robe smoothly draped and its halo an exquisite circle of clarity, glowing with captured light. So what if Jesse didn't like it? This was one little angel who deserved a home.

Robin carried the figurine to the counter and did a quick job of boxing and wrapping it. Then, having run out of excuses to dawdle at the store, she left for home.

Her house seemed unnaturally dark and still when she entered it. No exuberant welcome from Philip, no long-winded description of schoolwork and snakes' diets, no pleading for sweets. It was like stepping inside a mausoleum, Robin thought with a wretched sigh.

She placed the gift-wrapped angel beneath the tree, took off her coat, and went upstairs to the attic storage area to gather up the gift boxes she'd been hiding there. After changing into her jeans and a loose-fitting sweater, she carried the boxes downstairs and dumped them under the tree as well.

"All right, Santa's been here," she muttered to her absent son. Her voice resounded hollowly in the empty house, and she tried to conjure an image of Philip shrieking with delight at the sight of all the colorful packages.

Instead she was visited with the sound of his voice: "The star-shaped ones. Those are his favorites."

"All right," she said again, marching to the kitchen. She might as well bake the damned Christmas cookies and get it over with. She wasn't hungry—she'd fix herself a snack later, if she felt up to it.

Her fingers were crusted with gooey dough when the telephone rang twenty minutes later. "Have you eaten?" Jesse asked cheerfully.

The sound of his voice invigorated her. She was not going to mope, she was not going to sulk. She was not going to wallow in self-pity, as he had rightly accused her of doing a few days ago. "Not yet," she told him, feeling her gloom dissipate at the realization that she wasn't as alone as she'd feared. She couldn't be alone when she had Jesse. "I haven't gotten around to dinner. I'm too busy making cookies."

"Cookies! If I come over with a pizza, do I get to lick the bowl?"

"Whatever lickings there are, they're yours."

"Give me fifteen minutes," he said before hanging up.

He was coming. He would be here. She wouldn't have to bake the cookies—or face Christmas—all by herself. A wonderful, selfless, arguably too-tolerant man was going to face it with her. And she felt joyous, truly joyous.

Abandoning the kitchen, she hurried to the living room and plugged in the tree lights. Then she lit the red candles in the windows. This was the way Christmas was supposed to be, she reminded herself, striding to the den and turning on the television in search for a Christmas special. She supposed she ought to buy some Christmas records, but until she did, the TV would have to provide the carols.

She flipped through the channels, stopping at the first Christmas music she came to. The screen featured a huge choir robed in blue and standing in a horseshoe formation, singing "Joy to the World" in a cappella magnificence. "Perfect," Robin rejoiced, turning up the volume and detouring to the downstairs bathroom to check her appearance.

Her hair was a mess, but she barely had time to brush it before the doorbell rang. Racing from the bathroom, her face radiant with happiness at Jesse's arrival, she swung the front door open.

His hair and the shoulders of his coat were damp from the drizzle, and his arms cradled a steaming white box from which rose the spicy aroma of the pizza. He was smiling cautiously, peering past her at the tree and then at the flickering candles. She flung her arms around him, nearly knocking the pizza out of his hands, and drew him inside. "I'm so glad you're here," she murmured, planting a friendly kiss on his lips.

"I'm glad I'm here, too," he said, handing her the box and removing his coat. "How are you?"

He must have expected to find her in the doldrums, and she was pleased to have confounded those expectations. "I'm fine, Jesse, really. How was Newport?"

He shook his head and chuckled. "Ridiculous," he told her, hanging his coat in the closet. "It was as complicated as a bail hearing just trying to get the kid released. But I did it." He took the pizza back from her and started toward the kitchen. "Where are those cookies?"

"I haven't baked them yet," she said, following him through the house. "The dough's all ready. We'll get them into the oven after we eat." Jesse seemed to have brought her appetite with him. All of a sudden she wanted to dive headlong into the box and stuff her mouth with melted mozzarella.

He put the box on the table and surveyed the counter where she'd arranged the bowl of dough, her rolling pin, containers of red and green sprinkles and an assortment of cookie cutters. "You've been busy," he observed, impishly plucking a dollop of dough from the bowl and tasting it.

"You're just as bad as Philip," she scolded, slapping his hand away. "Is a fondness for raw dough a sex-linked trait?"

Rather than meet her playful teasing, Jesse abruptly grew tense, a cloud darkening his face. He tilted his head and frowned, listening. "What the hell is that?"

"What? The music?" If Jesse didn't like Christmas carols—especially carols performed so beautifully—then he'd just have to tough it out. Robin wasn't going to shut off the television.

His frown deepening, he spun around and stormed to the den. Robin raced after him, prepared to defend the music to the death. As soon as he saw the television screen he froze, then cursed. "You're not watching this, are you?"

"I'm listening to it," she clarified. "Their singing is absolutely gorgeous."

"That's the Grace Cathedral Choir."

"It is?" She moved to his side and gazed at the robed choristers. They were now singing "Oh, Little Town of Bethlehem," their voices sublimely blended and their harmonies pure. "They're fantastic."

"This is the Grace Cathedral annual Christmas special," Jesse said tautly, not at all moved by the spellbinding music. "Turn it off."

She caught herself before blurting out that she absolutely wouldn't turn it off. Perhaps the show had been produced by Jesse's former girlfriend; perhaps his sudden grimness was a result of some old heartache not yet healed. He had been so sensitive to Robin's sorrow lately; the least she could do was sympathize with his discomfort.

She started toward the television, but before she reached the on-off button, the choir came to the final cadence of the song and was replaced on the screen by the Reverend Robert Shepherd. Robin recognized him only because she'd occasionally caught glimpses of his shows, and because his picture appeared in the newspapers every once in a while, often shaking a politician's hand. He was a fine-looking man, with regally silver hair, dark eyes, a hawklike nose and a sharp, square chin. For this Christmas special he was dressed in a majestic royal-blue velvet robe with gold satin trim, and he stared out from the screen with an almost unnerving expression of omniscience.

"Brothers and sisters," he orated in a rich, melodic baritone. "Thank you for joining us in this, our celebration of the birth of Jesus Christ."

Robin hesitated, unable to turn the television off.

Something about the minister's voice, about his towering height, his proud bearing, the piercing darkness of his eyes...

"As you know," Shepherd intoned, "Christmas is a time of giving. At this time of year, we remember what Jesus Christ gave to free us from our mortal ignorance. He gave that most valuable gift—His own life—so that we might know the Lord."

There was something eerily familiar about the man on the television. That smooth, sonorous voice...

"Turn it off," Jesse said softly.

The quiet steel in his tone caused her to flinch. "Not yet," she implored him. She didn't know why she wanted to continue to watch the show. She didn't know what she was looking for, what she was sensing. All she knew was that she had to keep watching.

"I can tell you what he's going to say," Jesse remarked. "It isn't worth your time."

"Not yet," she repeated, turning back to the screen.

"...and so we mark this day by giving. We give to our loved ones, our families and friends, our co-workers and neighbors. The splendor of the Grace Cathedral Choir gives us their inspired music. In the spirit of Jesus Christ, we give."

"What's wrong with that?" Robin defended the sermon to Jesse. Shepherd hadn't said anything she could take issue with.

"He's just warming up," Jesse said, stuffing his hands into the pockets of his jeans and leaning against a bookcase, regarding the television from a distance. "Give him a chance—he'll get to the point soon."

"...and while you're giving, you must ask yourselves, what am I giving to the Lord? What am I giving to those who do His work, who spread His word?

You've just spent twenty dollars on a bottle of perfume for your mother, forty dollars on a G.I. Joe toy for your son, fifty dollars on Barbie's dream house and swimming pool for your daughter, a diamond for your wife, golf clubs for your husband...and where, in that, is your gift to those who do the work of the Lord? Where is the true gift, the gift that will bring Jesus to those who need Him most?

"Think about it, my friends. Think about what you can give, and then give it. We at the Grace Cathedral have seen with our own eyes the miracles that God can perform, and we ask you to help us. In the spirit of Christmas, in the spirit of Jesus, we ask you to give. Call the toll-free number that appears on your screen, and make a pledge. Or send a check to the address that appears above the phone number. Whatever you can afford—five dollars, ten, twenty, a hundred—every little bit helps us to do our work, to bring God to millions of people around the world, people who need Him as much as you do.

"And now, I'll turn you back to our choir. Let their spirit awaken the spirit within you, the spirit of giving."

The address and telephone number continued to flash on the screen as the camera cut back to the choir. They began a lush arrangement of "The First Noel," but Robin hardly heard them. Closing her eyes, turning out her ears, she pictured the Reverend Shepherd as he'd appeared on the screen, his stunning eyes, his mellifluous voice. His plea for money had been a bit heavy-handed, sure. But it wasn't what he'd said that so unnerved her. It was how he'd said it, how he'd sounded, how his dazzling, thickly lashed eyes had reached out to her...

She glanced at Jesse, inexplicably fearful of what she

would see. He was staring not at the television but at her. Reaching to her with those same dazzling, thickly lashed eyes. "Well," he said in his distinctive voice, a voice uncannily like Shepherd's. "Now you know."

Chapter Eleven

"What?" Robin asked frantically. "What do I know?"

Jesse's expression was inscrutable. "Don't tell me you didn't notice the resemblance."

She couldn't help but notice it, with the two men so closely juxtaposed, their faces confronting her from opposite ends of the same room, their voices merging in the air around her. That she hadn't noticed the likeness between Jesse and the TV evangelist before was only a result of her never having paid much attention to the Reverend Robert Shepherd. "Are you related to him?" she asked, realizing at once that it was a stupid question.

"He's my father."

"Your father!" For no good reason, Jesse's revelation made her feel even more stupid. "But—but his name is Shepherd."

"His stage name," Jesse clarified. "He legally changed his name to Shepherd when he took the job with Grace Cathedral. In fact, he changed all our names."

"Why did he do that?"

Jesse chuckled dryly. "Shepherd," he emphasized. "What could be a more suitable name for someone leading the flock?"

Robin shook her head, amazed that she'd never made the connection before. "And your name is Lawson, because you're a lawyer," she guessed. "Is that some sort of family gag? You all take last names based on your professions?"

"No," Jesse replied. "The family name was Lawson before my father changed it to Shepherd. I decided to change mine back right after I finished law school. In my case, it was just a coincidence."

"Why did you change it back?" Robin asked, totally at sea. "I don't understand any of this, Jesse."

He stared at her for a minute, his eyes glittering enigmatically, his mouth curved in a humorless smile. "It's a long story," he said. "And the pizza's getting cold."

"Then we'll eat and you'll tell me," Robin resolved, leaving the den for the kitchen. Her appetite had fled her again, but she hoped that if she ate something she would stop feeling so light-headed and addled. She covered the cookie dough with plastic wrap and placed the bowl in the refrigerator—the last thing she could cope with right now was baking—and then gathered plates, glasses, napkins and a bottle of cola and set the kitchen table. Jesse pulled two wedges of pizza from the box, distributed them, and sat across from Robin.

Ignoring the food in front of her, she watched him while he bit into his slice. She was unnerved by the steady force of his dark eyes, so similar to Shepherd's, and equally unnerved to find herself picturing Jesse thirty years from now, when his thick shock of black hair would turn silver, when time would deepen the laugh lines radiating from the corners of his eyes and the creases bracketing his lips. If he took after his father, however, his voice wouldn't change with age. It would remain low and silky and persuasive.

"I'm waiting," she reminded him as he swallowed a mouthful of pizza and reached for his soda.

He drank, then lowered his glass. "He changed his name—he got the job at Grace—when I was nine years old. Before that, he was a minister at a relatively small Baptist church in Oroville, up in the mountains in northern California. He had developed a reputation for being a passionate speaker with a lot of charisma, and he was approached by Grace and asked to audition for the opening they had. They were a local operation then. They broadcasted a half-hour show on an independent station every Sunday morning, but they were thinking of expanding. They had hired another guy for the position, but he wasn't working out well and they intended to fire him. His name was Larsen. When they hired my father, they asked him to change his name from Lawson so viewers wouldn't confuse him with Larsen."

"And he chose Shepherd," said Robin.

Jesse nodded. "Not exactly subtle, but then again, standing before a national audience and haranguing them to send you their hard-earned dollars isn't subtle, either. My father's producers didn't care about subtlety—they cared about effectiveness. And my father's very effective. He raised the money to build that monstrous cathedral. He gave Grace clout. He gave its broadcast the numbers—the ratings to enable it to go national. My father's an emcee, an entertainer and a businessman rolled into one."

"He's also a minister," Robin commented, nibbling on her pizza.

"Right. How could I forget?" Jesse scoffed.

"I'll grant you, a big, gaudy cathedral filled with television cameras isn't the same thing as a cozy white clap-board church on the town green, but still…that doesn't mean you have to reject the religious part of it.''

"I was having problems with the religion long before we moved to Los Angeles,'' Jesse confessed. He rolled up the sleeves of his flannel shirt and helped himself to a second slice of pizza. "My best friend in Oroville was a kid named Mickey Santangelo. He lived down the street from me, and we did everything together. My parents told me he wouldn't go to heaven because he was a Roman Catholic.''

"No!'' That parents would say something that cruel to an impressionable young boy shocked Robin, and she laughed. "Roman Catholics believe in heaven.''

"Not the way fundamentalists do. It's such a strict denomination. I began to have my doubts when my father changed our name to Shepherd. I never got used to that. My two younger sisters didn't care—they hadn't spent so many years being Lawsons. But Marybeth and I had real problems with the name change, and the move, and being taken out of public school and sent to a private Christian academy. And then, two years after we arrived in L.A., Marybeth got sick.''

He fell silent, submerged in a memory of his sister's illness and death. Robin's curiosity about his childhood was far from satisfied, but if it hurt Jesse too much to talk about his sister's passing, she wouldn't press him. She brushed her fingers comfortingly over the back of his hand and murmured, "Jesse…''

Shaking off his sadness, he pulled his hand from hers and took a bite of his pizza. "Marybeth understood,'' he said. "She had the same doubts I did, the same ques-tions. But once she was diagnosed, she returned to the fold. She kept telling me that she had no choice, that

she was too weak to fight it and so she may as well
trust in prayer. It was such a betrayal, Robin—it was
like losing Marybeth twice, losing her to my parents'
church and then losing her to death. If only she had
trusted herself, maybe she would have beaten the can-
cer. Maybe she would have pulled through. Some leukemia patients do. But she gave up. She stopped fighting
and prayed for God to put her out of her misery."

"Jesse," Robin said, "you can't blame her for that.
None of us know how we'd react to such a dreadful
disease unless we've been through it ourselves."

"I know that," Jesse agreed contritely. "I don't
blame her, I don't judge her. All I know is that, once
she was gone, what little faith I had was gone as well.
My father threw himself even more energetically into
denouncing sinners and raising money for the cathedral,
and my mother—well, she's just a simple God-fearing
woman, a clergyman's wife out of her depth. Whatever
my father tells her to do, she does. After Marybeth died,
Mom turned our home into a domestic cathedral, with
prayer corners and iron-clad rules. She spent most of
her time hosting fund raising luncheons and leading parents' groups protesting textbooks that mention evolution
or sexual equality."

"And you became a lawyer for your father's
church," Robin remarked.

Jesse nodded. He tossed a crescent of crust onto his
plate and shifted in his chair, hooking one arm over the
back of it and perusing Robin, trying to gauge her reaction to what he was telling her. She wasn't yet certain
of her reaction, other than bewilderment and surprise—
and a strange, undefinable relief that, at last, she was
learning what she had to know about Jesse.

"You've talked about the importance of traditions,"

he pondered. "Well, this was ours: you finished your schooling and went to work for G.C.E. Or, at least, that's how it went for me. My sisters didn't take jobs with the company—proper ladies are supposed to marry and stay home and raise families. But they both married G.C.E. people. Lillian's married to the musical director of the choir, and Martha's married to one of the accountants. And I became a lawyer and signed on."

"But first you became Jesse Lawson again," Robin pointed out. "Didn't that upset your father?"

Jesse glanced skyward and groaned. "My father's spent almost as much of his life being upset with me as he has raising money and praising the Lord. He knew I had a rebellious streak; he was always punishing me for it. When he found out that I was sneaking to the public library after school in order to read all the books that were banned in our house, he locked me in my bedroom for a week. The only time the door was unlocked was to pass in a tray of food. When I met a Jewish girl one summer at the beach and asked her out for a date, I got locked up again. Each time in my room I had only the Bible to keep me company."

Jesse searched Robin's face. It was turned up to his— open and caring—as she listened intently to him and tried to understand.

"When I was in college," he continued, "we had some ferocious debates about the Vietnam war. I kept asking my father why he wasn't preaching more sermons on peace. He kept telling me that fighting against Communism was the same thing as fighting for Jesus, that our side was God's side and he doing his part by praying for the lives of our boys overseas. By the time I told him I was going to law school instead of divinity school, he had all but given up on me. Changing my name back to Lawson was anticlimactic.''

''But after all that, you still went to work for him.''

Jesse reached for his glass of soda and settled in his chair. He watched the bubbles rising to the surface, drank a bit, and shrugged. ''He was my father, and that was the way things were done.''

Robin eyed him skeptically. ''Not good enough, Jesse,'' she said. If he could have stood up to his father so many times on so many issues, why couldn't he stand up to the man when it came to his career?

Jesse sighed. His attention remained on the fizzing bubbles in his glass, and his words emerged slowly, falteringly. ''I wanted to believe,'' he explained. ''Even after all the rebelling, all the questions…I wanted to. It was so much easier for them, having that structure, having answers to everything, knowing exactly what to do and how to do it, whom to embrace and whom to avoid. They belonged to something, and I—I wanted to belong, too.''

He looked so lost, so bereft when he revealed his secret desire. It was almost tragic, this man whose mind wouldn't allow his heart's desperate longing. Robin had wished that Jesse would bend in his views, but now she comprehended how hard bending must be for him. He had spent his entire life trying to bend, aching to bend for his family—and discovering that he couldn't.

''Then why did you change your name?'' she asked gently.

He set down his glass and sighed again. ''I had to,'' he insisted. ''I had never gotten used to being Jesse Shepherd. It never felt right to me. I was so anxious to figure out who I was—I couldn't believe in anything until I was sure of that. And I was sure that I was Jesse

Lawson, not Jesse Shepherd.'' He smiled pensively, his
eyes momentarily losing focus, growing distant. Then
they returned to Robin. ''Ultimately my father decided
that changing my name was a wise idea from a business
standpoint. If I was going to be negotiating contracts for
him, he thought it would look better if we didn't come
across as some hokey family project. He wanted people
to think he had lots of outside advisors—it gave him an
image of strength and professionalism.''

''So you dealt with his church's legal affairs.''

''It was basic contract law. I could handle it.'' Jesse's
smile twisted, becoming cynical. ''And then Anne Cot-
ter was hired on as a producer—straight from a stint
producing game shows, believe it or not—and we
started seeing each other socially. That was all right
with my father, too. Anne was a solid employee. The
fact that we weren't married bothered Dad, but he rationalized it by saying that, since we were both doing
such indispensable work for G.C.E., God would forgive
us our sins. Anne viewed things that way, too. I seemed
to be the only person who didn't.''

''You wanted to marry her?''

''I...I wanted to live a consistent life, not a hypocritical one,'' Jesse explained. ''I'm glad I didn't marry
her; it would have been a lousy marriage. But I felt
strange about our relationship. Obviously, my interpre-
tation of right and wrong differed from Anne's, and
from my parents', and from everyone else's at Grace. I
finally came to recognize that when I told my father I
wanted to take a sabbatical from G.C.E. and work with
the poor. He flew into a rage. So did Anne. They told
me that I was doing God's work at G.C.E., and that that
was where God needed my talents. And...'' He exhaled

and smiled wryly. "At that point, it occurred to me that the indigent might need me even more than God did."

"So you quit God and signed up with New Haven Legal Assistance," Robin summarized. It sounded stark when she put it like that, but she couldn't rationalize his actions any other way. "Jesse, it seems as if you rejected God only because it was a way of rejecting your father."

Jesse grunted a laugh. "I rejected God because I'm me," he argued. "*If* God exists, and *if* He created me, then He created me to have the sort of personality that can't accommodate God."

"Q.E.D.," Robin muttered sardonically. "It's not that simple, Jesse. We all go through torture trying to separate ourselves from our parents. I had a real love-hate relationship with my father for most of his life. I loved him because he was my father, but I hated him because he was always putting his job and his country ahead of the needs of his family. My mother and I had our ups and downs, too. She used to drink too much, I told you that. It wasn't until I grew up and developed some perspective that I could accept that she had a reason for drinking. It's always hard to make the break with your parents, but it's part of becoming an adult." Robin smiled wistfully. "Sometimes, when I look at Philip, I wonder what it's going to be like for him, how he's going to rebel and cut his ties. I don't know what's going to happen, but I know something is. I don't think there's any way around it."

"Maybe," Jesse conceded. "Maybe that's what my rebellion was all about. But when the man you're trying to cut your ties with claims to have a direct line to God, it makes the cut a great deal more complicated."

"I'm sure it does." Robin reached for Jesse's hand

again, and this time he rotated it to grasp hers. "Why didn't you ever tell me about this before?" she asked.

"I told you about my work for G.C.E."

"But not about your father." Her gaze met Jesse's and held it. He no longer looked bereft. His eyes were lucid, returning her direct scrutiny, and his smile was receptive and sincere. "Is it...is it that you're ashamed of your father?" she asked.

"No, of course not," he answered swiftly.

"Then what?"

His eyes remained locked onto hers, unflinching. His mouth flexed as he searched for the right words, the right response. "Perhaps...perhaps I'm a little embarrassed that it took me thirty-four years to do what most people do when they turn twenty-one."

"There's no time limit on growing up," Robin assured him. "Besides, growing up isn't the same thing as rejecting your father. It only saddens me to think that after all this, you're left with so little. You haven't got your family and you haven't got any faith, either."

"I have myself," Jesse noted, his tone subdued. "In the end, that's all any of us ever has."

Robin's gaze broke from his. She turned to view the counter, where her rolling pin and cookie cutters still sat, a reminder of the fact that Philip was gone, that every other room in her house was empty, that she was alone. In the end, Philip had departed and all she had was herself.

Jesse's fingers tightened on hers. Her head swung back to him, and she felt a sudden burst of warmth inside her. She wasn't alone. "We have more than ourselves, Jesse," she whispered, her face illuminated with joy at her epiphany. "We have each other."

An unspoken communication passed between them, a

tacit understanding of what existed between them—a bond, a friendship, a defense against solitude. Jesse stood, circled the table and pulled Robin to her feet. His lips covered hers and coaxed them apart, permitting the intrusion of his tongue. For an immeasurable instant Robin's identity seemed to blur with Jesse's in the heat of their kiss. When Jesse drew back, his eyes were as bright and clear as hers, his smile hesitant but enraptured.

Without a word, Robin led him to the stairs and up. His fingers remained laced through hers, his hold seemingly unbreakable. Not until they had entered her bedroom did he release her. His hands rounded her shoulders and rotated her to face him. "Are you sure about this, Robin?" he asked.

She peered up at him. "Yes," she swore, convinced that she had never been more sure of anything in her life. She had known for a long time that she loved Jesse, and tonight she knew why. She knew that being with him was the way to stave off her loneliness, that his presence could give her life new meaning just when everything had begun to seem meaningless. She knew that taken separately, she and Jesse were two drifting souls, unsure of what to believe in, but that together, they could believe in each other, in "us." She knew, finally, who Jesse was and why he meant so much to her.

His mouth found hers again, moving possessively, instilling in her the comprehension that he offered an answer to more than just the recent loneliness she had suffered since Philip's decision to go to Orlando. She had been living with a different loneliness, one that she had endured for so long she was hardly conscious of it anymore. From the day Ray had chosen a new job and forfeited their shared dream of creating a home, Robin had been alone.

That loneliness had been evanescing ever since Jesse had entered her life. His visits, his calls, his attentiveness to her… It wasn't merely that she needed a man in her life. It was that she needed Jesse, a true friend, someone who cared, someone who mattered.

And tonight, she would have him. They would have each other.

His arms surrounded her, one ringing her waist and the other her shoulders. Her head fell back, and he raveled his fingers through her hair as his tongue probed deeper. When her fingers groped for the buttons on his shirt, he groaned. "Do you know how much I want you?" he whispered hoarsely, sliding his hand beneath the ribbed edge of her sweater to stroke the skin of her back.

"Not as much as I want you," she replied.

He groaned again, her words obviously arousing him. With a quick movement, he yanked her sweater upward. She lifted her arms, helping him to remove it. He snapped the clasp of her bra, which followed her sweater onto the floor.

His hands floated forward to caress her breasts. During her recent meditations about renewing her sex life, she had wondered, with some worry, about how a man might react to the toll that time and childbirth had taken on her body. Hers were not the firm, perky breasts of a young girl, but were soft and small.

Yet with Jesse, she didn't feel self-conscious about her body. His fingers danced across her flesh with almost reverential sensitivity, exploring the warm valley between her breasts, teasing her nipples. He backed up to the bed, pulling her with him, and lowered himself to sit. Then he brought his mouth to one nipple and sucked.

The friction of his tongue on her caused a sharp spasm of desire to rip through her. She gasped, reeling from the wonderful sensation, then once again reached out to undo the buttons of his shirt. This time, Jesse offered his assistance in opening his shirt. Within an instant, it was gone.

His torso was hard and magnificently proportioned. Robin's hands celebrated the muscular contours of it, twirling through the fine dark hairs that curled enticingly across the upper half of his chest and then rising to the knotted ridges of his shoulders. She bowed to kiss the top of Jesse's head, and he took her kiss as a cue to unfasten her jeans.

As soon as she was naked, he shed the rest of his own clothing. Then he urged her down onto the bed beside him, rolling her onto her back and running his hands the length of her compact body. "This is your last chance," he murmured as he molded his palm to the flaring curve of her hip. His lips grazed her chin, tasting its delicately sculpted angle. "I want you to be sure."

Robin sighed brokenly. It wasn't only the warmth of his mouth on her, the pressure of his fingers against her upper thigh, the erotic tug deep within her, anxious with yearning... It was more than that that made her sure. She was sure of Jesse, sure that she knew him, that they needed each other, that this was right. She wove her fingers into his hair and stroked down to the nape of his neck, to the thick bones of his shoulders. "I am."

"I..." His lips nibbled lower, tasting the underside of her jaw, her throat, the arch of her collarbone. "I didn't come here expecting this," he murmured, his breath caressing her skin. "What I mean is…I didn't come prepared."

She laughed, from both surprise and gratitude. Jesse's thoughtfulness and responsibility only magnified her love for him. "It's all right," she assured him, her hands roaming along his back, following the chain of vertebrae to his waist. "I'm protected. I did assume something like this would happen, sooner or later."

"Did you?" His fingers continued to roam down her leg, describing a circle around her kneecap and then rising along the inside of her thigh again. "I didn't."

Robin's eyes widened. "You didn't?"

Jesse's hand paused, and he raised himself to peer down at her. "I never assumed I'd find someone like you," he explained. "I never assumed I'd find something this special."

The extravagance of his compliment rendered Robin speechless. What Jesse said was true. She hadn't dared to dream she'd find a man as special as Jesse.

She curved her hands around his head and pulled him down to her. Their lips fused in a ravenous kiss. The sheer force of it left Robin shifting impatiently beneath Jesse, her body demanding to share in the intimacy her lips and tongue had experienced. The movement of her leg against his hand prompted him to set his fingers free on her thigh again, sketching a twisting line upward.

His fingers combed through the downy golden hair between her legs. When he found her, every muscle in her body tensed reflexively, then melted into his caress. She moaned, surrendering to the fluid pulsing inside her body, the damp rush of hunger for him.

Her hand slid between their chests and down over the taut stretch of his abdomen. He was already fully erect, and when she tightened her fingers around his swollen flesh he gasped. "Slow," he pleaded on a broken breath, fighting to maintain his self-control. "It's been so long for you. I don't want to hurt you."

Robin began to protest that he couldn't hurt her, that at this point she doubted she could go slow anymore. But as his finger gently entered her, preparing her, the only sound she was able to make was a breathless cry of pleasure. Her body clenched around him, every nerve sparking crazily to vibrant life, every impulse centered on the need to have Jesse, all of him, to absorb him and surround him with herself, to deliver her soul to him. "Now," she implored, guiding him fully onto her. "Please, Jesse..."

He pulled his hand away and covered her body with his. His hips surged convulsively, pressing, invading, conquering. For a moment, he became still deep within her as he struggled to contain himself. Then he withdrew and thrust again, less wildly this time, allowing himself to savor the enveloping warmth of her body, the comforting warmth of her love.

Her legs twined around his, and her hands settled at the base of his spine, resisting him every time he drew back. Whenever his body left hers, she felt herself glimpsing her loneliness...and then he would return to her, plunging deeper, demanding more, and she believed she would never be alone again.

His pace increased, driving her to a pinnacle, pushing her to an instant of perfect unity with him. With a sigh, she surrendered to the deluge of throbbing sensation, the glorious pulses of completion rippling through her, transporting her, soothing her. It had been too long, much too long since she'd felt anything like this—and yet she willingly would have waited even longer if she'd known that, ultimately Jesse would be the man to bring her here.

He peaked as she did, his body wrenched by the explosive force of his climax. Groaning, he sank into her arms and let her hold him. His heart thudded savagely against her breast, and his breath was shallow and ragged. She wrapped her arms comfortingly around him, waiting for him to recover, wondering whether she herself ever would.

Eventually his muscles relaxed. He propped himself up on his arms and gazed down at her. "Are you all right?" he asked in a hoarse whisper.

She answered by raising her head to kiss him. Then she nestled back into the pillow, overcome with resplendent weariness.

He tenderly brushed a few stray golden hairs from her cheeks. His eyes journeyed over her face, examining her, easily comprehending the bliss in her shimmering eyes and her astonished smile. "Angel," he breathed.

"What?" A vision of the lovely crystal angel she'd bought for Jesse flashed across her brain. How did he know what she'd gotten him for Christmas?

Grinning, he shook his head. "Nothing," he murmured, rolling off her and gathering her into a snug embrace. "I was just thinking about how much I love you."

Robin needed no further explanation for his cryptic remark. He loved her. Nothing else mattered.

NOTHING ELSE MATTERED, that is, until she woke up the next morning. Her clock buzzed its alarm through her skull, jolting her awake. She slammed her fist onto the button that silenced the clock, sat up, and looked around.

Jesse was gone. She knew she hadn't dreamed the previous night's rapture, because the pillow next to hers still bore the impression of his head, and the sheets were still warm on his side of the mattress. But whatever had happened last night, this morning she was alone.

Shaking her head, trying to ward off the sudden sense of emptiness that seeped through her, she stood and retrieved her bathrobe from the closet. The house's silence troubled her; she considered turning on the alarm again, just so she would hear something. Stepping into her slippers, she shuffled out of her bedroom, halted at the top of the stairs, and listened. Not a sound.

She knew she ought to go downstairs, but instead, she found herself stalking to Philip's bedroom. The door was open, and she stopped at the threshold to stare in at the crisply made bed, the closet door, the clear surface of the desk, the shelves stacked neatly with books and toys that usually lay scattered across the floor. The irritating hush filling her house had as much to do with Philip's absence as with Jesse's unexplained disappearance. Right now Philip ought to be bouncing on the bed, smearing toothpaste all over the bathroom sink, hollering at Robin to shake a leg so she wouldn't be late for work, cheering about the impending arrival of Santa Claus.

Last night hadn't changed a thing. The day before Christmas had arrived, and Philip was gone.

Robin felt a veil of gloom descend around her, cloaking her in its dreary weight. Sighing, she turned her back on Philip's uncharacteristically tidy room and plodded down the stairs. At the foot of the staircase she caught a whiff of coffee. She followed its tempting scent to the kitchen.

Jesse was standing by the coffeemaker, filling two

cups with the fresh brew. He was wide awake and fully clothed. At the sound of her entrance, he spun around. "Good morning!" he greeted her robustly. "I was going to surprise you with coffee in bed."

"It's a nice surprise, even if I'm out of bed," she said with false cheer. Seeing him, remembering the ecstasy they had shared last night, recalling his confession of love…why couldn't that dispel the doubt creeping over her?

Jesse loved her—that wasn't what she doubted. Nor did she doubt that she felt strongly about him. But was it love that had drawn her to him yesterday, love that had lured them upstairs and into her bed? Or was it loneliness? Had she come to Jesse in the hope of affirming her love for him, or in the hope of assuaging her misery?

He had pulled out a chair for her at the table, and she slumped into it. "I'm an early riser," he said apologetically, handing her a cup of coffee. "Something tells me you're a bear in the morning."

"Not always," she mumbled, hiding her face behind the cup so Jesse couldn't see the torment and confusion in her eyes. "I'm not used to waking up to the alarm clock, that's all. Usually Philip wakes me up."

"Work today?" Jesse asked, sitting across from her and sipping his coffee.

Robin nodded.

Jesse lowered his cup and appraised her, his smile fading. "That bad, huh," he murmured sympathetically. "If it makes you feel any better, I've got to go to work today, too."

"It isn't work that's bothering me," she corrected him.

Something flickered in his eyes, a flash of fear or

annoyance, or something—Robin couldn't tell. "Then what's the problem?"

She offered a bleak smile. "Oh, Jesse... It's just that I'm a novice at this," she explained. "I don't know how to deal with the morning after."

Jesse set down his cup, pulled hers from her fingers, and folded his hands around hers. "There's nothing to deal with," he said gently. "It isn't the morning after. It's the morning *before*."

"The morning before what? Christmas Eve?" Hearing herself enunciate those two emotion-laden words made her shudder.

Jesse continued to study her. After a long minute, he sighed. "Forget about Christmas Eve, Robin," he said dryly. "One day isn't worth torturing yourself over."

His words stung, and she couldn't shake the suspicion that he'd intended them to wound her. Perhaps he was trying to shake her out of her malaise—or perhaps he really meant what he'd said. Christmas was just one day to him, worth nothing more than any other day.

How could she possibly love a man who believed such a thing? How, even after making love with him, even after finding refuge from her loneliness in his arms, could she really love Jesse?

Chapter Twelve

She looked stricken.

Jesse gave himself a mental kick in the rear end. What had possessed him to say such a thing to her?

He'd wanted to drag her out of her torpor, that was all. He'd wanted to rescue her from the depression that was closing in around her. If he'd spoken a bit too sharply, a bit too bluntly, it was only because he couldn't stand to see her sinking into despair about the holiday all over again. Derogating Christmas came as a reflex to him. Robin ought to have grown accustomed to his views by now.

Watching her as she slumped in her chair, her downcast face framed by hair as pale and fine as cornsilk, her slim, lovely body hidden beneath a fleecy bathrobe, Jesse admitted that his harsh words had arisen from an impulse more complex than simply the desire to elevate her mood. As egotistical as it was, he had hoped that last night had been marvelous enough to dispel her misery about her son's absence. He had hoped that one night in his arms had been enough to vanquish her sorrow. Making love with Robin had been so rhapsodic, so indescribably splendid; he had presumed that if it had been half as beautiful for her, she wouldn't need anything more.

What a conceited fool he was. He ought to have enough sense to realize that Robin's passion for him couldn't replace her grief over Philip's absence. At best, Jesse had offered her a delightful distraction for a few hours. He wished he could have offered her more, but apparently he hadn't—and the realization hurt. That was why he'd lashed out.

It was too late for him to retract his bitter words. The moment was gone, beyond salvation. He'd have to make it up to her somehow. "What time does Woodleigh's close tonight?" he asked in a placating voice.

"Six," she said dully. Her eyes were opaque, her lips taut as she shaped the solitary word. A narrow crease lined her brow.

It broke his heart to see her this listless. He would make it up to her. He had promised that he'd do his best to make her Christmas bearable. Now, more than ever, he was determined to live up to that promise.

"I'll see you this evening?" he half asked.

"If you want."

Her unenthusiastic delivery wrenched his heart again. He tried to console himself with the thought that he hadn't personally caused her sadness. No, of course he hadn't. All he'd done was to shoot his damned mouth off and exacerbate her mood.

"I've got to go," he said, gulping down his coffee and rising. "I have to stop off at home and change my clothes for work."

Robin shrugged.

"Robin." He moved to her chair and bent down beside her. He was close enough to notice the teardrops beading along her spidery eyelashes. *Please,* he prayed, not even questioning whom he was praying to, *please, let me make it better for Robin. Please show me the way.* He enclosed her in his arms and kissed her lightly. "I love you," he whispered. "We'll have a good Christmas, Robin."

She nodded, batted her eyes and looked away. Jesse could do nothing more for her now. He straightened up and strode out of the kitchen.

He was scheduled to meet that morning with the gas station owner who had bilked Jesse's client of back wages. It was the kind of appointment that called for a suit and necktie; Jesse wanted to intimidate the proprietor, to compel him to compensate his employee promptly and save them all the hassle of a protracted legal battle. The total amount owed came to less than three hundred fifty dollars—a pittance in the circles in which Jesse used to travel, but a fortune to the young man he was currently representing.

After the session with the gas station owner, Jesse would have to attend to a mess of paperwork at his office. Negotiations with Cabot's attorney seemed to have reached a stalemate, and Jesse feared that not long into the new year his Newhallville clients might find themselves homeless.

In the meantime, however, he could see to it that they had decent Christmas dinners. Jesse wasn't good at celebrating Christmas himself, but he was willing to help others celebrate it. He intended to buy those needy tenants some food.

He wanted to indulge Robin, too. He would do whatever he could to make sure she celebrated her holiday.

His meeting with the gas station owner went better than expected. As he'd hoped, Jesse overwhelmed the tight-fisted man with his impeccably tailored suit and a cascade of awesome legalese gibberish. By the time he was finished reciting his list of contingencies, estoppels and adjurations, the poor man had his personal checkbook in hand and was busy punching numbers into his calculator, figuring out the precise amount of wages and interest he owed. Jesse drove directly from the service station to his client's apartment to deliver the check.

The young man's elation at receiving his money bolstered Jesse. But his satisfaction was tempered by the phone message awaiting him at his office, from Cabot's attorney. After investigating the cost of performing the necessary repairs to the tenement, according to the message, the landlord had decided not to improve the building. He'd take his chances in the civil court.

Jesse cursed. Five hundred was a spectacular batting average in baseball, but not in life. Jesse had gotten a gasoline jockey his back wages, but he hadn't gotten Cabot to make his property livable for his renters. Jesse had brought Mrs. Selby's son home for Christmas, but was powerless when it came to Robin's son.

Jesse had won Robin's love last night, but he'd lost it this morning.

On the other hand, he mused, the old guy supposedly pulling the strings from above wasn't doing much better. The sky was a clear, cold blue, the streets clean and dry, the few expanses of grass in downtown New Haven naked, in a frozen grayish-brown state of hibernation. The least God could have done was given Robin some snow for Christmas.

WOODLEIGH'S REMAINED frenzied until five-thirty. Then, as if answering some silent command, the customers vanished, toting their purchases with them. At ten minutes to six, one final, hysterical customer en-

tered, snatched up the last three soldier nutcrackers, paid
for them in cash and whisked away. And then it was
over.

After bidding her staff a happy holiday, distributing
bonus checks and shooing the clerks out the door, Robin
locked it and turned to survey the shop. The place was
a shambles: merchandise picked over, shelves empty, a
pewter pitcher resting upside-down on a table.

There would be time enough for cleaning up and sorting the leftovers, Robin meditated with a sigh as she
crossed to the cash register and released the drawer. The
store would be closed tomorrow, but she could come in
early on Saturday to organize the place before the expected rush of returns. Or she could come in tomorrow,
she thought glumly. Other than stopping by at Joanna's
house to exchange gifts, Robin had no holiday festivities
planned.

Christmas would be easier to live through if she were
sure of herself, she thought dismally. But she was sure
of nothing at the moment, nothing but the fact that
spending the night with Jesse had been sublime. If she
didn't love him, she couldn't have responded so gloriously to his lovemaking. Yet if she did love him, she
would have to accept some basic concepts about him—
most significantly, that he shunned the things she considered most important and valuable.

A tap at the door startled her, and she swore generally
at all the idiots who left their Christmas shopping to the
last minute. Sliding a stack of ten-dollar bills back into
their slot, she shut the register drawer and turned toward
the store's entry.

Jesse stood outside the door, cupping his hands
around his eyes as he peered through the glass. His coat
was unbuttoned, and he had on a suit underneath it, with

his tie hanging loose and his shirt collar unbuttoned. His breath emerged as small white puffs of vapor in the evening cold.

The sight of him brought on a sudden rush of happiness within her. She ought to have been just as troubled by him now as she'd been that morning—and she imagined that once the wave of joy receded, she would be. Even so, she darted around the counter and raced to the door to let him in. A transient joy was better than no joy at all.

As soon as she opened the door he pushed inside, eager to escape the frigid evening air. His lips were cool but comforting as he kissed her cheek. Slinging an arm around her, he scanned the store. "If it's closed, how come you're still here?" he asked.

"Maybe I was waiting for you." Robin wasn't certain that was true, but she felt good saying it. Seeing how much her statement pleased Jesse made her feel even better.

"This is a strange place to wait," he argued good-naturedly. "I stopped by your house, assuming that you'd be there. But you weren't, so I cruised over here to see if you'd decided to keep the store open an extra hour."

"You came straight from work," Robin observed, scrutinizing his outfit.

"Yes, well, I've got an errand to run. I thought I ought to take care of it first, and then go home and unwind."

"What errand?" Robin asked. Maybe she could join him. Running around town with Jesse would take her mind off the Christmas decorations and untouched gifts for Philip that were waiting at her house.

"I've got some food to deliver to my clients in New Haven. Would you like to come along for the ride?"

"Food?" she questioned. "Food baskets, you mean?"

Jesse chuckled and glanced through the glass front wall to his Volkswagen, which was parked by the curb. "Food bags, actually. I stopped at the supermarket and picked up a few things I thought they could use. Being their lawyer, I know what their finances are like. I didn't want them to be stuck eating hot dogs and peanut butter for Christmas."

Robin's eyes narrowed on him. This man, this Grinch who thought Christmas was just one more day, had purchased Christmas feasts for his indigent clients. What a phony he was! Blustering about his lack of faith, his rejection of God and religion—and here he was, the personification of Santa Claus himself!

Jesse met her quizzical gaze and smiled sheepishly, clearly attuned to what she was thinking. "It's just some stuff in cans," he said. "Don't get the wrong idea."

"I'll tell you what the wrong idea is," Robin asserted, feeling her energy and her sense of purpose revive. "The wrong idea is to give people their food in bags instead of baskets. If you're going to do this, Jesse, you'd better do it right."

"Uh-oh," he grunted, his smile widening. "Okay, Robin. How do we do this right?"

"First, we get some baskets," she said, jogging across the store to the display of woven wicker baskets. Most of the fancy baskets, the ones with lids and compartments for chilled wine bottles and glasses, had already been sold, but a few plain, open-top baskets still stood on a low shelf. "How many do we need?"

"Four," Jesse told her, taking the baskets as she handed them up to him.

"They don't match," she said.

"It doesn't matter. We'll use this larger one for the Selbys. They're a big family—I bought them a bigger ham."

"Ham?" Grinning, she stood and marched down the side of the store until she came to the remaining Christmas linens. "You're the one who's a hypocrite, Jesse. Pretending to hate Christmas, and you went and bought these people hams!"

"I'm not a hypocrite," he retorted. "I've never objected to giving, Robin. All I object to is concentrating a year's worth of giving on this one day, and then not giving for the rest of the year."

"Sure," Robin scoffed in disbelief as she plucked four red-and-green tablecloths from a shelf. "And how many other days of the year do you give your clients hams?"

Jesse conceded with a grin. "I think it would mean more to them on Christmas than it would at some other time. They're the ones who are celebrating, not me."

Robin laughed. "Of course, Jesse," she said with fake solemnity. "Your act of giving isn't any sort of celebration, is it?"

"Lighten up," he protested, although he was laughing, too. "You're the one who's fixing up these ridiculous baskets."

"They aren't ridiculous," Robin maintained, folding the linens to a manageable size and then using them to line the baskets. "If you do a thing, you do it right."

"Who's going to pay for all this stuff?" Jesse asked, smoothing out the corner of one of the tablecloths.

"I am," Robin said simply. Before Jesse could object, she went on. "I get an employee discount. Or better yet, I'll convince Jack Woodleigh to give them to us at cost. It's for a good cause."

"Even at cost, this stuff must be expensive," Jesse muttered, running his fingers over the delicate straw weave of the largest basket.

"If your clients deserve a ham dinner, then they deserve to receive it in style," Robin maintained. "Go get the food."

By the time he returned to the store, after two trips' worth of bulging paper bags, Robin had added to each basket a clove-scented candle, a brass candlestick, and a carved wood tree ornament shaped like a snowflake. The truth was, none of the items was terribly expensive at wholesale. If Jesse knew how much Woodleigh's marked up its merchandise he'd be horrified, so she thought it best to leave him in ignorance.

"Here we go," he said, dumping the bags onto the counter and unloading them. Along with the hams, he had bought canned sweet potatoes, canned string beans, and tins of fruitcake and hard candies. Robin and Jesse distributed the food among the four baskets, then folded the flaps of the tablecloths over the tops of the cans.

"Let me get my coat," Robin said, untying her pinafore as she strolled to the staff room at the rear of the store. Humming "We Wish You a Merry Christmas" to herself, she removed her barrette and brushed out her hair, smoothed her cowl-neck sweater into the waistband of her skirt, and pulled her coat from its hanger. After slipping it on, she turned off the light and joined Jesse in the store. "I'll leave my car here," she decided, gathering up two of the smaller baskets while Jesse lifted the third small one and the large one. "We can pick it up later."

It wasn't until they were on the turnpike, traveling to New Haven, that she wondered what had happened to her melancholia. She had been so busy arranging the baskets attractively that she'd forgotten how lonely she was without her son. Delivering food baskets to indigent strangers had never been one of her precious holiday traditions, but she was delighted to be doing it. Indeed, she thought it would be a lovely ritual to add to her annual Christmastime routines.

She wondered, too, what had happened to her doubt about Jesse. That he deliberately twisted the radio dial to a grating rock-and-roll program the minute he heard a fragment of the "Hallelujah Chorus" on another station didn't bother her in the least. She'd gladly provide the carols—over his objections, if necessary. She'd provide the tree and the gingerbread house and the pretty gift-wrapped boxes, as long as Jesse provided the Christmas spirit. And that he was doing, grandly.

Robin didn't often have occasion to visit New Haven, and even less often did she drive through the part of town Jesse was now entering. The multifamily dwellings were by and large seedy, and aged, battered cars were parked along the dimly lit roads. Jesse steered past a public housing project, a block of dilapidated two-family houses and a row of gloomy apartments, finally coasting to a halt in front of a rundown, four-story building with a few cracked and boarded windows gracing its front wall. Robin cringed at the realization that people actually lived inside such a dark, foreboding building.

To her surprise, Jesse seemed inordinately pleased by the sight of the place. "They collected the garbage!" he shouted, swinging open his door. "It's about time!"

"You mean, it could have been worse?" Robin

blurted out, trying to picture the building with the added blight of garbage heaped around its front door.

"It *has* been worse," Jesse said, leaving the car and moving around to her side to help her out. They walked together to the back of the car, opened the hatchback and pulled out the baskets. "I wonder what prompted Cabot to pay for the garbage removal. He's the landlord—the guy we're suing."

The Christmas spirit prompted Cabot, Robin contemplated. But Jesse might think she was needling or nagging him if she mentioned anything that corny, so she only smiled and followed him inside the grim apartment building.

Jesse knocked on a door in the first-floor hallway. A stocky young man holding an open bottle of beer answered. "Mr. Lawson?" he asked, speaking loudly to drown out the babble of voices and Salsa music emerging from somewhere inside the apartment. His gaze flew to Robin, and his eyebrows rose. "Who's this? Another lawyer?"

"Hello, Mr. Martinez. This is a friend of mine," Jesse replied. "We brought you some food for tomorrow, in case you want to make a Christmas dinner." He took one of Robin's baskets and handed it to the man, who peeked underneath the linen and whistled in amazement. "I wish I could have come with good news about Cabot," Jesse added, "but this was the best I could do."

"If this is the best, it's pretty damned good, Mr. Lawson," Mr. Martinez said, his eyes glowing with gratitude. "*Gracias*, Mr. Lawson. My mother, she's gonna love this, she'll make us a big feast. *Gracias! Felice Navidad!*"

Jesse mumbled something unintelligible, then took Robin's hand and escorted her down the hall to the stairs. He wouldn't dare to say Merry Christmas, she thought, amused. If he did, someone might actually think he believed in what he was doing.

"Can't we take the elevator?" she asked as Jesse began climbing to the second floor.

"It's broken," he told her.

Bracing herself for the steep climb, she inhaled deeply and followed him up the long stairway, glad that she had only one basket to carry.

On the second floor, Jesse knocked on another door. A wizened, elderly woman cracked it open, squinting at him above the chain lock. Satisfied by his familiarity, she closed the door to release the chain, then opened it a few inches more. "What is it, Lawson?" she asked suspiciously. "You got our settlement money?"

"I'm sorry, but that's a long way off, Mrs. Stokes," Jesse said apologetically. "What I've got is some food for tomorrow."

The woman turned her dubious gaze to the basket Jesse extended to her. "Hmm," she grunted. "What's the basket for?"

Jesse turned to Robin for assistance. The baskets had been her idea, after all. "You can use it for whatever you want," Robin noted, figuring that this testy woman was not the sort who would make a habit of going on picnics or picking berries.

"Hmm," the woman said again. She eyed the basket in Jesse's hand. "You brought one for *her*?" she asked, angling her head toward a door across the hall. "She ain't home. She's out doing heaven knows what."

"Well." Jesse took the other small basket from Robin and handed it to Mrs. Stokes. "Perhaps you could give this to her when she comes home."

"Yeah, sure." Mrs. Stokes pulled the basket inside.

"Heaven knows when she'll be home, carrying on the way she does," she said with a haughty sniff.

"Mrs. Stokes, it's Christmas," Jesse said awkwardly. "Have a little charity."

"Yeah, sure." Mrs. Stokes grumbled something that resembled a thank-you and slammed her door.

"What a strange woman," Robin whispered as they strolled back down the hall to the staircase.

Jesse chuckled. "She's pretty grumpy, all right. And she never passes up an opportunity to complain about Sheena—she lives across the hall. I think Sheena's a prostitute, but I'm not sure."

Robin didn't know what to say to that. This impoverished inner city environment was a far cry from the safe, wholesome world of army bases where she had grown up.

When they reached the third-floor hallway, Jesse stopped and gaped at the lightbulb glowing in the ceiling. He scowled. "Gerald," he muttered.

"What?"

Not bothering to answer, Jesse knocked on one of the doors. It swung open to reveal a strapping young man in jeans, his hair cropped short. The baby he held on his hip was wearing an oversize sailor cap that drooped adorably across his eyes. "Mr. Lawson!" the man hailed Jesse. "It isn't time to go back to Newport yet, is it? Me and my nephew are having too much fun."

"Tomorrow night," Jesse said, hovering on the threshold. "Gerald, did you replace the lightbulb in the hall? I told your mother—"

"Uh-uh, it wasn't me. Mama said some guy was by this morning, changing the bulbs and checking the lock on the front door. Said Mr. Cabot sent him, and he wanted to take care of a few things. Come on in, ask

Mama yourself.'' The man waved Jesse and Robin inside.

The cramped living room of the apartment echoed with the sound of Bruce Springsteen singing ''Santa Claus Is Coming to Town'' in his gravelly hard-rock voice. Four teenagers, three girls and a boy, were gathered around a flimsy-looking, propped-up limb of a tree, busily hanging the spindly twigs with tinsel. Next to the tree, a paper cutout of Santa Claus was tacked to the wall. A gray-haired woman was seated in a faded easy chair, but she rose at Jesse's and Robin's entrance. ''Mr. Lawson!'' she cried frantically, hurrying across the room to him. ''You haven't come to take Gerald back, have you?''

''No, he's got until tomorrow, Mrs. Selby,'' Jesse reassured her, extending the basket to her as the teenagers hung back shyly. ''We just dropped by to bring you this.''

As soon as Mrs. Selby took the basket, her children swarmed around her. ''Ooh, look!'' one of the girls shouted, pulling the wooden snowflake from the basket. ''Look at this! For our tree!'' She swooped down on the bedraggled-looking limb and attached the snowflake.

''Oh, my God,'' Mrs. Selby gasped, staring at the food in the basket. ''Oh, Mr. Lawson, we were gonna have nothing worth eating for supper tomorrow, and now this... I don't know what to say.''

''Say thank you, Mama,'' Gerald coached her. ''This is awfully kind of you, Mr. Lawson.''

''I praise God you came into our lives, Mr. Lawson,'' Mrs. Selby babbled, carrying the basket into the kitchen and setting it on the table. ''Let me empty out this basket so you can take it home—''

''No, the basket is yours to keep,'' Jesse corrected

her, arching his arm around Robin. "You can thank Ms. Greer for that. And for the candle and the table linen." Two of the girls had already removed the contents of the basket and unfolded the tablecloth. They squealed in delight at the red-and-green pattern of wreaths decorating the cloth.

Mrs. Selby dropped onto a chair, stunned. "You are too good to us," she said, sighing. "I thought all my prayers were answered when you brought Gerald home yesterday. And then that man came and fixed the light in the hall this morning. And now this…I just don't know what to say."

"Don't say anything," Jesse suggested, patting her arm. "We're on our way. You'd better get back to trimming your tree."

Robin's gaze passed from the gray-haired woman to Gerald and back again. Mrs. Selby had her son home with her for the holiday, and Robin hadn't. Yet she felt no envy, no resentment of the woman whose many prayers had been answered, thanks at least in part to Jesse. It was Christmas, and Christmas didn't have room in it for jealousy. It had room only for this: giving, making others happy, bringing joy.

Her eyes met Mrs. Selby's. "Merry Christmas," she said softly.

"Bless you," Mrs. Selby murmured. "May God bless you both."

The climb downstairs passed in silence. By the time Jesse and Robin reached the car, she was weeping. When he moved to unlock the passenger door for her, he noticed the tears streaking down her cheeks. "What's this all about?" he asked, drawing her against himself in a consoling embrace.

She rested her head against his shoulder and sniffled away her tears. "It's nothing, really. I'm all right."

He ran his fingers through her hair, thoughtful and concerned. "I'm sorry, Robin—I thought you'd enjoy this. It was something I wanted to do. Now we'll do something you want to do—sing Jingle Bells, roast chestnuts over an open fire…go to church, if you insist. Whatever you want—"

"No, Jesse," she said, her voice gaining strength. She tilted her head back so she could see him. "We've just done what I wanted to do."

His frown intensified. "Then why are you crying?"

She brushed her tears away with her fingertips. "It was so beautiful, what you did," she explained, her tone low but fervent. "Even that nasty woman who didn't have the good grace to thank you—I bet you knew she wouldn't, and you gave her the basket anyway. I've never seen anything so beautiful in my life."

Jesse gazed at her, his frown dissolving although his expression remained one of bemusement. "It wasn't so beautiful," he said modestly. "It was just something I wanted to do."

"Because it was Christmas," Robin noted.

"Because it was *their* holiday, and I thought they should have a good one. I don't have to believe in Christmas to do something for someone who does. And now—" he touched his lips to hers "—I'll do something for you. In fact, I'll do anything but put on a false beard. That was the deal we made."

"Listen to me, Jesse," Robin demanded impatiently. "I'm trying to tell you—you've already done something for me."

"What have I done for you? Cleaned out your store's supply of straw baskets?"

"You've made me realize that there's a whole lot more to Christmas than putting the tree in the same corner every year. And I love you for it, Jesse. I love you." Her arms coiled around his waist, beneath his coat, and she rose on tiptoe to kiss him.

He briefly returned her kiss, then pulled back and studied her. "You weren't crying because Mrs. Selby has her son and you don't have yours, were you?"

"No," Robin swore. She was honestly glad that her son was in Florida. As she'd just learned from Jesse, more than anything else Christmas meant doing something for someone who believed. Philip believed, and Robin had let him go. "I was crying, Jesse..." She tightened her arms around him, hugging him close. "I was crying because, for a while there, I was stupid enough to question whether I really loved you."

"Questioning isn't stupid," Jesse argued. "You know I respect people who ask questions."

"Yes, but that was one question that had an easy answer, and I shouldn't have had to keep asking it. I won't have to ask it anymore." She kissed him again. "And the other reason I was crying was because, after all these years, it took an avowed atheist to teach me what Christmas is all about."

"That makes perfect sense," Jesse commented, smiling whimsically. "We atheists have the objectivity you Santa worshippers are lacking."

"I'm not a Santa worshipper," Robin contradicted him. "I happen to like the Santa myth—"

"You admit Santa's a myth, then?" Jesse said victoriously. "That's a start."

"Don't try to convert me," she warned him with a laugh.

"What should I do?" he asked, his voice suddenly husky, his lips nearing hers.

"Take me home," she murmured. "We'll build a big fire in the fireplace, and we'll light up the tree, and—" her smile matched his in mischief "—I'll make a believer out of you."

"I already believe," he murmured before covering her lips in a searing kiss.

"And I believe in you, Jesse." She held him close, strengthened by her faith that they were a part of something bigger than themselves, that they were possessed by it. Maybe it was God, maybe love, maybe the power of two souls coming together, becoming one. Maybe all of those things.

Whatever it was, Robin would believe in it forever.

Epilogue

She was awakened by the ringing of her telephone. Groaning, she rolled out of Jesse's arms and groped for the receiver on the night table beside her bed. "Hello?"

"Hey, Mom! It's me!" Philip said gleefully. "Merry Christmas!"

"Philip!" Robin blinked awake and grinned. "Merry Christmas, Phil. Are you having a good time?"

"Yeah, it's been great. Yesterday we went to see this show at a place called Sea World, I think, and they had a whale that danced in the water, and dolphins that jumped through hoops and everything. It was really neat. We're just gonna hang out today, on account of it's Christmas, and tomorrow Dad's going to take me to Disney World."

"It sounds terrific," Robin said earnestly. "I'm so glad you're enjoying it."

"Our hotel room is neat, too. It's got this big color TV set, and they get the Disney channel here. I've been watching all the shows. Dad says he's going crazy."

"Maybe you'd better let him watch some football," Robin advised, sharing her newfound understanding of the holiday with her son. "Christmas means making other people happy, too, Phil."

"Okay, Mom. Did Santa come?"

"I haven't gone downstairs yet to look under the tree," Robin admitted. "But I'm pretty sure he did."

"Did you leave him some star-shaped cookies?"

Robin winced. The cookie dough was still sitting in a bowl in the refrigerator. It had probably solidified into a granite-hard mass by now. She considered confessing to Philip, then decided that a white lie wouldn't hurt. "I did, Phil, and I'm sure he ate them."

"Yeah, I bet he did," Philip concurred. "Are you going to see Jesse today?"

Robin turned to find Jesse awake, comfortably sprawled out beside her, his head propped up in his hand as he listened to her end of the conversation. His smile cut dimples into his cheeks, which were shadowed by an overnight growth of beard. The broad crest of his shoulder protruded from beneath the cover, reminding Robin of the fine body hidden from her view by the blanket. "I'll definitely be seeing Jesse today," she confirmed, winking at the man under discussion. He clasped her hand and drew her palm to his lips for a kiss.

"Well, listen," Philip said, "when you see him, make sure he does what he promised me he'd do. And tell him that if he sees Ms. Becker, he should tell her Merry Christmas for me, all right? Because she had a nice wreath on her door, and I'm gonna try not to think she's so boring anymore."

Philip's long-winded instructions made Robin dizzy, but she obediently responded, "I'll tell him."

"And tell him Merry Christmas from me, too."

"I will."

"I love you, Mom," Philip said. "I'm gonna go now. Dad said I could have pancakes for breakfast every day. Goodbye!"

"Goodbye, Phil. I love you, too." Robin sensed that her son had hung up before she finished speaking, but that didn't matter. Philip knew she loved him.

"How's he doing?" Jesse asked, pushing himself up to sit.

"Having the time of his life." Robin slid across the mattress to him, wrapped her arms around his waist and planted a kiss on his warm chest. "He said to wish you a merry Christmas, among other things."

"I'll forgive him for that," Jesse said magnanimously.

Robin frowned, trying to decipher the rest of Philip's cryptic message. "He also said that you promised to do something for him."

"Do something for him? I wonder what that's supposed to mean." Jesse frowned as well, but it looked like a fake frown to Robin. "It was sweet of him to take time out from his revels with Mickey Mouse to wish you a happy holiday."

"That's one of our traditions," Robin explained. "You call the members of your family who can't be with you. I'll be calling my mother in a few hours. With the time difference between here and Hawaii, I can't call her this early. And Philip will probably call her from Florida, and he'll call his other grandparents in Arizona. We always run up horrendous phone bills on Christmas."

"Some calls are worth the expense," Jesse allowed. "I can see how much Phil's call meant to you."

Robin leaned back from Jesse and examined his face.

She could discern in his features a reflection of his father, the similar eyes, the similar nose and jaw, the thick, softly textured hair. "All parents like to hear from their children at Christmas," Robin remarked quietly. "Why don't you call yours?"

"My parents?" The idea clearly didn't appeal to Jesse. His lips twisted in distaste, and he began to shake his head.

"Jesse, it's Christmas. Your first Christmas away from them. Call them."

"After everything I've told you, Robin..." He shook his head again, more vehemently. "It's not that I absolutely refuse to call them ever again. But I can't on Christmas. Any other day, sure, but not today."

"You have to," Robin argued. "Why not today? You keep telling me that Christmas isn't such a special day."

"But they think it is."

"Exactly." Robin bore down on him, her bright, hazel eyes piercing the guarded darkness of his. "Give of yourself, Jesse. Make them happy. Do it because *they* believe."

He met her stubborn gaze, then relented with a nod. "All right, I'll do it. In a few hours—I've got time-zone problems, too. And they may just hang up on me—"

"They won't," Robin predicted. "They'll be as happy to hear from you as I was to hear from Philip. Take it from a mother, Jesse. They'll be delighted."

"They'll chat for a few minutes, say good-bye and pray for my soul," he grumbled. Then he smiled grimly and pushed back the covers, putting an end to the conversation.

Robin didn't press him further. She knew he would phone his parents, and she was proud of him. It would be a difficult call for him to make, but he was strong enough to survive it. More than survive it—he would feel wonderful for having done it.

Standing, she put on her bathrobe. Jesse donned his shirt and the trousers of his suit. Taking his hand, she led him from the bedroom. Perhaps he wanted breakfast, but some traditions wouldn't be broken. The first thing Greers always did on Christmas morning was to hurry downstairs and view the presents under the tree. This year, one of those presents would be for Jesse. Though she wasn's sure how he would react, Robin couldn't wait to give it to him.

What she didn't expect was to find the tree all lit up. She was sure she had unplugged the lights last night. But as she reached the bottom step, she was confronted with the sight of her Christmas tree blazing in all its glory.

And something else—there were two packages under the tree that she didn't recognize. With a bright red envelope lying on the carpet beside them.

"What's going on?" she asked, planting her hands on her hips and turning accusingly to Jesse.

He offered a boyish grin. "This one is my gift to Phil," he said, marching to the tree, dropping down on his knees and lifting the rectangular package. "It's a remote-control four-wheel-drive Jeep. When he threatened to buy one for Mrs. O'Leary, I figured it was something he wanted for himself."

"Oh, Jesse—he'll love it!" Robin was once again overwhelmed by his sensitivity. By now she ought to be used to it; by now she ought to expect such thoughtfulness from him. But every time she caught a glimpse of Jesse's generous soul—the soul he pretended he didn't have—she was amazed, nearly moved to tears.

Not wishing to drown them both in a maudlin display, she effected a matter-of-fact smile and pointed to the other unfamiliar package, which was oddly shaped and crudely wrapped. "What else did you buy him?" she asked.

"That one's for you, from Phil," Jesse explained, setting the rectangular box back on the floor among the other presents for Philip. "Last week, he asked me to hide it at my house so you wouldn't find it. Then he ordered me to smuggle it into your house and under the tree on Christmas morning. I'm a man of my word, Robin, so…" He presented Robin with the oddly shaped package.

"When did you bring it in here?" she asked, sitting beside Jesse and gaping at him.

"While you were still asleep. I had it hidden in my car." At her astonished stare, he elaborated. "As a matter of fact, when I went out to get it, I nearly got run over by some obese old guy in a funny red hat. He kept making this stuttering noise at the back of his throat, kind of a ho-ho—"

"Jesse!" Robin laughed and poked him in the arm.

"Seriously," Jesse maintained, his expression deadpan. "I think the fellow was plastered—his nose was all red. And he drove like a maniac. When he wasn't making that silly ho-ho-ho sound, he was muttering about how Californians didn't know how to stay out of the way of other drivers in winter weather—"

"Snow!" Robin erupted, springing to her feet and hastening to the window. She pulled back the curtain and was greeted by the sight of her front lawn, an expanse of frozen grass, devoid of the picturesque white covering she prayed for every Christmas eve.

She hadn't prayed for it last night. White Christmases made for sentimental songs, but they weren't important when it came to what Christmas was *really* about. "So you ran into Santa, did you?" she said, playing along with Jesse's joke.

"He ran into me. It isn't the California drivers who cause all the problems—it's these hot-shot New Englanders."

"Santa isn't a New Englander—he's from the North Pole," Robin declared, returning to Jesse's side. She tore the wrapping paper off Philip's gift to her and unveiled a bizarre humanoid object made of clay and painted orange. It featured disproportionately large ears, stiletto-shaped toes, wings and a halo fashioned out of wire. "Don't tell me it's an angel!" she blurted out before succumbing to more laughter.

"According to Phil, it's a boy from Gleek," Jesse told her.

"Of course. That was my next guess," Robin said, still chuckling at the grotesque statue. "I love it. I'll use it as a centerpiece in the dining room—once you eat that gingerbread house I knocked myself out making for you." She set the Gleek boy aside and lifted a small, neatly wrapped box. "This is for you, Jesse," she said, abruptly solemn.

One of his eyebrows quirked in surprise as he took the box from her. Robin watched nervously as he unwrapped the box and raised the lid. Cushioned in a nest of tissue paper was the crystal angel she'd chosen for him. Jesse picked it up and raised it to the tree, gazing at the array of multicolored light reflected in its facets. "This," he said soberly, "is definitely not a Gleekian."

"It's an angel," Robin murmured, trying unsuccessfully to read his mind. "That seems to be a running theme this year."

"It certainly does," Jesse agreed, lowering the angel and closing his arms around Robin. He kissed her tenderly. "I don't think you can begin to know how much it means to me."

"You called me an angel once," Robin reminded him, looking down at the figurine cradled in his large hand to avoid having to look directly at him.

"More than once," Jesse acknowledged. "I don't believe in angels—except for you."

"I'm not an angel," Robin protested. "I'm not nearly good enough—"

"You don't have to be good," Jesse asserted. "You just have to be able to work miracles every now and then. And that you do, Robin. That you do." He leaned away and scooped up the red envelope. "This is for you from me. I'm not sure if you'll like it, but..." He cut himself off and handed her the envelope.

She scrutinized him. He appeared as nervous as she'd felt when she'd given him her gift. But what could he be nervous about? A gift certificate was a perfectly acceptable present, if that was what the envelope contained. A card would be sweet, too. She doubted that he'd give her money...

"Open it," he ordered her.

She drew in a deep breath and pried up the flap. A slip of red paper fell out with the word "ME" written on it.

Puzzled, she raised her eyes to his. "I'm giving you

me, Robin," he explained haltingly. "Myself. I know it isn't commercial, and I didn't wait in line for hours at a store, but...when I thought about giving, when I thought about what I wanted you to have...all I could think of was myself. If you'll have me," he added, his voice fading uncertainly.

Jesse. Her and Jesse. *Us.* That was what he was giving her. "I can't think of anything I'd rather have," she whispered. "It's the most extravagant gift in the world. The only problem is..." Her eyes sparkled playfully. "You've been giving yourself to me all along. It's not really a Christmas gift."

"That's right," Jesse agreed, his smile gaining confidence. "I'd just as soon give on every day of the year. Today is simply a day like any other."

"It is not," Robin insisted, curling up in his lap and hugging him. "You may have been giving yourself to me every day, but today, I got your gift in writing. And let me warn you, it's one gift I'm never going to return."

"Promise?"

"Promise."

"In that case..." He filled his lungs with air and struck a dramatic pose. "I hope I don't choke to death on the words: Merry Christmas, Robin."

Robin observed him for a moment, her eyes sparkling mirthfully despite her concerned expression. "You didn't choke to death," she noted.

He cuddled her close to himself, folding his arms possessively around her and brushing his lips against the glistening golden tendrils crowning her head. "Thank God for that," he sighed.

"Thank *who*?" Robin pounced on the word.

Jesse's mouth flexed as he considered his reply. "A slip of the tongue," he muttered with a laugh.

Robin smiled and nestled deeper into his embrace. So Jesse Lawson had said "Merry Christmas" without choking, and he'd acknowledged God. And he'd given her the most wonderful gift in the universe.

Just a few more miracles to illuminate this miraculously fine morning.

MERRY CHRISTMAS, BABY

Pamela Browning

Chapter One

Mariel Evans cruised her car smoothly down the ramp from the interstate highway and peered anxiously at her surroundings.

There was no gas station in sight on this December afternoon two days before Christmas. And an ice storm was approaching from the west, with sleet and freezing rain already falling steadily.

A glance at the gauge reminded Mariel that the gas tank was almost empty, and she knew it would be foolish to attempt to reach the next exit.

Then she saw it—a rusty sign tacked to a tree.

GAS—EATS 2 MI, the lettering said. An arrow pointed left.

In this mountainous part of northern Virginia, Mariel's faithful little Chevy could probably coast the two miles. It might have to.

The rain was falling harder now, and the swish of the car's windshield wipers barely kept up with it. The crackling voice of the radio announcer informed her that this was the worst ice storm to hit the state in thirty years.

This news was hardly reassuring, but the farther north she traveled, the likelier she was to outrun the storm.

Now, watching anxiously for the promised GAS—EATS, Mariel proceeded with extreme caution. When the bright red sign of the Magic Minimart came into view, she breathed a grateful sigh of relief, but only until she realized that she'd have to pump her own gas.

Christmas was Mariel's favorite season of the year. Her heart was full of peace and goodwill. So why should she begrudge the Magic Minimart's employees their party?

Through the wide plate-glass window, she saw them inside, whooping it up. The cashier was draped over the cash register, flirting with a guy wearing a Santa hat. A boom box parumpa-pum-pummed "The Little Drummer Boy" so loudly that the music vibrated the concrete beneath Mariel's feet. A man on a ladder was decking the men's room sign with boughs of holly.

And Mariel's fingers were so numb that she couldn't force the gas nozzle to separate from the pump.

"Looks like you could use some help," said a cheerful voice at her elbow. She wheeled around, sure that only a moment ago there had been no one near.

The guy inside wearing the Santa Claus cap couldn't hold a Christmas candle to this roly-poly little man, whose bright blue eyes twinkled up at her over a bushy white beard and a short red jacket.

Before Mariel could say "Jolly old Saint Nicholas," the man had pried her fingers from the handle of the gas pump and was expertly uncapping her gas tank.

"Why, thank you," Mariel said, smiling at him. To look at him made her heart feel happy, as if the sun were shining. Which was ridiculous, considering the fact that rain was dripping down her neck.

"Terrible weather we're having," said the little man.

"I know. And I have to drive all the way to Pittsburgh. I couldn't find a motel room. I guess you'd say there was no room at the inn," she said, trying to make a joke of it.

The little man's eyes snapped with a kind of droll wit. "That happens." He stopped pumping gas and screwed the cap on the tank.

"This is really nice of you," Mariel said. But she couldn't figure out if he worked here. "Do I pay you, or do I go inside?"

"No charge."

"But—"

"It's Christmas," he said with a sage shrug of his shoulders. "Got to get into the spirit of things, you know."

"Well, thanks. And—and merry Christmas." Mariel prepared to get into the car.

"You know, I could tell you a shortcut back to the interstate," the man offered thoughtfully. His beard was rimed with ice.

"Could you? Oh, that would be wonderful!" said Mariel.

"Instead of going back the way you came, take this road in the other direction. When you get to the blinker, turn left, then left again."

"Left, then left again," Mariel repeated.

"It'll be a lot better for you," he said solemnly.

"Thank you. You've been very kind."

"Merry Christmas. And I hope you have a happy New Year, too," he said. He stepped back from the car, and Mariel drove away from the station. When she glanced into her rearview mirror before pulling onto the highway, she expected to see him. But no one was there.

Well. Now to get on with her journey. Even though all that was waiting for her in Pittsburgh was an empty apartment and friends with busy holiday agendas, she couldn't wait to get there. She'd bake cookies for the neighbors, she'd go out and cut lots of pungent evergreen branches to drape across the mantel, and she'd invite the neighborhood kids in for a story hour.

Christmas was always such a magical time. Mariel loved the season and the celebration of it; she looked forward to it all year. If she were granted a pocketful of magic wishes right now, she'd wish for a miracle— that she were already home. She'd wish that it wasn't raining so hard that she could see no more than three feet in front of her car. And she'd wish she could remember if that funny little man had told her how far it was to the blinker. She'd driven miles—or so it seemed—and she hadn't seen a blinker yet.

JAKE TRAVIS DECIDED to take a shortcut back to Tellurian.

He was about ten miles from the new house where he'd been putting the final touches on the finish carpentry so that the owners could move in on the day before Christmas. It was a big deal to them—they wanted to be in their own place for the holidays.

So he'd worked long and hard, and this storm had caught him by surprise. If he'd known it was coming, he would have left for home hours ago.

Old Blue, his aged pickup truck, hugged the curve in the road as he cautiously accelerated for increased traction. If he didn't have to slam on the brakes, Old Blue would do just fine.

Normally Jake took good care of things. That included Old Blue, the only constant in his life. Jake bought beat-up houses and refurbished them, selling them for a pretty penny, moving on when he had to. He didn't even keep a cat.

A truck with four-wheel drive would be nice in this kind of weather. Hell, *brakes* would be nice. Why hadn't he had these lousy brakes fixed last week, when he'd noticed the problem? It was those people, that family. He'd busted his buns so that they could be in their house for Christmas, and now look at him—paying the price for his generosity.

Bah, humbug, he said to himself, thinking that this road didn't look like the shortcut. He couldn't recall the shortcut tunneling through the midst of the forest; nor could he remember its being so dark. Driving this road was like navigating the inside of a cow, and he hadn't passed a house or another car since he turned off the highway.

He pumped cautiously on the brakes, which did little good. He'd have to be careful, the way ice was building up on the asphalt road. Mist swirled ahead of him, graying the landscape, which was probably just as well. The countryside wasn't much to look at.

What I wouldn't give for a cup of hot coffee, he was thinking when a rabbit darted in front of his wheels and he slammed on the—Oh, no! No brakes!

BACK TO THAT pocketful of wishes, Mariel was thinking as she noticed with some trepidation that the trees seemed to be closing over the road.

If she were granted three wishes right *now,* she'd wish for snow that lay "roundabout, deep and crisp and even," as in the carol "Good King Wenceslas." And she'd like a cup of hot spiced cider. *And someone special to share it with,* she thought. *Let's not forget that.* At the age of thirty, she'd begun to think that her special someone didn't exist. Or if he did, she'd never find him. Her standards, according to her friends, were impossibly high.

Blap, blap, went her windshield wipers, and then they stalled for a moment. They started again in time for her to see that this road merged with another up ahead, but it was not soon enough for her to avoid the streak of blue hurtling out of the fog.

Mariel heard a sickening crunch of metal. Her car skidded out of control toward the ditch, long gray tree branches stabbing at the glass of the windshield, and she clung to the steering wheel for dear life until the car stopped spinning.

Silence. Then she was aware of rain drumming on the metal roof, and a rhythmic roar in her ears that she knew must be her own blood pulsing in her veins.

She opened her eyes, taking stock. She was shaken, but she could move all her fingers and all her toes. The car was resting against a couple of trees, the two right wheels suspended over the ditch. She unfastened her seat belt and then felt as if her heart had stopped. It wasn't a ditch. It was a deep ravine. Treetops were barely visible below.

Panic sluiced over her, freezing her into inaction. In that moment, she knew sheer terror, knew it intimately. In her mind's eye, she could see her car careening into nothingness and taking her with it. In that moment, she felt utterly alone.

"Don't move!" shouted the man who appeared at her window, and she stared at him wildly, wondering if he was an apparition or—as unlikely as it seemed—a real person.

Whatever he was, he looked very worried. Mariel peered up at him on a slant, taking in high, craggy cheekbones and a squared-off chin, a prominent brow and a lone wet strand of dark hair escaping his stocking cap. The man's brown eyes were intriguingly flecked with amber, and they flickered with concern. Despite the cold and damp, Mariel felt a rush of heat. This man was gorgeous. And—no doubt about it now—he was real.

"Are you hurt?" he demanded.

"I don't think so," Mariel said, tentatively finding her voice.

"Keep still. I'm going to stand back now and take a look at this situation."

He scrambled across a boulder and studied the car. Carefully, and very, very slowly, Mariel clasped her seat belt around her again. The way her car was suspended half in space, she wouldn't be surprised if it lurched suddenly.

Through the rain, Mariel saw that the man was big and broad-shouldered. He wore a red-and-black plaid lumberjack jacket, and he appeared to be fit and strong. Below the jacket, well-worn jeans hugged his calves. He studied the position of the car intently, his brow furrowed in concentration. She tried to breathe deeply in order to calm herself, but without success. Her breath came in shallow little bursts, somehow inhibited by the sheer masculinity of this man who wanted to help her.

The stranger hurried toward her. She started to roll down the window, but he said sharply, "Don't do that!"

She must have looked startled, because his expression softened.

"I can get you out of here. But we don't want to take any chances, and the way your car is leaning against those trees, the slightest movement this way or that could change things real fast. Understand?"

She nodded mutely.

He loped off into the fog, and Mariel thought suddenly that she might never see him again.

The windows began to mist, and she resisted the impulse to wipe them clear with her hand. *If I had three wishes,* she started to think, but before she could clarify them, her rescuer was back with a tool kit and a long length of chain.

"I'll have you out of there in a few minutes," he promised. She only looked at him. Every time she allowed herself to glance toward the ravine, her stomach rolled over.

The man ducked beneath the car. She heard and felt the rasp of the chain against metal, and then he reappeared and wrapped the other end securely around a couple of immense trees.

He yanked at the end of the chain to test it. "I think that'll hold it," he said, coming around to her window again. He bent over and looked at her, and under the influence of his calm gaze she felt her shoulders relax.

"I tied the chain around the chassis in a couple of places. If the car falls, it can't go far," he said.

"What do you want me to do?" It occurred to her that this stranger could be some kind of nut, but he *was* trying to save her life.

He considered, gazing off into the treetops below for a long moment. "I'm going to see if I can get your door open. The metal's kind of crumpled, so it may not work," he said.

Sure enough, it didn't.

"Want me to try opening it from the inside?" she asked, wanting to show him that she was cooperating. It seemed important to her that he know that he could count on her.

"Go ahead."

She tried. The door wouldn't budge.

"I'll roll down the window, and you can reach in and try," she said.

The man nodded. Slowly she cranked the handle, and the window eased down. Fog floated into the car; the mist felt cool against her hot cheeks. The man reached in and exerted a steady pressure on the door handle. His hand was square, and his fingers were long.

"Excuse me for a minute. I've got to go get a tool out of my truck," the man said. He strode away, the red and black of his jacket weaving through the forest until he disappeared altogether.

Mariel almost released her seat belt again, then decided against it. The stranger seemed to be in complete control. She'd be better off following his directions, since he seemed to know what he was doing.

When he returned, he was carrying a tire iron. Again Mariel worried. There were a number of things you could do with a tire iron, and one of them was hitting somebody over the head. Though if that was what he had in mind, he was going to a lot of trouble to do it.

"You can take off the seat belt now," he said briskly. "Then I'm going to pry at the door. Be ready to move fast if you have to."

Mariel braced herself. He pried. Nothing happened to the door, but the car settled against its supporting trees with a tired wheeze. The treetops in the ravine spun sickeningly, and Mariel thought of her three wishes.

"A parachute. A hot-air balloon. And a can opener," she said.

"What?" asked the man.

"Just…um, making a few wishes," she said, feeling foolish.

His look was scornful. "If you're crazy enough to

think that wishes will work, how about wishing for the rain to let up?''

She frowned. Where did he get off, calling her crazy? Nevertheless, she canceled the hot-air balloon anyway, mentally adding "no rain" to her wish list.

"You'd think they'd make these car doors with pop-off hinges or something," he said.

"I doubt that designers of cars think about all the things that can happen," Mariel said reasonably.

"They should," he said with a grunt. "They should sit around and brainstorm all the worst things that could go wrong. They should say, 'What if one of our cars is dangling over a ravine with a woman inside?' All kinds of things can happen, you know. Driving is unpredictable."

"Life is unpredictable. Nobody makes *life* with pop-off hinges, either," Mariel returned.

"Yeah, well, you were talking about wishes. You sounded as if you believed wishing might work."

"Sometimes it does. I do believe in magic," Mariel said defensively.

He paused and studied her for a moment. "Weird," was all he said before inserting the tip of the tire iron in a new place between car door and frame.

"There *are* miracles," Mariel said.

"That so?" he asked, as if he weren't really paying attention. Mariel heard metal bending, but the door still didn't open.

"What do you call, um...well, for instance, springtime? When everything is fresh and new again, and flowers bloom, and grass grows, and—"

He spared her a brief look of disdain. "I'd call springtime a welcome relief at this point," he said succinctly.

Mariel sat back, thinking that what she had here was

a realist, not a dreamer. In these circumstances, she couldn't say that was all bad.

"There!" he said, jabbing the tire iron one last time. Something bent and snapped, and he peeled the door back. Mariel, seeing an opportunity, started to scramble out of the car.

"Stop!" he yelled, grabbing at her wrist and missing it.

The car rolled slightly forward, and Mariel screamed. He caught her wrist this time, and with a tremendous surge of strength he hauled her out of her seat.

She staggered against him, and he held her in his arms. The wool of his jacket was soft against her cheek, and the length of his body against hers felt warm and reassuring. She clung to him, aware of firm muscles beneath his jacket and his gaze riveted on her face.

"Whoa," he said. "That was some predicament." For the first time, she was aware of his unmistakably southern drawl. It felt gentle on her ears.

"It was close," she agreed shakily, looking back over her shoulder. Her poor little Chevy hung over the edge of the world, its left side sideswiped, one of its headlights dangling from the socket.

"You really are all right?" he asked, and she focused her eyes to see that his face was filled with concern.

"I'm okay. Didn't you see that yield sign where the roads met?"

"I—Well, it was those fool brakes. Should have had them fixed, but I neglected it."

Mariel rolled her eyes in exasperation. "You mean I was in that fix because you were too lazy to take your truck to the garage?" she asked incredulously.

"I had to finish the carpentry in a house where I was

working so the owners could move in before Christmas," he said defensively.

"Great," Mariel said through gritted teeth. "Talk about the designers of cars not thinking about all the things that could happen. Didn't it occur to you that brakes are important? That they need to be in proper working order?"

"I didn't think—" he began.

"Obviously," Mariel said, to cut him off.

His jaw was set in a grim line. "I'm glad you're not hurt. I'd never forgive myself if you were," he said, which redeemed him somewhat in Mariel's eyes.

"I don't know your name," she said.

"Jake. Jake Travis. And yours?"

"Mariel Evans," she replied.

"What a way to meet," he said glumly.

"What do we do now? I didn't see any houses, or a place where we could phone for help, did you?" she asked. The fog amplified her voice, and her words echoed back at her.

"No phones, I'm afraid. I must have taken a wrong turn, but how did *you* end up way out here?" He was eyeing her Pennsylvania license plate.

"I followed the directions of a man who helped me at a gas station near the interstate," she said. "I must have gotten them wrong. I have no idea where we are."

"Neither do I, and I live twenty miles away. Well, let's see if Old Blue will crank up." He grasped her elbow and started to steer her past the dank, dripping trees toward the patch of blue in the mist.

"Wait," she said, holding back. "I'd better get my purse out of the car."

"Oh, no, you don't. I don't trust the way it's leaning."

"I can reach in and grab it," she said evenly. She marched toward the car, but he was past her in a minute, opening the damaged door and peering inside.

"I'll do it."

"You're too heavy. If you lean your weight on the car, it's going to move," Mariel argued.

"Who said anything about leaning? Anyway, I tied the frame of the car to the tree as tightly as I could."

"The car moved when I got out," Mariel reminded him.

He heaved an impatient sigh. "All right. I'll hold your hand while you lean in. Don't touch the car, just grab the purse."

"And my tote bag from in front of the passenger seat."

"Okay, okay. Just get on with it," he said. "Hold on to me." He extended his hand.

Reluctantly she reached toward him.

"No, not that way," he said. "You hold my wrist, I'll hold yours. It'll be stronger." He demonstrated, and as her hand held tight to his wrist, she felt the sinews contracting. He seemed as strong as he looked.

As soon as they had a secure grip on each other, Mariel leaned gingerly into the car. Already her little Chevy, which had seen her through a marriage, a divorce and two cross-country trips, seemed alien, different, not part of her anymore. She picked up the purse and stuffed it into the tote bag, and Jake hauled her up and out of the car.

He didn't let go of her wrist right away. His hand was warm, and she felt her pulse beating against his palm. Flustered, she pulled her hand away.

"Let's go get in my truck," he said, so she slung the tote bag on her shoulder and followed him.

Jake's truck wasn't much newer than her own car, but it seemed well maintained. He got in and leaned over the seat to open the door on the passenger side. Mariel climbed in, giving Jake points for the cleanliness and neatness of the cab.

He noticed that she was shivering. "As soon as the engine is warm, I'll turn the heater on full blast," he promised. She nodded. Her relief and subsequent anger with Jake had evaporated, leaving her feeling perilously close to tears. She shoved her hands deep in the pockets of her coat and stared out the window.

Icicles were beginning to form on drooping tree limbs, and Mariel leaned her aching head against the cool window glass. Idly she noticed pale, parasitic clumps of waxy green leaves growing in the treetops, and recognized them as mistletoe. *How appropriate to the Christmas season,* she thought. She had never seen mistletoe growing in the wild before. She'd always been partial to the contrast of the ivory berries against the paler oval leaves. She usually used it liberally in her holiday decorating, and not only for its effect on her love life. She simply liked the way it looked.

But for now, holiday decor was the last thing she wanted to think about. She felt stiff and sore all over, and her head ached. A warm bed with an electric blanket turned all the way to "bake" would feel wonderful at this point.

The truck engine turned over but wouldn't start.

Jake jiggled the ignition key and tried again. Nothing.

"The battery's new," Jake said. He got out and raised the hood, disappearing under it for so long that Mariel began to suspect that the problem was major. When he climbed back in beside her, he looked worried. And when he tried to start the motor again, the battery only clicked a few times and died.

"That's it," he said, a grim tone to his voice. "We won't be going anywhere in Old Blue."

"This," Mariel said wearily, "is a nightmare."

"You said it," Jake answered.

They listened to the rain falling for a while, and then Jake said abruptly, "We can't stay here. It's going to get colder tonight. I think we should strike out and try to find a house. Otherwise..." His words trailed off, and Mariel understood that he considered it dangerous to stay in the truck.

For the first time, she realized their peril. They were lost in the woods, their vehicles out of commission, with the worst ice storm in thirty years roaring out of the west. Without a warm place to stay, they could freeze to death.

Jake regarded her across the wide expanse of vinyl seat. "I passed no place fit for human habitation on the road I traveled, and there's nothing where you came from, either. If we continue the way we were headed, I think we'll come to civilization. There's a major highway in that direction," he said.

"The interstate?" Mariel asked hopefully.

"I think the interstate is the other way. The road I'm thinking of is the highway into the town where I live."

Mariel sighed. "I'm game. I can't see sitting here and waiting for help to come along, when it may not."

"Good," Jake said, smiling at her. He had a nice smile; his teeth were very white. One bicuspid lapped slightly over the adjoining tooth, which only made the smile more interesting. Mariel wished he'd take off his cap so that she could see his hair.

When Jake hopped out of the truck cab, Mariel did,

too. "What are you doing?" she asked when he climbed up over the open tailgate onto the bed of the truck and opened a metal box.

"Getting a few tools."

"For what?" she asked. She had to crane her neck to look at him.

"I was a Boy Scout once. We believe in being prepared," he told her, jumping down.

Mariel couldn't resist smiling at him. She wondered how old he was. Thirty-two? Thirty-three? It was impossible to tell, but then he probably couldn't tell much about her, either. She was wrapped in her tan, all-weather coat with the wool lining, her hair tucked under the collar, a red scarf wound up to her ears.

Now she flipped a corner of the scarf over her hair to protect it from the rain.

"Ready?" Jake asked. He shrugged into a small backpack and tugged at the straps until it fitted comfortably over his jacket.

Mariel nodded. With a last look at the truck, which, even though inoperative, represented a dry place to shelter from the weather, she resolutely faced the road. Whatever her fortunes, she had cast them with this stranger.

There was no use looking back. Anyway, it was too much trouble. Her neck hurt.

With the freezing rain stinging her face, and wearing boots that were designed for style rather than tramping along an ice-slicked road, Mariel followed Jake into the eddying mist.

Chapter Two

The road beneath their feet was so icy that it was difficult to keep a firm footing, and Jake kept a covert eye on his companion. She marched up and down the hills like a trooper, thank goodness, and he had the feeling that she was determined not to slow him down.

"So, Mariel, what brings you to this part of the country?"

"My job," she said. "I'm a folklorist for a museum in Pittsburgh, and they sent me to a conference in Roanoke. I was on my way home—I thought."

A glance down at her revealed that her blue eyes were dancing with a kind of rueful humor. He was glad to see it; he had a feeling that she'd need it before this day was over. He didn't look away immediately, because he was suddenly fascinated with her face. He hadn't realized before what a good-looking woman she was.

"What do you do?" she asked.

"I'm a carpenter by trade. Thus the tools," he said, gesturing over his shoulder at the small pack he wore. In it were things he hoped they wouldn't need—matches, leftovers from his lunch, a flashlight, hatchet, hammer, rope, and a Swiss army knife. He didn't want to talk about himself, though. He'd rather learn more about her.

"Tell me what a folklorist does," he said, trying to sound interested.

"I collect legends and catalog them," she said easily.

"How'd you get a job like that?"

"Oh, I have a master's degree in history, and I wrote my thesis on the origins of legends."

"Sounds boring. I guess that's why I never went to college."

She smiled. "It's not boring to me. I'm gathering stories to show how Christmas legends developed. You'd be surprised how many of them evolved similarly in different countries."

"Such as what? And where?"

"Such as gift-givers in all sorts of cultures. We're familiar with the real Saint Nicholas, who was probably a bishop in Asia Minor in the fourth century and is the basis for our Santa Claus. And there was the ancient Roman hag, Befana, who searched the world, leaving candy for good children, stones for the bad. And there was Knecht Ruprecht, a straw-clad German spirit who gave gifts to good children—"

"Sounds pagan to me," Jake said mildly, interrupting her.

Mariel turned wide eyes upon him. "Many of our customs had pagan origins. Take Christmas customs, for instance. People in primitive times lived very close to nature, you see, and they were quite aware of the shortest day of the year, which is December twenty-second. They celebrated when the days started to grow longer, and so we have celebrations of winter cropping up in every culture."

Jake hunched his shoulders against the rain, which

was turning to sleet. "The middle of the winter's not much to celebrate, in my opinion," he muttered.

"Oh, but the celebration was to banish the winter doldrums, you see. To cheer everyone up," she said.

A curly blond tendril had escaped the scarf protecting her head, and Jake had the ridiculous urge to reach out and push it back.

"You and I ought to be celebrating, I guess," he said. "We could certainly banish *these* winter doldrums, and that's a fact." His words evaporated into a vapor trail; the air temperature was dropping.

She was silent while they walked another half mile or so. He thought maybe he had offended her, but in his opinion, the whole conversation was silly. Its only merit was that it helped him to know her better.

"I wonder how far we've come." He turned around and walked backward a few steps. The road behind them was shrouded in mist, and a tree limb fell suddenly, startling both of them.

"Strange that no one lives near here," Mariel said, her voice echoing eerily in the surrounding forest.

"I'm sure we'll come upon a house soon," Jake said, with more bravado than he felt. Mariel was still walking pluckily along beside him, but her step seemed less springy, and a tense line bisected her forehead. The veins beneath the skin at her temple were blue; her skin was milky white.

"This isn't supposed to happen at Christmas," she said. "We should be home among our friends and family, our cheeks nice and rosy, comfy-cozy, roasting chestnuts on an open fire."

"Right, but Jack Frost is nipping at my nose, and we'd better not slow down, or we're going to turn into snowmen right here and now."

She glanced at him sideways. "Oh, but you have to keep the Christmas spirit, no matter what happens. That's the whole idea."

"I've never cared much for Christmas," he said tightly. "All that family stuff—well, I never experienced it. As far as I'm concerned, this holiday is one where I get a few days off work, for which, since I'm self-employed, I don't get paid. If I'm lucky, on Christmas Day someone will take pity on me and invite me over for turkey dinner. Then the men of the family and I will watch a football game. Afterward I'll go home to an empty house."

Mariel seemed taken aback. "You're not married?" she asked.

"No. And I've never had any family. I grew up in a series of foster homes. For Christmas I usually got a few pairs of socks and some underwear. There was no Santa Claus for me—ever."

"No Santa? Why that's—that's…"

"That's the breaks of the game," he finished for her. "Do you think you could walk a bit faster? It's getting late, which means it's going to be dark soon."

"You set the pace. I'll keep up," she said stoically, and so he sped up. Walking slightly ahead of her, he was able to hide the expression on his face, which he was sure wasn't pleasant.

He just didn't like thinking about Santa Claus, that was all. The whole idea of a jolly little man who lavished gifts on people who already had everything they needed made him angry. If there really *were* a Santa Claus, he'd give things to people who needed them. The whole Christmas thing was enough to make him Santa Clauseated, which rhymed with nauseated, which was a pretty bad joke, and he already knew there was no point in saying it to Mariel.

THEY HAD BEEN WALKING for about an hour when Mariel spied something that looked like a roof through the trees. At first she couldn't believe her eyes. She'd begun to think they were walking along the most deserted road on earth.

"A house! Over there!" she exclaimed, clutching Jake's arm.

He clapped his hand over hers and broke into a smile. "I knew someone must live along here. Careful, don't trip in that pothole," he said, taking her gloved hand in his and pulling her along. Above them, bare, icy branches seemed to lock arms overhead, creaking and complaining with the rising wind.

A path, almost overgrown with bushes, led to the little house. Such a funny little house, Mariel thought, and she didn't see any windows or any lights.

Jake stopped so suddenly that she almost ran into him. "It's just an old hunter's blind, not a house at all," he said. "Look, the roof is crumbling."

"Oh," Mariel said on a soft sigh of disappointment.

They made their way around to the hidden side of the structure. "Why, it's nothing but a lean-to," Mariel said.

Jake kicked at a few loose boards. "There's no point in staying. This place wouldn't be any better shelter than my truck. Speaking of which, maybe we shouldn't have left."

"I don't know," said Mariel. "I'm cold and hungry and I ache all over. I wish somebody would come along and give us a lift back to the Magic Minimart where all my problems started, and—"

Jake interrupted her. "No more of your wishes. So far you're batting zero."

They both heard the cry at the same time.

"What's that?" Jake asked in alarm.

"It sounds like a baby crying."

"A baby? Here? No, it could be an animal, or maybe a bird, but a baby? No way," Jake said, as though there could be no doubt. "Come on, we'd better get out of here. This place gives me the creeps." He walked away, his hands deep in his pockets, his boots tramping down the wet brown leaves. The set of his shoulders was resolute, and he didn't look back.

Mariel readjusted the scarf over her hair and groped in her pocket for a tissue. She was stuffing it back into her pocket when she heard the cry again. Not the strong, full-bodied cry of an older child, but the high, thin wail of a small baby.

She looked toward Jake, whose bright jacket was barely visible through the wet tree trunks. She almost followed him. She certainly didn't want to lose him, and she didn't want him to think that she was slowing down. But how could she ignore a baby's cry?

"Mariel! Hurry up!" he called.

Impulsively Mariel pushed aside a rotting, rain-soaked board and entered the hut. It took her eyes a moment to adjust to the gloom, but when they did, she was astonished to see, lying on a bed of dry leaves and wrapped in a sturdy pink blanket, a tiny infant.

The baby's face was red and screwed up into a furious wail. Small fists flailed the air, and beneath the blanket little feet kicked.

"Jake!" Mariel called, falling to her knees and gathering the child into her arms. The baby stopped crying at once and stared, openmouthed, at Mariel.

She heard Jake crashing through the underbrush. He appeared at the entrance to the hut, his eyes wild. "What's the matter?"

For an answer, Mariel slowly rose to her feet and turned so that he could see the child. His eyes widened.

"It *was* a baby!" he said in a strangled voice.

The air between them seemed very heavy.

Jake's cap had fallen off, and he ran his fingers through his hair. It was dark brown and wavy, crisp with the cold, and it sprang up under his fingers as if it had a life of its own.

"I'll be damned," he said. He was regarding the baby with distaste.

"We can't leave it here," Mariel said.

"Of course not," he said. "How did it get here in the first place, that's what I'd like to know." Jake's sweeping gaze took in the dilapidated shelter, icicles forming where water dripped from the roof. His eyes met Mariel's. He looked angry and disgusted.

"Does it matter how she got here?" Mariel asked. She cradled the baby protectively in her arms and pressed her cheek to the top of the infant's head. Despite Jake's dismay, Mariel felt a thrill of excitement. She parted the blanket and counted ten fingers and ten toes. The baby was a girl, and Mariel thought she might be a month old. She wore a pink flannel nightgown and a dry cloth diaper. She had a curl of pale yellow fuzz atop her head, and she was beautiful.

The baby made little mewling noises, not unlike those of a newborn kitten. Mariel's heart turned over when she realized that she must be hungry.

"Where are her parents?" Jake asked with barely controlled anger. He stomped out of the hut and stared into the woods. Mariel followed, the baby in her arms.

They saw no sign of life other than themselves, only wet tree trunks half hidden in fog.

"Hello?" Jake called experimentally, hands cupped to his mouth. The word danced around them in echoes, but there was no answer.

"Is anyone there?" Jake shouted, but the forest only cried, "There…there…there," until the sound died.

"We can't leave this baby," Mariel said again.

Jake threw his head back in exasperation, staring up at the imprisoning branches as if hoping to find an answer. When, after a long moment, he looked back at Mariel, his eyes were grim.

"With the light fading, we can't let the baby slow our progress," he said, in a tone that struggled to be matter-of-fact.

"Of course not."

"And she's an added responsibility. I don't know anything about babies. Do you?"

Mariel bit her lip and gazed down into the chubby little face.

"Well, do you?" he demanded.

"Not a thing," she admitted.

"How are we going to take care of her?"

"We'll have to manage," she said, lifting her chin. "We can do it. We have no choice. We have to get her someplace warm and feed her and—and everything," Mariel said.

"What kind of person would leave a child out in this weather? I'd like to get my hands on him," Jake said. He pulled his cap securely down over his forehead. "I'd better carry her."

"But I—"

"Your feet were slipping and sliding on the ice, I

noticed. I'm wearing work boots with a tread. It's a matter of safety.''

''I am perfectly capable—'' Mariel began.

''Mariel,'' Jake said gruffly, ''give her to me. You're wasting time.''

Stung by Jake's tone, Mariel reluctantly handed the baby to him. The child settled against Jake's chest as if she felt perfectly comfortable there, the pink blanket incongruous against his bold plaid jacket. Mariel solicitously reached over and pulled a fold of the blanket over the baby's face to protect her from the sleet.

''Ready?'' Jake said. He held the bundle awkwardly, and his face was stony, unreadable.

Mariel nodded silently, her heart in her throat. She wasn't responsible for the baby's being there, but Jake seemed to be angry with her. This situation was hard enough without having to take that kind of flak.

Making her way at a slower pace, Mariel followed Jake back through the woods to the road. Water dripped from bare branches; patches of dense fog filled the hollows. It wouldn't be long before it was completely dark. The thought of being stranded in these woods in the cold and the dark with sleet falling all around made her shiver.

If she talked, maybe she could jolt Jake into a better mood. If she kept talking, maybe she wouldn't think about the danger.

''Tell me about the town where you live,'' Mariel said to Jake, struggling to keep her teeth from chattering.

''Why?'' His expression was uncompromising, and it only softened slightly when he glanced at Mariel. The baby was snuggled in his arms and wasn't making a peep.

"Because I want to know about it," she said.

"Now? While we're walking along in this sleet? Just after we find a baby in the woods?" he asked incredulously.

"I just want to talk," she said through gritted teeth. When he saw the dark look on her face—the first sign of negativity since they'd started out—he seemed to think better about resisting conversation and began to talk.

His voice was deep and reassuring as they walked through the darkening woods, the sleet cold and wet against their faces.

"Tellurian," Jake said, "is a picture-book town folded into a valley in these mountains, the Shenandoahs. I live on a tree-shaded street in a big, rambling house with old-fashioned plumbing and beautiful hardwood floors and a kitchen with oak cabinets that I built myself," he said, walking briskly to set their pace.

"Go on," she said, keeping her eyes on the road. Ahead was another hill, and she dreaded the climb.

"I buy houses and fix them up, then I sell them. I like working with wood, shaping a board into something beautiful. I like the clean smell of the wood, as well as the feel of it, and I like the way the people who buy my houses admire my handiwork."

"I can't believe you'd put so much of yourself into a house and then sell it," Mariel said breathlessly. They were walking so fast that she was having a hard time pulling enough air into her lungs. Jake was having no difficulty; he swung easily along beside her, planting his feet firmly, the baby hardly any weight at all.

"It's how I make money" was all he said, and she sensed that worldly possessions meant little to him. They walked on, tackling the hill. Mariel was too much out of breath to prod him with more questions. He looked down at her once or twice, and she tried not to let him see how tired she was. Once he slowed his pace slightly, which made walking easier. She sensed he was worried.

I can't let him down, she thought to herself, but at the foot of the hill, she slipped on loose rock and caught his arm, almost knocking him over in the process.

He steadied her, and she peered down at the baby. The infant was quiet, her face barely visible beneath the fold of the blanket. Jake looked at the baby, too, his expression grave.

"Mariel, we're going to have to come to a decision," he said as she leaned against him.

"About what?" she said wearily.

"About which way to go. If it were still only the two of us, I'd say let's forge ahead. But now that we've got this baby, I think we should go back to my truck."

Mariel's head shot up. "We've come all this way and you want to go back where we came from? No way," she said, starting to walk on and expecting him to follow. She hunched her shoulders and concentrated on moving one foot after the other, only to be halted by Jake's imperative tone.

"The truck's a place of shelter from the storm. We don't know how bad it's going to get."

She turned around. He was strong and stolid, standing there with sleet bouncing off his wide shoulders, the baby pressed to his chest. But was he right? *Should* they turn back?

"We already know there's no one for miles in that direction," she said stubbornly. "It's foolish to go back that way."

"We have no idea what lies ahead," he retorted.

''Could be better, could be worse. Back there—'' he jerked his head to indicate the road along which they'd come ''—there's my truck. I vote we go that way.''

''A house with heat sounds a lot more inviting. There's bound to be someone in this direction,'' she argued.

''Don't be stupid!''

''Stupid! May I remind you that we wouldn't be in this fix if you hadn't run me off the road?'' Mariel's feet were like blocks of ice now. Her knee and hip joints ached. Never had she felt more miserable.

Darkness was gathering around them, but she saw Jake's brows draw together. Fear stabbed through her. What if he decided to go back to the truck, leaving her to struggle on toward the unknown? Yet she knew in her heart that to turn back would be the wrong thing to do. They already knew there was nothing there, and while the truck might afford a place to shelter from the weather, it wouldn't be warm. She'd rather take her chances on finding a house with welcoming inhabitants up ahead.

Jake was silent for a long time. Too long. Mariel shifted her weight from one foot to the other, wondering if her feet would ever be warm again.

Reluctantly she walked back to where Jake stood and nudged the blanket away from the baby's face. The child looked up at her, blue eyes wide and trusting. In that instant, Mariel felt the full weight of responsibility settle slowly onto her shoulders.

''This baby needs food, Jake. No telling how long it's been since she's eaten,'' Mariel said, quietly but urgently. She let the fabric fall across the baby's face again, and the child whimpered and nuzzled against Jake's coat.

Jake stared down at the infant in his arms, his brows drawn together. Mariel watched the expressions flit across his face, one after the other—worry, doubt, anguish and, finally, concession.

"All right," he said at last. "You're the one with the college degrees. We'll do it your way."

"What kind of dig is that?" she demanded.

"I didn't mean anything. Let's go." He started walking.

Now that she had convinced him, Mariel felt uncertain. What if they were indeed headed farther into the wilderness? But, no, she instinctively felt that the worst thing they could do would be to turn back.

Quickly, before she could change her mind, she wheeled and caught up with Jake. Anxiously she looked at the bundle that was the baby.

"Do you think she's all right?" she asked.

"She's moving around."

"I guess that's good. I hope wherever we end up, they have clean diapers."

"Dream on," Jake scoffed. After a few minutes he said, "It's getting so dark I can hardly see ahead of us. Can you get the flashlight out of my backpack?" He stopped and turned his back to her, and her fingers struggled with the fastening. He waited patiently, but the baby began to wail.

"You'll have to bend down. I can't reach in," said Mariel.

He bent his knees, and she fumbled for the flashlight. Finally her fingers closed around its handle and she withdrew it and switched it on. The beam bounced around the treetops before settling on the road.

"What else is in that pack of yours?" she asked.

"Some things left over from lunch."

"Anything that would feed a baby?"

"A bit of milk in the thermos."

"We may have to feed her soon." Mariel shone the light on the baby's face as they walked. The infant's eyes were scrunched tightly, and her toothless mouth stretched wider with every wail.

Now that it was dark, Mariel was beginning to feel exhausted. Putting one foot in front of the other was starting to feel like too much of an effort, but she knew she couldn't stop now that she had insisted that they continue in this direction. She wanted to act confident, to make Jake feel as if this had been the right decision.

"I don't see any signs of people," Jake said after they had walked in silence for half an hour or more. The baby had stopped crying after he opened his coat and settled her inside. Mariel supposed Jake was getting tired of carrying the baby, but he hadn't complained.

"Does the road seem narrower to you?" she asked anxiously. She focused the flashlight ahead of them, where the road seemed to become part of the forest.

"I don't know," Jake said. "You look bushed. Want me to carry the flashlight?"

She shook her head. "I'm fine," she said doggedly.

His keen look told her that she didn't look fine, but she was beyond caring. The skin of her face felt raw from the sleet, and the scarf that was supposed to be protecting her hair was soaked through. As a therapeutic exercise, she tried to remember all the warm fireplaces she'd ever known, like the cavernous one at camp where they'd toasted marshmallows on rainy summer nights, and the marble one at the museum, which was used only for patrons' parties in the winter, and the small but cozy fireplace in her apartment, where she would like to be right now.

They walked another hundred yards before the road tapered into a hard-packed dirt track.

"Now what do we do?" Mariel asked in bewilderment.

"We should have gone back to the truck," Jake said tightly.

"We still could," she pointed out.

He glared at her in exasperation. "Look at you. You're barely able to stand up. There's no way you can walk that far."

She stared at him bleakly, knowing it was true.

When he spoke again, Jake's voice was kind. "We'll sit down on that fallen log over there and rest for a few minutes while we figure out what to do."

Mariel's knees buckled just as she reached it. She hoped Jake hadn't noticed.

The infant had been quiet for a long time.

"Is the baby—?" she began fearfully.

"Asleep. I think." Jake opened his coat. The baby's eyes were closed, and her fists were curled against her cheeks like small pink shells.

"Would you hold her while I look around?" Jake asked.

"Of course." Mariel unbuttoned her coat. "I'll hug her inside, next to my sweater."

Carefully Jake transferred the sleeping baby to Mariel's waiting arms, and she drew her inside her coat.

Jake couldn't help feeling tender toward both of them. The baby was so helpless, and Mariel's face was white and strained. He wondered how much longer she'd be able to hold up—and how much longer she would have to.

"You must be freezing," he said, thinking that Mariel was really quite small and more fragile than he had thought.

She nodded. She looked extremely uncomfortable, but not one word of complaint had fallen from her lips throughout this journey, and he had to admire that.

"I won't go far away. Maybe I'd better take the flashlight," he said, picking it up from the log where Mariel had put it.

"I won't be able to see you," Mariel said shakily. Her eyes were like bottomless black pools, and he saw in that moment how scared she really was.

"I'll call to you from time to time," he said, and she nodded. He thought for a moment of leaving the flashlight with her, but what good would that do? He wouldn't be able to see a thing without it.

"Go ahead," Mariel said, wrapping herself around the baby. He saw that Mariel's teeth were chattering, and that she was trying to conceal it from him.

"I hate leaving you here in the pitch dark."

"Just go," she said. "The sooner you leave, the sooner you'll be back."

"Mariel…" He wanted to tell her something to reassure her, but he couldn't think of anything.

"Go," she whispered, her voice barely audible above the sound of the softly falling sleet.

With one last look at both of them—it was a scene that Jake knew would be imprinted on his mind for all time—he turned and forced himself to walk away.

THE FLASHLIGHT made eerie shadows among the trees as Jake walked away from her, and Mariel bent her head down to protect the baby's. She had never felt so completely and awfully alone.

But she wasn't alone. She had the baby.

Jake called to her once or twice, and eventually she

saw the beam from the flashlight wavering in another direction. After that, she couldn't see Jake at all.

The baby fussed, and Mariel tried to see her face but couldn't. She felt water dripping off the tip of her nose, and the baby started to cry when it fell in her face. Mariel covered the infant's face with the dry end of her scarf and tried to comfort her, and eventually the cries tapered off into hiccups.

Now that she wasn't moving, Mariel realized the full extent of her exhaustion. She was so tired that she didn't have enough energy to get up off the log, but she thought she should rise and stamp her feet to get her circulation going. She forced herself to stand, surprised at how rubbery her legs felt. Somewhere overhead, a branch cracked under the weight of accu-mulated ice, crashing through tree limbs and landing on the ground behind her.

Mariel sat down again. She was trembling. There might be bears in these woods, or wolves. She hadn't seen the flashlight beam in a while, and Jake hadn't called. She hoped he was all right.

The cold had numbed her face and her feet and her hands. She thought of her parents, who had gone to Africa six months ago to help with famine-relief efforts. They would be warm. They might be on vacation for the Christmas holiday; her mother had written that they might go on a photo safari. It would be adventurous and different, she'd said.

I'll show you adventurous and different, Mariel thought. She wished she'd joined her parents for Christmas, as they'd asked her to. She wished she'd done anything but wander off the interstate and follow the directions of a bushy-bearded man at a Magic Minimart.

She closed her eyes, willing herself to be in Africa.

She saw gazelles leaping across her field of vision, antelopes, and an elephant lumbering toward a river in the distance. The weather was warm, and she was so tired that all she wanted to do was sleep.

Her head fell forward, and it was too much trouble to lift it. She would never open her eyes again, she would sleep here forever, and she would be warm....

"Oh, no, you won't," said a voice in front of her. "Open your eyes, Mariel."

She wanted to speak, but the words wouldn't come out. And her eyes wouldn't open.

"Mariel," said the voice, which was somehow strange and familiar at once.

With great effort, Mariel forced her eyelids apart. In front of her, only a few feet away, stood the little man from the Magic Minimart.

"Who—Who—" she stammered.

"You sound like a frozen owl. Get up! If you don't, you'll freeze to death!" The man's white beard bristled, and his blue eyes were stern.

"But—"

"Hurry up! You have to go find Jake!"

She didn't know what made her follow his instructions; certainly the last time she'd done what he suggested, she'd found herself in a mess. *This* mess. Nevertheless, she struggled to her feet.

"Now get going. No, not *that* way. The other way. That's right. Keep walking through the trees. You'll see the path. Take good care of the baby. She needs you." And with that, the man disappeared.

Mariel blinked her eyes. Had she really seen him, or had he been a dream, like the gazelles and the antelopes?

Her eyes had adjusted to the darkness. She saw a path

leading through the trees, a path that she could have sworn hadn't been there before, and she stumbled along it, unsure whether it was the right thing to do. Jake had said to wait for him. And she hadn't heard a sound from him for a long time.

"Jake?" she called, but her voice was so weak that she was sure he wouldn't hear, and she wasn't surprised when he didn't answer.

A MAN ALONE would have a better chance of making it to safety than a man burdened with a woman and a child. Jake couldn't help it; he thought about hoofing it back to his truck, solo. Yet he knew he would never actually do it. Jake Travis was a man who lived up to his responsibilities, and he considered it his fault that Mariel was in this predicament.

He regretted his gruffness toward Mariel back at the hunter's blind, but he'd had to get her moving somehow, and being short with her had seemed like the only way to do it, considering all the commotion she was making over the baby. She sure liked that kid; she didn't seem to mind that the baby might slow them down.

Jake wasn't much for praying, but he found himself doing it. He had to find a place where they could get out of the sleet, a place where they could stay warm. He would probably survive a night in the open, but Mariel might not. No telling what being out in this weather would do to the baby. Jake hadn't mentioned it to Mariel, but the kid hadn't moved much after the last time it cried.

The dirt road continued for fifty yards or so. He veered off the path where a huge fallen tree blocked it, and he changed direction a few times, memorizing his path so that he would be able to return to Mariel and the baby.

The woods were thick here, and icicles had formed on all the branches. When he realized that he had wandered away from the road, he stopped and beamed the flashlight upward. He was shocked to see that he had come up against a sheer rock cliff.

He whistled under his breath. They wouldn't be moving on in this direction, at least. He stood there, taking stock. Perhaps the downed tree he had passed earlier could form the basis for a shelter. They could dig out the ground beneath the trunk and crawl under it.

"Jake?"

He heard Mariel's voice close behind him. "Mariel, how did you find me?" he asked, because he had taken a circuitous route and had had no sense of her following him.

"It wasn't hard."

As Jake swung around, the beam from his light pinned Mariel's pale face in its glare, and he realized that she was barely able to stand. The baby made no sound, and that frightened him.

"You should have stayed where you were," he said, more sharply than he'd intended.

"I was worried. I called, and you didn't answer." She moved toward him, a wraithlike figure in the fog, and he reached out and drew her to him.

"Looks like this is the end of the road," he said, swinging the beam of the flashlight along the face of the cliff.

Mariel didn't answer, and when he looked down at her, he saw that the light had gone out of her eyes.

"Can you take the baby?" she asked shakily. "I want to sit down someplace."

He reached for the bundle, but as he did so, the dimming circle of light from the flashlight picked out a shadow on the face of the cliff.

"Wait," he said to Mariel, sprinting past her. He scraped his knuckles on the rock as he pulled away brambles. He discovered a waist-high hollow in the wet rock, and when he shone the light inside, the hollow expanded into a small cave. The remains of a camp fire were scattered across the sandy floor.

"Hey! I've found something!" he shouted. A glance at Mariel told him that she was swaying as if her feet would no longer support her weight. He rushed back to her and slid a supporting arm around her shoulders.

"Come on, you can make it. It's a cave, and inside it looks dry."

Wordlessly she let him propel her to the opening, and he carefully took the baby and handed her the flashlight to light her way. She stumbled once as she tried to climb into the opening, which formed a downward chute ending in the larger room of the cave. He felt helpless to assist her, and, since she was carrying the flashlight, he couldn't see her. All was dark.

Light returned when Mariel finally dragged herself into the cave. Carefully shielding the baby's face from the prickly brambles, Jake crawled through the chute. He literally fell into the cave, regaining his balance by grabbing a projecting overhang near the entrance.

The cave was about a foot higher than his six feet, and, judging from the evidence of old camp fires, a place where other people had found shelter in the past. It was dank and damp and smelled of wood smoke, but their having found it was nevertheless a kind of miracle.

The baby stirred against his chest. Mariel sprawled on the sand floor, clutching the flashlight.

Safe, Jake thought. *We're safe.*

Chapter Three

Mariel was shivering violently. A thread of blood trickled down the side of her face from a scratch inflicted by the brambles. She slumped against the smoke-blackened wall of the cave, scarcely able to sit up.

"Mariel? Are you all right? Mariel?" Jake crouched beside her, and the baby in his arms whimpered.

Mariel couldn't answer. She had thoughts, but they wouldn't shape themselves into words. She was thinking *dry,* and *hungry,* and *baby,* and then, finally, *What should we do about the baby?* which made her, with the utmost effort, focus her blurred vision on Jake and the infant nestled in his arms.

"Can you hold her for a minute?" Jake was saying urgently.

With difficulty, Mariel adjusted her position to form a lap, her gaze locked on Jake's. With his face only inches from hers, she was all too aware of the complexity of the emotions flooding his dark eyes. In that moment she wanted nothing more than to sink into their warm depths, but she denied herself that comfort. Right now, there was the baby to think about.

The infant was thrashing her head fretfully from side to side, and her tiny lips were tinted blue. Jake was alarmed about her condition. He had expected her to be rosy and pink, the way she had been when they found her.

"You can't hold the baby against your wet coat," Jake said. Mariel fumbled with her coat buttons with weak fingers until Jake said, "Let me."

Cradling the baby in the crook of one arm, he shed his soggy glove and, one after the other, slid the buttons through their buttonholes. Under her coat, Mariel wore a white lamb's wool sweater that buttoned up the front. The collar of the sweater was damp, but the rest of it was warm and dry. She wore corduroy slacks, and Jake carefully laid the baby in her lap.

Jake didn't know who worried him most, the baby or Mariel. The thing was, neither of them was in good shape. Mariel, with her difficulty in unbuttoning her coat and her vague, slurred speech, was showing symptoms of hypothermia, and as a camper from way back, Jake knew the dangers. Hypothermia, subnormal body temperature, could kill.

He had to raise her body temperature, and the baby's, too. Mariel was a small woman, fine-boned, with little body fat to keep her warm. The shivering would help, it was a good sign, but it wasn't enough.

Mariel's scarf had fallen away to reveal a mass of pale curls tumbling across her shoulders. The scratch on her face was still bleeding, and without thinking, Jake reached out to rub the blood away. His thumb caressed her cheek, and if she hadn't been shivering so much he might have forgotten his purpose. At the moment, all he wanted to think about was the rose-petal texture of her skin.

"The baby," she whispered.

Jake slid his hands between the tiny body and Mariel's thighs. The baby began to wail, and Mariel made a nest of her arms. As soon as the baby felt Mariel's warmth, she quieted.

"Her blanket is so wet," Mariel said, but the words gave Jake hope—if not for the child, at least for Mariel. She was thinking, and that was a good sign.

Jake stripped the baby's blanket away. A quick inspection told him that the child's long flannel nightgown was damp around the bottom, but dry everywhere else, so he decided it was safe for the baby to wear. But he knew he'd better check Mariel's clothes, too.

"Jake," she said, moistening her lips with her tongue in a gesture that was unconsciously erotic. "I want to hold the baby next to my skin. We could warm each other."

"You want me to unbutton your sweater?" he asked.

"Please." She plucked at the tiny mother-of-pearl buttons marching in a straight row down her sweater front, but it was clear that she didn't have the strength to undo them herself.

Jake hesitated.

"Can you help?" she asked. Slowly he reached out and slid the top button out of its buttonhole. Damn, but the skin of her throat was soft.

It didn't take him long to part the sides of her sweater. Her bra seemed to be made out of cobwebs; he could see through it to the pale pink nipples, puckered from the cold. Mariel was exceptionally well endowed for a small woman, and Jake looked away, entirely unnerved by what the sight of her did to him. He wanted her. It was crazy. In her present state, he could easily take advantage of her, but of course he wouldn't. If only she weren't so beautiful and so desirable and so spirited; if only he weren't so powerfully attracted to her.

He forced himself to attend to business. He slid his arms under the baby and lifted it to Mariel's chest, guiding her arms around it. The baby hid her breasts, and he sighed in temporary relief.

He felt the bottoms of the blue corduroy pants that Mariel wore. The cuffs were cold and wet. He slid his hand upward to check the extent of the dampness, noting that she stiffened slightly as his hand went higher.

Her slacks were wet to the knee. "You're going to have to take these off," he said.

"Wh-what?"

"Take off those slacks. In your condition, it could be deadly to wear wet clothes," he said, clipping his words. He wasn't sure he was making any sense to her; hypothermia victims sometimes lacked judgment and reasoning power.

Mariel's only response was uncontrolled shivering, and that, added to the fact that she obviously was unable to do anything for herself, told Jake that he'd better act swiftly.

"I'm going to pull off your boots and socks and hang them up to dry," he told her. Mariel made no objection, and he slid the boots off her feet, then her cotton socks. Her feet were slim and white, dainty and well formed.

"Now the slacks," he said, reaching under her raincoat. "I'm going to pull these down over your hips. Help if you can."

He unfastened her belt buckle and yanked at the zipper, which immediately caught on a lace flounce in her underpants.

Swearing, Jake wiggled the zipper fastener, which refused to let go. It was firmly stuck.

He glanced at Mariel. Her eyes were open. She was watching him, her chin resting on the baby's head.

"Just what I need," he said tightly. "Another problem."

"Go ahead and rip it if you must," she said, looking embarrassed. He couldn't imagine *why* she would feel embarrassed. She was beautiful, her skin sweetly scented and inviting, her abdomen gently rounded between her hipbones. The triangle of lace that was giving him so much trouble did little to hide the pale curls beneath.

To his relief, when he again tried easing the zipper pull down the slide, the lace sprang free without tearing. In a moment Jake was shimmying the corduroy over Mariel's hipbones. She lifted her hips slightly, her eyes closed.

Jake found it difficult to look at her as if she were an object instead of an attractive woman with considerable sex appeal. He wasn't prepared for the way the sight of her body sent lightning sparking along every one of his nerve endings, and he had to resist to the fullest his impulse to let his fingers stray from their task.

"Tough duty," she said, as he was hanging her corduroys from a convenient rock projection, and he realized that she was trying to make light of the situation for his sake, as well as hers. When he turned back to her, she had already wrapped herself modestly in her coat. Her feet looked shriveled and cold, and that reminded him of his next task.

"I've got to build a fire right away," he said. Mariel's only reply was a nod.

Jake inspected their shelter. The cave was about seven feet wide and perhaps ten feet deep, its walls ledged, its floor a combination of rock and sand. As it played across the back of the cave, the beam of the flashlight picked out a small stack of firewood, which Jake knew was their salvation. It would be impossible to find dry wood outside.

He looked back at Mariel. She was still shivering, but not as violently as before. Her hair was drying in soft, fetching ringlets around her face; the folds of her coat barely hinted at the sweet curves of her body.

Tough duty, indeed, he thought to himself. It was going to be very hard for him to keep his behavior within the bounds of respectability. Mariel Evans was an exceptionally lovely woman. And he was a healthy, red-blooded American male.

MARIEL KEPT her eyes closed while Jake went about the serious business of building a fire. She was shaken by the force of her feelings. Jake's hands had touched her skin as little as possible, and yet, as innocent as his touch had been, she felt physically disturbed by it.

The warmth of the baby against her breasts felt oddly erotic. Jake's scent drifted up from the baby's skin—a woodsy after-shave underlaid by the pungent odor of wet wool. The baby's head pressed tightly against a nipple, engendering a heat that coursed through her veins and made her think about the crisp efficiency of Jake's hands as they had undressed her. The cold must have affected her in a very strange way. Who else in this predicament would be fantasizing about a man whom she had met only hours ago?

For once she regretted her penchant for wispy underwear. It was her secret indulgence. Now she thought she would have been better off with something utilitarian and opaque. Jake had gotten an eyeful, despite his feigned disinterest.

The baby made little snuffling noises, and she realized suddenly that it was rooting against her bare skin, searching for something to eat. It was basic instinct for a baby to do this, she figured. But suddenly she couldn't bear the stimulation of the warm, seeking mouth against her breast, and she abruptly changed position so that the baby's face rested against the soft cable knit of her sweater.

"I need something to use for tinder," Jake said, breaking into her thoughts.

Mariel was grateful for this reminder of practical matters. "Look in my bag. There's a notepad I seldom use."

Jake found the pad and crushed the paper into wads. When he dug into his pack and emerged with matches in a waterproof canister, Mariel thanked her lucky stars that she was sharing this experience with an outdoorsy man who had some survival skills.

The tinder caught fire, and the flames, carefully nurtured by Jake, spread to the kindling. Mariel watched him as he blew on the flames, coaxing them to life. His face was rugged, his nose blunt, his mouth mobile. Not like the baby's tiny rosebud mouth, but well-shaped, the lower lip slightly pendulous, the upper one deeply grooved.

He saw her watching him, but made no comment. The fire was burning brightly, sending tongues of yellow flame leaping toward the ceiling of the cave. "How are you feeling?" he asked gruffly.

"Better."

He picked up her hand and closed his fingers around her wrist. "I want to check your pulse. I'm worried about you." He kept his eyes on his watch, and Mariel felt her pulse beating against his fingertips.

"You're fine," he said finally. He dropped her wrist and took a thermos from his pack. He poured milk into the metal cap and heated it over the flames. Mariel slid her feet even closer to the fire and flexed her toes in pleasure.

"Here," Jake said gruffly, holding out the cup of warm milk.

"We should save it for the baby."

"You need it. I'll heat some for her after you're through," he told her.

But Mariel's hand shook so much that she couldn't wrap her fingers around the cup.

"I'll help." Leaning toward her, Jake placed his hand over hers and guided the cup to her lips. She drank slowly, the milk warming her as it went down. It was no more than two or three ounces, but Mariel immediately began to feel stronger, and soon she stopped shivering. The fire was a roaring blaze now, the smoke disappearing into a crack in the cave's ceiling.

Jake's expression was unreadable in the firelight. He knelt beside her, his jacket open to reveal a gray turtleneck sweater that defined the firm pectoral muscles underneath. Mariel drew a long, deep breath, hoping to infuse her addled brain with clarity and judgment. The tingle she felt was not due to the return of warmth to her half-frozen limbs; it was directly attributable to the presence of Jake Travis.

She pulled herself together when the baby began to whimper. "We'd better feed her," she told him, gazing at the bundle in her arms. She wondered what, if any, effect exposure to the cold had had on the child. She looked better now, Mariel thought.

"Aren't babies supposed to drink formula from a can, not cow's milk?" Jake asked anxiously.

"We don't have any formula," she reminded him.

"I don't want to harm the baby, that's all," he said.

For someone who had reacted with anger at his first sight of the baby, Jake had softened quite a bit. He looked so concerned that Mariel's heart went out to him.

"We're talking survival here. We have no choice," she said.

"How much milk would a baby drink at one feeding, anyway?"

"I have no idea," Mariel admitted. They both looked at the baby, trying to assess her capacity.

"She's not very big. Her stomach couldn't hold much," Jake said.

"Three ounces?"

"Maybe," he agreed. "How are we going to feed her?"

"I don't know."

They looked at each other blankly.

"Maybe if we soaked a piece of cloth in the milk, she could suck on it. I saw that in a movie once. Trouble is, they were feeding motherless puppies," Jake said ruefully.

"I carry eyedrops in my purse," Mariel said. "Maybe the eyedropper?"

"It might work."

"Get it, please. There's an unopened package of eyedrops in my cosmetic bag," she said. The baby began to cry, the noise ricocheting off the cave's walls so that no more discussion was possible.

"This must be it," Jake said, holding the box aloft. He tore off the cellophane wrapper.

Mariel raised her voice to be heard over the baby's wails. "The eyedropper should be wrapped in plastic," she said.

Jake held it up for her inspection. "Is it sterile?"

"It says so on the box," she said. "How about the

milk? Do you suppose it needs to be sterilized?'' She had a vague memory from her childhood of a neighbor boiling baby bottles in a big pan on her stove. She didn't know if anyone still did that.

''Does milk have a lot of germs?''

Mariel didn't know. She shrugged her shoulders.

''I could boil the milk in my thermos lid,'' he said. ''That might take care of it.''

''What about the taste? I think boiled milk tastes awful.''

''We don't know if she'll drink cow's milk anyway, boiled or unboiled,'' Jake said. They both regarded the baby, whose face was red from crying. She looked furious.

''If she doesn't eat something, she'll die,'' Mariel said.

''So back to the question—do we boil the milk?''

Mariel tried to think. She had friends who had babies, but she'd never paid much attention to their care. It seemed to her that her friend Carole had fed her baby canned baby formula, then switched to cow's milk poured directly into the baby bottle from a milk bottle kept in the refrigerator. Had that been at three months? Or had the baby been on formula for six months?

Mariel couldn't recall. She also didn't know the age of this baby, who appeared to be only a month or two old. But then, Mariel didn't know anything about babies. Her college degrees hadn't prepared her for a situation like this one. All she knew was that they'd better make a fast decision.

She decided. ''We'll warm the milk and give it to her as it is, but first, you'd better sterilize the thermos lid by boiling water in it, don't you think?'' she asked Jake.

''I don't know what I think,'' he said through tight

lips. "Mostly what I think is that we're ill-equipped to take care of a kid."

"I couldn't agree with you more," Mariel said, failing to control the edginess in her tone.

Jake went outside for water. While he was boiling it in the metal lid, the baby's crying grew louder and more frantic, straining their frayed nerves to the breaking point.

"Can't you keep her quiet?" Jake asked sharply.

"I'm trying," said Mariel over the din. "Hurry up, will you?"

Jake growled, "I'm doing this as fast as I can," whereupon Mariel regretted her own testiness. She turned her attention to the baby again, smoothing the golden hair, rubbing the little back under the nightgown, all to no avail. The baby was hungry, and that was that.

Jake poured out the boiled water, since there was nowhere to keep it, and sniffed the thermos lid. Mariel almost smiled, thinking that smelling it wasn't going to tell him if germs were present, germs not necessarily having odors.

Anyway, what kind of germs were they worried about? Didn't babies put all kinds of things in their mouths, such as key chains that had dropped on the floor, and the dog's chewy pieces of rawhide? And didn't most babies survive such adventures? Someday Mariel would look up the answers to all these questions. She realized that baby care was a great gap in her knowledge.

Jake, apparently satisfied that the lid from his thermos was clean enough, heated a bit of milk and drew some of it into the eyedropper.

"Here," he said, carefully transferring the dropper to

Mariel's outstretched hand. She smiled a silent thank-you when their hands touched.

With Jake watching over her shoulder, Mariel dribbled a few drops of milk into the baby's open mouth. The infant stopped crying immediately and looked mystified.

"There, that's better, isn't it?" crooned Mariel. The baby closed her lips around the eyedropper, her eyes never leaving Mariel's face.

The dropper wasn't the best feeding apparatus in the world, because it wasn't suited for sucking, something that the baby expected to be able to do. As fast as Mariel filled the eyedropper, the baby drank, but it was frustrating to watch the baby trying to suck on the hard plastic tube and to listen to her fussing while Mariel refilled it.

"Damned inefficient," Jake said.

Mariel glared at him. "Would you like to try it?"

"No, no," he said, backing away. He watched them for a few more moments. "I feel helpless," he said, giving her the idea that it was an admission that he seldom, if ever, made. "Usually when something needs doing, I can make something to do the job. I'm a fair plumber, a pretty good electrician, and a bang-up carpenter. This has me stumped."

"Me too," she offered, and he grinned at her.

After she had swallowed three or four ounces of milk, the baby stopped eating and puckered her little face as if she were going to cry again.

"Uh-oh," said Jake. "I think something's wrong."

"She has to be burped."

"Burped? How?"

"She's supposed to be patted on the back. I think it brings up the air bubbles."

"Give her to me. I'll try it."

Carefully he took the baby from Mariel.

"You'll have to drape her over your shoulder," Mariel said.

"There, there," Jake said to the baby in a soothing voice.

"She's waiting for you to do something," Mariel told him. She wanted to giggle; Jake, so masculine and rugged, looked absurd with the baby slung over his shoulder. He was holding her as if she were a sack of wood chips.

Jake thumped the baby between the shoulder blades, producing nothing but a startled look.

"Not so hard," Mariel hastened to say, and when Jake experimented with a few tentative taps, the baby obliged by producing a sonorous belch.

"That was pretty good, wasn't it?" Jake asked, sounding smug.

"Better than I could have done," Mariel said, meaning it.

The immediate problem of hunger solved, Mariel reached over and gingerly felt the baby's diaper.

"She's sopping wet."

"Nowhere in this cave have I found a stack of diapers. Have I?" Jake said to the baby, who yawned.

"If my scarf weren't so wet, we might use it as a diaper," Mariel said, though she wasn't at all sure about it's suitability.

The discarded scarf lay in a damp heap on the sand, its fringe clumped together. "It's too stiff and woolly. Babies' diapers need to be soft, like cotton. At least I know that much," Jake said. He was still jaunty from his success at bringing up the baby's air bubble.

"Well, we've got to think of something," Mariel

said, staring pensively at the baby, who looked back at her unblinkingly and with great interest. There was trust in that gaze, and Mariel wondered how on earth they were going to meet the complex needs of an infant using only the things they had on hand.

"I know," Jake said suddenly.

"What?"

"What we can use for diapers."

"Is it bigger than a breadbox?" Mariel asked, with more than a hint of sarcasm.

"Never mind. Here, take the baby and turn your head," he told her.

She took the baby, but what he'd said didn't register until he began unbuckling his belt.

"You're not going to take off your clothes?" Mariel blurted out.

"Only my long johns. They'll make good diapers," he replied, seemingly unperturbed.

"Oh," Mariel said faintly. There was nowhere in this cave where he could go for privacy. He'd have to take his pants off in front of her.

"Don't worry—I'm wearing briefs underneath. I often dress warmly at this time of year. In my job, I sometimes have to work in unheated areas."

Mariel could have sworn that she saw the hint of a grin. "Don't we have something else we can use?" she asked skeptically.

"Do you have a better idea, Mariel?"

She realized the futility and folly of objecting to what he had in mind. "No. *No.* It sounds fine. Just do it, okay?"

"Don't look at me, if it'll embarrass you," he said, mollified.

Mariel turned her head away and tried to ignore the

sounds of his undressing until she discovered that, by squinting out of the corners of her eyes, she could see him clearly by the light of the fire.

First he shucked off his boots, and then his wool socks, which he hung to dry above the fire. Then, slowly and deliberately, he unbuckled his belt.

She managed to close her eyes before he glanced sharply in her direction, but at the sound of the zipper, she peeked under her lids.

Jake's worn jeans were molded to his body as if they had grown there, and their dampness revealed the firmness of his thighs, the compact curves of his buttocks.

As graceful as a panther, he stepped out of the jeans and dropped them onto the ledge next to his socks. As he pulled down his white cotton-knit long johns, Mariel saw that his thighs were muscled and lightly furred with dark hair. The briefs he wore underneath were brief indeed, revealing a tapering V of hair that disappeared under the waistband, near the well-defined bulge below. She could hardly pull her eyes away as he stood, clad only in turtleneck and briefs, the hard contours of his body limned by firelight and gilded by its glow.

She caught her breath at the sight of him, thinking that she'd never seen a man who so exuded sexuality. Even here, in this miserable cave, Jake Travis had that indefinable animal magnetism that made woman weak, and though it could be argued that she was already weak, her ordeal hadn't caused the catch in her throat when she looked at him, or the tension vibrating just below her skin.

She had been aware of his arresting good looks from the moment they met. His mere touch had been enough to banish her cold-induced stupor. Now that she was being treated to the full impact of his physical presence, she was brought up short by a confusing tangle of emotions.

He caught her staring at him. It might have been her imagination, but he seemed to draw himself up to his full height, a desirable male exhibiting himself more fully to a female who was clearly admiring.

"I thought you weren't planning to look," he said, sounding amused.

"I'm not *looking,*" she lied. "I have to aim my eyes somewhere, after all."

"I never thought about it that way," he said, but she knew he was laughing at her.

Let him, she told herself. She'd have had to be deaf, dumb and blind to ignore the chemistry between them, but she was well aware that in this survival situation it could only make things more difficult.

"I think I'll leave my jeans beside the fire until they dry," he said. She made no comment.

Jake anchored his jeans to a ledge above the fire with a rock, and then he knelt and withdrew a knife from his pack, his movements swift and economical. The firelight emphasized the braided muscles of his thighs and calves as he squatted and spread his discarded long johns across his knees. His hair was dark, and longer than she had thought at first; it had sprung into a shining frame for his face. Intent on his task, he didn't look up, seeming totally unaware that she was observing him so closely.

There was something strange and elemental in this scene. Mariel could almost imagine that they were cave dwellers in some ancient age, making do with what was available. He was the provider and she the mother of the child who slept in her arms, snug and warm....

She awoke with a start. Jake was shaking her arm, his face contorted with fear.

"Don't go to sleep!" he said.

"I only—"

"It's all right," he said, the sparks fading from his eyes and his shoulders slumping when he realized that she had only been drowsing.

"I must have dropped off for a moment," she began, but he silenced her with a finger across her lips.

"One moment you were wide awake, watching me work, and the next minute your head was nodding and you didn't hear me say your name. I thought—"

"I'm fine," she said. She shifted her position to avoid the rock that was biting into her backbone, wondering how she could have slept while so uncomfortable.

He checked her pulse, holding tight to her wrist. "Normal," he pronounced.

"I told you I'm okay," she said.

"I'm still worried about hypothermia. You shouldn't sleep yet—it could be dangerous."

"I'll try to stay awake," she promised. She nearly told him about the appearance of the man with the white bushy beard in the woods earlier, when she had almost fallen asleep. Jake didn't seem to be in the mood to hear a fanciful story, but she couldn't help musing over what she had seen. Was the little man real? Or had he been a dream?

Jake went back to the fire, squatting there as he contemplated the destruction of his long underwear.

"I wonder what size a diaper is," he mused.

"She's a small baby," Mariel answered. "Cut them into large pieces, and we'll fold them to the size we need." The baby in her arms slept openmouthed, her small puffs of breath stirring the fuzz of Mariel's sweater. Her upturned nose was smaller than the tip of Mariel's thumb, and her cheeks were fat and round. She looked like a little cherub, and already Mariel knew that if it were necessary, she wouldn't hesitate to put her life on the line for this baby.

She would have liked to ask Jake if he felt the same way, but he was making short work of cutting up his long johns, holding up the resulting pieces of fabric for her approval.

"Okay," she said when he had finished. "Let's change her diaper."

"You deserve the honors," Jake said.

"I've never diapered a baby."

"Neither have I," he confessed.

Mariel sighed. "All right, I'll try. We need a clean place to lay her down," she said.

There was only the sandy floor. "Here," Jake said, spreading his jacket over the sand. The inside was warm and dry, and Mariel carefully lifted the baby out of her coat and laid her on the jacket lining. She quickly closed her sweater over her breasts, but not before Jake saw a tantalizing glimpse of her lacy bra.

Mariel unpinned the diaper. The baby awoke, fussed briefly, then saw Mariel's face and began to kick and coo.

"She acts as if life's going on as usual," commented Jake, who looked on from above, his arms folded over his chest.

"Maybe that's why she's here. To remind us that it should," Mariel said briskly, sliding the clean white cotton knit beneath the baby's buttocks.

Mariel's observation took Jake by surprise. For one thing, it made him look at this situation in a new way. For another, it clued him in to Mariel's thought processes. He liked her knack for putting a positive spin on things.

"There," Mariel said, smiling down at the baby. The child waved her fists in the air, and Mariel gathered her into her arms. "Is her blanket dry yet?"

Jake checked. "Nope," he said, hoping that Mariel would open her sweater again.

While he was thinking that, Mariel said, "You'd better put this dirty diaper outside. If only we had something to wash it in, like a pan of some kind."

Jake went back to the stack of firewood and emerged from the shadows triumphantly, a beat-up old tin pot in his hand. The bottom was fire-blackened, but as far as Jake could see, it didn't have any holes.

"I'll set it out to catch water," Jake said, and, to his disappointment, Mariel had already snuggled the baby inside her sweater when he returned.

"Are you warm enough?" he asked her.

She nodded, barely able to keep her eyes open.

Jake regarded her for a moment. Her cheeks were rosy again, and she had brushed her hair behind her ears. She had Dresden-doll coloring, delicate and comely, and her eyes sparkled. It was all he could do not to bend over and kiss her pink lips.

He did lean closer, using the baby as an excuse. "She's pretty, isn't she?" he asked, but he wasn't looking at the baby. He was studying the cleft in Mariel's chin, hoping she wouldn't notice.

"She's a wonderful baby," Mariel agreed. "You like her, don't you?" She watched Jake anxiously for his response. Somehow it seemed important that he love this infant, that he harbor the same tender feelings toward her that she did.

Jake didn't answer right away. "She's okay, I

guess," he said reluctantly, but from his tone of voice
Mariel knew that he was as taken with the baby as she
was.

They sat silently, watching the baby breathe. Smoke
curled up from the fire toward some unseen outlet in
the cave roof, and sparks danced in an occasional gust
of wind that penetrated the sheltering brambles at the
entrance. Outside, the sleet continued to fall, holding
them prisoner.

"There's half a sandwich in my pack," Jake said
quietly.

"We'll split it," Mariel said, and soon he had cut the
sandwich into two portions and was handing one to her.
Jake heated water in the thermos cap, and they sipped
alternately from it.

"I have an apple, too. We can eat it in the morning,"
Jake said.

Mariel nodded, and after a while he saw her head
falling to one side. She jerked it up again.

"Let's talk, so you won't go to sleep," he said.

"You talk," she said.

"That would put you to sleep for sure. Tell me about
where you live, your family, your job."

Mariel sighed and shifted position again. "I live in
an apartment with a bay window overlooking a garden—" she began, but he interrupted her.

"What kind of garden? Vegetables? Flowers?"

"Both, but I love the flowers best. Do you know that
the Victorians wrote a language of the flowers? Mistletoe, for instance. It means 'Give me a kiss.' " She
stopped talking suddenly, looking flustered.

To fill the gap in the conversation, Jake said, "Is your
apartment big? Small?"

"Two bedrooms. And it's not far from the museum where I work," she told him.

"I never knew anyone who was a folklorist."

"I'm surprised. In this part of Virginia, there are probably all kinds of stories the local people tell, legends to be collected."

"Maybe so. I don't run into them much, that's all. I've only been in Virginia for a short time—moved here from Atlanta around Christmastime three years ago, in fact. I think I left Atlanta mostly *because* it was Christmas, because that way I could avoid all the hoopla that I wasn't part of," Jake said.

"Well, my family was small, since I was an only child, but I always loved the 'hoopla,'" said Mariel.

"Must be nice," Jake said noncommittally.

"I guess I was spoiled, in a way. Everything I wished for—no matter how silly—somehow came true at Christmas. A bicycle once, a puppy another year, my grandparents flying in for a visit—all were wishes of mine."

"I think I would have wished for a Lamborghini when I was sixteen, and maybe a football scholarship, even though I never played," Jake said with a grin.

"Well, my wishes had to be within reason. I mean, it wouldn't have done any good to wish for the moon on a silver platter, because it's an impossibility."

"These three wishes you're always making... Now that you're an adult, don't you feel ridiculous doing it?" he asked curiously.

"Why would I? Wishes *can* come true, Jake. Magic *can* happen. There *are* such things as miracles," she said.

"Hogwash," he said amiably.

"Hogwash! Listen, Jake Travis, it was no mere co-

incidence that you found this cave when we needed it.
Or that we happened along when the baby needed us.
And let me ask you this—how often do you have milk
left in your thermos after lunch?''

His eyes shone mischievously as he bent to stir the
fire. ''Often, in fact. Sometimes the guys on the job go
to a convenience store and pick up a six-pack of cola.
Or, like today, it's cold and somebody offers us a hot
drink for lunch,'' he said.

''Okay, so I struck out on that last one. But there's
still the cave and the baby. Don't forget that,'' she said.

''It's probably safe for you to sleep now.''

''You're ready to shut me up, right?'' she asked him
with a glint of humor.

''Not exactly,'' he hedged, thinking that he could go
on listening to her high musical voice all night long.
She had a way of talking that slid up and down the
scales, a sound most pleasing to the ear. To his ear, at
any rate.

''I'm glad to hear that. Tomorrow I may want to talk
a lot more. You're a good listener, Jake.''

It was a compliment he hadn't heard before, or at
least couldn't remember hearing, which amounted to the
same thing. He wasn't sure if he should say thank you,
so he only nodded his head slightly. Mariel wasn't like
any women he knew; most of them were practical and
down-to-earth. Not that Mariel wasn't, but she had another, more evanescent quality too, one that he couldn't
quite put his finger on. She had a lot of charm, that was
for sure.

''There's no place to stretch out except on the sand.
If you'd like, I'll hold the baby while you get settled,''
he said.

"At least we're not out in the cold," she answered as he took the child in his arms.

"And to think it's all because of magic," he said, teasing her.

"I'm glad you're starting to think my way," she tossed back, her eyes sparkling at him, and he knew that she knew that he didn't really believe, and that it was all right. He wouldn't put it past her to work on him some more, and for some reason, he was actually looking forward to it, to sparring with her, to watching her expressive face as she spoke so earnestly.

"I'm ready," she said when she had arranged herself on the sand, and Jake handed the child to her. Mariel tucked the baby inside her sweater again and lay down on her side, flexing her legs to curve her body protectively around the child and pillowing her head on her tote bag.

"Aren't you going to sleep?" she asked, looking up at him. Her eyes were bright and glowing.

The two of them had established a camaraderie, a rapport. He hoped she felt it as strongly as he did.

"I'm going to sit up for a while. I want to keep an eye on the fire," he said, because he knew that he could not lie down beside her without touching her.

The fire crackled and spit, and he saw Mariel tenderly stroking the pale golden hair on the baby's head. He wished it was him she was comforting.

Mariel seemed to represent everything that he didn't have in his life, everything that other people lived for, not him. He wasn't normally a sentimental guy, so maybe it was that she had taken such care to remind him of the Christmas season, or maybe it was that she looked so Madonna-like with the baby in her arms. He tried to swallow the lump in his throat, but it wouldn't go away.

When Mariel was asleep, Jake got up and brought in the thermos cap, which he had set out earlier to catch water. He heated the water and sipped it slowly, resting on his haunches. After a while, he dropped another log on the fire and lay down as far from Mariel and the baby as he deemed necessary, wrapped in his wool jacket. He was sleeping lightly when he heard Mariel moan. He shot up, instantly alert.

"Mariel?" he said.

"Cold," she muttered, and was quiet.

He felt her corduroys, which were hanging from the ledge, but they were still damp. All Jake could think of to do was what he had wanted to do all along. He nestled himself against the back of Mariel's body and twined his legs around hers for warmth. She murmured something indistinct, and he reached under her coat and slid his warm hands up along her rib cage. Her ribs seemed not like mere bones, but like a house to enclose her beating heart.

Her heart throbbed beneath his fingertips, and his thumbs brushed the soft underside of her breasts. After a few moments, his breathing automatically synchronized with hers. He smelled the wildflower scent of Mariel's shampoo, blended with the sweet, milky fragrance of the baby, and it was all he could do not to bury his face in the nape of Mariel's neck.

Jake didn't know if Mariel realized he was there, but it didn't matter. All that mattered was her warmth, and her softness, and that neither of them was alone in the dark.

Chapter Four

When Mariel awoke, she didn't know where she was. Her joints and muscles hurt, and a baby was crying.

She opened her eyes. A few feet away, glowing coals were a red eye in the dark.

All at once, Mariel remembered. The accident. Their trek along the icy road. The baby. The cave. Her exhaustion. And Jake. Where was he?

Something moved behind her, and she stiffened in alarm before she realized that it was Jake and that his legs were wrapped around hers. She twisted away as he sat up and said in a groggy tone, "Maybe the baby's hungry." He went to stir the fire, and it blazed brighter.

"You were—" she began.

"I was keeping you warm. You were cold."

"I was asleep," she said, with as much dignity as she could muster.

"So was I," he said. He got up and felt his jeans, which still hung by the fire. They were still wet, and he moved them closer to the flames, his back toward her.

"I didn't ask you to keep me warm," Mariel said.

"You cried out in your sleep." He turned and leveled a serious gaze at her. "I was only trying to help."

Mariel didn't know whether to thank him or not, but

at that moment the baby started wailing at the top of her lungs. Thankful for the distraction, Mariel sat up and studied the infant. She was putting all her energy into screaming, and one tiny pink foot had escaped the nightgown.

Jake was bringing a fresh log for the fire. "Jessica," Mariel said, raising her voice over the baby's cries. "I'm going to call her Jessica."

Jake looked harried. "Is that the most important thing you can think about, with her carrying on like that?" he asked, his eyebrows lifting.

"She has to have a name. We can't keep calling her 'the baby,'" said Mariel. Carefully she spread the baby on her lap and checked the diaper. Soaked. No wonder she was crying.

Jake had already poured milk into the metal cap and set it on a hot rock to warm.

"Diaper time again," Mariel said. Jake's hair was standing up in clumps, and he needed a shave. She didn't look so terrific, either, she imagined. She felt grungy and disheveled, and she needed to relieve herself.

Jake brought another piece of his long johns, took off his jacket, and spread it out. Mariel laid the baby— *Jessica,* she reminded herself—on it.

Jake felt one of the baby's arms. "She's cold. We should keep her covered while you're doing this," he said. He brought the pink blanket, which was finally dry, and folded it across Jessica, who was punching her arms and legs into the air as if against an unseen assailant.

"Your turn for this chore," she said to Jake above the noise. His mouth dropped open.

"I can't—"

"Of course you can," she said, smiling encouragingly.

"I told you, I've never changed a diaper," he said in bewilderment.

"Neither had I until last night," she reminded him.

"But she's kicking," he said, eyeing Jessica's flailing legs. He looked up at Mariel, who had started pulling on her boots while he was voicing his objections. "Where are you going?" he demanded.

"Out." She stood up, surprised that she felt so strong. Her knees gave nary a wobble. She took a few experimental steps, testing them out.

"Why are you going out?"

Mariel regarded him with exasperation.

"I don't see any facilities in here," she pointed out.

It was almost comical, the way he clamped his mouth shut.

"Oh," he said. "Well, uh, when you get outside the cave, turn to your left. There's a chunk of rock that provides shelter from the wind. And you'd better take the flashlight," he said. He was still looking at Jessica's wet diaper, steeling himself to remove it.

She bent, picked up the flashlight, and said sweetly, "Be careful not to stick her with a pin, won't you?" She was rewarded by a perplexed expression, and it was all she could do to keep from laughing when she emerged from the cave.

It had stopped sleeting, but at this predawn hour, it was still dark. Mariel found the boulder, took care of business and, mindful of the scratch on her face, negotiated the brambles at the cave entrance with care. Once safely inside, she switched off the flashlight and sat down beside Jake.

"How'd you do?" she asked. He was squeezing a

dropperful of milk into Jessica's mouth, concentrating mightily on the task.

"It'd be a lot easier if you could nail diapers on kids. I didn't poke *her* with the pin, but I stuck myself." He held up his pricked finger for her to see.

"But you survived," she pointed out.

"Barely. So did the baby—barely. That was supposed to be a pun," he said.

"Cute, Jake. Very cute. How much milk is left, by the way?" she asked.

"A few ounces. I'm not going to give her much this feeding. We'll need some for the morning."

"What time is it now?"

"Three o'clock in the morning."

"It doesn't seem like it. I feel so wide awake," Mariel said. She drew her bare legs under her for warmth and watched Jake's hands as they ministered so gently to the baby. They were capable hands, and she would trust them with her life. In fact, she had. She felt a warming toward him and wondered how he felt about her.

"Why did you name her Jessica?" Jake asked.

Mariel was surprised. She hadn't expected conversation. "I've always liked the name," she told him.

"Any special reason?"

"When I was in high school, dreaming about a home and family, as many girls do, I chose the names for all four of my children," she said.

He lifted his head and grinned at her. "Four?"

"I was going to have a station wagon, and I wanted to fill it with kids. I'd take them to swimming lessons in the summer, to children's concerts in the park, and all kinds of things. Jessica, Mark, Joanna and Matthew.

Those were their names. But—'' she sighed ''—I never bought that station wagon.''

"Regrets?"

"A few. I love my job. I just wish there was something *more.*"

"Like a Jessica?" he probed, glancing at her.

"I've thought about becoming a single mother. I haven't quite figured out how, that's all.''

"Shouldn't be too hard, for a woman who looks like you," he said quietly.

"Oh, that's not the problem. But there are only so many ways to go about acquiring a child. If a single woman wants a baby, she can be artificially inseminated, but it's too expensive for me to contemplate. Or she can ask a male friend to be the father, but then, what if he expects to be part of the child's life, as he has every right to do? Would I have to invite him to birthday parties and Christmas dinners for the next twenty years? I've never known a man that I wanted to put up with for that long. So that leaves adoption," she said.

Jake fed Jessica the last drops of milk from the thermos cap. "I guess you've thought about it a lot."

"And then I find a baby in the woods. It seems—it seems like a kind of gift," she said.

"She belongs to someone," Jake said, turning the drowsy infant over his shoulder.

"But to whom? And why was she there? It's almost as if someone knew we would come along to save her," Mariel said as Jessica twisted her head around to look at her. Jake was patting the baby's back, to no avail.

"She doesn't want to burp," he said.

"She will. Won't you, Jessica, darling? Come on, burp for us," coaxed Mariel.

As if on cue, Jessica brought up a bubble of air and triumphantly waved a fist in the air.

"Let me hold her for a while. You can go back to sleep," Jake said.

Mariel propped herself against the wall of the cave. "I'm not tired. I must have really been out of it before," she said. She was remembering how cozy and warm she'd felt; now she knew that it had been because of Jake's closeness. It had been his warmth, his body heat seeping through her clothes, making her comfortable, letting her sleep.

"You were dead to the world," Jake confirmed. He had derived great comfort from her. He'd have liked her to know that. And yet it seemed inappropriate to talk about it.

"It's stopped sleeting," Mariel said.

"Then we can get an early start. We should leave as soon as the sun rises," he replied.

"Sunrise is only a few hours away."

"That's why I think you should sleep," he said. "You'll need all your energy for whatever happens."

"What do you think will happen?" she asked, looking slightly alarmed.

"I don't know. But if anyone had predicted when we set out during the storm that we'd be spending the night in this cave while trying to figure out how to take care of an infant, I would have accused him of partaking of illegal hallucinogens."

"Have *you* ever done that?"

"No. What kind of question is that, anyway?" he said, halfway offended.

"One designed to find out about your habits."

"Not smart. Besides, I could have lied."

"You wouldn't."

"How do you know?"

"Because you aren't that kind of guy. You were up-front with me from the beginning by admitting that the accident was your fault, that your brakes didn't work. Any lawyer would caution you not to admit liability, but you had to tell the truth. It's in your nature," she said.

He found this conversation fascinating, not only because of where it was going, but also because it covered new territory. Usually women asked if he had been married, if he'd fathered any children, and if there was a serious relationship in his life. Also how much money he made; the answer often caused them to beat a hasty retreat.

"So," he said easily, massaging Jessica's back, "are you always so good at instant character analysis?"

"Most of the time. Men don't like it."

"Why?"

"They don't like being figured out."

"Do I?"

"You're humoring me, so you'll put up with it," she told him.

"Hmm..." he said, sliding the baby into his lap. He moved his forefinger back and forth in front of the tiny face, and the baby's Wedgwood-blue eyes tracked it.

"It's Christmas Eve day," Mariel said, stretching. "It doesn't seem much like it, does it?"

He shrugged. "What's the big deal?" he said.

She stared at him. "Well, tomorrow we will celebrate the birth of Christ, for one thing," she said. "Aren't you a Christian?"

"Supposedly. I lived in a couple of so-called Christian foster homes when I was a kid. They believed in

'Spare the rod, spoil the child,' which forever spoiled Christianity for me.''

"They beat you?"

"Me and the other kids who lived there," he said.

Jessica was sound asleep in his lap. She looked sweet and innocent and supremely helpless.

"Well, my experience of religion was Sunday school and church picnics and marching in place in front of the pew when we sang 'Onward Christian Soldiers.' And later, serving as an acolyte and reading part of the Christmas Eve service. Besides," Mariel added, "I can't understand anyone who would hit a child."

"It shouldn't happen. Ever. For any reason," Jake said tersely.

"In my house, it wouldn't. I mean, if I were lucky enough to have a child." She gazed longingly at Jessica.

"If *I* had a child, I wouldn't fill her head with all this Christmas nonsense. Santa sliding down the chimney, bringing gifts for good little girls and boys. What if you've been good and there are no gifts?" Jake asked. He meant the question to be rhetorical, and he was surprised when Mariel shot back an answer.

"The child would be soured on the whole Christmas idea, right? Like you, right?"

"Right." The word was no more than a growl deep in his throat.

"Well," she said, "no matter what you think, it's still Christmas Eve day. And I'm going to keep the season, no matter what." To Jake that seemed like a silly statement, considering that they didn't know what the day would bring. He only hoped she wouldn't break into several choruses of "Deck the Halls with Boughs of Holly" while they were confined to this damn cave.

"I'm going to catch a few more Zs," he told her, thoroughly annoyed with all this sweetness and light.

"Maybe that's a good idea," she agreed, but he thought it was mostly because she didn't want to talk to him anymore.

"Who's going to hold the baby?" she asked.

"I will. In fact, I think we should sandwich her between us. The fire's getting low, and we only have a few sticks of firewood left. It's bound to get colder in here."

She seemed uncertain, looking at him out of the corners of her eyes.

"Go ahead, lie down. I'll settle Jessica. It won't be much different from before," he said.

With one last, unfathomable look, Mariel lay down and pillowed her head on her tote bag, the way she had earlier. She jackknifed her knees and wrapped the folds of her coat close around her so that all Jake could see was the soles of her boots peeking out from under the fabric.

Carefully he wrapped the baby in the front of his coat; Jessica didn't even wake up. He slid down next to Mariel so that the baby occupied the space between her back and his chest.

"Comfortable?" he asked as he propped his head on his arm. Mariel shifted so that he felt the rounding of her derriere against his thighs. He was unprepared for his sudden arousal, and he leaned away from her under the guise of readjusting Jessica's blanket.

"Well, this isn't the Comfort Inn, you know," Mariel mumbled.

He didn't reply.

"Jake?"

"Hmm?"

"Did you remember to lock the door?"

He felt her shoulders shaking and realized that she was laughing. In a moment, he was laughing, too, and as he did, he realized that the burden of the situation had lightened with her mood.

In his experience, women always took everything so seriously. He had seldom come across one who could laugh in the face of adversity. He wanted to wrap his arms around her and pull her to him.

After a few moments, he heard Mariel's steady breathing. He should have slept, but he didn't. He was thinking that Mariel was a woman he'd like to get to know, and yet their backgrounds were so different. She was college-educated, and he wasn't. She was from a big city, and he was small-town. And if he cared about his own happiness, he'd better nip these thoughts in the bud.

THE GRAY SHAFTS OF LIGHT creeping in through the mouth of the cave woke Mariel first. She lay quietly, listening to Jake breathe. She felt Jessica resting snugly against her back, and she wondered if the bit of milk left in Jake's thermos would be enough for the baby's breakfast. One thing was certain—they would have to find civilization soon.

Civilization…people…home… At her apartment in Pittsburgh, the neighborhood kids would soon be knocking on her door, looking for handouts of candy canes. When she wasn't there, they would be disappointed. She always asked a few of them inside to help her decorate her tree. Would they tell their parents when she didn't answer their knocks? Would anyone think to notify the authorities that she was missing?

She wouldn't be missed at work; she was supposed

to be on vacation through New Year's. She had no close relatives other than her parents, who at this very moment might be going about their appointed task of feeding starving children. Little did they know that their own daughter was hungry back home in the good old U.S.A. At the moment, her stomach was so empty that it was nibbling on her backbone.

Jake sighed in his sleep. She wouldn't wake him. The baby would do that soon enough.

Jake shifted position, and she almost spoke to him. Then, her cheeks burning, she was glad that she hadn't. She could feel his erection through her coat. It was pressed hard against her back, and there was absolutely no mistaking what it was.

He apparently wasn't aware that he was pushing against her, and she had no idea whether to move away, thereby waking him and probably embarrassing both of them, or if the proper thing to do under these circumstances was to lie still and feign sleep.

She feigned sleep. She regulated her breathing, trying to keep it even, willing her stomach not to make hungry noises, when all the while her heart was racing and her head was spinning. Not to mention the rest of her, which, heaven help her, was responding the way any healthy woman's body would respond to a sexual stimulus from a good-looking man.

He awoke with a start. Mariel squeezed her eyes shut and held her breath.

Taking the baby with him, he rolled away from Mariel and lay quietly as Jessica fussed herself awake. Mariel didn't move. She remained as if frozen until Jake began to prepare the last of the milk for the baby. Then she sat up and blinked her eyes, smiling with what she thought would pass for supreme innocence.

"Good morning," he grunted, more interested in Jessica than in her. That should have pleased Mariel, but instead she felt slighted.

"How about handing me a clean diaper?" he suggested.

Silently she got up and went to the stack of dry cotton rectangles, folded two together and presented them to him. He unpinned the diaper that Jessica was wearing, looking as if he were all thumbs.

"Those diapers look dry," he said, nodding toward the ledge where they hung. "You might as well fold them up and stuff them in my pack. The way this kid goes through these things, we're going to need them." He slid the clean diaper under the baby's buttocks and drew the fabric up between her legs, pinning the corners haphazardly, his brow furrowed in concentration.

Mariel fought the urge to smile at his awkwardness and did as he suggested. As she was withdrawing her hand from the pack, the apple rolled out. She held it up. "Did you say we could eat this for breakfast?" she asked.

Jake had finished his diapering chores and had begun the slow, laborious process of feeding the baby. Jessica was fretting because she couldn't get the milk fast enough; Jake was concentrating on speeding up the process. He spared Mariel a quick, impersonal glance. "Sure," he said. "My knife's in the pack, too."

Mariel sliced the apple into quarters. She held one out toward Jake, but his hands were full.

"Here," Mariel said, holding the apple to his lips. After a quick look at her, he bit from it, chewed, and swallowed. "There's more," said Mariel, and he opened his mouth, letting her pop the bit of apple into it.

"Thanks," he said.

"Want the other piece?" she said, waving it in front of him.

He eyed it briefly. "Maybe not. I'll save it for a few minutes, and that way it'll seem like I've eaten more than I really have."

"Suit yourself," Mariel said, but she ate her half of the apple all at once, savoring every last morsel. She was just as glad that she hadn't had to feed him the last part of the apple—it seemed too intimate by far for her to be putting food in his mouth. His lips had brushed her fingertips, and it had sent shivers through her, shivers that had nothing to do with the chill and damp of the cave. Maybe he had noticed it, too, since he hadn't wanted her to feed him the rest.

Mariel busied herself with cleaning the knife while Jake finished feeding Jessica. She felt the corduroy of her slacks and found they were still too damp to wear. She moved them closer to the fire, and Jake said, "Are my jeans dry yet?"

She felt them, unable to avoid a mind's-eye picture of Jake peeling them off last night. What was wrong with her? Why wasn't she handling this better? She shouldn't be unnerved by this man—she hardly knew him.

And then she thought about waking up with him, about his erection pressed against her, and she realized that she knew him, knew some things about him well, and that her awareness was normal. But it wasn't comfortable. That was the problem. It wasn't comfortable at all.

"Well, what about my jeans? Dry or not?" Jake demanded.

"Almost," she said, dropping the fabric as if it burned her hands.

Jake ate the last quarter of the apple and stood up abruptly, leaving the baby lying on his jacket, crowding Mariel in her space. She fled to the other end of the cave, keeping an eye on him as she put the knife back in his pack and, for something to do, rearranged the things in her tote bag.

Still facing away from her, Jake pulled on his jeans. She turned her head, her hair falling over her face, as he zipped the fly with a quick flip of the wrist.

After pulling on his socks and boots, Jake took the empty thermos lid outside, which gave Mariel the opportunity to compose herself before he came back with icicles to melt. By that time, Mariel was kneeling by the fire, holding Jessica in front of her like a shield.

Mariel murmured to the baby as Jake pulled a disposable razor out of his pack and began to shave. He had no mirror, but his strokes were swift and sure. He seemed quiet, thoughtful, perhaps even dour.

At first she didn't plan to speak to him, but she couldn't stand the silence. Finally, for the purpose of testing his mood, she observed, "You travel well prepared."

"Habit," he said. He poured water over the razor to rinse it, dried it on his jeans, and returned it to the pack.

"You always carry a backpack?"

"Only when I know I'm going to have to trek miles and miles through a winter storm," he said.

"Seriously," she said, trying to cajole him into the kind of banter that had made them both feel better earlier.

"Things happen. That's why I keep it in my truck. I work far from home sometimes, and I carry the stuff I'll need if I have to spend the night. That's all," he said. He looked at her, then looked away. She had the feeling that he was edgy about being cooped up here with her and the baby, with diapers hung up to dry, nothing but the rocky floor to sit on, and not enough to eat.

As if to verify her thoughts, he said gruffly, "I'm going outside for a minute."

The call of nature or merely a longing for fresh air and a bit of freedom? Mariel didn't know. She tried to think, which wasn't easy on an almost empty stomach. What she thought was that they had to get out of here. Not only for Jessica's sake, but also so that she and Jake wouldn't end up at each other's throats.

JAKE CRAWLED through the tunnel to the outside, toward fresh air. He'd felt cramped all of a sudden: he'd felt crowded. The atmosphere inside the cave was so worrisome and tense. Mariel was beautiful and unconsciously provocative. Had she known what it did to him when she allowed her fingers to touch his lips while she was feeding him that piece of apple? Hadn't she felt the electricity vibrating between them when their eyes met, when they spoke to each other?

Maybe she was too worried about their circumstances to notice. But he noticed, and that was why he'd put on still-damp jeans. He could no longer wear only his underwear around her without giving himself away, long jacket or no.

He emerged into the cold, still thinking about Mariel, when he suddenly realized the beauty of the scene before him. The ice storm had wrought a miracle. Icicles hung from every tree branch and from every projection on the cliff, glittering in the sun. Each individual needle of the surrounding evergreens was coated with ice, and it glimmered and shimmered brighter than the tinsel on a Christmas tree. On the ground, water ran in crystalline rivulets; the air was filled with the tinkle of ice as it fell from the trees.

He wanted Mariel to see it. He called her name, his voice filled with excitement.

As Mariel came out of the cave with Jessica in her arms, Jake held back the brambles and helped her get her footing. He watched her eyes widen as an expression of delight spread over her face.

"Oh, Jake, isn't it beautiful?" she murmured, her breath frosty in the air.

"Like a winter wonderland," he agreed in a hushed voice.

"Didn't I tell you about miracles?" she asked him.

"Miracles," he said staunchly, "had nothing to do with this. A winter ice storm, that's what did it. It could have happened on any night."

"But we found the baby last night, and now this," Mariel reminded him.

"And this morning we have nothing to eat. If someone were granting miracles, I think he'd leave us a box of granola, at the very least. Or maybe a few sticks of firewood, since we're getting low," he said wryly.

"Let's gather up our things and leave here as soon as we can," Mariel said.

"Too late," he said, gesturing at the clouds gathering behind the mountains in the distance. "Another storm is on the way."

"Another! But it can't be! We just had a storm," she said, though the clouds were all too visible, hunkering on the horizon.

"Just another one of those miracles of yours," Jake said with a sly look that Mariel ignored. "Besides," he said, "you should be happy to have a safe place to ride out this new storm. Remember yesterday? I don't think either of us wants to go through something like that again.''

"I'm sick of that cave. And Jessica needs something to eat. We can't stay here any longer. We've got to go.''

Jake could see that Mariel was prepared to be stubborn about this, but he was no longer sure that there were houses around here.

"Go? No way. A few hours and the storm will have passed over,'' he said. He cocked his head and assessed the clouds with an experienced eye before sliding a comforting arm around Mariel's shoulders. "We'll be on our way by early afternoon,'' he said soothingly.

"What's Jessica going to eat? What are *we* going to eat?'' she said, her inflection rising unnaturally at the end of each sentence. She didn't want Jake to notice, but she felt as if she were going to cry.

"We'll have water to drink,'' Jake said calmly.

"Water! Maybe we can survive for a while on water, but what about the baby? And we only have one stick of firewood left,'' Mariel reminded him, exasperated that he wouldn't see this her way.

"I was thinking that I'd walk along the face of the cliff and try to figure out where we should go when we leave here. I'll try to find some dry firewood then.''

"Jake, let's make a run for it. We can outrun this storm, I know we can!''

"What if we can't? No, Mariel, we're staying where we are.''

Mariel gazed down into Jessica's trusting eyes. How long could a baby Jessica's size go without food? She had to make Jake understand that they couldn't continue to stay in the cave.

"Jake,'' she said desperately, "can't you see? It's

Jessica's life we're talking about. If she doesn't get something to eat soon—real baby formula, I mean—she'll get weaker and weaker, and she may die. We can't do this to her, Jake. We've got to leave. We've got to!''

"And what if we get stuck in a snowstorm, Mariel, the way we were caught in the ice storm last night? What about that? What if *we* die? Jessica has precious little chance of survival without us. Don't you realize that?'' He shook off Mariel's arm and disappeared into the cave, emerging in a few moments wearing his backpack.

Mariel's eyes stung with unshed tears. She turned her head away so that he wouldn't see.

"Go back in the cave and try to keep the fire going. I'm going to find some dry wood before the snow starts," Jake said. With that, he stalked away along the track, his boots crunching on fallen icicles and acorns.

Mariel stood stunned, the baby in her arms, her fear a metallic taste in her mouth. She was hungry. So hungry. And suddenly she felt very, very tired.

Jake had disappeared into the forest, and he hadn't even looked back.

Chapter Five

Mariel crawled blindly into the cave, scarcely able to think. But she *had* to think.

For one thing, she had to see if there was anything left from Jake's pack to feed Jessica, anything at all. Jake had been worried about the storm, but there was one thing they hadn't discussed. During their impassioned discussion of the coming storm, neither of them had mentioned that once the snow stopped, they might not be able to get out of here at all. They could be marooned for days.

The temperature in the cave was warm compared to that outside, so she pulled on her dry corduroys, slipped off her coat and zipped out the wool lining. She wrapped the baby in the coat lining and set her down beside the jumble of things that Jake had dumped out of his pack, hemming the baby in between the cave wall and her own tote bag so that she couldn't roll. Jessica suddenly became absorbed in studying her tiny fists, which was all to the good. It left Mariel free to explore Jake's belongings.

She set the empty thermos aside. Next, she inspected the waterproof canister of matches, and a camper's set of interlocked fork and spoon, which almost made her laugh. At the moment, it seemed to be the last thing they needed.

There was also a small roll of cash—also virtually useless unless they burned the bills to keep the fire going—a hammer, and a rope.

Great, Mariel said to herself, *just great.* He had left nothing that could be useful to her at that point.

Next she rummaged through her purse. In it was a roll of mints, unopened, and an overlooked package of crackers. Deep in the zippered side pocket she found a small packet of sugar.

These things promised some sustenance, but not much. How long until Jessica began crying with hunger? At least, with the ice storm of the night before and the approaching snowstorm, there would be no lack of water.

Mariel had to keep up her spirits or she'd go crazy. She'd taken another look at the scudding clouds overhead, and she knew that the snow would not hold off for long. The fire was rapidly dying; she hoped Jake would be back soon with dry firewood.

She picked up Jessica and held her in her arms, rocking her gently until she fell asleep. Then Mariel placed the bundle in the nest between her tote bag and the wall and crawled out of the cave. How long had Jake been gone? Half an hour? More?

As she stood in front of the opening, snowflakes began to sift from the sky, gently at first, then borne on a biting wind. Mariel's eyes searched for Jake's familiar red-and-black lumberjack jacket among the tree trunks, but she didn't see him.

She wrapped her arms around herself, too cold to stay outside and yet too worried to go back in the cave. Where was Jake? Why didn't he come back?

JAKE WAS HEADING into unknown country, all right. Without a map, with only the sun to give direction, he didn't know if he would run smack into a river, rough terrain or a road. After he stubbed his toe against an upturned stump, he kept his eyes on the ground and wished he were at home watching TV, his feet propped on his favorite footstool.

Adventures like this were tailor-made for television. They did not happen to real people. He shouldn't be following a winding trail through the woods, trying to keep the direction of the cave in his mind while his stomach complained that it hadn't been fed lately. He wondered how long he'd be able to keep up his strength if he didn't get something to eat soon.

There were deer in these woods. And rabbits; he knew that from his disastrous experience yesterday, when he'd tried to brake for one. Jake wasn't a hunter, and he knew nothing about trapping. His survival skills did not include converting live animals into food. Still, if it came down to feeding Mariel...

Mariel. He said her name out loud, there in the silent forest. He liked to say her name.

He shouldn't be thinking about her. One of the benefits of having to gather firewood was that he was able to get away from her.

He needed to figure out what to do. This morning, when he'd awakened, it would have been so easy—and so stupid—to reach for her lush curves and fit himself to them. Warming the baby between them had been his idea, and it was for the baby's benefit. But it was also supposed to serve the purpose of keeping him away from Mariel. It hadn't worked.

Those last few dark hours before light, during the second time they'd huddled on the cave floor trying to stay warm, he'd hardly slept at all. Mariel had; her breathing had been slow and even. That was good. What wasn't good was that he had lain awake, thinking about the tantalizing smoothness of her skin, the creaminess of her breasts, so inadequately concealed by that wisp of a bra, and the curve of her waist, flowing so delectably into the roundness of her hips.

He'd only met her yesterday. What would she think about a man who was supposed to be getting them out of this mess but could hardly think of anything except the details of her body and how longingly he wished to abandon himself to their exploration?

When they had slept together the first time, his hands on her rib cage, her heart fluttering beneath them, it had taken a supreme act of will not to slide his hands upward and under that lacy bra to cup her lush round breasts. He already knew how they'd lie heavily in his hands, how they'd taste sweet to his lips. He had wanted to nuzzle beneath the soft trailing hair on her neck and nibble gently at the fragrant skin there, his breath teasing her ear. He had wanted to hear the soft whisper of her skin against his as she turned within the circle of his arms until the two of them rested front to front, lips together.

He could imagine brushing aside those bikini panties and seeking the silken wet center of her, making her quiver with desire. She would reach around him and pull his hips toward hers, her fingernails cutting into his flesh as she felt him surging against her. He would begin to move, and she would, too, and then—no. He couldn't think about it. He *wouldn't*. If he did, he'd march back into the cave and—What was that quaint expression? Oh, yes, he'd have his way with Mariel.

A dream. All of it. A fantasy that had nothing to do

with reality. The reality was that they had to stay alive and find their way out of here after the snowstorm had passed.

Jake looked around, trying to determine his location. The mountain directly above looked like the peak that was known, for some unfathomable reason, as Old Barker. This was a rural area, thinly populated, and the interstate highway that Mariel had been looking for was miles away. He had no idea how to get out of these woods.

The track he was on wound through the dense forest; he saw where a lumber cut had been made through the trees. He jogged along it, and eventually he saw what he was looking for: a tall tree with branches placed so that he could climb it.

He jumped up and gained a grip on a lower branch, sending a thin coating of ice tinkling down the trunk. Then he swung up his legs and pulled himself onto a sturdier branch, dislodging even more ice. He continued upward until he had a fairly good view of his surroundings.

He glanced back in the direction from which he'd come. He saw the cliff and tried to pick out the entrance to the cave, which would be difficult, because it was so small. He detected movement, and that was when he saw the tiny figure in the tan all-weather coat, its drabness broken by a red scarf blowing in the wind. *Mariel,* he thought, a thrill of pleasure rippling through him. He wanted to wave, to shout, but he thought it might frighten her.

Mariel looked no bigger than an insect from this vantage point. Suddenly Jake was afraid she was planning to strike out on her own in the snowstorm. The thought terrified him. She wouldn't do that. Or would she? She was a woman who was accustomed to making her own decisions, after all. Why should she listen to him? He watched the figure that was Mariel, but it didn't move.

He didn't want to take his eyes from her, for fear that she'd disappear, but he couldn't stay there forever. Telling himself that she'd have more sense than to move on alone, he tore his eyes away from the Mariel-figure and scanned the opposite direction. He was looking for a puff of smoke that would indicate a chimney, a driveway that led to a house, a road, a movement, *anything*. All he saw was bare-branched trees, their trunks dark with melting ice.

Then he saw something that wasn't a tree. Neither did it seem to be a house. At first he thought it was part of a distant mountain, but then he looked again. It was…a tower?

He eased himself upward to the next branch for a better view. It was *probably* a tower, he decided, and it seemed to be constructed of gray stone.

His precarious position in the tree afforded him only a glimpse of it. But at least it gave him hope that there was help ahead. That, for the moment, was enough.

He glanced back at the place where he'd seen Mariel, but she was gone. She'd disappeared. Had she gone back into the cave, or had she left?

He made haste down the tree trunk, stopping to snatch a bit of mistletoe from one of the branches and shove in into his coat's breast pocket. He thought it might amuse Mariel. He had to keep thinking that she'd be there.

MARIEL'S TEETH were chattering from the cold. Or maybe it was fear. She knew that Jake wasn't coming back.

Was she afraid for him? No, she was afraid for all of them. They would die out here. It was Christmas Eve day, and they were going to die.

Jake must have decided that he would go on without her and the baby; certainly it would be easier for him not to have a woman and a child to drag along. So he had walked out into the face of a blizzard. They had argued, and he had been so angry that he'd left.

She looked at Jessica, so pink and sweet, sleeping as if she hadn't a worry in the world. *Poor little thing,* Mariel thought. *Abandoned in the woods, and now this.*

Mariel gathered a few twigs and pieces of bark from the place where the firewood had been stacked, and she found another log in the far corner of the cave. She noticed with some surprise a previously undetected crevice from which dank air seeped, but she didn't want to waste the precious flashlight battery to investigate what it was.

She tossed the bark on the fire, knowing that it wouldn't keep the flame going for long. But she did want to boil the water in the thermos lid for Jessica. At least she could offer the baby that.

She huddled at the edge of the fire, listening and waiting. Waiting and listening. And still there was no sign of Jake.

ON HIS WAY BACK to the cave, Jake found a good-size fallen tree and rolled it over to expose the dry wood. Using his trusty hatchet, he managed to split off several reasonably dry, seasoned logs.

There was an ominous feeling in the air as he started back to the cave, the firewood in his arms, and he kept his eyes on the encroaching clouds, knowing that if they blocked the sun he'd be in trouble. The sun was his only directional guide. He hadn't taken time to notch the trees as he walked, so he might wander off the track if snow fell hard enough to obscure his vision.

He should feel more successful than he did. He was returning with wood that would burn, wood that would keep them warm until after the snow fell. They would be snug in their cave.

But he, too, was worried about how long the baby could survive without food. As he trudged through the woods, unbidden pictures flooded his brain, freeze-frame images that made him quicken his step. He thought about Mariel carrying the baby through snow-drifts, unable to see in the whited-out landscape. He thought about them falling down, and Mariel unable to get up again, and the baby crying until suddenly the crying stopped.

He was angry with himself for not having made things clear before he left. He should have extracted a promise from Mariel that she wouldn't take the baby and leave. Why hadn't he taken that precaution? Why had he been so rash and bullheaded?

Snow began to fall. *If Mariel and Jessica are still in the cave, I'll never get drunk again,* he promised himself, though it wasn't much of a promise. He hadn't been drunk since a buddy's bachelor party five years ago.

If Mariel and Jessica are still in the cave, I'll never argue with her again, he decided. The whole exercise reeked of "Step on a crack, you'll break your mother's back, step on a line, you'll break your mother's spine," childish doggerel that had stuck with him to this day.

If Mariel is still there, I'll pull her into my arms and kiss her was Jake's final offering. And that was one promise that he fully intended to keep.

JESSICA BEGAN TO SQUALL, and Mariel, giving up on the eyedropper, used the spoon from Jake's pack to ladle sugar water into her mouth. It kept her quiet while Mariel tried to think.

If Jake didn't come back, she would wait until the storm passed and then dig her way out of the cave. Then she and Jessica would head toward her car.

Not that it would be easy, with snowdrifts covering the road. Considering the fact that they seemed to be in a completely deserted part of the world, she could hardly expect a snowplow to come through and clear it.

After she'd swallowed most of the sugar water, Jessica was due for a diaper change, which Mariel was able to accomplish more easily now that she'd gained experience. She rocked Jessica until she fell asleep and laid her in the nest she'd made from the lining of her coat.

Mariel felt cold; without its lining, her coat wasn't particularly warm. She crept closer to the fire, which was now reduced to a bed of glowing coals.

For lack of anything else to do, she used a bit of precious light from the flashlight and went to look for a scrap of bark, or a bit of paper, or anything else that would burn. And then she saw the log.

There couldn't be another log there. It was impossible. Jake himself had said they'd used the last piece of wood earlier, and Mariel had figured that the log she'd found a while ago, a spindly, meager log, had simply been overlooked. But here was another.

It felt strange to be picking up the log and putting it on the fire, and she wondered how she could have missed it earlier. Then she felt a blast of cool air from the cave entrance and went to check on the weather.

When Mariel emerged from the cave, snowflakes

were drifting down in clumps, almost covering the ground. The sky was the shade that her mother had always called tattletale gray, only this sky was telling no tales. Neither were the trees. She saw no sign of Jake.

She thought she had prepared herself never to see him again, but now that she knew that there was virtually no hope he'd return, her heart sank to the pit of her stomach and settled there like a rock.

Well, she couldn't blame him for trying to get out of here. She had no doubt that he'd send someone to rescue her and the baby. In fact, that might have been his purpose in leaving. Now she could only hope that he'd find help—and find it fast. But who could get through in the face of the second major storm in twenty-four hours? Only Santa Claus, she thought, trying to feel lighthearted. Santa Claus and his airborne reindeer, soaring through the sky.

Jake would laugh at her. She was almost laughing at herself. But what if Jake didn't get through to someplace where there were people? What if he was in worse shape than she and the baby were, lost somewhere in these vast, uninhabited woods?

She wouldn't think about that. No point in dwelling on the problems. Time to get on with business. Time to think about how they were going to make it through the rest of the day, and probably longer, without food.

But when she went back in the cave and saw Jessica sleeping so peacefully, it was Mariel's undoing. She didn't mind all of this so much for herself. After all, she was a grown woman, thirty years old, and had experienced some of what life had to offer.

But Jessica was a baby. An infant. She wasn't even old enough to creep or crawl, and she couldn't hold her head up to see what the world was about. She'd never had a chance, and if they died in this awful cave, she never would.

Mariel buried her face in her hands. It was so unfair. So, so unfair...

JAKE STRUGGLED toward the cave, seeing no sign of Mariel. The snow was falling so heavily now that there was no way he would have been able to detect her departing footprints even if they were there.

Then he was at the entrance of the cave, dropping pieces of wood in his eagerness to see within. It was silent inside, a forbidding sign. If Mariel and the baby were in there, the baby would be hungry and she would be crying. Or Mariel would be talking to the baby and he would be able to hear her as he made his way through the opening.

He pressed through the brambles and crawled through the tunnellike entrance. And then, as his eyes adjusted to the gloom of the cave, he saw the flames and the hunched-over shape beside them.

Jake fell into the cave, firewood scattering in every direction.

"Mariel!" he cried, unable to believe that she was there. She was really there. He had talked himself into believing that she was headstrong enough to leave.

The figure rose as he staggered to his feet. "Jake! Oh, Jake!" she said, and the fire was bright enough for him to see the tears drying in salty streaks on her cheeks.

Then, with no warning, she was catapulting into his arms, laughing and sobbing at the same time. She flung her arms around his neck, unmindful of the snow clumped on the shoulders of his coat, and pressed her body tightly against his. His heart began to throb so strongly that he thought it would burst out of his chest.

"I thought you had gone," she said, sobbing into the front of his jacket. "I thought you had left us."

"I wouldn't," he said, wrapping his arms solidly around her and drawing in her warmth. Her sweater was soft, her body voluptuous, her hair tickling his mouth. He moved his head slightly, only to precipitate the uplifting of her face to his. Her eyes were silvery blue, the pupils defined by rims of a darker hue. They were shining with happiness.

"I thought you might be planning to send someone to rescue us," she said in a choked voice.

"I was sure you'd left. I saw you standing outside the entrance of the cave earlier, and I figured you had waited until I was out of sight and had taken the baby, looking for a safer place. When I thought that, I was so scared—"

"You? Scared? I don't believe it," she said, her eyes searching his face.

He enfolded her more tightly in his arms. He could feel her heartbeat, see the pulse of it at her temple. All at once he knew that he would sacrifice his life for her or the baby if need be. He had read about people who did things like that, but before, from his limited perspective, that altruistic mind-set had meant nothing to him. He certainly hadn't thought he would ever feel that way about anyone himself.

"I—I made all kinds of promises to myself while I was on my way back with the wood and thinking you wouldn't be here," he said unevenly.

"Like what?" Her voice was almost a whisper.

"Like—*this,*" he whispered back, bending his head over hers.

Her fingers fluttered at the back of his neck and were still. He fitted his lips to hers, so perfectly, so beautifully, and slid one hand up her spine to weave it into the loose curls hanging below her shoulders.

She sighed, her breath gentle against his cheek, and drew his head down even farther. He deepened the kiss as her mouth opened to his, the textures of her lips and teeth and tongue a powerful aphrodisiac. They were instantly lost in the moment, clinging to each other, pouring themselves into the connection between them. Jake forgot his physical hunger and gave in to a more elemental one, wanting to feast, but not on food. In that moment he realized that she wanted him as much as he wanted her, and he was so wildly happy at the thought that all he wanted to do was to follow his instincts, which would take them both into realms that he had so far only imagined.

She slid her hands into his coat, her fingers finding their way, moving under his shirt, searching for warm skin. He felt as if he were floating in a warm dark world where normal rules didn't apply and where pleasure was the only sensation. He felt her knees buckle and wrapped his arms around her to lower her to the sand.

And then the baby cried.

It took a moment for the noise to register. Time and place seeped back into their consciousnesses; they remembered. The storm. The cave. The baby.

Jake was the first to speak. "Is she all right?" he asked.

Mariel only breathed deeply, a kind of gasp, and then she righted herself. Her hands dropped to her sides, and she closed her eyes for a moment as if to clear her head.

And in that moment, Jake saw that it was regrettably inappropriate in this time and in this place to think that they could relate to each other in any way that didn't ensure their survival and the baby's. While making love might make them feel gloriously and completely alive, it wouldn't solve their problems. It would only make them go away temporarily.

"The noise woke her," Mariel said, sounding like her ordinary self as she backed away, smoothing her hair self-consciously. In a few seconds, she was kneeling in front of Jessica, murmuring sweet nothings in that solicitous voice she always used with the baby and ignoring Jake completely.

Jake waited until his body returned to normal and then bent and retrieved the firewood. Mariel, he had discovered, had a strong motherly instinct. Yet he couldn't help feeling disappointed; he wanted to hold her in his arms, to whisper fiercely that he would never let anything harm her, that he would give his life for her if need be.

But he couldn't do anything of the sort. Mariel was changing the baby's diaper. The storm was roaring outside the cave. Jake made himself wedge a few sticks of firewood on the fire and deposited the rest where the old woodpile had been.

"You know, after you left I found another stick of firewood. And then, just a while ago, another," Mariel said, lifting her head. Apparently she had chosen to act as if nothing had passed between them. Well, he didn't know any better way to handle it, and two could play that game.

"That's impossible. I put the last stick on the fire this morning before I went out looking for wood."

Mariel didn't notice his reluctance to pursue the topic. She went on talking, her hands busy with the baby. "It was strange, and I thought I must have overlooked those two logs this morning,'' she said.

He detected an unnatural brightness in her tone. She *had* been affected by what had happened between them. The thought gave him hope.

But at that moment he couldn't ignore what she was saying, because it was, he knew, bald fantasy. ''Mariel, Mariel...'' he said gently, genuinely concerned about her. What was this? Was her mind playing tricks on her?

''Well, it happened,'' she said flatly.

''It *is* Christmas,'' he said, hoping to gloss over this disturbing development. He *knew* there had been no other logs this morning. There was no doubt in his mind.

She shook her head and laughed. He was relieved to see the corners of her mouth tilting upward, even though it reminded him that he could still taste her on his lips.

Mariel, quietly efficient, had bundled the baby into her arms and was swaying back and forth, murmuring endearments.

Jake removed his coat and spread it on the sand.

''We might as well both sit on my coat. This storm may take its own sweet time in passing.''

Jessica fussed and fretted until at last she dropped off to sleep. ''I scraped up a package of mints and another package of crackers while you were gone,'' Mariel told him. ''And I fed Jessica sugar water.''

''She seems okay.''

Mariel studied the baby's face, a frown bisecting her forehead. ''I think so.''

Jake made himself concentrate on other things besides Mariel's closeness. He didn't want her to see how worried he was, so he stood up and began to pace back and forth at the back of the cave. He still couldn't believe her claim that she'd found two more pieces of wood after he left. He kept glancing at her out of the corner of his eye, searching for some sign that she was becoming mentally unstable. She seemed completely normal. And sexy, though he didn't think she realized it.

"How's our flashlight doing?" he made himself ask.

"Almost gone," Mariel said.

He reached down and switched it on, mostly for the hell of it. The circle of its beam was orange and dim.

"Oh, by the way, I found a fissure of some kind in the wall," Mariel said.

"No kidding! It can't be very big," he said, unable to square what she was saying with what he knew to be true. He had thoroughly vetted the cave last night. He hadn't seen any fissure.

"I think we didn't notice it before because it's way at the back of the cave and could have been partly obscured by the woodpile," she said.

Jake, with marked reluctance, took a look. He couldn't believe his eyes when he saw it. Sure enough, there was a crack in the rock.

"Why, there is something here!" he exclaimed.

"Did you think I made it up?"

"I don't know what to think anymore." He saw that the fissure was barely wide enough for him to slip his arm through, and he didn't know what made him do it, but he reached into the crack. As his hand groped within the dark space, his fingers closed around a cylindrical shape. Cautiously he withdrew it, then stared at the object in his hand. Then he reached back in and pulled out two more cans, scarcely able to believe his eyes.

"What are you doing?" Mariel asked. He was blocking her view.

"Bringing home the bacon," Jake replied, in a

choked voice as he turned to show her a can of Vienna sausage, a can of date-nut bread, and a can of evaporated milk.

Chapter Six

"Where did those come from?" Mariel asked in sheer disbelief.

He nodded his head toward the crevice. "They were in there."

"Why?" she asked, turning the can of milk over and over in her hands. It was exactly what they needed, and she could hardly believe that it had been there all the time.

"I don't know *why,* Mariel. Can't we simply be grateful that it *was?*" he said, sitting down beside her. He could no longer think there was anything wrong with Mariel's mental faculties, not when everything she'd said had turned out to be true. He was beginning to wonder if his own mind was playing tricks on him instead.

"The milk has to be diluted for drinking. We can mix it with melted snow. It should get Jessica through the rest of the day, at least," Mariel said with a kind of awe.

"The other stuff is for us," he said. "I hope you like Vienna sausages."

Mariel wrinkled her nose. "Under normal circumstances, I wouldn't touch them. But I'm hungry. Very hungry,'' she added.

"And the date-nut bread,'' he said. "Actually, I've always liked it, especially when it's spread with cream cheese.''

"Did you try sticking your hand further into the crevice? You might find some,'' Mariel said impishly, and he laughed.

They ate ravenously, and when Jessica woke up, they were ready with milk, which they had mixed with an equal amount of water. The baby was greedy, rooting for the eyedropper and fussing each time Mariel refilled it. Feeding her was a tedious job.

The feeding accomplished, Jake took Jessica from Mariel and balanced the infant on his upraised knees. "Too bad babies don't come with blueprints to tell us what's where and how it works,'' he said.

"Or instruction books.''

"Or user's manuals.''

"Do you think we're doing everything right?'' Mariel asked anxiously.

"I don't know,'' Jake said. "But doesn't she seem okay? She's smiling. Look.''

"She is! Well, I think she likes us,'' Mariel said.

"I know she does. By the way, what's the status of the storm?''

Mariel sat down beside him. "Still raging.''

"We need to plan what to do when we leave here,'' Jake said, becoming so serious that Mariel didn't speak but waited for him to continue.

He told her quickly about the tower he thought he had seen when he climbed the tree, and he suggested that they head in that direction when they left the cave.

"Was there any smoke near this tower? Any sign of life?" Mariel wanted to know.

Jake shook his head. "Not that I could tell."

"How about in any other direction?"

"Nothing at all."

"Jake, where *are* we? You're from around here. You should have some idea."

"We're lost, but we're going to get out of here today. I promise you that," he said with an air of determination.

Her eyes were troubled, and Jake reached out and enclosed her hand in his. "I promise," he repeated in a firm voice, and because he sounded so sure, she was, too.

THE SNOW STOPPED before the hour was out, and, fortified by their meager lunch of Vienna sausage, they set out.

With Jake leading the way, they waded through the freshly fallen snow, breaking a trail. Jake carried the baby inside his coat, and Jessica peeped out in round-eyed astonishment.

Mariel smiled at Jessica, thinking what a cute baby she was. Then she laughed at Jake.

"What's wrong?" he asked.

"You look so funny," she said, still grinning. "You look pregnant, carrying her in front of you like that."

"I kind of wondered what pregnancy would be like," he told her, and she laughed.

"How do you like it?"

He made a face. "It's tolerable," he drawled, which only made her laugh again.

"You should stop laughing and talking so much," he said sternly. "You'll get exhausted again."

"Oh," she said, feeling liberated by the sun peeping out from behind the clouds, and the bright snow, and the sky, washed as blue as bottle glass. "Let me enjoy this. After all that time in the cave, I feel as if I can breathe again. I want to dance and sing and play the way I did when I was a child!" She bounded through the snow until she was walking backward in front of him, her eyes sparkling.

"You can dance and sing if you want," he said, trying to keep a straight face, "but I can't. I'm pregnant."

She laughed merrily, the sound reminding him of silver bells.

She looked so beautiful, so carefree, so different from the way she had looked in the cave. At the moment, all he wanted to do was to pull her into his arms and kiss her.

She threw out her arms, as if to embrace everything, and he thought he had never seen anything as beautiful as Mariel welcoming herself back to the world after an ordeal that both of them had thought might be the end of them.

Then she skipped back to him and took his hand. "I'll behave now. I wanted to get all that out of my system, that's all," she said with uncharacteristic meekness. He wondered if she knew that even the presence of her hand in his aroused him, then decided she didn't. If she knew, she wouldn't do it so casually.

He decided to stick to business. "Mariel, it's not a matter of behavior. It's a matter of conserving your energy in case of a problem," he said.

"You mean, in case that tower you saw was a mirage?"

"I don't *think* it was, but I didn't *think* there was firewood left in the cave, and then there were two more pieces. The things I take for granted don't seem to be true anymore, and things that I thought *weren't* there, including the food I found in the cave, *were*," he said.

"Magic," Mariel said. "It's Christmastime, you know."

He didn't answer, and they walked on quietly for a few more steps until Mariel realized that Jake wasn't going to rise to the bait. She decided to try a new tact.

"I wonder what it's really like to be pregnant. I don't mean just carrying a baby inside your coat," she ventured.

"It's not as if I would know," Jake pointed out.

"I think it must make a woman feel special to be pregnant."

"I think it must make her feel fat," he said in all honesty.

"A baby is not classified as fat," Mariel said indignantly.

"Did you hear that?" he said into the front of his coat. "A baby is not classified as fat."

"Wah," said Jessica.

"Oh, my gosh, did you hear that? She said something!" he shouted.

"All she did was get her vocal cords into gear while she was yawning. It doesn't mean anything."

"Knowing what I now know about babies, it probably means 'Change my diaper,'" Jake said, with more than a touch of irony.

"We only have one clean diaper left."

"If you're still in the wish-making business, you should wish for a box of Flubbies, or whatever they call those disposable things babies wear."

Mariel dissolved into laughter. "They're not called Flubbies, but that's close enough."

"I'd hate to turn her over to her parents with a full-fledged case of diaper rash."

"I don't think she has any parents," Mariel told him seriously.

"Of course she does."

"Well, they're not anywhere around."

"She didn't appear out of thin air. She had to come from somewhere."

"Do you suppose she was left in the woods by a stork who was reluctant to risk dropping her down someone's chimney at this time of year?" Mariel asked innocently.

"Well, according to you, chimneys have been pre-empted by a VIP who has unorthodox ways of gaining entry into people's houses, so what's a stork to do? Look, Mariel," Jake said earnestly, "maybe this baby is the answer to your question. You know, the one we were discussing last night. How does a single woman get a child? We thought we'd covered all the possibilities, but there was one we didn't think about—finding one in the woods in the middle of an ice storm."

She favored him with a keen look to see if he was teasing her, but he stepped up his pace, and the snow was drifted high on this part of the trail, so she had to struggle to keep up.

The glare of the sun on snow was beginning to make Mariel's eyes ache when Jake suddenly stopped walking. "I see something!" he called excitedly over his shoulder.

"A house?"

"I'm not sure if it's a house, but I think it's what I saw earlier."

Mariel plunged through the snow and came to a halt behind him, looking over his shoulder at the tower.

It was visible through the treetops, a high, round gray

stone structure rearing up against a bright blue sky. Pale yellow sunlight played over the walls, glittering on the snow frosting clinging to the spaces between the stones. Mariel caught her breath.

"It's a *castle*," she said, dazzled by the sight.

Jake drew her close by slipping an arm around her shoulders, something that she welcomed. She wondered if there was a chance that he would kiss her again, then decided that there wasn't. He had been acting matter-of-fact ever since they left the cave, and in spite of his teasing and their banter earlier, he didn't seem to recapture the highly charged feelings that they'd shared when they kissed. The realization left her with a mounting sense of disappointment.

"It's a castle, all right, unless we're both seeing things," he said.

"But what's it doing here? Where are we?" Mariel asked.

He squeezed her shoulder. "I don't know, but it's shelter. Come on," he said, taking her hand again.

They walked as fast as they could into the very heart of the woods. The track twisted and turned, sometimes doubling back upon itself, so that occasionally the tower was over Mariel's right shoulder, occasionally her left.

And then they came around a curve, and a clearing opened up in front of them. The castle was cupped in a hollow, as if within the palm of a hand. For a brief moment, birdsong trilled through the air, stopping suddenly and leaving them in pristine silence with nothing but the castle to fill their gaze.

The castle was complete with gatehouse towers reaching toward heaven, a huge, nail-studded oaken door, and a sagging drawbridge leading across a twenty-foot-wide moat. Speechless, Mariel and Jake stood and stared.

It looked like something out of a fairy tale. Somehow they expected people or horses to burst through the gate and run across the decrepit drawbridge, welcoming them with a fanfare of trumpets. But nothing like that happened. They saw no one, and they heard nothing but their own breathing.

And then Mariel saw the candle flickering in the gatehouse tower window. "Look."

"Someone's here."

"The candle is guiding us to shelter," Mariel said with certainty.

"If you say so," Jake said doubtfully.

"It's a Christmas custom in some countries to light a candle to guide travelers to a safe place," Mariel said in a rush. "They think that Christ wanders in the guise of a stranger to test the hospitality of people along the way. At Christmas, no one is turned away."

"I'm certainly glad to hear that," Jake said with great deliberation.

"You don't think much of the story, do you?" she challenged.

"At the moment, all I think is that I'm as hungry as a beast. Do we stand out here in the cold, or do we go in and— What did you say? Test their hospitality?"

Mariel knew that, inside, he was laughing at her. She kept her eyes on the candle flame. "We go in," she said, leading the way.

She hesitated at the start of the drawbridge. It was covered with snow, so they couldn't see the actual boards underneath.

"Do you think this bridge is safe?" she asked dubiously.

"You can hold the baby, and I'll go first." Jake prepared to divest himself of Jessica, but her loud wail rent the air.

"Better not," he said hastily, tucking Jessica into the front of his jacket again.

"I'll go first," Mariel decided, but in Jake's mind, the welcoming horses had become stallions intent on trampling to death anyone who got in their way, and the hounds a yapping horde, sure to tear her to pieces.

"We'll all go together," Jake said, and, mindful of every creak, they made their way across the drawbridge until they stood in the walled outer ward in front of the gatehouse.

It was three stories high, with two elongated twin towers connected by a roofed-over passageway. The top of the walls was crenellated, giving the effect of a giant set of teeth with every other tooth missing. The spaces between the crenellations were banked with snow.

A smaller door had been cut in the massive nail-studded oak door, and a rusty gong to their right presumably notified the occupants that they had visitors.

"Shall I ring it?" Mariel wanted to know.

"Let 'er rip," Jake answered. She picked up the waiting mallet and gave the gong a hard whack, sending a flock of birds fluttering off the battlements in panic.

"I don't think anyone's coming," Jake said after a few minutes had passed.

Mariel walked back to the edge of the drawbridge and looked up at the gatehouse window. "The candle is gone!" she exclaimed.

"Maybe they got a look at us and decided they didn't want to lodge such a scruffy-looking group," Jake said ruefully.

"I don't think that's it. The flame must have blown out."

"Well, do we stay here or go on?" Jake asked, shifting Jessica's weight impatiently.

"We're not in a position to leave. We have to feed Jessica," Mariel said. "We have to go in, whether anyone is here or not."

"Try the door. Maybe it's open."

Mariel pushed at the smaller door within the apparently immovable larger one, and was surprised when it swung open with little effort.

"After you," Jake said, standing back, and so Mariel went in first.

Once inside, she was overcome by the aura of the place; there was a haze of unreality about the castle. Mariel paused for a moment, glancing at Jake to see if he felt what she did, this kind of heightened awareness, as if she were breathing rarefied air.

Jake looked as if nothing were amiss, and so she shook off whatever imaginary effect she thought she'd felt and took notice of their surroundings.

They stood in a passage between the two towers of the gatehouse. Mariel saw a staircase leading up, but it was in deplorable condition, and she didn't see how anyone could have gotten upstairs to light the candle.

Puzzled, she stood on tiptoe to peer through a window in search of an inside stairway, but all she saw was the remnants of one, its boards strewn around the floor. While she was still wondering how anyone could have reached the upper story of the gatehouse with the staircases missing, she was startled to see two long ears waggling at her.

"There's something in here!" she said, turning to Jake.

Jake cocked his head to one side. "Animal? Vegetable? Mineral?"

"Animal, but I can't see *what*," Mariel said as she continued through the passage to the castle courtyard, where she saw a doorway into the first floor of the gatehouse.

The actual door was missing. They could see directly inside. On a pile of straw, backed into a corner, was a goat.

"Bleah-h-h," went the goat.

"That's exactly the way I feel," Jake said in a conversational tone.

"Why, she's scared to death," Mariel said in concern. She didn't know how to behave around a goat; she'd never, as far as she could remember, met one before. She did, however, know that this goat was female, because of her large, swollen udder. The goat was gray and white, with great golden eyes, which were presently rolling around in their sockets to express extreme agitation.

"She's tame," Jake said.

"She probably belongs to the people who live here," she said, looking around for food or water and seeing none.

"Let's go find them." Jake couldn't wait to get to a warm place, where he could relax on a deeply cushioned chair and use the telephone.

Reluctantly Mariel followed him into the castle courtyard. The goat trailed after them, bleating all the while.

They were much too awed by the castle to pay attention to the goat. The courtyard was wide, and snow had drifted into all the corners. There was no sign of any inhabitants.

Mariel sized up her surroundings and determined that this one was small as castles went, with the inner courtyard about the size of two basketball courts. On their left were lean-tos built against the wall; to their right, more of the same.

"The bakehouse," Mariel said as they passed one door. A section of a thatch-roofed building elicited the comment. "That's the stable."

Jake couldn't resist asking, "How do you know?"

"I deal in legends. Legends take place in castles. I took college courses in medieval studies."

"I'm not so much interested in what's what as I am in where the people live."

Mariel pointed to a larger door directly ahead. "I'm sure that's the great hall. That's where people eat and spend leisure time. We should try there first."

Jake followed Mariel's lead, noting the stained-glass windows adorning the small enclosure to their right.

"That must be the chapel," he said. His brilliant deduction should show her that he knew something about medieval castles, too, but Mariel was forging ahead of him, leaving small, neat footprints in the snow.

"I don't see a doorbell," Mariel said as she stood in front of the door, and Jake had to laugh at the perplexed expression on her face.

"A doorbell? In a medieval castle?"

"Modern people must live here. You'd think there would be modern conveniences."

Jake shook his head. "No mod cons in this place. I don't see any telephone poles, or wires, or signs of any connection with the outside world."

Mariel's face fell, but only fleetingly. "All I hope is that they have a bathtub and water," she said firmly.

Jake knocked on the door, and the sound resounded hollowly within. No one answered. He knocked again, trying not to notice Mariel's look of discouragement.

Finally he said, "There's no one here."

She stared at him. "This big castle, stuck way out in the middle of the forest, and there's no one home? Why would anyone go to the trouble to put it here?" she asked in exasperation.

Jake looked at the blanket of snow, and at the icicles as long and as thick as his forearm hanging from the roofs of the nearby buildings. "I bet they've gone to Florida for the winter. I know *I* would," he said gloomily.

Without saying one more thing, Mariel marched around the courtyard, trying the locked chapel door, poking in corners, and jumping up to peer in windows, which were narrow and few. Jake followed her, being patient and consoling Jessica, whose diaper had reached the saturation point.

"You'll have to break in," Mariel said, looking panicky, when Jake reluctantly told her about the sorry state of Jessica's diaper.

"Bleah-h-h," went the goat.

"At least you didn't suggest that I go down the chimney," Jake said, but Mariel only wrinkled her nose at him.

"Anyway," he said, "this place belongs to someone who might not take kindly to breaking and entering, so maybe it's not a good idea."

"But this is an emergency," Mariel insisted. "Whoever lives here wouldn't want us to stay out in the freezing cold with a baby whose diaper is approaching flood status."

To emphasize her point, Jessica made a sound that was something like "glug."

"Okay, we'll take a look at the door to the great hall," he said.

Mariel found it difficult to keep up with Jake as he

strode across the courtyard. The goat cavorted in their wake, something urgent in its manner. Mariel had no time to think about the goat; she was far more concerned about what they would do if they couldn't get inside the castle. Camp in the courtyard? Bed down in the gatehouse? Neither option seemed any more desirable than spending the night in a cave.

Jake studied the heavy door, and in a moment, using nothing more than a hammer and a Swiss army knife, he was pushing the door open. They stomped the thickly caked snow off their boots before Mariel followed Jake inside.

Once she was standing inside the great hall, Mariel realized that no one could be living there. It was long and dreary, dark and musty. The ceiling was vaulted in stone, and occupying one end of the room was a massive fireplace big enough to roast an ox. A dais at the other end held a long table with smaller tables arrayed below it, and a pale winter sun picked out the details of the faded tapestries on the walls.

"It's cold in here" was the first thing Jake said, his voice echoing back from the high ceiling.

Mariel, amazed at the authenticity of the place, was studying the elaborate tapestries. They were embroidered in warm browns and reds, with occasional flashes of yellow and blue here and there. The panels depicted stories—a hunt, the arrival of noblemen amid waving banners, knights jousting.

Jake's spirits were sinking. He might as well scrap the idea of a soft chair and a television set. The most modern convenience he saw was a packet of matches tossed carelessly on the hearth.

"Hello?" called Mariel, thinking she'd better make their presence known, in the unlikely event that someone was around. When no one answered, she looked at Jake and shrugged her shoulders.

"It's not much," Jake said with an audible sigh, "but we call it home. Let's take a look to make sure there aren't any more goats wandering around and to see if there's anything to eat." He took off at a fast clip for the far end of the hall.

"If this is like most castles, we won't find a kitchen. They always put the cookhouse far away from the hall and its apartments because of the danger of fire," Mariel was saying as Jake led the way into the room behind the dais, but she stopped and breathed, "Ooh," when she saw what was there.

"A kitchen," Jake said in an unbelieving voice. "An honest-to-goodness, real-life kitchen."

"With a stove," Mariel said. "And a refrigerator!" Things were looking up.

And in a matter of seconds, she was looking up—at Jake. He wrapped his arms around her, pulling her close.

"We're going to be all right, Mariel. We'll manage here," he said, and she knew then that he was going to kiss her again.

She didn't try to stop him. She wanted it. He ran his fingers through her hair first, tilting her head back before dipping his head and covering her mouth with his. An ache curled up from somewhere below her stomach, making her nipples tighten into hard little points. It was a potent and exuberant kiss, a celebration of their safety. It was a kiss that could have gone on and on, except for Jessica's squirming presence between them.

Reluctantly Mariel leaned away from Jake. "That's one way to raise the temperature in here," she said, holding on to the front of his jacket for balance. "But

I think we'd better find a more appropriate heating device.''

Jake shook his head, as if to clear it, and although his lips smiled, his eyes reflected a more serious mood.

He moved away and bent to study the stove. ''It's run by propane gas, and I'll need to get it fired up,'' he announced before taking a look at the refrigerator. ''This is run on propane, too. There's no electricity, which explains the kerosene lantern and that box of candles on the table.''

''With a way to cook, there may be food around,'' Mariel said.

While she checked the cabinets above the stove, Jake threw open a pantry door.

''A gold mine,'' he said. ''Mariel, look at this!''

Mariel saw a cabinet filled with canned goods of every description. There were baked beans, garbanzo beans and kidney beans. There was noodle soup, cream of celery soup and bouillon. There were cans of tuna and sardines and baby clams. In short, they would survive.

''I don't see any canned milk,'' Jake said suddenly.

Mariel's happiness turned to dismay. ''We have to have it for Jessica. Is there baby formula?''

Jake shoved the cans around. ''No. Nothing.'' His expression was bleak.

''What are we going to do?''

''I don't know.''

They stared at each other for a moment.

''Well,'' Jake said finally. ''At least I can do something to improve our comfort level. I'm going to build a fire in here.'' He handed Jessica to Mariel and headed toward the kitchen fireplace, whose wood box was filled with apple logs.

Even here, far from the door, they could hear the bleating of the goat.

Mariel jounced Jessica expertly. "We'll be nice and warm soon," she promised the baby, who was holding up remarkably well, she thought.

"That goat's probably hungry," Jake said as he built the fire. "I wonder how she ended up here, or if the people who live here left her."

"I don't think anyone has lived here for a long, long time." Mariel watched as the flames leaped up to embrace the logs.

Jake rocked back on his heels. "Do you want to take a stab at fixing something to eat, or shall I?"

"Before we do anything, I'd better change Jessica's diaper. Maybe you could look around the kitchen for a cardboard box or someplace where she can sleep." She wished fervently that their cursory search had turned up a few dozen clean diapers. Jake's cut-up long johns were really not equal to their task.

Jake returned from his search carrying a drawer that he had pulled out of a cabinet in the pantry. Over one arm was draped a pile of white huck towels.

"Look," he said, tossing the towels down beside Mariel. "These will make dandy diapers. And I didn't find any boxes, but won't this do for Jessica's bed?" He placed the drawer at the far edge of the wide hearth.

Mariel was thrilled about the towels, which could be folded to the right size and were thick and absorbent. The drawer was sturdy and scarred, but suitable. "It's better than nothing," she said.

"Let's eat something before we figure out what to do next." With Jessica settled in her drawer-bed, he and Mariel feasted—there was no other word for it—on canned tuna, smoked oysters, artichoke hearts and beets from the store in the cupboard.

"I hate beets," said Mariel, munching happily.

"Me too."

"This is a horrible dinner," she added as she claimed the last artichoke heart.

"Awful," Jake agreed.

They looked at each other and laughed. Their stomachs were full, and their spirits were rising.

"This might not be such a bad Christmas after all," Jake said, and Mariel smiled.

"There's no such thing as a bad Christmas," she said.

Chapter Seven

While Mariel fed Jessica the last bit of the canned milk they had found in the cave, Jake built another fire in the great hall. When he came back, he said, "Now that we're getting the place warmed up, let's take a look around."

Jake had lit candles in the wall sconces in the great hall, which mellowed it more than Mariel could have imagined earlier. It was furnished sparsely, as great halls should be, with a few wooden chests and a couple of settees for sitting in front of the fire.

With Jake carrying Jessica, they set out to explore the castle. A small corridor off the great hall led to the chapel, jeweled with light from the huge stained-glass windows. Pews were small, and the ceiling was high. On the other side of the chapel was a small room lined with shelves of books. Mariel looked at them more closely. She saw *Ivanhoe,* and a book of recipes, and something called *Your Infant.*

"A book about baby care!" she said triumphantly, gingerly edging it out of its dusty place beside the others.

"It looks awfully old," Jake observed as she leafed

through yellowed pages, one of which proved him right by stating the publication date as 1908.

"People knew how to take care of babies then. If they hadn't, you and I wouldn't be here." Mariel hugged the book to her chest as Jake led the way through the corridors and back to the great hall, where a staircase led to an upper gallery.

They were awed by the dusty collection of armor and the display case full of swords. Rooms opened off the gallery, bedchambers furnished in the medieval manner, with immense high beds draped with heavy curtains. Without benefit of fires in the fireplaces, the chambers were cold and damp, and both Mariel and Jake were so uncomfortable with the chill that they quickly returned to the great hall.

After a few minutes of warming themselves in front of the now-roaring fire, Jake started toward another set of steps.

"Shouldn't we explore the tower?"

"Let's," Mariel agreed without hesitation. "At least we'll be able to survey the countryside from the highest point around. Maybe we'll see signs of life nearby."

The narrow tower steps were built into the wall and spiraled to the top. Jake was about to comment on their steepness to Mariel, who was bringing up the rear, but he stopped, speechless, when he stood in the doorway to the tower room.

There were toys everywhere. Dolls were heaped upon rocking horses; toy dump trucks carried loads of blocks; a sled leaned against the wall; a harmonica rested on a child's rush-seated chair.

"It looks as if we've happened upon Santa's storehouse," Jake said wryly. In his arms, Jessica, too young for toys, gawked at all the bright colors.

"I can't for the life of me figure out what's going on," Mariel said, bewildered by the array. "There's no one for miles around, and now we find *this*." She knelt and picked up a stuffed unicorn. "These are new toys, Jake. Not toys that might have been played with by children who once lived here, the children whose mother consulted the baby book, but *new toys*."

"It just goes to show you that Santa Claus lives," Jake said. He bent and scooped something out of one of the dolls' arms. "And he wants Jessica to eat properly. Will we be able to feed her with this?" He held a doll's bottle out to Mariel.

It wasn't the size of a regular baby's bottle, but it was marked for ounces and had an ordinary rubber nipple on top.

"It will work, I think," she said, but then her face fell. "If only we had something to feed her."

"We'll think of something, Mariel."

Mariel was still assessing the contents of the room for usefulness. "I'm taking more than a bottle. Jessica needs clothes, too," she said. She swiftly stripped the baby dolls of their nightgowns and held one up. "This'll fit perfectly."

"And it matches the blue of Jessica's eyes," Jake said approvingly. "Come on, let's go downstairs. I can't figure out what these toys are doing here, and I'm not sure I even want to try."

They trooped downstairs and basked in front of the fire, warming their hands and feeling satisfied with their discoveries. While they were congratulating themselves, they became aware of the piteous crying of the nanny goat in the courtyard.

"Poor goat." Mariel opened the door. "She probably needs to be fed. I wonder what we can give her."

Jake followed her to the door, holding the baby in his arms. "Our discarded tin cans," Jake said helpfully from over her shoulder, earning him a skeptical look from Mariel and a toss of the head from the goat.

"They eat hay," he offered. "Grain, maybe."

"You know this for a fact?"

"I lived on a farm once with some foster parents."

"Wasn't there hay in the gatehouse?"

"What I saw was dirty and trampled. Would you eat it?"

"No, but I'm not a goat."

As it occurred to Jake what was wrong with the goat, a light bulb went on in his head. And then he saw fireworks. Why hadn't they thought of this before?"

"She needs milking," he said in a rush. "And Jessica can drink the milk."

Mariel, looking down at the distressed goat, didn't know whether to laugh or cry. "If we can milk her, it will certainly solve a huge problem. I'm a city girl, however, and I have *no* idea how to go about milking a goat!"

"I told you I've lived on a farm," Jake said.

Mariel grinned widely. "In that case," she said, standing aside, "she's all yours."

Jake confronted the goat, who was regarding him uneasily from the other side of the doorstep.

"First, we'll have to wash her udder," he decided with false heartiness."

"With what?"

"Water. And soap. I saw soap in the kitchen," he said.

"I hate to say this, Jake, but she doesn't look as if she's going to allow you near her," Mariel said. She had stepped forward and was scratching the goat gently behind her ears, a service that was only barely tolerated. The goat, swaying to and fro on tiny, anxious feet, kept tossing baleful glances in Jake's direction.

"How about if you put Jessica to bed while this goat and I make friends?" he said, transferring the baby to Mariel.

Jessica hiccuped. "We'd better leave him to it," Mariel told the baby, who only hiccuped again. Jake thought he detected a hint of skepticism in Mariel's expression as she went back inside.

After Mariel and the baby were safely out of sight behind the closed door, he crouched in the snow and tried to get the recalcitrant nanny goat to regard him as a friend, not an enemy. He put on his most goat-friendly smile. He mimicked her bleat, softly, so that Mariel wouldn't hear. He put his hands up to his ears and flapped them, goat-fashion. But every time he got within arm's length of the goat, she shied away.

He kept saying, "Whoa, Nelly, whoa," even though he had no idea if the goat's name was Nelly or if you said "whoa" to a goat. He recollected that people talked about saying boo to a goose, but that was another matter. Did you say boo to a goat?

He tried everything he could think of. Nothing worked. By this time, he regretted telling Mariel that he'd once lived on a farm. When he'd lived on that farm, the only cattle his foster father had kept were three geriatric cows. Besides, Jake had been all of three years old.

WHILE JESSICA DROWSED in her makeshift bed and Jake tried to worm his way into the goat's good graces, Mariel read the baby-care book.

The book offered all sorts of advice, one welcome bit about how to prepare goat's milk for drinking.

"'Cool the milk quickly in the icehouse,'" Mariel read out loud, hoping her words would lull Jessica to sleep. "'Bacteria must not be allowed to multiply.' Well, we don't have an icehouse, though at the moment it seems as if the whole world is one."

"Wah," said Jessica.

"I know, I know, but you're stuck with me and Jake. We don't know much about babies, but we'll learn," Mariel said soothingly.

"Nah," said Jessica.

"You doubt it, of course. But you just wait and see. Didn't we find milk for you? And Flubbies?"

"Dah," said Jessica.

"Hmm... I believe that's Russian for *yes.* Anyway, Jessica, you usually make your needs known loud and clear," Mariel said, smiling fondly at the baby.

"Blfdghbf," Jessica said, which Mariel figured was untranslatable into any known language.

Mariel read more of the baby-care book, poring over words such as *colic,* and *cradle cap* as she wondered if she'd ever need to know about them.

When at last Jessica was sleeping peacefully, and after tucking her blanket securely around her, Mariel took soap and water outside to Jake.

When she stepped into the courtyard, Jake was circling the goat, which in turn was trying to circle him.

"She doesn't seem to like you," Mariel said.

"Understatement of the year." Jake slipped on a patch of ice and swung his arms wildly as he tried to keep his footing.

This frightened the goat, who spotted Mariel and trotted directly to her, becoming docile and nuzzling her hand. This only made Jake angry.

"Why does she like you and hate me? And besides, I can't milk her out here in the snow," he pointed out. "I'd have to lie on my belly in order to reach her udder."

"Udderly impossible," Mariel said seriously, for which she received an impatient look from Jake.

"Look, Nelly seems to like you, so why don't you lead her into the stable?"

"Nelly? You've named her Nelly?"

"It was all I could think of. She has to have a name, if we want to be friends with her," he explained.

"Come along, Nelly," Mariel said, holding her hand toward the goat and walking backward across the courtyard, toward the stable. The goat followed, eyeing Jake distrustfully all the while.

Once in the stable, Mariel backed the goat into a corner.

"She's practically begging you to milk her," Mariel told Jake by way of encouragement.

"If that's true, why is she trying to escape?" The goat was scrabbling at the stable wall, sending a shower of stones raining onto the earthen floor. He tried approaching, his hand held out in an attempt to mollify the terrified goat; when that didn't succeed, he clasped his hands behind his back and tried again.

"This isn't working," he said when Nelly rent the air with a terrified squeal.

"I'll hold her head," Mariel offered, grasping Nelly's neck. The goat struggled for a moment and then was still. But when Jake approached her hindquarters with the soapy cloth, she wheeled and tried to wrench away.

Mariel did the only thing she could think of. She began to sing to the goat.

"Silent night, holy night," she began, and Nelly calmed immediately.

"All is calm, all is bright," she went on, heartened by the results. Jake crept closer to the goat, cloth in hand, one eye on the goat's udder, the other on her hooves. At this distance, Nelly could kick him clear into tomorrow if she put her mind to it.

Nelly stood quietly now, Mariel scratching her head. "Sleep in heavenly peace, sleep in heavenly peace," sang Mariel.

"Again," said Jake, reaching for the udder.

Mariel began singing the second verse of the Christmas carol, and Jake sudsed and rinsed, then slowly slid the pan Mariel had brought under the goat and crawled closer for a better look.

"Shepherds something at the sight," Mariel sang.

"Quake," interjected Jake. "Shepherds *quake* at the sight." He was quaking at the sight of this udder. There weren't four teats, like a cow's, but two. That should make it easier, but he had no idea how to express the milk.

"Glorious beams from heaven above," Mariel continued. Jake thought of singing "Glorious streams from udders above," which might get a laugh from Mariel but wouldn't get the job done.

"Don't stop singing," he said, seeing that the goat was virtually mesmerized by Mariel's voice. Mariel sang another verse.

Jake stuck out a hand and curved it around one of the teats. The goat didn't move. Jake squeezed. Nothing happened, except that the goat became startled and almost planted one hind foot on the palm of his non-squeezing hand.

"Silent night?" Mariel sang anxiously. "Are you all right?" She bent to look at him, her brow furrowed in concern.

"I'm okay, don't take fright," he assured her in his chesty baritone.

"Hurry this up, she won't stand still long," Mariel sang, fitting the words to the carol's tune.

"This isn't easy, the fit is all wrong," he sang, wedging himself between the wall and the goat, and Mariel went on singing while he wrapped his fingers around one of the teats again.

This time he followed an instinct that told him he'd get better results if he squeezed from top to bottom. He clamped the top of the teat with the thumb and index finger and pulled. Again, nothing happened, but Nelly remained calm. She seemed to expect him to do this right.

By now, Mariel was starting on another verse of "Silent Night." Jake clamped his other hand around Nelly's second teat and squeezed one, then the other. Much to his amazement, a stream of milk squirted from each, hitting him squarely on the top of one boot.

Hmm... he thought, *I'll have to improve my aim.* The next time, he pointed the ends of the teats straight down toward the stainless-steel pan, and was rewarded by two steady streams clanging against the metal.

He was jubilant. "Did you see that?" he yelled. Nelly promptly kicked the pan, sending the bit of milk flying.

Undaunted, he tried again. Mariel switched to "Joy to the World," and after that, things progressed satisfactorily. Finally, Jake triumphantly held the pan aloft.

"Congratulations," said Mariel, and he beamed.

They fed Nelly from a bag of grain they found in the stable, and on the way back to the great hall he kept one arm companionably around Mariel's waist.

"I'd better get this milk to the kitchen," she said. "I'll want to strain it and cool it, and—"

"Not so fast." Jake carefully set the pan on one of the long tables and pulled her close. "I think I should tell you that you're one of the most versatile women I've ever met. I don't know too many women who look as beautiful when they're keeping a fire going in a cave as they do when they're singing to a goat, and I can't imagine anyone else of my acquaintance keeping her sense of humor. You're very special, Mariel," he said, gazing into those eyes that had captivated him almost from the first moment he laid eyes on her.

"Jake, I—"

He didn't wait for her to finish. Instead, he pulled her into his arms and rested his cheek against her hair, listening to the beating of his own pulse in his veins. He thought that he had never shared so much with any other woman; nor had he ever wanted a woman as much as he wanted Mariel.

She pulled away slightly to look up at him, and he lowered his head until his lips moved lingeringly against hers. Her lips were the sweetest he had ever tasted, full of what he had come to know as the essence of Mariel, and he drank from them as if from a spring that he feared would run dry. He felt his knees go slack, and he knew he would melt into her without any effort if this went on for much longer.

The baby was sleeping. They were alone in the big relic of a castle, and likely to be so for some time. The very thought of saying goodbye to her once they found their way back to the real world made him feel slightly crazy. Then the inevitable would happen; she would leave. Why would a well-educated woman from Pittsburgh want to have anything to do with a simple carpenter from rural Virginia?

He let her go. He dropped his hands, but his face remained only inches from hers, taking in every detail of her expression. For a moment, he thought she was going to fling her arms around his neck and press her body along the length of his, and then it would be all over. If she had done that, there would have been no point in fighting it. Nature would take over, nature and—might as well admit it—passion. He would take her right there on the wooden table, with the baby sleeping nearby.

But she only masked whatever she was feeling and said, "Well. I suppose we'd better see what we can do about cranking up that refrigerator." She reached for the container of goat's milk, and then she bustled away, leaving him to his regrets and his imagination.

MARIEL STEADIED HERSELF against the kitchen counter, hoping that Jake wouldn't follow her.

She had to get a grip on herself. She had no business lusting after Jake Travis. She didn't know who he was or what he was; all she knew was that he looked good in his skivvies and built a decent camp fire. And that he could milk a goat.

Which reminded her that she needed to refrigerate the milk. The refrigerator door was closed, unlike earlier, when it had hung open. She opened it, surprised that the inside light was on and that the air inside was cool. *Funny,* she thought. *When did Jake find the time to turn the refrigerator on?*

Thoughtfully she set the pan inside and closed the door again. Something strange was going on here.

"Mariel, I think we'd better talk about this," Jake said, bursting in the door.

"Did you turn the refrigerator on?" she asked.

"Refrigerator? No. Didn't you?"

"No."

Jake opened the refrigerator door and closed it again. "It's on. You must have done it."

"Didn't you say that it's run on propane gas? I wouldn't even know where to begin."

"When would I have done it, Mariel? You've known where I was every minute." Jake folded his arms across his chest and waited for a reply, which wasn't forthcoming, because she realized he was right.

They stared at each other uncomfortably. Finally Mariel threw her hands in the air and said, "I give up. Neither of us started the refrigerator. It's working. Chalk it up to something, I don't know what."

Jake checked the stove. "While you're chalking, I'm going to make coffee, because the pilot light's on here, as well."

"I'd like a cup of coffee, too," Mariel said, and Jake busied himself filling an old coffeepot while she strained the goat's milk into a glass pitcher. Soon the aroma of coffee filled the air, and she sat across the kitchen table from Jake, who handed her a mug of coffee and stared down into his own mug thoughtfully.

Jake didn't speak, and Mariel was determined that they wouldn't embark on any heavy discussions about their relationship.

"When do you think we'll be able to leave here?" she asked.

Jake lifted his eyes to her face. His expression was

impassive as he lifted the mug to his lips. "I don't know."

"Tomorrow? The next day?"

"At the moment, we still have no idea where we are. I can determine direction from the sun, and I think we should probably head west, but the mountain is there. Probably the safest thing to do is to wait until someone comes to rescue us."

"How long will that be? Tomorrow is Christmas."

"No one will come looking for me. I'm pretty much a loner, and all my buddies had out-of-town plans. How about you?"

"Unless some of the neighbors happen to check on me, I won't be missed. Even if they realize I'm not home, they'll think I've gone somewhere with a friend," she said slowly.

His eyebrows shot up. "Any special friend?" he asked sharply.

"My girlfriend Ellie—" she began, then realized that what he wanted to know was if there was a man in her life. "No, not the kind of friend you mean," she finished.

"And Ellie wouldn't wonder where you are?" he probed.

"She'll be with her husband. They were going to her grandmother's in Ohio."

"It looks as if we'll have to depend on someone wandering by if we hope to be discovered."

"How long can we hold out here?"

"If the baby drinks goat's milk, she'll be all right. As for us, there's plenty of food to last a couple of weeks."

"We're lucky," she said.

They drank in silence, each apparently unwilling to say anything more, each thinking private thoughts.

Finally, without comment, Jake went to rinse his cup at the sink. He couldn't see how Mariel studied the way his muscles rippled beneath the gray turtleneck, and he couldn't know her thoughts. She was thinking that she might be safe from the elements. But she didn't feel safe from the most capricious danger of all—her own runaway emotions.

JAKE WANTED to talk to Mariel about what was happening between them. He wanted— But what was the use?

He wanted a relationship. He'd known a lot of women in his life, but he'd never been really close to any of them. Now here was a woman, a woman for whom he was beginning to care deeply, and, thrown into close proximity with her, he was beginning to see how much he'd missed in his life.

When he'd followed her into the kitchen, he hadn't planned to talk about why the refrigerator was running when no one had turned it on. He'd planned a confrontation during which he'd lay his cards on the table.

All that had happened was that they'd had a civilized conversation over coffee. Now she was sitting in front of a fire in the great hall, playing with the baby. Soon it would be time to rustle up dinner. All he could think about was how soft and willing her lips had been when he kissed her.

"Come see Jessica play pat-a-cake," Mariel said, turning to him. Her skin had a golden glow in the firelight.

"How do you know how to play with a baby?" he asked as he sat beside her.

Mariel laughed. "Everyone knows how to play pat-a-cake," she told him, guiding Jessica's little hands through the motions.

"I don't," he said before he could stop himself, and she looked over at him, surprised.

"Because you were a foster child?" she asked.

"Maybe," he said with a shrug.

"Well, here. You play with Jessica," she said, shifting the baby to his lap. She rose to stir the fire with the poker, sending tiny sparks up the flue, and he grinned at her when she resumed her seat beside him.

He looked down at the baby, who blinked at him and kicked her legs. He felt like an idiot, batting the kid's hands together and saying, "Pat-a-cake, pat-a-cake, baker's man," but Jessica cooed, and Mariel smiled. The three of them were warm and safe as dusk grew thick outside the castle windows.

"Everything's going to be all right, isn't it?" Mariel said, tilting her face toward him.

"Not unless we have a diaper handy," he said, grimacing as he felt the dampness seeping through the baby's blanket. Mariel laughed as she went into the kitchen to get a clean one.

A warmth settled around Jake's heart, and he found himself thinking that here in this castle, this strange, out-of-the-way castle, something odd and yet reassuring and wonderful was going on, something he couldn't quite explain. Everything *was* all right—maybe for the first time in his life.

Chapter Eight

"It doesn't seem like Christmas Eve," Mariel said later as they sat in front of the fire, watching over the sleeping Jessica.

"We could hang up our stockings by the chimney with care," Jake told her.

"In hopes that Saint Nicholas soon would be there? No, thank you, I'd rather keep my socks on. Cold feet, you know." Mariel smiled at him, thinking that she had cold feet in more ways than one. Here she was, sequestered with a guy who could have been a pinup, and she was reluctant to let nature take its course. Some might call it stupid; she called it prudent. She'd never believed in rushing into things.

Jake had pulled one of the dusty velvet settees close to the fire, and Mariel was curled up on it. He sat at her feet. Jessica was at the far end of the hearth, where she slept in warmth and safety. Although the castle had many rooms, they had decided to spend the night in front of the fire in order to conserve firewood. They had no idea how long it would last, and Jake wasn't willing to chop down trees that belonged to someone else.

"What do you usually do on Christmas Eve?" he asked.

"My parents and I would go to the midnight service at our church."

"What's it like?"

"Haven't you ever been to one?" she asked in surprise.

"I never lived with a family that did that," he explained. For a moment, Mariel could see Jake as a boy. He would have been vulnerable and he would have been lonely.

"We light candles and sing Christmas hymns. Afterward—in my church, anyway—people hug each other and wish each other a merry Christmas. And then we all go home to sleep, and when we wake up, it's Christmas morning," she said dreamily.

"And then what?"

"Mother and I cook a turkey. And Dad mashes the potatoes. And I bake a cake."

"What kind?"

"Dad likes coconut, and we like to humor him on Christmas, so that's what it usually is. We always have turkey and stuffing and mashed potatoes. I miss them so much at this time of year. I won't be seeing them for six more months."

"Families should be together for the holiday."

Mariel sighed. "It's the first time in my life that I haven't been with my parents for the holidays," she said.

"Even though I don't have parents, I can imagine how you must feel. Not to mention having to spend the night in a cave."

"You know something? That time we spent in the cave—it wasn't so bad."

He focused unbelieving eyes on her. "How can you say that? Your face is scratched from the brambles, we had to care for a baby without the proper equipment or supplies, and we almost starved," he reminded her.

Mariel thought for a moment. "Those things are true," she agreed. "But you left something out. You didn't mention how kind you were to me, or how good it felt to provide for Jessica. You didn't say anything about how it felt when you came back into the cave, after I had been thinking that you had deserted us and you had been thinking that I had left, and we were both still there."

He stared at her, unsure what he should say or do, but she took care of that for him. She reached for his hand across the space between them and squeezed his fingers.

"I need you, Jake. And you need me. Jessica needs both of us. Those truths were brought home to me in the cave."

Jake hadn't known that Mariel realized how important they all were to each other. He didn't know how to react.

"It's almost midnight," Mariel said softly. "Would you like to join me in our own special Christmas Eve candlelight service?"

"I wouldn't know what to do."

"I'll show you," she told him, and got up from where she sat.

He gazed into the flames while she went into the kitchen. He heard her rummaging around, but he didn't want to follow her. He didn't want her to see that he had tears in his eyes or to know that, on this Christmas Eve, Mariel Evans had touched him to the depths of his soul.

JESSICA SLEPT DEEPLY beside the fire, and Mariel insisted that she and Jake repair to the cold chapel for their ceremony. Jake put on his jacket and held Mariel's coat for her. Her scarf was caught in the sleeve, and he pulled it out.

"Don't you want to wear this?" he asked.

She hesitated for a moment, then wrapped it around her head. Jake stared at her, fathomless eyes fixed on her face. To break the mood, she bent to light a candle that she had affixed to a saucer with melted wax.

When she straightened, he was still staring at her as if he couldn't pull his eyes away. "You look..." he began, then stopped.

"I look what?" she asked, something stilling inside her.

"You look beautiful in the candlelight," he finished softly.

This was not the way this was supposed to go. She didn't want to encourage Jake Travis; nor did she want to give herself false hope. Tonight she wanted to celebrate the meaning of Christmas and give thanks for their safety, and that was all.

"Come with me," she said quietly. Taking Jake's hand, she led him through the small corridor to the chapel.

The altar was wide, surmounted by a stained-glass window featuring Jesus, Mary and Joseph. Candelabra holding old parchment-colored candles flanked the altar, and Mariel lit the candles one by one. They cast a warm glow over the room, highlighting the wood grain of the pews and giving enough light to read the print on the pages of the large Bible that stood on the altar.

Mariel cleared her throat. "First," she said, "we thank God for his protection, and we ask for his blessing. Would you like to—?"

Jake shook his head.

Mariel bowed her head, and Jake followed her example. "Heavenly Father, thank you for letting us find Jessica in the woods. Thank you for guiding us to the cave last night and for providing food for us and for Jessica. Thank you for helping us find this castle. We ask your blessing on all of us, and for your guidance in the days to come." She paused. "Is that all?" she whispered to Jake.

"Thank you for the goat," he reminded her.

"And thank you for the goat."

"Amen," Jake said hastily, and Mariel added her own "Amen" to his.

"Now I'll read the Christmas story." Mariel picked up the Bible and leafed through it until she came upon the age-old story, so familiar to her, but perhaps not to Jake, who stood beside her, his attitude cooperative but otherwise unreadable.

"'And she brought forth her firstborn son, and wrapped him in swaddling clothes, and laid him in a manger; because there was no room for him in the inn,'" she read. The story had more meaning than ever for her now, because of Jessica.

When she finished, she laid the Bible on the altar.

"Now we should sing a Christmas carol," Jake said, surprising her, and he started with, "Hark, the Herald Angels Sing." She chimed in with her sweet contralto, and their voices blended so that the notes reverberated from the high ceiling in joyous accord.

"Let's sing another carol," Mariel said, gazing up at Jake, and he smiled and took her hand.

"Your choice this time."

Mariel sang "Away in a Manger," because it had been her favorite when she was a child. She had become unaccountably nostalgic while reading the Gospel, re-membering how her father had often read it to her, not only at Christmas but at other times during the year, because she loved to hear about the baby being born in a stable.

"One more prayer, I think," she said in a low voice, and she tried to think of the formal benediction from church, but her mind had gone blank. She looked ques-tioningly at Jake.

"And thank you for each other," he said. "Amen."

Mariel gazed up at him, surprised and touched. "Amen," she said, and he squeezed her hand.

The chapel was no longer cold. The air was warm, warmer than it should have been from the heat of a few candles.

"What time is it?" she asked Jake.

He glanced at his watch. "It's three minutes after midnight."

"Merry Christmas," she said, unwilling to look into his face.

But he had no such compunctions. Slowly he lifted his hands to her shoulders, and slowly he turned her to face him. His gaze was hard and penetrating, the set of his jaw firm.

She shook her head, denying what she read in his eyes, but it was too late.

"Merry Christmas, Mariel," he said, as he lowered his lips to hers.

She let him kiss her, but she held back. She didn't dare let herself participate, because she knew all to well what that would mean.

His lips were warm, and his hands found their way beneath her coat and adjusted to the slender curve of her waist. She wanted to slide her arms around him, to feel the wool of his coat against the palms of her hands, to feel the play of the muscles of his back. But her hands only hung at her sides.

Her mouth parted helplessly as he explored all the warm, sweet textures of lips and teeth and tongue. He kissed her so thoroughly and with so much unexpected passion that her heart trembled beneath her ribs and her skin caught fire.

Stop, Mariel thought. I don't want to do this.

But even as the thought seared her consciousness, she knew it wasn't true. His mouth was insistently seductive, and with supreme effort, she steeled herself to push him away. For one last, sensual moment, she was lost in the scent and taste and touch of him, and then she caught herself, just in time to wrench herself from his grasp.

"No," she said shakily, "I can't." Her boots clattered on the stone floor as she ran from the chapel.

Jake waited for a moment to see if she would return. He didn't know how she'd had the strength to put a stop to the mystical flow of passion and emotion between them, and he didn't know why she would want to. This was something special, this relationship, and he wanted to encourage it, to nurture it, and to embellish it. He couldn't imagine why Mariel wouldn't feel the same way.

He sat down in one of the pews to contemplate the situation, staring up at the stained-glass window of Jesus, Mary and Joseph above the altar. Mary held the infant Jesus in her arms, and Joseph stood behind Mary, his hand placed lovingly and protectively on her shoulder.

A family group. He had a rare flash of insight, unusual for him. He didn't know where it came from. He didn't know why it chose this moment to stun him into understanding. But now he knew what the hoopla of Christmas was all about.

It wasn't only to celebrate the birth of the Christ child. It wasn't just tinny Christmas carols piped into the grocery store, or toys on Christmas morning. It was a celebration of family.

For Jesus's birth had made Mary and Joseph a family. Not just a couple, but a man, woman and child. It was simple, really, because family was the basic building block of society. Nothing could change that. It had always been that way, and always would be.

His thoughts flew to encompass Jessica. She had made them a family, too. A temporary family, maybe, but it was the family that Jake Travis had never had. Families could come in all shapes and sizes. Single parents and their children were families, grandparents who were raising their children's children were families, and sometimes people who were unrelated were families. Like Mariel and Jessica and himself.

He was overcome by this feeling of kinship. One by one he blew out the candles, and then he went to find Mariel.

WHEN SHE FLED from the chapel, Mariel checked on Jessica and found her sleeping blissfully in her drawer on the wide hearth. She didn't want to have to talk to Jake; anything she might say would only make things worse between them. So she hurried into the kitchen and began to fill the huge tin bathtub she had found hanging in one of the pantries.

The castle didn't have adequate bathroom facilities. Toilets and miniscule sinks had been installed, apparently as an afterthought, under stairwells, and every time

Mariel used one, the flushing rattled the pipes into a cacophony. She had a fear of causing a miniature Niagara and eventually having to explain to the owner of this castle how she had managed to flood it.

So she was relieved that there were no built-in bathtubs, only this tin tub. She heated water on the stove and poured it into the tub until there was enough for a bath.

Mariel couldn't recall ever having felt so grimy before. She was caked with two days' worth of dirt, overlaid with the smell of a camp fire and the dank odor of the cave, which clung to her hair and skin.

She peeked out the kitchen door and saw that Jake wasn't sitting with Jessica, which surprised her. He was probably still sulking in the chapel, which was fine with her. If he was like most men, his ego was wounded. He'd probably never try to kiss her again. She only wished that thought didn't make her feel so depressed.

JAKE, after coming out of the chapel, was surprised not to find Mariel with Jessica. Jessica was sleeping on her stomach, her mouth open. She looked like one of the dolls in the tower; she really was a lovely baby.

He sat to wait for Mariel. When she didn't return after a reasonable length of time, he made his way toward the kitchen, seeing a glow behind the door as he approached.

The door was ajar, and it didn't occur to him to knock. This was, after all, the kitchen, and he thought that Mariel would be preparing a bottle for Jessica. He had no idea that she would be taking a bath, and when he saw her, he froze, spellbound by the sight of her.

In the light from the kerosene lamp on the table, Mariel's skin glistened like oiled silk. Her hair was dark from the water, and slicked back, making her eyes seem bigger. He was used to her fluffy curls, not this sleek cap; he was accustomed to seeing her wrapped up for cold weather, not totally naked. She was so achingly beautiful that she took his breath away.

Somehow reality evaporated like mist; there was no castle, no baby, they weren't lost, and he knew exactly what he was going to do. Only the two of them existed in the world, and he was going to do what any man would do under those circumstances. He was going to make Mariel his, incontrovertibly and forever.

In his mind he was striding forward, and she was turning her head toward him, slowly, slowly, as if in a dream. Their eyes met, and he was drawn into the warm azure depths of hers as a moth, utterly doomed, seeks the hot blue center of a flame. She smiled and held out her hand, droplets of water scattering like diamonds in the flickering lamplight, and when their hands met, she rose up out of the water like a nymph, smoothly and quietly, and somehow she was in his arms.

He had magically shed his clothes, and their bodies met, melding contours, flowing together. Her breasts brushed against his chest, their nipples wet and warm, and her mouth merged with his in an exquisite mating. He slid his hands down her smooth sides and cupped her bottom, urging her close. She moaned, deep in her throat, and so did he, and he pressed himself against her, lifting her so that she could wrap her legs around him, holding him so tightly, tightly, the two of them wrapped in the enchantment of the moment....

Of course, all this only happened in his mind. What really happened was that Mariel reached for the soap, which was resting on a nearby wooden stool, saw him standing in the doorway and screamed.

"Sorry," Jake said, his dreams bursting like a soap bubble. He retreated, feeling like a fool. She must think he was no better than a Peeping Tom—which, come to think of it, might be the truth. He was so angry with himself that he brought his fist down hard on one of the tables as he was passing, whereupon Jessica woke up and began to cry.

"Okay, okay..." Jake said, rushing to pick her up. If the truth were told, he was glad of the ruckus. At least taking care of Jessica gave him something to do besides put himself down for acting like an idiot.

Mariel shot out of the kitchen, a towel wrapped around her.

"What happened to Jessica? Is she all right?" she shouted, running up the aisle between the tables. Drops of water sprayed everywhere.

"She got scared," he said, trying not to look at Mariel. She hadn't taken time to dry herself, and her flesh rose up in goose bumps. It didn't make her any less attractive to him, unfortunately.

He picked up the baby, who was making more of a fuss than was warranted.

"Time for a diaper change," he said with false cheer. He reached for the stack of towels that served as Flubbies.

Mariel's teeth were chattering. "What was that awful noise?" she said.

"I hit the table with my fist," he said calmly.

"Why?"

"I was angry," he said.

"W-with me?" she asked.

"No," he said, efficiently pinning one corner of the towel together. He was getting good at this diapering business, but Mariel never seemed to notice.

"With the baby?"

"With myself," he said shortly. "Don't you think you'd better put some clothes on?"

Her eyes shot daggers at him. Then she turned and, with the utmost dignity, stalked back into the kitchen and shut the door firmly after her.

Jake had no idea what Mariel's look meant, but he was pretty sure what it *didn't* mean.

Jessica began to cry. It was the wail that he had come to know as her "feed me" persuasion.

"All right, little one," he said tenderly, kissing the top of the infant's head. And then he added, with a kind of wonder that he was saying it at all, considering the way things were going with Mariel, "Merry Christmas, Jessica. Merry Christmas, baby!"

AFTER Mariel came out of the kitchen to dry her hair by the fire, Jake went to take his bath.

Mariel knew he hadn't meant to walk in on her when she was bathing, and she didn't know why she had reacted by screaming. He'd startled her; when she'd looked up and seen him standing there, mesmerized at the sight of her, she'd been momentarily caught off guard. She'd felt foolish afterward. It wasn't as if Jake Travis hadn't seen her body before.

She'd try to reassure him and let him know that she had no hard feelings over it. In fact, it was just the opposite. She was so strongly attracted to him that she felt caught in some kind of spell, unable to resist, though she knew she had no business thinking about him in that way. They had almost nothing in common except the baby and their goal of survival—why, they wouldn't have spared each other more than a passing glance if they had happened to stand next to each other at the bus stop in Pittsburgh.

Pittsburgh. It seemed so far away.

Mariel picked up Jessica and fed her. The baby adjusted to the doll bottle and drank the goat's milk without a peep, and Mariel was so engrossed that she didn't hear Jake when he came out of the kitchen, fresh from his bath. She looked up to see him standing before her.

"Mariel, I think I should sleep upstairs, in one of the rooms off the gallery," he said without preamble.

"It's so cold up there!" she exclaimed in dismay.

"I can build a fire."

"Jessica will wake up again in four hours. I thought we'd take turns feeding her, and if you're sleeping upstairs, you won't hear her cry."

He thought for a moment. "A good enough reason," he said grudgingly.

"We'll toss for the settee?" she said, favoring him with a brisk smile.

"That's not necessary. You can have it."

Mariel nodded toward a window. "I saw blankets in a chest over there."

Jake went to look and returned with his arms piled high with cushions, a comforter, and several woolen lap robes. "These should do," he told her. He tossed the cushions on the hearth and sat beside Jessica. When the baby was asleep, he punched the cushions he'd spread on the hearth into a semblance of a bed.

Mariel held the comforter to her cheek. "This smells of lavender," she said.

Jake ignored her. "I'm going to turn in. It's been a long day," he said. He lay down and tried to carve out hollows in the cushions with his hips and shoulders, his back to her.

"Is everything okay? Was your bath all right?" she asked.

"Yeah. I'm just tired." He threw a lap robe over himself and said nothing more.

Mariel curled up on the settee and pulled the comforter up over her shoulders. It was quiet, the only sound the crackling of the fire.

"Jake?" Mariel said, her voice too loud for the silence.

"What?"

"You know those toys in the tower?"

"I only met them today," he said gruffly, but he sounded slightly amused.

"Don't be funny. Anyway, why do you think they're there?"

He sighed audibly. "For all I know, this is Santa Claus's distribution point for northern Virginia and all points south. Mariel, how the hell would I know what they're doing there?"

"I just wondered," she said. He didn't speak. "Are you comfortable?"

"Mm-hmm" was his muffled reply.

"At least this is cozier than last night," she said.

"I'm not so sure," he answered, leaving her to ponder his meaning. Last night, she thought he meant, she had slept beside him, warmed by his body. It had felt good, *so* good....

Soon she saw his shoulders rising and falling rhythmically, and she knew he was asleep.

After a while, she slept, too, a deep, wintry sleep filled with slippery dreams. Nothing in them seemed concrete; everything was wispy images.

Until suddenly the white-bearded man from the

Magic Minimart bent over her, wearing a fur-trimmed red cap and looking as solid as anyone could.

Mariel stared. He didn't fit into this dream. He was too real.

He *wasn't* real—was he?

Chapter Nine

"You made so many wishes, I wasn't sure *what* you wanted for Christmas," said the little man. "I had to guess. How did I do?"

Mariel felt disoriented and confused, and at first she was reluctant to answer. This was a *dream*. She didn't want to participate.

But she knew the man represented Santa Claus. She was in awe of him, the way she'd been when she was a little girl and her parents took her to the city's biggest department store to sit on Santa's knee. The little girl in her felt obligated to answer, even though she was half scared to speak up, just as if she were still a child.

"Well?" Santa said. "Aren't you going to talk to me? I don't have all night, you know."

"I don't like to complain," Mariel said.

He *ho-ho-ho*ed. "Seems to me you made a big fuss the Christmas when you were ten, because you didn't get a chemistry set," he replied.

She had. She was surprised that he'd remembered.

"You did okay this year, but I could have done without the sleet and the cave," she said grudgingly.

"Some things can't be helped. Anyway, don't you

think Jessica's better than any of those baby dolls I used to bring you?" And then he winked and disappeared.

At that moment, Jessica started to cry and Mariel opened her eyes. Jake was sleeping, and Jessica had kicked off her blanket. It must be time for her feeding. Jake stirred as Mariel struggled out from the comforter.

"Don't get up," she said, mindful of how tired he'd been. "I'll take the first turn." Still wondering about her dream, she crossed the long hall and went into the kitchen.

The coals in the kitchen fireplace radiated warmth into the room, and Jake had left the kerosene lantern burning on the table. She found Jessica's bottle in the refrigerator, already filled. Jake must have prepared it earlier. Grateful for his foresight, Mariel warmed it quickly in a pan of water on the stove.

Jessica broke into a full-fledged wail as Mariel reentered the great hall, but Jake had already lifted her from her bed and was cuddling her in front of the fire and murmuring consoling words.

"I've got her bottle," Mariel told him. "I can feed her while you go back to sleep."

Jake looked bleary-eyed, but he took the bottle from Mariel. "I'm doing this."

"It's my turn," she protested.

"You go back to sleep," he said. "It's been a long day."

"Jake, I'm wide awake."

"That can be remedied soon enough." He smiled at her, and she sank down on the settee. She pulled the comforter up to her chin, but she didn't close her eyes. Jake was urging the baby to take the bottle, his head bent, his voice low as he murmured encouragement.

They looked so cute together, the man and the baby,

and she wished she had a picture of them. But then, she was always wishing something.

That was when she remembered the little man with the beard who had appeared in her dream. Santa Claus. Santa Claus? She forced herself to sit up straight.

"Jake..." she began, but then she knew she couldn't ask him if he'd seen Santa Claus too. She had no doubt that Jake would seriously doubt her sanity if she so much as hinted that she wasn't sure whether the man was a dream or reality.

Jake looked up at her. "I thought you were going to sleep," he said.

"I told you I'm too wide awake," she said. "I don't think I can sleep anymore."

"In that case, would you mind giving Jessica her bottle? I'll find us something to drink." Mariel moved to the warm hearth, and he carefully transferred the baby to her arms before disappearing into the kitchen.

Jessica drank eagerly, her eyes on Mariel's face.

"A bottle's better than an eyedropper, isn't it, Jessica?" Mariel whispered, and she thought that Jessica smiled momentarily.

She wondered if it was normal to bond with a baby so quickly when the baby wasn't even hers. She loved Jessica so much; before, she would not have believed that she could adore a tiny baby so completely.

"I love you, little Jessica," Mariel whispered, trying the words on for size and liking the way she felt inside when she said them. "I love you."

She was startled when Jake appeared suddenly, holding two steaming mugs.

"What's that?" she asked.

"I dug around in our host's cellar and found several bottles of burgundy, one of which was perfect for my own recipe for mulled wine. I thought we might as well try to be festive," Jake said with a smile. He set one of the mugs down beside her on the hearth and cupped the other between his hands as he sat. He leaned his elbows on his knees and looked ruminative.

"Jessica was a good baby. She drank all her milk," Mariel said after a while, holding up the empty bottle.

"Let me hold her for a while." Jake set his cup aside. "She doesn't look any sleepier than you do."

Mariel handed Jessica to him, and Jake rested her on his knees. Jessica bicycled her legs vigorously, and he laughed. Jessica cooed. He laughed again and tickled her under the chin.

Mariel treated herself to a sip of wine. It was good, warming her all the way down. Jake had spiced it with something—canned oranges from the pantry, perhaps, and cloves and cinnamon. "You two look so right together," she told Jake, and she meant it.

Jake shot her a quick sideways glance. "I was thinking the same thing about the two of you when I came out of the kitchen and saw you holding her. You look like a Madonna. Even your hair. It could be a halo."

"Oh, my hair..." Mariel said disparagingly. Her mother had often said that she didn't appreciate her naturally blond hair, which curled of its own accord, and maybe her mother was right. Mariel had always wanted straight hair, as fine and glossy as corn silk. Most of her friends thought she was out of her mind.

"What I said was meant to be a compliment," Jake said.

"I—well, I do feel comfortable with Jessica. I'll be going home to Pittsburgh after all this is over. Will you let me know how she fares?"

"Of course."

"Where she is, what her parents are like, how they live, all those things?"

"I'll even try to find out what kind of Flubbies she wears," he promised.

"I'm serious, Jake. This has been an experience I could never have imagined. I'll never forget Jessica. Or—" She had almost said "you."

There was silence for a few beats. Jake cleared his throat. "I was thinking that we could keep in touch," he said at last. "Not just about Jessica," he added in a rush, when he saw the fleeting expression of doubt that crossed her features.

"Mmm…" Mariel agreed noncommittally. She wasn't sure what he meant. Phone calls back and forth between the two of them? Letters? Visits?

She couldn't picture Jake in the city where she lived. She tried to imagine him swinging along her street, wearing blue jeans and his red-and-black lumberjack jacket, and the idea made her want to smile. Jake would feel out of place there, although she was certain that none of the other men of her wide acquaintance would outshine him. She'd be proud to show off Jake Travis to her friends. But she didn't think he'd like being put on display, like one of the artifacts at the museum where she worked.

"You might want to visit me in Tellurian," he said. "I'd show you the house I'm working on, and some others I've finished. We could even go spelunking and reminisce about old times."

"Spelunking?" the word didn't ring a bell.

"Exploring caves," he said, grinning.

"No spelunking," Mariel said firmly.

"When would you like to visit?" He was pushing her, and she didn't know how to deal with it. She couldn't imagine herself in rural Virginia any more than she could picture Jake in Pittsburgh.

"Oh, Jake, I don't know." She was wary of making a promise that she couldn't keep. She was attracted to him, but what did it mean? She needed to sort out her feelings. Right now she didn't know what she felt; all she knew was that she wouldn't mind kissing him again.

He look chastened, and she thought she might have hurt his feelings. She wished he didn't look so crestfallen.

He sat Jessica up in his lap, rubbing her back. She burped noisily. Jake wiped her face gently and then rocked her against his chest.

He's so good with the baby, Mariel thought. *How many men do I know who would share this experience so completely?* She didn't know any men who were this comfortable around babies.

Jessica's eyelids immediately began to grow heavy. Mariel thought that Jake's heartbeat must have a calming effect on the baby, because whenever he held her that way, she became drowsy and fell asleep. Mariel had a notion that it would be a very pleasant way to fall asleep, listening to Jake Travis's heartbeat.

"What do *you* think will happen to Jessica?" she asked idly. The baby's eyes drifted shut, and Jake settled her in her bed before answering.

"After we get back to civilization, we'll have to tell the police how we found her. She was abandoned in the woods, which is clearly a case of child neglect. If they can find her parents, perhaps they'll be prosecuted. Jessica could have died in that hut," he said.

"And if the authorities don't know immediately who her parents are? What will they do then?"

"Call in a social service agency, and they'll see that she's put in a foster home, I suppose," he told her.

"I can't bear the thought of that."

"Why?"

"Because—because I'm so fond of her," Mariel said in a low voice.

"Well, so am I. I'm a product of foster homes myself, and it's not an easy way to grow up."

"I suppose not."

He looked up at her. "Remember what I said, Mariel? Maybe Jessica's the solution to your problem. Maybe she's the baby you always wanted."

Mariel gazed into space for a moment. "There's something I didn't mention," she said at last.

"Oh?" he said, sounding surprised.

She forced herself to look at him. "I was married once," she said. "I could have had a baby then, but I refused. If I'd had a baby, I wouldn't be so alone now, that's for sure." She tried not to sound too regretful. She didn't want his pity. She only wanted him to know what few people knew about her.

"Do you want to tell me about it?" he asked gently.

Mariel leaned her head back against the stone of the fireplace and gazed at the tapestries, half hidden in the gloom at the opposite end of the great hall. Jake waited while she gathered her thoughts.

"My husband was an officer in the air force, and we lived in California," she said finally, half wishing she hadn't opened this chapter in her life to Jake, but nevertheless feeling compelled to continue. She paused to take another sip of wine, covertly observing him from beneath her lashes, wanting to see how he was responding. His face showed no expression, and his eyes were thoughtful.

"My husband wanted a baby right away, but I resisted, because I thought we needed time to get to know each other."

Jake nodded. "That's understandable."

"Something else upset me, as well. He was drinking too much, and I worried about bringing a child into that situation." She let her sentence trail off, then took a deep breath and went on. "He drank more and more, and in the end he became abusive."

"He hit you?"

"Only once. I left and filed for divorce. He was killed two days after the divorce was final. He drove head-on into a tractor-trailer rig. He was drunk at the time." She bit her lip, remembering how demoralized she'd been by the whole experience. She'd thought she'd never get over the end of her marriage, and her ex-husband's death had sent her into a deep depression.

"I'm so sorry, Mariel," Jake said. He reached for her hand.

"I'm all right now," she said. "I feel as if I missed out on something that was rightfully mine, that's all. I feel cheated out of a home and children."

"I know how you feel. I've felt cheated out of a home all my life," he said.

"What happened to you—all that moving from one foster home to another—wasn't your fault. It *was* my decision not to have a baby," Mariel said earnestly.

"Ah, but, Mariel, I didn't know that all the shifting around wasn't my fault. When I was a kid, I was told I was bad for not eating all my vegetables, for leaving my shoes in front of the TV, for skipping school on the day of a test I wasn't ready to take. Naturally I felt that I must be bad, if I wasn't fit to stay in a foster home. It was easy to blame myself."

"Childhood probably isn't an easy time for anyone," Mariel said softly.

"Probably not. Though I know some people who claim to have had a happy childhood."

Mariel smiled. "I'm one of them. My parents were wonderful."

"Chances are," he said, tracing one of the veins on the back of her hand with his thumbnail, "you'll be a wonderful mother yourself. Since you've had a positive role model," he added.

"I may not get the chance," she reminded him. She bent over, and with her free hand she smoothed Jessica's nightgown. "I hope Jessica's parents will be good to her. I hope she'll be happy," she said wistfully.

The warm wine in her stomach was doing a wonderful central-heating job, and her fingertips were beginning to tingle. But maybe it wasn't the wine. Maybe it was Jake's touch that was sending warm waves of pleasure through her body. Whatever it was, it felt wonderful.

The stone of the fireplace was cool and bracing against the back of her head, and she closed her eyes. The fire crackled nearby, and the faint, sweet, woodsy odor of burning apple logs wafted over them. She still tasted the full-bodied wine on her tongue; whimsically she wondered if it was a magic potion. Whatever it was, it was potent stuff.

She felt Jake's hand brushing her hair away from her face, and she opened her eyes to find his head only inches from hers. She didn't have to read his mind to know what he wanted, because at the moment she wanted it, too. She wanted to be lost in the illusion that this could be more than a one-night stand, that this wasn't really a transient relationship. She wanted to know in her heart of hearts that a simple carpenter from rural Virginia and a sophisticated, college-educated woman from Pittsburgh could find enough in common to fall in love and make it last a lifetime.

If only she could believe! But how could she risk emotional involvement with someone she was sure she would never see again?

He cupped a hand around her face, staring deep into her eyes, and she felt the whisper of his breath on her cheek. Outside the wind blew, and the castle creaked around them. These were realities. She should have refused to be bewitched. She should have fought her way out from under Jake's spell. She should have, but she didn't.

Because in his eyes, there was magic.

Her heart turned over as he began to kiss her expertly and in a leisurely way, as if they had all the time in the world to explore their physical attraction. Maybe they did, she thought fuzzily. Maybe this, too, was a dream, maybe none of this was happening, maybe she would wake up soon.

His mouth tasted of wine and cloves and cinnamon, and his breath fluttered softly against her skin. His face smelled faintly of soap.

His hands rested lightly around her waist, but they began to move upward, exploring her ribs with excruciating slowness. A shiver sliced through her, a delicious tremor of anticipation. One of his hands slid upward and wove through her hair to cradle the back of her head, and the other rested lightly on her back, caressing in small, repetitive circles.

She felt so confused. She loved what he was doing to her, she loved the way she felt while he was doing it, and yet she worried that what was happening wasn't in her best interests. Or maybe it was. Maybe this was what she needed—a fleeting encounter with a man she liked. For too long she had been looking for the right man—preferably a PhD—and a love that would last a lifetime. Perhaps a handsome hunk of a carpenter and a *like* that lasted for a few days was good enough.

Jake shifted his weight so that his chest molded to hers, and he slid his hand lower to urge her toward him. Her head fell back as he traced the outline of her lips with his tongue in a foray that left her breathless.

She didn't know when she began kissing him back, but she was no novice, taking as well as giving, until he moaned with desire. His kisses became wilder and deeper, and soon her kisses matched his.

For the life of her, Mariel could think of no reason now to avoid this; she only knew that she had survived an automobile accident, a trek through an ice storm, a night in a cave, and an excursion through snow to this castle. She had taken on the responsibility for a small baby, and at times, though she would never have admitted it to Jake, she had been frightened out of her wits by their plight.

Now she wanted to celebrate their survival by feeling good again, by feeling alive, by unleashing the passions that had built up between her and this man, this Jake Travis, who might not be a permanent fixture in her life but was, by God, important to her.

She sighed deeply and he trailed a row of kisses down her neck to the hollow of her throat. She slid her hands down over his heavily muscled back, clutching him to her. His hands parted the neck of her sweater, and he lavished kisses in the sensitive hollow between her breasts as he undid the buttons.

His hands moved reverently beneath the soft lamb's

wool to cup her breasts, still confined by the transparent lace of her bra. She was trembling as he reached around and unhooked it.

"Mariel..." was all he said, looking deep into her eyes, and she thought that she had never wanted a man so much in her entire life.

Her nipples ached for his touch, and when he rested the tips of his fingers on the sensitive underside of her breasts, she moved closer, until his hands completely encompassed the soft mounds of flesh. She slid her own hands under his clothes, and he moved away for one swift moment to divest himself of his sweater.

His chest was smooth, and bronzed by the firelight, and she slid her hands up over his nipples, gently rubbing until they rose into hard nubs beneath the palms of her hands.

"Ahh," he said, "that feels so good." He helped her to shrug out of her sweater, and her nipples were hot peaks beneath his fingertips.

They fell back against the cushions, her mouth opened beneath his and her hand went behind his neck to urge him closer, closer.

They were going to make love. It was what she had wanted to happen with every fiber of her being, though she still doubted the wisdom of getting involved with someone she'd only have to leave. And now, with the flicker of the firelight the room's sole illumination, and given the attraction that had flowed between them from the first, it seemed only natural and inevitable that they come together.

Jake's mouth was urgent and demanding, and his hands were knowing and insistent. She breathed in his warm, clean, male smell, wondering how it was that men could smell so different from women. Each had his own distinct natural fragrance, too, and Jake's was like no other man's she had known. She tried to identify it, but couldn't; she knew only that it was a woodsy, wild scent, and that it was, at the moment, compelling her to act with uncharacteristic wantonness, as if she weren't Mariel Evans, but a bolder, more seductive, more daring version of herself.

He slid both hands up to fan her hair across the cushions in a flow of spun gold. He gazed down at her, murmuring her name. She thought she had never heard anyone say it so beautifully.

Luminous flecks, so fascinating to watch, surfaced in his dark eyes. His hands cupped her face, and his eyes searched hers. "Oh, Mariel, you are all I've ever wanted in a woman," he breathed.

This is the way it should always be, she thought. She slid her hands between them, fumbling with the fastening of his jeans. He helped by lifting himself away so that she could unzip them, and he slid out of them as she shimmied free of her corduroys.

He knelt before her and slowly rolled her panties down over her hips and legs.

"You are so beautiful," he whispered, his eyes taking her in. He brushed his fingertips lightly across the soft wisp of curls where her legs met. "Lovely," he said, his hand seeking the hot center of her.

Her hands splayed over his flat belly and then moved lower, her fingers encasing his dusky hardness. He was hot, even hotter than she was, and very hard. As he strained against her hands, she felt a rush of heat in her lower abdomen, and she opened to his questing. His fingers found molten honey, and she arched beneath him, guiding the way.

She heard his sharp intake of breath as he lowered

himself over her with agonizing slowness, supporting himself on his elbows as he took fierce possession of her mouth.

"Do you…want…?" he gasped close to her ear, and all she could do was cry, "Please…oh, yes…oh, yes…"

He moved a hand beneath her and paused for the space of a heartbeat, an eternity, before rearing back and, guided by her fingers, plunging into her with all his strength. She felt a white-hot throb of joy as he penetrated to her very center, and she gasped with pleasure against his mouth.

Their two bodies were one as, again and again, he rocked against her, his breath harsh against her ear. She felt dizzy, she felt hot, she felt wet and superbly energized. The thought flashed through her mind that somehow, in every past relationship she had ever known, she had missed out on what lovemaking could be, and she felt a sense of loss over those past futile fumblings. She wrapped her legs around him, lost in sensation and riding the sweet waves as they broke over the two of them, dissolving in a crest of pleasure.

She heard him cry out in exultation and heard her own answering sob, and then the sounds merged and were one and she didn't know where Jake ended and she began. As he pulsed within her, she gave herself over to the ecstasy, wanting this moment to go on forever. She had never before felt so wild and abandoned.

He fell against her, spent and sated, her fingers entangled in his damp hair. As he became conscious of time and place, he tried to roll his weight away, but she clutched him tightly around the waist.

"No," she murmured. "Not yet."

He covered her face with kisses, nuzzled her earlobe,

and came to rest with his head pillowed on one breast, his finger slowly circling the other.

She couldn't believe it was happening so soon, but she was becoming aroused again. Her nipple rose between his fingertips, a small, swollen berry, and he laughed and took it between his lips, sucking, tasting, kissing. She let him, lazily giving in to the sensations.

"I never knew it could be like that," she said dreamily, and he lifted his head. His eyes were bright.

"I didn't, either."

"You were...wonderful."

"And so were you." He kissed the tip of her nose.

"So, if you feel like doing it again..." she said, because she already felt him rising against the smooth flesh of her hip.

She was ready for him, but this time it was different. It was more controlled, more knowing, and their eyes seldom left each other's. Once, when she glanced to make sure that Jessica was still sleeping soundly, he tipped a finger under her chin and turned her face back toward him.

"Don't," he said tenderly. "I want to look into the heart of your soul." He held her eyes with his as he moved slowly within her, the flames from the fire illuminating her own reflection in his eyes.

This time he waited for her to climax first, taking in the flush of her face, the widening of her eyes, the gasps that she couldn't, didn't, want to control, and then he sought his own peak. She pulled him close, inhaling the sharp, tangy scent of his skin as he cried out. He buried his damp face in her neck and murmured her name over and over again in a voice husky with passion.

Afterward, he pulled the comforter off the settee and

settled it over them in a flurry of warm air, cradling her in his arms when they were both snug beneath it.

"Well," he said, "I guess this proves Santa Claus isn't the only one who's coming," and Mariel dissolved into giggles interspersed with kisses.

"We should get up and prepare the bottle for Jessica's next feeding," she whispered, but he only smiled against her cheek; she could feel the corners of his mouth turn up.

"Jessica will make sure we get up soon enough, and the bottle only takes a few minutes," he said. "For now, let's sleep."

Mariel wanted to stay awake, savoring this experience to the utmost, reliving the joy of these moments over and over. There was no doubt in her mind that this was special, that no two people had ever experienced such passion, and that nothing could ever compare to it.

But it was only two or three minutes before she slept, safe in the confines of his arms.

Chapter Ten

Jake didn't wake Mariel at dawn. Instead, he eased out from under the warm comforter, dressed quietly, and went to the stable. There, he fed and milked the nanny goat who was docile and welcoming. Then he walked into the woods, dug up a beautiful blue spruce tree, and dragged it across the wobbly drawbridge to the castle.

Jake planted the tree in a dilapidated bucket that he found in the stable. He wanted to surprise Mariel with it. It was Christmas Day, and she must have at least one gift; the tree would be the perfect present for the perfect day.

The sun was shining, melting snow and icicles. Avalanches of snow kept sliding from the sloping roofs of the castle buildings, the intermittent dull roars resounding like distant thunder. It looked as if they were in for a thaw, which meant that soon they'd have to walk out of here. The thought that this idyll would soon end, whether he liked it or not, was the only flaw in the perfection of his world on this day.

He carried the tree into the great hall, but Mariel wasn't there. Nor was Jessica sleeping in her makeshift bed. He heard Mariel singing in the kitchen, and hearing her silvery voice cheered him considerably. Christmas wasn't over yet. Not by a long shot.

"Mariel!" he called.

She bustled out of the kitchen, a towel across her shoulder, the baby in her arms. She looked radiant this morning.

"Jake, I—" She stopped when she saw the tree. He thought she would have clapped her hands if she hadn't been holding the baby. "Oh, Jake! How lovely!" she exclaimed.

"It was practically begging me to take it inside to be your Christmas tree." He grinned at her, pleased with himself. Her eyes sparkled as she walked toward him.

"Here," he said, holding out his arms. "Let me see the baby."

He took Jessica into his arms so that Mariel could inspect the tree more closely. He loved Jessica's warm baby smell, and he touched his lips to her forehead. "She smells so fresh."

"I was heating water on the stove, so I poured some of it into the smallest washtub and bathed her. She liked it," Mariel said.

Jake hummed "Rockabye Baby," mostly because he remembered that it had something about a tree in it. Then he remembered what it was, and he didn't hum the rest of it. In the song, the bough broke, and down came baby, cradle and all.

"Who would write a song like that for a baby?" he said indignantly.

"What song? Oh, that rockabye-baby one," Mariel said. "It's an old English folk tune."

She circled the tree. "What a good job you did in choosing this one," she said with satisfaction.

"Sadistic thing," Jake mumbled, holding Jessica more snugly.

"The tree, Jake?"

"No, no. The *song*," he said. "Sounds like something one of my worst foster parents dreamed up."

"Well, sing Brahms' 'Lullaby.'"

"I don't know that one," he told her.

"I'll teach you. While we're stringing popcorn into garlands for the tree."

"I've never done that."

"It's about time you did. And we'll prop the toys from the tower beneath it and pretend they're for Jessica. Oh, Jake, it will be such fun."

He pulled her to him and buried his face in her hair, unable to embrace her with as much enthusiasm as he really would have liked, because he was holding the baby. Memories of the night before danced in his head.

"Better than visions of sugarplums," he said, his voice husky, and Mariel pulled away and looked at him quizzically.

"The toys, you mean?" she asked.

"Last night, I mean. It was beautiful, Mariel. I'll never forget it."

"Magic," she said. "It was magic."

A smile lit his features. "If that's what you want to call it, that's okay with me."

They walked arm in arm to the fire, which Jake had fed before he left. It was blazing now, the flames roaring. "I found hot cereal in the pantry," she told him. Two large bowls of cream of wheat stood steaming on the hearth, along with two mugs of coffee and two glasses of juice. "It was the best I could do," she explained.

Jake laid Jessica in her bed and picked up one of the

bowls. "Let's eat," he said. "Then maybe we should go for a walk in the woods, see if we see any signs of people."

"We could gather berries and things to decorate our tree," said Mariel, her eyes shining. Then her face fell. "We can't. We can't carry decorations for our tree, and Jessica, too."

"I saw a sled in the tower room yesterday," he reminded her.

"So did I. Good, we'll pull Jessica along on that."

She looked so excited and happy that it was all he could do not to lean over and kiss her. He wasn't sure how she'd respond to such a gesture. Passion in the night was one thing, but kisses in daylight were quite another.

He finished his cereal. "That was good."

"I checked the store of canned goods. The prospects for dinner are dismal, unless you like chop suey. I wish we could eat a real Christmas dinner today," she said pensively.

"Is that one of your three wishes?" he asked her with a twinkle.

"It should be."

"Well, one of mine is that we get going on this tree-trimming mission of ours. I'd better run up to the tower room and bring down the sled."

When he left, she was bending over Jessica, the soft womanly curve of her breast outlined by her sweater. The sight of her reminded him that he wasn't so eager to be rescued after all. He'd like at least one more night with her, one more night to hold her close, one more night to—

He stopped in the door to the tower room. He couldn't believe his eyes.

"Mariel!" he called in a startled voice.

After a moment, he heard her mounting the stairs behind him, the heels of her boots rapping sharply on the stones.

"What is it?"

"Look," he said, standing aside, and behind him Mariel gasped.

Not one toy was left in the tower except the sled. And beneath the window stood a pair of tall black boots.

"Where—?" Mariel was as mystified as he was.

"I don't know," Jake said, striding into the room.

Mariel went over and picked up one of the boots. She inspected it carefully. "This boot is damp inside. Feel the lining," she told him.

He did. It was soft and fuzzy and definitely wet. Whoever had worn those boots—someone who wore a man's size 6, apparently—had been tramping around in the snow.

"No one could get in here," he said, trying the latches on the windows one by one. One swung open when he pushed at it; beyond it was the leaded roof over the chapel, denuded of snow by an avalanche earlier, while he was milking Nelly.

With the practiced eye of a master carpenter, he judged the distance. Someone could climb into this room from the chapel roof if he had a mind to—but who would? And how would he get up there, anyway? The wall on one side of the building was sheer and ended in the moat. The wall on the other side offered no handholds for climbing. There was no ladder that he could see. And, of course, with the snow gone from the roof, there were no footprints.

"Well," Mariel said with remarkable calm, "maybe the toys weren't here in the first place."

Jake turned to her incredulously. "You saw them. *I* saw them. Even Jessica saw them! They couldn't just get up and walk away!"

"Maybe—" Mariel began, but then she bit her lip. Just then Jessica began to cry, and they both hurried down the steps again.

Mariel picked up Jessica and soothed her. "We left you all alone, didn't we? And you knew it, didn't you? Sweet Jessica, how would you like to go for a walk? Outside in the snow? Wouldn't that be fun?"

Jake went outside to prepare the sled for the baby while Mariel got Jessica ready for their walk. After he'd finished, he stood in the middle of the courtyard and studied the tower above the great hall, where the toys had been. How in the world had someone managed to remove them without his and Mariel's knowing about it?

Sure, their lovemaking had made the rest of the world go away, but certainly he and Mariel would have noticed someone hauling toys down the tower stairs. It didn't make sense. It didn't make any sense at all.

MARIEL AND JESSICA, who was wrapped in blankets to the tip of her winsome pug nose, joined him in the courtyard a few minutes later.

"The snow may last only a few more days," Jake said. "From the balminess of the weather, it looks like we're in for a thaw."

"Well, it can't possibly all melt today, and I'm glad. There's nothing like a white Christmas."

Jake had rigged up Jessica's drawer-bed on the sled, hammering in a few well-placed nails to hold it. Now he fastened Jessica securely, so that she wouldn't fall out.

Nelly the goat trotted out of the stable and right up to Mariel, nuzzling her hand. Mariel scratched her ear affectionately, and the goat trailed in their footsteps as they made their way through the gatehouse passageway. But Nelly balked at the drawbridge. They left her behind and headed into the woods, Jake pulling Jessica on the sled. Mariel looked ecstatic.

"Say, isn't that holly growing over there, near that dead tree?" Jake asked after they'd walked half a mile or so.

"Oh, Jake, it will look so beautiful heaped in vases on the hearth!" exclaimed Mariel, her eyes alight with enthusiasm.

"Vases? Dream on," Jake said.

"I saw them in a kitchen cupboard. Or maybe they were big pottery jars. Does it matter? The holly will look so pretty." She ran through the snow, exclaiming over the abundance of berries while Jake, faintly bemused, followed after her, with Jessica on the sled.

Jake cut several boughs of holly with his hatchet. Careful not to prick herself with the points on the ends of the leaves, Mariel stuffed the branches into one of the many large bags they'd found in the kitchen.

Mariel rushed ahead, her hair as bright as the sunshine. "Wait for me," Jake called, because he didn't want her to get too far ahead.

"Oh, I see a fallen spruce tree!" she exclaimed, and with that she was off and running, leaving Jake behind.

"Let's take home some of these big lower branches," she said. "And a few smaller ones." She gathered them as fast as Jake could cut them.

"What are you going to do with those?"

"Drape them all about. The great hall will look so

lovely when we're through decorating.'' She smiled up at him.

"*You* look so lovely now.''

"I feel happy. As if I could fly. Watch me.'' She was off again.

"Look,'' she called from somewhere up ahead, "I'm making a Christmas angel!'' When he reached her, she was lying in a snowbank at the edge of the meadow and energetically moving her arms and legs up and down. She sat up. "Why don't you make one, too? We'll write our names in the snow underneath.''

"I'd rather watch you.''

To his surprise, she wadded up a handful of snow and sailed it past his head. The next snowball was more accurate and hit him in the chest.

"I wouldn't do that if I were you,'' he warned. It was too late; she managed to land the next one squarely in his face.

"If you don't want more of the same, I suggest you make your own angel,'' she said, laughing up at him.

For answer, he bent down and scooped up some snow of his own, molding it quickly.

"Oh, no, you don't,'' Mariel said, rolling quickly to one side, annihilating the snow angel she had just finished making.

He tried to hit her with the snowball, but it exploded directly to her right, and with that she was on her feet and scooping up great clods of snow.

"We'll see who can make the biggest snowball,'' she said, but this time he managed to hit her, and she threw a handful of loose snow at him.

"I'll fix you,'' he said, and he grabbed her by the collar and washed her face with snow until she twisted away and fell in a snowbank, whereupon he lost his balance and fell on top of her.

"Who fixed whom?" she said, grinning up at him, and then they were rolling over and over in the snow. She tickled him, and he retaliated by pinning her down, his hands holding her wrists, his leg across her thighs.

Suddenly it seemed very quiet. All they could hear was the sound of their own irregular breathing.

He was aware of her beneath him, of all her gentle curves, of the bones beneath her skin, of the sublime softness of her lower lip. Her eyes were as blue as the sky, and her skin was pink from the cold. She smelled of evergreens.

"Mariel," he whispered, and then he kissed her, tasting her, tentatively at first, then more forcefully. Her arms went around him, and he felt her warmth through the layers of clothing they wore. With any encouragement, he would make love to her here in the snow, with the whole forest looking on. The heat from his body would be enough to keep them warm.

"If only it could be Christmas forever," he said against her cheek, and she turned her head and looked deep into his eyes. He was dizzy with desire for her, but she pushed him away.

"We're not acting much like angels," she said lightly.

"Do we have to?" he asked, but she was already standing up and bending over the sled to check on the baby.

"What's this?" she asked, holding the thermos he had tucked in the side of Jessica's bed.

He brushed snow off his clothes. "Hot chocolate. For our lunch."

"You brought lunch?"

"A package of saltines and some canned pudding from the pantry." He pulled the cans and crackers out of the blankets around Jessica's feet.

"Let's sit down on that rock over there and eat," Mariel said. Jake could think of things he'd rather do, but even he had to admit that they were impractical. He followed Mariel and endured the peculiar lunch. Mariel insisted on spreading her chocolate pudding on saltines. He ate his separately, watching her and realizing that she was actually enjoying the meal.

"I'll bet we can find some things around the castle to decorate the tree with," Mariel said.

"I noticed scraps of aluminum foil stuffed into a crack in one of the windows. It'll be fine for a star. And if we can find wood, I might be able to make a few ornaments. I used to be a pretty good carver," he told her.

"This part of Virginia is so beautiful." Mariel gazed at the mist-shrouded mountains in the distance. "If this hadn't happened, I would have missed sitting here with you and enjoying the peacefulness of this snowy landscape. Isn't this better than watching a football game in the company of a bunch of guys?"

"You'd better believe it" was Jake's heartfelt reply.

"What would you do tonight if we weren't here?" she asked him.

"Sleep off the effects of a huge dinner. Chop suey at Christmas may have its good points. After an hour or so, we'll have to remind our stomachs that we've eaten."

Mariel made a face and tucked her arm companionably through his. "The chop suey wouldn't be so bad if we only had some rice. And noodles. And maybe a couple of fortune cookies."

"There you go, wishing. Aren't you aware you do it?"

She laughed and shrugged. "No. You know, I dreamed I saw Santa Claus last night," she told him.

"I dreamed I heard hoofbeats on the roof," he said, completely deadpan. He was obviously teasing, but she wanted to be serious.

"No, Jake, I honestly did," she insisted.

"Okay, and what did the old guy have to say?"

Mariel could tell he was humoring her, but she wanted to share this with him; for some reason, it seemed important.

"He asked me if I didn't think that Jessica is better than any of those dolls he used to bring me," she recounted, and her face flushed.

"Ha! I hope you told him that the dolls didn't wet their diapers every fifteen minutes."

"No. He disappeared." Mariel was feeling slightly disgruntled, and she thought she had been foolish to tell Jake about the dream.

"I would too, if I were him. If he hadn't, you might have given *him* the sack of dirty diapers. Speaking of which, it should be fun to wash them by hand. I didn't see a washing machine."

"I can do it," Mariel said. She was disappointed that he hadn't taken her seriously, but at least it made it clear that they were two different types. Jake was down-to-earth, elemental; when he'd told her he didn't believe in magic, she should have believed him.

He took her hand and pulled off her glove, pretending to inspect her palm and fingers carefully. "You'd wash diapers and roughen these lily-white hands? Oh, no, you won't. We'll share."

She smiled at him, feeling better now. "I think it's

good the way we divvy up the work of taking care of Jessica,'' she said, determined to put his previous teasing out of her mind.

"Isn't sharing the modern way to bring up a baby? Isn't that what fathers are supposed to do? I suppose that old baby book you found doesn't tell you that.''

"But you're not—'' She stopped. She didn't want to hurt his feelings.

"I'm not Jessica's father, you were going to say. No, Mariel, I'm not. And you're not her mother. But living together in the castle, it's almost like we are. I never told you, but after we left the chapel last night, I suddenly knew what Christmas was all about.'' He told her how he'd felt when he was looking at the stained-glass portrayal of Mary, Joseph and Jesus. Mariel seemed subdued, so he put his arm around her.

"And you know something?'' he went on. "I like being a family, even if it's just for Christmas.'' He looked away across the field, his eyes on the outline of the mountains rising against the milky blue sky.

"But would you still like it if it was the same old day-to-day routine?'' Mariel kept her own eyes on Jessica's face, her dear, sweet, beautiful face.

"I don't know,'' Jake said honestly. "And it's not something I need to think about, is it?'' He stood up; looming over her, he seemed to fill the sky.

Mariel licked her lips, her mouth suddenly dry. His remark had brought her to her senses. She'd been deeply affected by Jake's revelation, and it made her more aware of her own mind-set. She had, without being really aware of it, been thinking about what it would be like for them to be Jessica's parents and to share the responsibility of her upbringing.

Jake reached down and pulled Mariel to her feet. He

wasn't wearing his cap today, and his hair fell in an unruly mass over his forehead. It gave him a roguish appeal and emphasized the rough-hewn quality of his features.

"Is everything all right?" he asked, looking puzzled.

"Yes, but I think we should continue our foraging. It'll be time to feed Jessica soon." She turned abruptly and headed into the woods, pulling on the glove he'd removed from her hand and walking too fast for him to keep up with her.

She had to think, and she wanted to do it as far away from those warm brown eyes as possible. Because, now that they were out of any real danger, living together in the castle was too comfortable by far. It was easy for them to fall into playing the role of mother and father to an oh-so-adorable baby. It was easy to think that this could go on forever.

But it couldn't. She and Jake Travis were totally different types. They led lives so far apart that there was no way to merge them, ever. She'd better face up to that. She'd better not start thinking that it could be any other way, because if she did, she would only be heartbroken.

She picked up some pinecones and gathered a few fallen evergreen boughs. Jake, pulling Jessica in the sled, was narrowing the gap between them when she pointed to a mass of pale green leaves and pearly white berries high in the leafless branches of an old oak tree.

"Jake, look!" she exclaimed, glad of a distraction. "It's mistletoe!"

Jake's gaze followed her pointing finger. "It certainly is."

"Oh, I wish I had some. It would look so pretty on our Christmas tree," she said, but she knew the mistletoe was too high up to reach, and the tree didn't look suitable for climbing.

"I wonder," he said thoughtfully, "if it's the same variety we usually see hanging over people's doorways during the holiday season."

"Oh, I'm sure it is," Mariel told him. "Did you know that mistletoe was revered in olden times as a plant of peace? If enemies met beneath a bough of mistletoe in a forest, custom required them to dispense with their hostilities and observe a truce until the next day."

"Mariel," Jake said, "you don't have to tell me what mistletoe is for. It's for this." And with that he swept her into his arms and kissed her until her knees went weak.

When his lips released hers, she gazed up at him. "What—what was that for?"

"For mistletoe. And for magic."

She struggled to regain her composure. "You don't believe in magic," she reminded him.

He smoothed her hair back from her face, his hand warm against her cool cheeks. "It's getting so I believe in it more and more," he said before kissing her again.

"Jake," she said when he released her lips, deciding that it was time to lay it on the line, "this is more than I can handle. Last night was wonderful, but now I need some space. Everything's happening so fast." She looked up at him helplessly.

"You think we need a cooling-off period."

"Yes."

"Don't you know I really care about you? About what happens to you?" he asked fiercely. His arms were still locked around her, and he seemed unlikely to let her go.

"I believe you do," she said, meaning it. "It's just

that I'm afraid of starting something that we both know we won't be able to finish.''

''Didn't you feel something special last night? Or was it just the same old same old?''

She twisted away from him. ''You know it wasn't. You know it meant something to me, too.''

''Then why do we have to pretend that it didn't?''

''Because there's no future in it. Can't you see?'' she cried. Tossing the bag of forest gleanings over her shoulder, she marched away from him, toward the castle.

''Who says? Why can't there be? Is it because I'm not as educated as you are?'' he called after her in exasperation.

Mariel whirled in her tracks. Her voice shook when she spoke. ''Let's get this straight once and for all, Jake! I'm well aware that it was *your* skills that saved us in the woods. It so happens that I respect people who work with their hands. But I won't apologize for my education! My father held down two jobs to send me to a state university, and my mother worked in a day-care center. I was lucky. But I don't look down on people who haven't been to college, okay?'' She turned her back on him and headed toward the castle.

He hailed her with a shout as she approached the drawbridge. She didn't think about the bridge's construction—she was too intent on ignoring him. Suddenly, when she was about halfway across, she felt one of the boards snap beneath her feet.

She was flooded with panic as she felt the bridge lurch beneath her and heard part of the board fall into the moat. She was only a few feet from the land at the end of the drawbridge, and she lunged toward it. When she looked back she saw that a hole had appeared in the snow, and through it she spied the rotted edges of the old board. The black water of the moat swirled below.

Jake had already stepped onto the other end of the drawbridge.

"Don't—" she warned him, but it was too late. Jake's strides were long, and by the time she spoke, his boot had struck what remained of the rotted board.

Only then did he realize what was happening. He tried to catch his balance, but, as if in slow motion, he toppled over the side of the drawbridge and into the icy water below.

Chapter Eleven

Fortunately, Jake had had the presence of mind to drop the rope that pulled the sled before he went over the side of the drawbridge. Jessica was safe, and, best of all, she was unaware that anything had happened. She snoozed amid her blankets, bundled tightly against the cold.

"Jake?" Mariel called. She felt frozen in place; she didn't know whether it was safe to move toward Jessica on the treacherous drawbridge. Jessica wasn't in any immediate danger. That couldn't be said of Jake.

Mariel hung over the battlemented fence of the outer ward and peered down into the water. Widening circles told her where Jake had plunged, but he had vanished. Her heart stilled in her chest.

Thoughts chased through her mind; she imagined Jake knocked out by the fall, his body drifting to the bottom of the moat. Did he know how to swim? She imagined him so cold that he couldn't move his arms and legs.

The drop from the drawbridge was a good twelve or fifteen feet, and, despite the thaw in the air, little fragments of ice floated on top of the water, broken off from the thin shell around the edges. As Mariel was wondering how long someone could survive in such cold water, Jake's head popped up.

He saw her immediately. "The water must come out of a pipe that comes directly from the North Pole!" he gasped, treading water.

"Are you all right?" she asked anxiously. She was flooded with relief at the sight of him. And he must not be hurt, if he could joke.

"As all right as someone can be when weighed down by a heavy, waterlogged wool jacket."

Mariel knew that she had to keep from panicking. She knew that, but the sight of Jake trying to keep afloat in the icy water almost unnerved her.

"Get Jessica off the drawbridge," he said.

Mariel took her eyes from Jake long enough to spare a brief glance at the sled, which was still where he had left it. She felt torn, not knowing what to do first. It took her only a split second to come down on the side of Jake, who was in immediate peril.

"Jessica's all right," she said distractedly. She looked around for a rope or a pole—anything to help Jake with. She knew she had to find a way to rescue him from the water immediately.

"*Jessica,*" Jake said in a tone that brooked no resistance and made his meaning perfectly clear.

Maybe Jake was right. Maybe she'd better tend to the baby. Barely managing to keep her senses about her, Mariel ran to the edge of the drawbridge. How safe was it for Mariel to step on the drawbridge and pull Jessica's sled the rest of the way across? Would the other planks bear her weight?

"Stay toward…the middle of…the bridge," Jake called. Was it her imagination, or was his voice flagging?

If something happened to her, Mariel knew both Jake and Jessica would be in grave peril. Jake's rescue and the baby's well-being depended solely on her. Yet in that moment, she realized that the baby's safety was more important than either Jake's or hers.

If only she could see the condition of the broken board beneath the snow! She had no idea of the extent of the damage. But there was no time to sweep the boards clean, not with Jake waiting patiently below, so she stepped out onto the bridge.

All one hundred and five pounds of her tensed as she carefully tested each step before investing it with her full weight. Every creak seemed magnified in the crisp clear air, and she waited for the *crack* that would mean that one of the boards had broken beneath her feet.

But finally she was close enough to Jessica's sled to grasp the rope and pull Jessica to safety. When at last the sled stood within the outer ward, she said a silent prayer of thanks and ran to hoist herself up on the wall again so that she could see how Jake was doing.

But now, where Jake's head had broken the surface, there was only dark water reflecting an endless blue sky.

Her heart fell to her boots. What had happened? Had he slipped beneath the water? Was he alive?

"I'm over here!" she heard him say, and when she looked carefully she saw his head, wet and seal-like, at the edge of the moat. He was clinging to a rock that formed part of the foundation of the castle.

"Can you climb out?" she asked frantically.

"I can't get a grip on these rocks! They're too slippery!" he gasped.

She remembered the rope in Jake's backpack. "I'll get the rope," she said. "Can you hang on?"

She thought he answered, "Yes."

This was no time to wait around and clarify things, she thought to herself as she bore Jessica on her sled through the gatehouse passageway and into the castle courtyard. She didn't want to leave Jessica out here in the cold; she wanted to set her inside by the fire.

Nelly the goat greeted her outside the gatehouse and, wagging her tail, capered wildly after the sled. Inside the great hall, Mariel parked Jessica—now awake and gnawing on her fist—in her sled beside the hearth.

"I'll be back," Mariel told Jessica as she fumbled in Jake's pack for the rope. "I'll be back *soon*. I promise." Not that Jessica could understand, but she hoped the baby would know that she wasn't deserting her.

She had been gone for only a matter of minutes, but Jake looked visibly more tired when she returned, his face white, his teeth chattering like a pair of castanets.

"I'm going to tie the rope around this iron ring in the castle wall," Mariel called down to him.

"Have you been p-practicing your c-clove hitches?" Jake hollered back.

"Don't make jokes," she ordered, not knowing what a clove hitch was, but sure that she'd never practiced any.

She fumbled with the knot, taking so long that the plaintive plea rose from the moat: "Mariel...can't you...hurry?"

By way of an answer she ran to the edge of the moat and dropped the end of the rope over the side, testing it from her side of the wall with her own weight. It held to the ring.

The end of the rope dangled above Jake, and she paid it out as quickly as she could, watching as Jake made several unsuccessful attempts to grab it.

"Are you okay?" she asked anxiously. His fingers seemed stiff with cold.

"As okay as...a Popsicle..." he managed to say.

"If you can make dumb jokes, you're fine."

Finally Jake caught the rope and wrapped it around his wrist. Then, with an enormous surge of strength, he hauled himself out of the water and began to pull himself hand over hand up the rope, bracing his feet on the rocks.

When he approached the top, Mariel added her weight to the rope, pulling him up and over the wall. Jake fell to the ground and lay there gasping for a moment. Mariel found a tissue in her pocket and wiped his face. She could hardly bear to think about what might have happened to him.

He rolled over on his back, and it was all she could do not to gather him into her arms and hold him. That would, however, serve no practical purpose, so instead she helped him up. He was soaked through, and his lips were blue.

"Don't you know you're not supposed to *wear* a moat?" Mariel said as he put a wet and dripping arm around her shoulders. She didn't care if she got wet. She didn't care about anything except that Jake was safe.

"I was only trying it on for size. Th-thank you, Mariel. You did a f-fine job," he said, his teeth still chattering. They started toward the gatehouse, Jake walking stiffly at first.

"It was my fault you fell in," she said.

"No."

"I shouldn't have—"

"*No.* Don't blame yourself. Neither of us knew that those boards were rotten. If anyone should have checked it out, I should have. I'm the carpenter in this group, remember?'' The color was returning to his lips, and for that Mariel was thankful.

They heard Jessica's wails from the moment they stepped into the courtyard, and they hurried toward the great hall. The baby had kicked off all her covers, and her face was red and wrinkled from the effort of crying. Mariel picked her up and cuddled her close.

"I think I'll take a hot bath," Jake said.

"Good idea. And Jake—I'm sorry for the way I acted in the woods."

"I think we have some things to talk about."

"I think so, too."

"Later?"

She returned his smile. "Later."

While Jake took a hot bath, Mariel went outside and brought in the holly and evergreen boughs, and she shut Nelly up in the stable for fear that the goat would change her mind about the drawbridge and wander into danger.

When she returned, Jake was wrapped up in the comforter on the settee and holding Jessica. The fire was blazing in the fireplace, and their Christmas tree stood ready to be decorated. He was holding the bottle for the baby, who was sucking greedily, the fingers of one hand wrapped trustingly around his thumb.

"I'm none the worse for my winter swim," Jake said, craning his neck to look at her.

Mariel was hovering over the two of them like a mother hen. "Are you sure?"

"Positive. I even made tea and left it on the stove for you."

When she came back, Jake was singing Jessica to

sleep with a Christmas carol. He stopped when Mariel entered the room.

"Go on," she said. "I like hearing you sing."

He hesitated for a moment, then went on singing the rest of the verse.

"Doesn't she look happy?" he asked.

"Jessica? Of course."

"Why shouldn't she? Two grown-ups are knocking themselves out to keep her that way." He laughed, clearly enjoying himself.

The comforter had slipped, exposing Jake's shoulder and part of his chest. Mariel stood up, suddenly unnerved. Of course he had no clothes on; there was nothing dry for him to wear. And if she sat here long enough, they would end up making love again.

It was what she wanted. No, it wasn't! If she let it, their lovemaking would become a drug, making her lose track of the rest of her life.

"I think I'll go exploring upstairs for things we can use to decorate the Christmas tree," she said unsteadily, slamming her mug down on the hearth so that tea sloshed over the rim.

Jake turned and stared after her as she fled to the unexplored gallery of rooms above them.

"I thought I'd—" Jake started to say, but she didn't wait to hear what he thought. Instead, she ran past the suits of armor, past the sword collection and into one of the large chambers off the gallery. She slammed the door behind her, cutting him off in midsentence.

AFTER MARIEL ran upstairs, Jake put the sleeping baby in her bed.

Mariel's behavior was erratic, to say the least. She blew hot, then cold, which was different from him—he blew hot all the time. He twisted, trying to get more comfortable. Ever since they had been in this castle, he became aroused embarrassingly often. Maybe he'd better find something to keep him busy. Obviously cold dunks in water wouldn't do it; after his impromptu swim in the moat, he desired Mariel as much as ever.

What could he do? Something to occupy both his hands and his mind, he thought. Carpentry would be good.

He'd make Jessica a proper bed. Or a cradle, so that she could be rocked to sleep.

He inspected the drawer where Jessica slept. With the addition of two curved pieces of wood, it would *be* a cradle. His mind grappled with the problem.

Suddenly there was nothing that he wanted more than to create, with his own hands, a cradle for this baby. He had given Mariel a Christmas tree, and now he wanted to give the baby something, too.

He started to stand up, then fell back. He'd forgotten. He wasn't wearing any clothes.

SHE WAS GOING to have to stop this, Mariel reflected as she sat on the edge of the cold bed in the middle of the cold room and stared out the mullioned window at the tops of trees.

She was sending Jake mixed signals. She was letting him get too close, making the relationship seem all warm and fuzzy, and then finding excuses to put distance between them. She ought to be more mature.

But it had already gone too far. After last night, he would only be hurt if she tried to withdraw, or he'd doubt his prowess—and there was certainly nothing wrong with *that.*

So, why not let it run its natural course? Okay, so she

might be falling in love with this guy. He didn't have to know. After they got out of this place, after they no longer had anything in common, it would be over of its own accord. Why precipitate a crisis now?

At least this point of view helped her to feel more cheerful. Now she'd better look around up here and see if she could find something with which to decorate the Christmas tree. Doing that would take part of the afternoon, leaving them less time to get involved in doing other things, such as what was on her mind, and probably on his, right this minute. The memories of the previous evening were very vivid.

She opened a big wardrobe against one wall, looking for scraps of lace, or buttons, or anything else that could be used to trim the tree. In the bottom, below the clothes hanging there, she discovered several bright-colored satin and velvet sashes, red and green and blue, and she held them up to the light for inspection. They would become garlands for the Christmas tree.

After setting those carefully aside, she threw the wardrobe doors open wide, and out tumbled garments fashioned not only of silk, but of velvet, satin and lace, as well.

She picked up one of the articles of clothing and held it up to the light, fully expecting to see moth holes. Though she turned it this way and that, none were evident. In fact, the dress looked almost new.

It was a long-sleeved velvet gown of midnight blue, the bodice joined below the low-cut neckline with golden laces. Bound up with it was a floor-length surcoat of a paler blue, also velvet.

A tissue-wrapped package fell out of the folds, and when she unwrapped it she found a small, pearl-encrusted cap and a pair of soft slippers the same shade of blue as the gown. They looked as if they'd fit if she stuffed bits of tissue paper into the toes.

Mariel held up the dress. There was no mirror, but the gown looked her size.

Suddenly she was seized with eagerness to try it on. It was cold in this gallery room, but she moved into a patch of sunlight and took off her coat anyway. In a matter of moments she had sloughed off her dirty corduroys and the lamb's wool sweater and was pulling the velvet dress over her head.

It smelled of lavender, just like the blankets from the chest downstairs. When she'd adjusted the velvet-and-pearl cap on the back of her head and slipped her arms through the sleeveless surcoat, she felt as if she were in another age, an enchanted age. She couldn't wait to show Jake.

A search through the clothing turned up a man's red tunic, which she paired with purple breeches and matching soft-soled shoes. A golden surcoat and hat completed the picture. She thought Jake might rather die than be seen in any of it—but he would have to admit, at least, that it would solve the problem of his having nothing to wear.

She burst out of the gallery room as suddenly as she had disappeared into it. She saw Jake wrapped up in the comforter, his bare feet warming on the hearth.

"Jake!" she called. "Look what I found!"

She ran lightly down the gallery stairs and tossed the clothing to him. "These were in the wardrobe upstairs," she explained, whirling for his inspection. His mouth fell open at the sight of her. Jessica, she noticed, was awake, and her expression mirrored Jake's. The baby clearly didn't know what to make of this new Mariel.

"You look wonderful," Jake said when he could

speak, and Mariel laughed, the notes echoing back from the vaulted ceiling.

"Evidently the people who own this place entertain themselves with costume parties. Put those on, and we'll trim the tree," she said, dancing away when he would have clasped her hand.

"I can't wear these." Jake held up the tunic, surcoat and breeches in distaste. "This is a skirt. These look like a pair of panty hose. And this other thing looks exactly like a bathrobe. I'd look like a jackass."

"But a *warm* jackass," she reminded him.

"We can't wear things that belong to someone else."

"Didn't you say that we'd explain that we had to use their things because it was an emergency? You won't be able to wear your clothes for hours," Mariel pointed out.

"There's no underwear," he said peevishly.

"Does it matter? I'm going to go cook our chop suey Christmas dinner while you get dressed. Bye." She waved her fingers at him as she made tracks for the kitchen.

"Mariel, I can't possibly—" he was saying, but by that time Mariel couldn't hear him.

Actually, she thought the breeches would do a lot for Jake's legs. A pair of blue jeans hardly did them justice.

"YOU CAN COME OUT NOW," Jake called.

Mariel, who had been reading the directions on the chop suey label, set the can on the counter and, mindful of her long skirt, swept out of the kitchen.

"If you aren't a sight," she said, barely able to contain her laughter.

Jake glared at her and adjusted his breeches. The surcoat came only to his knees, and his tunic looked as if it might be on backward.

"Well?" he said.

"You look perfect," she said warmly. She went to him and adjusted the front of the surcoat. "The color becomes you, my lord," she said, dropping a curtsy.

"You make me feel as uncomfortable as hell," he told her.

"But, my lord, 'tis the Christmas season. We should keep it with good cheer, do you not agree?" Her eyes danced playfully, and that only seemed to goad him.

"Dammit, Mariel, it's all very well for you to play queen of the castle, but I don't feel much like a king." He tugged at the neck of the tunic.

"Nevertheless, there is this strange pagan custom of decorating a tree, and I do believe that we should get on with it. Hast thou found the bit of aluminum foil that thou saidst would do for a star? If so, please do bring it to me," Mariel said. She was enjoying this immensely.

"I'll go get it," Jake said through clenched teeth, and he stalked away, albeit silently, in his velvet slippers.

He might feel ridiculous, but if anything, Mariel thought the medieval costume accented his rugged masculinity.

Jessica grunted and waved her arms, and Mariel checked her diaper. Amazingly, it was clean and dry. Jake must have changed her.

"Now we're going to deck the halls," she told Jessica, and she had already heaped evergreen branches on the mantel and flanked the fireplace with jars of holly when Jake returned.

By this time, he looked more at ease in his costume, and he even managed to grin at her. "I hope we don't get rescued before my clothes dry,'' he said. "I couldn't bear for the guys to see me wearing this.''

"I like the way you look,'' she said honestly.

He picked up her hand and kissed the inside of her wrist, unnerving her completely. "And I like the way you look, as well, my lady,'' he said, making her heart flip over and her knees go weak.

She yanked her hand away. "So,'' she said, too hastily, "see what you can do with those pieces of foil while I pop corn on the stove.''

"I thought we were going to do that in the fireplace,'' he called after her.

She replied over her shoulder, "We don't have anything to pop it in,'' which was true.

The whole time she was popping the corn, she was thinking about the damp flick of his tongue on the tender inner part of her wrist, and how easily it would have been to let things escalate.

But now the baby was awake. They couldn't make love with Jessica watching. It wouldn't feel right.

Mariel wondered how long it would be before Jessica fell asleep again. A baby couldn't stay awake forever.

WHEN MARIEL WENT BACK into the great hall, Jake had fashioned a big, lopsided star out of the foil and was admiring its position at the top of the tree.

"That's good, Jake.'' Mariel set down the pot of popcorn and produced a large needle. "Thank goodness for my travel sewing kit,'' she told him. She also had a long length of thread, which she'd purloined from the torn hem of one of the gowns in the wardrobe upstairs. She began to string the popcorn.

Jake sat at her feet, helping. "About what we said in the woods…'' he said uneasily.

"I meant what I said," she told him. "I don't look down on you. There are different kinds of education, you know."

"*I* know. I wasn't sure *you* did," he said quietly.

"So will you quit with the remarks?"

"Yes. If you'll quit dropping popcorn kernels in my hair," he said, grinning up at her. She grinned back. The subject was closed.

The popcorn chains joined the garlands and the holly berries on the tree, along with a few simple ornaments that Jake had whittled from scraps of wood. When they stood back, the three looked so festive that Mariel clapped her hands in delight.

"When will we eat our Christmas dinner?" Jake wanted to know.

"As soon as I heat it up. Want to help?"

Jake shook his head. "I'm going to see if I can knock together a surprise for Jessica. For her Christmas present," he said.

"I'll play with her for a while, so she won't be lonely."

Jake took off for unknown parts of the castle, and soon Mariel heard hammering from somewhere beyond the kitchen.

She picked Jessica up and held her in her lap. The baby seemed to love the caress of velvet against her cheek and Mariel was totally absorbed in Jessica until she heard a knock on the door.

The noise was completely unexpected. It startled Mariel so that she almost let Jessica roll off her lap.

"Jake?" she asked, leaping to her feet with the baby in her arms. She'd heard no sounds indicating anyone's arrival, perhaps due to the hammering from the direction of the kitchen, which had now stopped. But why would

Jake come around to the door of the great hall and knock on the outside when he was already in the castle? It made no sense.

Warily she stood up, and, after securing Jessica in her bed, she hurried to the door. Again came the knocking, more forceful this time.

"Who—who is it?" she asked.

"Your friend from the Magic Minimart" was the answer, and it was with surprise that Mariel recognized the voice of the little bearded man.

They were rescued! Someone knew they were here! How and why, she had no idea, but she knew they were safe. She flung the door open, ready to fall into their rescuer's arms.

But she couldn't. He was holding a sack slung over his back and had no arms available for her to fall into.

"Merry Christmas! I thought you could use this," said the little man, and Mariel turned and called to Jake.

"Jake, hurry, there's someone here!" she said excitedly. She turned her back for only a split second, but when she spun around again, the man was gone.

Chapter Twelve

"Someone found us?" asked Jake, appearing at once.

Mariel looked from him to the empty courtyard. She was speechless.

"I thought you said someone was here," Jake said in a faintly accusatory tone.

"He was. He—" she began, but then she saw the sack that the little man had dropped in front of the door.

"What's this?" Jake said, instantly alert. He bent over and opened it. "Food?" Jake said incredulously. "A turkey? A can of coconut?"

"Christmas dinner," Mariel said faintly. "He brought us the ingredients for Christmas dinner."

"Who did?" Jake demanded.

"It was the little man from the Magic Minimart. He looks like Santa Claus."

"And I look like the king of this castle, which we both know I am not. So who was this guy?"

"I can only tell you what he looks like."

"Santa Claus," Jake said, sounding baffled.

"Yes." Mariel felt slightly light-headed. She stepped outside the door, looking for footprints. They had been in and out of this door so many times that the snow was trampled into slush.

"Well, how did he get in? And where did he go? Anyone could see that the drawbridge is out of commission."

"I realize that," Mariel said helplessly. "He can't have gotten far. Let's go look for him."

"We'll need to put on our boots." Jake cast a doubtful glance at Mariel's long skirt. "Do you want to change clothes?"

"There's no time," Mariel said, rushing inside.

"What about Jessica?" Jake looked down at the baby in her drawer-bed as they pulled on their boots.

"We'll take her," Mariel decided swiftly, sliding her arms through the sleeves of her all-weather coat.

Jake bundled up Jessica in one of the warm lap robes, and the three of them set out, rushing across the courtyard. They saw no sign of anyone in the outbuildings; nor was anyone lingering in the gatehouse.

"Let's check the drawbridge," Jake said.

They hurried out of the gatehouse and into the walled outer ward. The melting snow on the drawbridge showed no evidence of anything other than their own footprints, and a gaping hole was still evident where their feet had broken through the rotten wood.

"No one would have crossed the drawbridge when it's so clearly broken," Mariel said with great certainty.

"There's no other way into the castle, other than swimming the moat, and I can promise you that no one would do that willingly on a cold day like this," Jake said, looking around.

Mariel walked a short distance along the outer ward gazing across the moat, toward the trees in the forest.

"'Not a creature was stirring, not even a mouse,'" she quoted.

"If we didn't have the food, I wouldn't believe there had been anyone here," Jake said thoughtfully.

"We might as well go back in. And yet..."

"And yet we don't know what happened," Jake finished.

"At least we won't have to eat chop suey for Christmas dinner."

"Who's cooking?" he asked, eyebrows lifted.

"I am. It's my turn to give you a gift, and Christmas dinner is it."

Surprising her, Jake swept the hat off his head and bowed low in imitation of a courtier. "I accept, my lady," he said. When he lifted his head, his eyes were dancing.

His eyes seemed full of light, and, held in his spell, she stood motionless as he dipped his head and kissed her. His lips were cold and fresh with the tang of winter, but his breath warmed her cheek.

Jessica stirred against her, and Mariel broke away from the kiss. Jake's hands came up to frame her face.

"You're always fighting it, Mariel," he said softly. "Why?"

How could she explain? How could she tell him that she couldn't see herself with this man for the rest of her life? How could she tell him that she was afraid that, after all this was over, they wouldn't have anything to talk about? She didn't want to hurt him.

She only shook her head, willing the silent tears gathering behind her eyelids not to fall.

"We both know it's special," he went on. "It doesn't have to end after we leave this place."

He must have seen the perplexity in her eyes, because he stepped backward and let his hands drop to his sides.

"We'd better go in," he said gently. "We both have work to do."

She couldn't argue with that statement, at least, and so she murmured reassuringly to Jessica and, careful not to look at Jake, walked with him back into the castle courtyard.

IN THE KITCHEN, Jake set the sack of food on the counter beside the stove. While Mariel warmed herself and the baby in front of the fireplace, Jake dug in the sack and pulled out a small stuffed turkey. There were potatoes and milk and butter, so they would have mashed potatoes. There was a can of cranberry relish, a bunch of raw carrots, a can of green beans, and the makings of a coconut cake.

"Oh, I almost forgot," Jake said, after the riches of the sack had been revealed. "I made something for Jessica." He disappeared briefly into one of the keeping rooms off the kitchen. When he returned, he was carrying a small cradle, crafted from a drawer similar to the one Jessica usually slept in.

"I thought she'd like to rock to sleep," he said with an abashed look as he set it in front of the fireplace.

"So that's why you were doing all that hammering," Mariel said, marveling at the cradle. Jake had fashioned wooden rockers from pieces of scrap lumber and had fastened them to the bottom of the drawer.

"If I were making a real cradle for her, it would be wider and longer, so that she'd have growing room. And I'd carve a design with her name into the headboard," he said.

"Maybe you'd better see if you can repair the drawbridge, in case we have any more visitors," Mariel said quickly.

"Good idea. I'll clear out of here while you cook dinner."

"A pleasure, my lord," Mariel said demurely, dropping a curtsy. He only grinned at her and went to get his tools.

"So," Mariel said briskly to Jessica, "you and I have work to do."

But Jessica was already sound asleep.

LATER, Jake came in noisily, stomping his feet and rubbing his hands together against the cold.

"The drawbridge poses no threat," he told her. "Only two of the boards were rotten. Others looked as if they'd been replaced recently. I managed to do a creditable patch-up job, so we don't have to worry about falling into the moat again. Mmm…is that frosting for the coconut cake?"

"Yes. It's only canned coconut, but it's better than nothing. I suppose they didn't have a fresh coconut at the Magic Minimart," she replied.

Jake leaned on the counter. "Mariel, do you think this guy was merely a delivery person for the Magic Minimart?" he asked skeptically.

"Well, what else could he logically be? Meals on Wheels?"

"Trays on Sleighs."

Mariel shot him an exasperated look. "Whoever he was, I wish I knew how he figured out that we were here. Or that we needed food for a decent Christmas dinner. And why didn't he rescue us? Why did he leave us here?" she said in a rush.

"Because he gives gifts to good little boys and girls," Jake said. "Because we've both been good, and he's giving us the gift of each other."

Mariel stared at him, dumbfounded. "You're not joking, are you? Do *you* think it was really Santa Claus?"

"At the moment, that theory makes a lot more sense than believing he's a delivery person for a convenience store. In case you've never noticed, Magic Minimarts don't deliver," Jake said.

He eased up behind her where she stood at the stove and planted a kiss on her cheek.

She twisted around in his arms. "What was that for?" she asked.

"For hello. And this one's for how nice it is to come home to a warm kitchen and the smell of dinner cooking." He bent his head and kissed her again. It was a kiss that she felt powerless to resist.

"Now," he said, drawing the word out in that drawl that fell so pleasantly on her ears, "wasn't that nice?"

"More than nice," she whispered against the front of his tunic.

"Do you suppose it's like this for people who are married?" he asked whimsically.

"You've forgotten—I was married once," she said, her mood dashed by the reminder of a part of her life that she would have preferred to forget.

"I haven't forgotten," he said. "Was it like this?"

Mariel moved away from him and busied herself measuring out confectioners' sugar. "At first," she allowed. "Not for long, however."

"If I were married, I'd want it to be like this all the time," he said.

Mariel could think of no adequate reply. Because she was happy, too, happier than she'd ever been in her life. But it was a feeling she couldn't trust. It was a feeling that could melt away as fast as the snow, which was thawing even now.

MARIEL INSISTED on using a snowy white linen tablecloth on the table, and where she found the silver goblets, Jake never knew. He only knew that Mariel, wearing her blue velvet gown and with the glow of candlelight gilding her face, was more beautiful than he had ever seen her as she bore the turkey to the table and set it steaming before him.

Jake carved the turkey, taking his time about it and savoring his own happiness. He was almost afraid to admit to himself that he *was* so happy. It was such an unfamiliar feeling.

But now here was Mariel, and here was Jessica, and he felt himself settling into the role of the paterfamilias, and he liked it. He, Jake Travis, who had never had a real family of his own, was finding it comfortable to be the acting head of an acting family.

At the moment they sat to eat, Jessica woke up.

"I'll get her," Mariel said. "You go ahead and start eating."

"No, I'll get her," Jake said, and they both stood at the same time and headed for Jessica's cradle, near the hearth.

The baby was crying lustily, her face red and wrinkled, her fists clenched. "Is it time for her feeding?" he asked anxiously.

"She just ate two hours ago. Could she be hungry again?"

"I don't know. Do you suppose the cooking odors woke her?"

"Do babies wake up when they smell something good to eat? How can they? It's not as if they ever ate turkey, so how would they know it tastes good?" Mariel asked in a burst of logic.

"I don't know. Maybe she has colic. Do you know

anything about colic?" He stared down at the baby, a perplexed expression on his face.

"I read about colic in the baby book, but it didn't say much, except that it makes babies cry," she said. She picked up Jessica and checked her diaper. "Well, she does need a diaper change."

"Here, Mariel, let me do it. You've worked so hard to cook the dinner, and it'll get cold if we don't eat it," Jake said, reaching for Jessica.

"I cooked it for you," Mariel objected. "It's supposed to be your Christmas present."

He saw in that moment that she felt about the dinner the way he had about the Christmas tree and the crude cradle he had fashioned—she had wanted to do something in the spirit of Christmas for the two people most important in her life at the moment.

"Go on," she said, shooing his hands away, and so he went. But he felt uncomfortable sitting at the big table without her, watching her changing the baby's diaper at the other end of the room.

"I'll put her in her cradle," Mariel called to him over the din. "Maybe that will soothe her. I don't know what's bothering her."

"I'm not enjoying this," he said suddenly, almost shouting, because he didn't think she'd hear him otherwise. Mariel was so startled that she wheeled around and regarded him with an expression of mild apprehension, which only made him more determined that Mariel not have her Christmas dinner ruined.

He stood up and strode the length of the hall until he stood before Mariel. "I'll take care of her. *You* eat."

Mariel hugged the baby to her chest. "I don't mind taking care of her, really I don't."

Jake spoke to her in a gentler tone. "Let's bring the

cradle to our end of the hall. I can rock her with my foot while we eat,'' he said, and Mariel, her lower lip caught between her teeth, nodded in silent agreement. Jessica, however, was anything but silent. She was still crying so hard that he could see her tonsils.

He lifted the cradle and tucked it under his arm, smiling faintly at Mariel. ''Is this what parents go through? Do babies often interrupt mealtimes?''

''Given the nature of babies, it's entirely possible,'' Mariel said, trailing after him with the baby, her long skirt sweeping the floor.

They put Jessica in her cradle beside the table, but she continued to scream. Mariel had eaten only a few bites of carrots when she set her fork down, looking miserable.

''I can't stand it, Jake. I can't eat when she's crying.''

He had managed a few mouthfuls of turkey since he returned to the table. It was good, but he couldn't enjoy eating, either.

Jake picked up the baby from the cradle. Jessica immediately stopped crying and blinked at him. He wiggled his eyebrows at her; he crossed his eyes. Jessica appeared fascinated.

''You're not going to be able to eat if you hold her,'' Mariel said.

''If she's this amazed at the faces I make, wait until she watches me chew,'' Jake said, shifting the baby to one arm and picking up his fork.

He ate slowly, because he held the baby, but Jessica's eyes tracked every bit of food from plate to mouth.

''She likes you, Jake,'' Mariel said. ''She likes you a lot.''

''If only I were able to hold your attention the way I do hers,'' Jake said without thinking.

"How do you know you don't?"

"Oh, come on, Mariel." He couldn't bring himself to admit that her indifference hurt. He hoped she'd take the hint.

She got up and cut the cake, setting the first piece in front of him. "The only thing that takes my attention away from you is the baby," she said. "We *are* alone together here, after all."

"Alone—but sometimes not very together."

"What do you mean?" she asked, sounding as if she really didn't want to hear his answer.

"I mean— Oh, look, Mariel, she's gone to sleep." Jessica's eyes were closed, and she looked peaceful and contented in his arms.

"Now who isn't paying attention to whom?" Mariel said waspishly, and she got up and flounced into the kitchen.

Jake stared at the place where she had been.

"I don't think I understand women," he said to Jessica, who slept on, unaware.

He wondered if Jessica would wake up if he slid her gently into her cradle. He wondered if there was some way to warm the blankets in the cradle so that the cool shock of them after being held against a warm body wouldn't awaken her. He wondered why he was wondering all these things, when what he really wanted to do was go to Mariel and gather her into his arms.

Taking his chances, he deposited Jessica in the cradle as gently as he could. She sighed and made little sucking noises with her lips, lapsing into what appeared to be an even deeper sleep.

He picked up the cradle with Jessica in it and tiptoed to the fireplace, where a steadily burning log threw out an agreeable warmth. He turned around as Mariel came out of the kitchen, her face pale but composed.

"Come here," he said, holding his hand out toward her.

"Where's Jessica?"

"Sound asleep. I think we need to talk."

"You haven't finished your cake."

"I haven't even *started* my cake, but it doesn't matter. We have other, more important, unfinished business. I've taken your comment that we don't know each other to heart, Mariel."

She glided toward him, petite and dainty and looking very much the medieval lady. Behind her, the tapestries on the wall, stirred by a draft, rippled. The candles flickered in their sconces. Jake hoped that she would notice the yearning in his eyes, which was only about half of what he felt in his heart.

"Darling Mariel," he said, taking her hand. "Let's get to know each other better, much better."

"My lord—" she began, but he was tired of play-acting. He wanted something real. He swept her into his arms and kissed her, smothering the words upon her lips.

"Is my lady pleased?" he demanded when he released her lips.

She stared into his eyes, and for a moment he wasn't sure what he read in her face. Then, with a playful look, she said, "I could be pleased more," and he laughed in relief and swept her into his arms, mounting the steps to the gallery two at a time before she caught her breath.

"Where—?"

"To my lady's chamber," he told her, and before she knew it, he was kicking open the door to the room where she had found the clothes they were wearing.

"I wanted this to be special. For you, Mariel," he said, and then he carried her into the chamber.

The room had been transformed. Jake had built a roaring fire in the fireplace, and the room was toasty warm. He had lit candles in the wall sconces, and the bed was turned down and waiting for them.

"When did you do this?" she asked as he laid her gently on the bed. The sheets were redolent of lavender, and the fragrance blended with that of the evergreens that Jake had heaped on the mantel.

"After I repaired the drawbridge. We can leave the door open and hear Jessica if she begins to fuss," he said, smoothing her hair. "Mariel, are you happy?"

"I wish—" she began, but he silenced her with a kiss.

"Don't wish anything right now, unless it's for me," he murmured, somewhere in the vicinity of her ear.

She felt a fluttering in her stomach as he bent over her, and a rush of heat rose to meet his lips as he kissed the firm rise of her breasts above the low neckline of the velvet dress.

She was acutely aware of Jake, of everything about him—of the strong, rugged planes of his face, of the yearning in his eyes. Heat radiated from his body to hers, and, lifting his head, he brought his fingertips up to trace the delicate line of her jaw from her ear to her chin.

She had never realized how much she loved to be touched before. Jake's hands, so big and capable, knew all the subtleties of touch, from the quick, deft turn of fastenings to make clothes fall away, to the light brush of fingertips upon skin primed for love.

Time slowed down, became part of her, drifted away on a tide of sensation. She didn't know what time it was or what else she should be doing. She knew only the lazy, languorous exploration of love.

Jake's skin was taut and smooth and golden in the firelight. Her lips trembled slightly, and he brushed them gently with his thumb, his touch like the graze of a butterfly's wing.

"I've never been able to talk to anyone the way I talk to you. Does that mean anything to you?" he asked.

"Where is this going, Jake? What are we doing?" She was so unsure of him, and of herself.

"We're feeling the magic," he said, his eyes solemn with truth. "The magic of Christmas."

"You don't believe," she breathed.

"That was before I met you. Before we found Jessica. Before we ended up in this castle. Before I was truly alive, Mariel," he said with the utmost sincerity.

She swallowed. He was so handsome, and so earnest, and so wrapped up in her. Was she only lost in the admitted thrill of having a man show desire for her?

But this was Jake. Jake, who had sheltered her with his body and guided her to this castle, who had taken on the responsibility for both her and Jessica, when he could have left them in the woods or the cave. Feeling his desire for her was different from feeling his commitment, but both existed.

"So sweet," he whispered, unlacing her bodice with hands that were firm and sure.

By the time he had finished, she was trembling, and as he parted the fabric to reveal her breasts, she said, "Now you," and she helped him out of his surcoat and tunic until he knelt before her bare-chested.

He slid the dress from her shoulders, then bent and took the tip of one breast between his teeth, teasing it with his tongue. He caught her other nipple between his

thumb and forefinger and applied gentle pressure until
it hardened into a tight round bud. She gasped and
arched against him, winding her fingers in his hair.

His lips upon her breast made her undulate with pleasure, and when he felt her body start to move, he trailed
a line of slow, erotic kisses upward to her lips. She
moaned softly as his tongue slid into her mouth, and
she opened herself to it, tantalizing him with the exquisite mating dance of her own tongue, delighting in the
play of flesh against flesh until she felt him trembling
with desire.

He eased her downward and slid a leg between hers,
pressing the hardness of his thigh tight against her. Mariel heard her breath escaping her in sharp gasps, and she
felt his hands beneath her, holding her close. She
wrapped her arms around him fiercely, wanting to bond
him to her, wanting to be part of him, not only now,
but forever.

"I think I never knew real passion until now," she
whispered against his shoulder.

"Neither did I," he said unsteadily. The pulse of his
heartbeat pumped in the vein above his temple, and she
impulsively lifted her head to kiss it. He slid his hands
beneath her head, twisting his fingers in the silky
strands. His breath stirred the tendrils around her face.

Slowly he began to kiss her, breathing little kisses
along her jaw, nibbling at her earlobe, probing the sensitive spot at the corner of her mouth with the tip of his
tongue. He seemed determined to kiss every inch of her,
to explore all of her, and the waiting was excruciating.

His hands moved lower, over the ripe curve of her
hips, spreading a warm, pulsing sensation deep into her
abdomen, lingering a moment before sliding her dress
down. She didn't know how he managed to dispense

with the lace barrier of her panties so swiftly, but soon she shivered in his arms, conscious not of the cool air, but of the heat emanating from his body to warm her.

When he slid out of his breeches, she couldn't have looked away if her life had depended upon it. In his nakedness, Jake Travis was magnificent, and she felt as if all her senses had become magnified as he took her hand and placed it on his hardness.

"Do you like to touch me, Mariel?" he whispered, and she said, "Oh, yes," and he smiled and moved himself between her fingers as she kissed his forehead, his chin, his chest, in silent tribute.

"Now I want to touch you," he said, and he caressed the soft curls between her thighs, seeking the silken sweetness within as he drew her into a deep, impassioned kiss. He easily found the sensitive heart of her and stroked gently, so gently, until she was damp with wanting him.

"You are so responsive, Mariel, so ready for love," he said as he bent down and pressed his lips against her abdomen.

His mouth, moving lower, kindled wildfires in her veins, made her into someone she hadn't known she could be. She could not get enough of him, and she tangled her hands in his hair to pull him closer to the center of her. She felt the whisper of his breath and the warmth of his lips, and then, with the skill of an expert, his tongue found her molten core and coaxed her almost to her peak before stopping.

She moved against him, unable to help herself, and as he positioned himself above her, she wrapped her legs around his, longing to feel him inside her, but still he stroked with his fingers, watching her with half-closed eyes. It was such exquisite pleasure, such delicious sensation, but it was a kind of torture, too, and Mariel longed to be released by her tormentor.

She clung to him blindly, unable to speak, unable to move, totally in his thrall, until with a victorious cry he filled all the emptiness she had ever known with his own hard and satisfying need. She heard him cry out, speak her name, but she wasn't really conscious; all she wanted was to feel and feel and feel, to be entered again and again in time to the elemental rhythm pounding in her veins, to give herself so completely to this man that she would never again be the same person she was now, not ever.

He was much more aware than she, much more ready to pace himself to her passion. They found a flow, a way of giving and receiving happiness, that surpassed the ordinary and approached the sublime.

At the moment when Jake pushed a damp strand of hair away from Mariel's face, their eyes met, completing their union. His eyes were so dark that Mariel could see no iris; all she saw was the reflection of her face, blurred with passion, in their depths. At that moment, with a fusion of spirit, a meshing of bodies, a blending of souls, their climax exploded inward and outward, leaving them drowning and helpless, safe in each other's arms.

Mariel was limp with exhaustion, but at the same time she felt a fierce, proud joy in her heart at what she and Jake had achieved together. They had transcended the boundaries that usually separate two people and had become one in a state of mind and body that she knew was the rarest of human accomplishments. She nestled close to him, as if by maintaining a connection she could make this moment last forever.

She must have slept, though she didn't know how long. When she awoke, Jake's arms still held her close.

She thought she would like to lie just this way in his arms forever, languidly savoring the joy of their mating. She was just beginning, slowly and lazily to figure out the implications of this feeling when she heard the explosion outside the chamber window.

She was alert instantly. Jake jumped to his feet.

"What was that?" she asked, clutching the covers to her breasts.

"Gunfire, I think. Someone is shooting outside the castle!"

Chapter Thirteen

Mariel struggled into her sweater and slacks, and Jake raced downstairs to Jessica, who had been awakened by the gunshots. The baby was screaming at the top of her lungs.

Mariel had barely reached them when there was a loud pounding on the door. Mariel looked wildly at Jake, who was zipping up his jeans, grim-faced.

"Who do you think it is?" she said.

"It doesn't sound like some kindly, mild-mannered old gentleman with a beard," Jake replied, his voice muffled by the turtleneck he was pulling over his head.

"Are you going to the door?" Outside, someone was shouting, and they heard another blast of gunfire.

"I'd better, or they'll break it down."

Mariel picked up the crying Jessica and cradled her in her arms. "Hush. Everything's all right," Mariel said, though she did not quite believe it herself.

Jake was at the door now. "Who is it?"

"Open up, open up, we want to wish you a merry Christmas!" was the shouted demand.

Suddenly Jake's features lit with recognition and relief. "It's okay," he said to Mariel. "They mean us no harm."

"But they're shooting guns! What are they doing here?" Mariel said, shocked that Jake was going to open the door without asking more questions.

Jake shot the bolt. "Quaint local custom," he said, smiling broadly. "You'll see." To Mariel's dismay, he flung the door wide.

It was dark, and a full moon illuminated the scene. Mariel could make out one or two grinning male faces, and other people, men and boys, carrying old-fashioned muskets, were milling in the courtyard, laughing and jostling one another.

"Merry Christmas! Merry Christmas!" they shouted when they saw Jake, Mariel and the baby in the doorway.

"Where is Mr. Nicholas? Is he home?" asked one of the party.

"Won't you come in?" said Jake, and Mariel stared at him in disbelief.

"Jake—" she said, but he quieted her with a glance.

"Ah, it's a cold night. We don't mind if we do," said the leader, and Mariel had no choice but to stand back as twelve men and boys trooped past and headed for the fireplace.

The leader looked from Jake to Mariel and held out his hand. "I'm Barney Sims," he said.

"Jake Travis. This is Mariel, and the baby is Jessica. Frankly, we need your help."

"What can we do for you?"

"Mariel, please, will you make us some hot chocolate?" Jake asked. So Mariel listened from the kitchen, Jessica propped against her shoulder, while she stirred hot chocolate and Jake told Barney Sims and his party the story of their accident, being lost in the woods, and their subsequent walk to the deserted castle.

When she came out of the kitchen, she arranged the now-sleepy Jessica in her cradle and carried in a tray holding cups of hot chocolate.

"Funny, I thought it was, when we saw a light on the second floor of the gatehouse. We didn't expect anyone to be here," said Barney.

"A light in the second story of the gatehouse? We didn't—couldn't have—put a light in the gatehouse. The stairs aren't—" Mariel began, but Jake threw her a warning look. It said, *Don't tell crazy stories.* It said, *Don't tell them something they won't—or can't—believe.*

"Mr. Nicholas, the old guy who owns this place, usually goes away during the winter, but somehow I had a hunch I'd better check on him. He's an old fellow, you know, and healthy enough, but neighbor looks after neighbor around here," said Barney, oblivious of the byplay between Mariel and Jake.

"Neighbors? We didn't see any houses around," Mariel said.

"We came by Jeep. It's not easy to get in and out of this place," he said. That was certainly not news.

"If only we could have found you when we were lost," Mariel said, sitting down on the hearth beside Jake.

"We live on the other side of the mountain," said Barney Sims.

"Can you give us a ride into Tellurian tonight?" Jake asked.

"Wish we could," one of the men said, "but we've got three Jeeploads with just the bunch of us, and bags of mistletoe to take back besides, and no room left over for three more people. What we'd better do is send a

Jeep in tomorrow morning. You're safe here for the night, aren't you?''

"Safe enough," Jake said.

Jake went to make more hot chocolate. Mariel leaned forward, eager to talk to the men about their reason for roaming around on Christmas night, shooting off old muskets.

"It's tradition, that's all I know," Barney Sims said, clearly warming toward her. "I heard it started when the old-timers went to gather mistletoe. It grows so high no one could climb up and get it, so they had to shoot it down."

"But why on Christmas Day? Why not before?" Mariel asked.

"The mistletoe's got to be fresh for the big party on Christmas night," said one of the boys.

"Yeah, the women like to hang it up so they get plenty of kissing."

"Aw, Barney, it's not just the women who like the kissing," said one of the men.

As a collector of Christmas folklore, Mariel didn't often find something totally new, and yet she had never heard of this custom before. She borrowed a piece of paper and a pen from one of the men and wrote down everything they could tell her about the origin of the custom of shooting down the mistletoe, scribbling until they said they had to go.

"Look for the Jeep early in the morning," Barney said by way of parting. "We'll get you and your family out of here, safe and sound."

Mariel hung back, busying herself with Jessica, until the visitors had gone and Jake had returned.

"Well," he said with a certain finality. "We're rescued, Mariel."

"Yes," she said in a curiously flat tone, her excitement having evaporated now that reality was beginning to sink in. "I suppose we are."

He waited until she laid Jessica in her cradle before pulling her down beside him on the hearth.

"In a way," he said, gently taking her hand in his, "I've felt rescued ever since I met you."

She tried to pull her hand away. She wasn't up to any declarations right now. Her lips were still swollen from his passionate kisses, and her body was still primed for love.

"Mariel, listen to me," he said. She would have turned away, but he grasped her by the shoulders and made her look at him.

"Mariel," he said. "I never thought I'd be in love with anyone, but what has happened between us has changed my mind. I'm crazy about you, Mariel. When we came out of that cave into a world all fresh and new, it was as if I'd left the dark part of my life behind, too. I don't want to let you go. If we were together, every day could be like Christmas."

"I don't know what to say," she said, helpless under the restless scrutiny of those warm brown eyes.

"Say you feel the same way," he urged. "Say you love me."

"I—I *want* to say it," she told him, and he relaxed his grip on her shoulders and pulled her into his arms. She heard his heartbeat—or was it hers? She couldn't distinguish whose was whose anymore.

"Then why don't you make us both very happy? It's only three little words. Three very simple, easy words. You love me, Mariel. You know you do!" He held her fiercely, and she couldn't see his face.

"If I say it, then we have to do something about it. You have your life, and I have mine."

"We can combine them. I know we can! You and me and the baby—"

"She isn't our baby, Jake," Mariel said quietly. "Have you forgotten that?"

He eased away so that he could look at Jessica and then back to Mariel. "I *have* forgotten, yes, in the same way I've forgotten what my life was like before I had you."

"You were the one who kept reminding me at first that Jessica has parents somewhere," Mariel said, perilously near tears.

"We could have lots of babies of our own."

"It's what I've always wanted, a home and children," Mariel said. "But how can I make any promises? Everything has seemed so unreal, with toys disappearing and roly-poly little men showing up and then leaving without a trace, and men shooting muskets in the courtyard. How can I know if what we feel is real, Jake? How can I?" Tears began to run down her face, and he gathered her in his arms.

"It's real, believe me," he said. "As real as what we feel when I do this."

He kissed her. It was a long, sweet, lingering kiss that spoke of caring and passion and happiness to come. It promised forever and eternity and a life filled with love. And magic. It captured all the magic of the hours they had spent together and made it seem, in that moment, more real than anything else in Mariel's life.

But the kiss ended. As their life together would end tomorrow.

In a moment, she was sobbing in his arms, and he was kissing and consoling her, and all she could think of was that here was an eligible, handsome, kind, considerate man, and she was a fool for not telling him she loved him. But she couldn't lie. She didn't know if she loved him or not.

He lifted her in his arms. "Come to bed," he said, and she made no objection.

He carried her upstairs, this time setting her down gently amid the rumpled, sweet-scented sheets, adding another log to the fire before covering her body with his. Sparks flew up the chimney like golden fireflies, and Mariel held him in her arms and watched them go, like so many memories turning to ash.

After a while, he kissed her face tenderly. Her tears were wet against his lips. Then, because they couldn't help it, because this was to be their last night in the castle, they coupled, slowly and gently, in a celebration of their time together.

To Mariel, who was lost in a haze of desire, the scene had a dreamlike quality of illusion—Jake's dear, wonderful face hovering above her, the candlelight and fireglow playing across the curves and planes of their bodies, shadows leaping and blending on the wall. There was delicious excitement and overwhelming passion; there was joy and exuberance, and finally peace.

That night they slept in each other's arms, waking and sleeping, making love and just looking at each other, whispering and murmuring all the age-old endearments that lovers have shared in their mutual enchantment since the beginning of time. In the castle they were secluded, lost, far away from mundane worries. Tonight, they didn't have to think about tomorrow and the changes it would bring. Tonight, all they had to do was love.

When the pearly light of dawn crept into the room, Mariel was startled awake.

Jessica, she thought, alarmed. Jessica hadn't cried all night.

Jake was lying with his head pillowed on her shoulder, one hand thrown carelessly across her breast. Carefully she lifted his hand and set it aside, and he whispered her name. Her hair spread across his chest like a golden cloak, and he stirred when she slid out from under the robe covering them.

But he didn't wake up, and, mindful of her responsibility to the baby, Mariel clutched another blanket around her shoulders and crept down the stairs to the great hall.

Jessica was sleeping peacefully, and Mariel realized that the infant had slept through the night. This was a milestone her friends had often mentioned when talking about their own babies.

Mariel went swiftly into the kitchen and warmed Jessica's bottle, wondering as she heated the milk what would happen to the goat when they left. They would have to send someone to get Nelly; otherwise, she might starve. Unless the owner of this place returned, and Mariel didn't know how likely that was.

Mr. Nicholas, the mistletoe shooters had called him. They hadn't seemed to know him well, though they had appeared to like him well enough. Mr. *Who* Nicholas? Mariel wondered. They hadn't given him a first name.

Jessica woke up while Mariel was warming the bottle. As she gathered the baby into her arms, Mariel was glad that she was awake before Jake so that she and Jessica could enjoy this moment of closeness together.

"Jessica," Mariel said, and Jessica seemed to recognize her name. A sense of melancholy settled over

Mariel. What was Jessica's real name? Or what name would foster parents give her, assuming that her real parents couldn't be found?

Mariel knew she'd always remember Jessica, how her warm little body snuggled so close, how her tiny, seeking mouth had pushed against her breasts on that first night in the cave. Now that she had sampled motherhood, it was going to be hard to give it up.

She held Jessica over her shoulder and burped her, then settled her in her lap again. Jessica was dressed in doll clothes from the tower room. She looked so pretty, the pink of her cheeks echoed in the pink of the polka-dot flannel doll's nightgown she wore.

When Jessica had drained the bottle, Mariel couldn't bear to put her back into her cradle. Instead, she carried her upstairs to the room she had shared with Jake.

Jake had been up to put another log on the fire, and he was sitting up in bed when Mariel came in.

"Good morning," he said, smiling at them. The sun had risen so that a slat of lemony light lay across the pillow, which he patted invitingly. Mariel climbed up on the bed and laid Jessica between them.

"What time to you think the Jeep will come?" Mariel asked.

"I don't know. Barney Sims said it would be early," Jake replied.

"We should get dressed," said Mariel.

"We should," he agreed, sliding his arm around her and pulling her close.

"Jake…"

"I just want to feel your skin next to mine."

"It leads to other things."

"Only this, at the moment," he said capturing her lips for a kiss.

She pulled away. "We'd better eat breakfast."

"I'm not hungry." He slid a hand around her neck and pulled her down beside him on the pillow. "You mean so much to me. I really do want to keep seeing you," he said, gazing deep into her eyes, as if he were trying to work his way into her very soul.

"We will," she said helplessly, though she knew it wasn't true.

"Wouldn't you like to see each other? Say in a couple of weeks, in order to catch up?"

"I—I'm not sure," she hedged.

Jake was silent for several minutes. "I'm not going to pressure you," he said finally. "But I know—and I hope you know—that I'm not going to change my mind. I'm not going to stop loving you." *And I'm not going to let you get away with this,* he thought. If Mariel noticed the determined set of his chin, she gave no sign.

Between them, Jessica stirred. Mariel sat up and took the baby into her arms.

Jake felt a wave of longing wash over him. "That's the way I want to remember you," he said softly. "With the baby in your arms, looking like a Madonna."

"Please, will you hold her while I get dressed?" Mariel asked. She was on the verge of tears.

Jake nodded, his eyes bright, his look solemn, and she shifted the baby into his arms. Clutching the blanket around her, she slid out of bed.

He watched her as she dressed, and once he said, "You're the most beautiful woman I've ever seen, Mariel," but all she could do was look at him. She didn't want to provide any encouragement for him to think that they had a future together, because she didn't think they did.

Later, she cooked a makeshift breakfast while Jessica

watched from her cradle. Jake replanted the Christmas tree in the woods and, using pen and paper borrowed from their visitors, wrote a note to the owner of the castle, scrawling his name and address at the bottom so that he could be charged for the items they had used. He left the note under a salt shaker in the kitchen. Mariel was washing up their coffee cups when they heard the honk of a horn at the drawbridge. At the sound, she felt a sense of impending doom. She had known it was coming, but she couldn't welcome it.

"Whoever is driving the Jeep probably doesn't want to attempt the drawbridge," said Jake grimly, and he went to talk to the person, who came back with him a few minutes later.

"Mariel, this is Barney's cousin, Hoke Sims," he said, his voice neutral, not giving away his feelings. "He's going to take us to Tellurian."

Mariel said hello, and Jake shrugged into his backpack. He held Mariel's coat for her, and they looked around the great hall one last time. They avoided looking at each other.

"Big old barn of a place, this castle," said Hoke Sims. "Big old *ugly* place, if you ask me."

"Oh, you get used to it," Mariel said.

Jake gave her a sharp look. "I'll carry Jessica out," he said, going to get the baby.

"I want to take a last look around. To see if I left anything."

Jake spared her a curt nod, and he and Hoke Sims went out, leaving her alone in the great hall.

Mariel fought to gain control of herself. She wasn't going to cry; she wasn't going to let her emotions run away with her. She blinked back tears, and when her vision cleared, she found herself staring at the tapestries hanging on the wall.

To her regret, Mariel had never taken the time to look closely at the tapestries before. Now, while she was trying to quell her tears, while she listened to Jake and Hoke outside the door, discussing what to do about Nelly the goat, she couldn't help but notice them.

At this early hour, a shaft of light from one of the narrow windows illuminated the wall hangings, making the rich embroidery gleam. At first, the illustrations on the fabric seemed to be standard tapestry fare—a unicorn surrounded by a group of ladies, a formation of knights and a depiction of a joust, a dancing bear and a juggler in a great hall that resembled this one.

"Mariel? It's time to go," Jake said from the door, propping it open. Jessica was in his arms, wrapped warmly in her pink wool blanket.

"One moment," she called back, wiping her eyes, her back turned to him. "I've been wanting to take a look at these ever since I got here."

She had reached the last tapestry and was ready to turn around when she noticed that it was different from the others. No veiled ladies here, and no knights, just an artistic view of a castle that looked very much like this one. A drawbridge, a moat, a strikingly similar gatehouse and—

"Jake!" she called uncertainly. "Come look at this!"

But the door swung on a cold wind that swept through the hall. Jake had left, presumably to go to the Jeep. She heard the Jeep's motor start up, and she knew that it was no use to call Jake.

She took one last look at the tapestry, which pictured something she knew she would never forget.

"Mariel," called Jake.

She had to leave. Her time here was over. One last look around the great hall, and then she pulled the door firmly shut behind her.

"What took you so long?" Jake asked from the back seat as she climbed into the front seat of the Jeep.

"Just looking around one last time," she said.

"And what did you see?"

"The tapestries. By the way, what did you decide to do about Nelly?" she asked briefly, leaning over and chucking Jessica under the chin. The baby looked so sweet, her cheeks pink and glowing, her eyes wide and wondering.

"I suspect that she belongs to my brother-in-law," said Hoke. "He has a herd of goats, and this one probably wandered away."

"In winter? During two violent storms?" murmured Mariel, who found this hypothesis unlikely.

"We thought that the goat might belong to the castle's owner," Jake said.

"To Mr. Nicholas? No, he's not here enough to keep any animals, though he used to breed some kind of exotic deer," Hoke said. The Jeep bumped over a rutted track, now turned to mud with the thaw.

"Tell me about this Mr. Nicholas," Mariel said.

"Oh, he's a nice guy, but a recluse of sorts. No one sees him much."

"He's away most of the winter?" Mariel ventured.

"Yeah, that's what I've always heard. The rumor is that his family won a lottery in Europe years ago, and the present Mr. Nicholas's father was a student of medieval studies. He built the castle on a kind of a whim, and he lived here for a long time. In fact, I think he was the one who started breeding the deer."

"What kind of deer?" Jake asked.

"Reindeer," Mariel said under her breath, and Jake looked at her sharply.

Hoke, who seemed not to have heard, shook his head. "No one knows. You hardly ever saw them. Maybe a glimpse now and then through the trees, that's all, according to my grandfather, who knew Mr. Nicholas's dad. The deer didn't like to be around people much."

"When do you expect this Mr. Nicholas back?" Jake asked.

"Who knows? He's a hard guy to figure. Kind of eccentric, and all that," Hoke said philosophically.

They rode on another mile or two, and Mariel mulled it all over. There were no firm answers, but she thought she knew who the mysterious owner of the castle was. She didn't think she could talk to this Hoke Sims about it. No, she'd better keep quiet.

"I'd like to hold Jessica," she said after a while, and Jake handed the baby over the seat. Mariel buried her face in the infant's neck, telling herself that her eyes were watering from the cold. Behind her, Jake rode silently, his eyes on the back of her head. They didn't speak to each other all the way into town.

"So," JAKE SAID in front of the Department of Social Services office building as Mariel was about to get in the car she had rented, "you won't change your mind and come see my house?" His southern drawl seemed even more Southern than usual; she had grown so accustomed to it that she'd almost forgotten about it.

"I want to go home," she said, keeping her eyes on the distant mountains.

"The social worker was good with Jessica, don't you think?" Jake asked. They'd had to answer a battery of suspicious questions, but finally, because of their sincerity, they'd been believed. *Yes,* Jake and Mariel had said when interviewed separately and together, *we really found this baby in the woods. No,* they had both said, *we don't know who she is or where her parents are.* Because there was no evidence to the contrary, and because Jessica had obviously been well cared for, the social worker had taken their word about what had happened and found a foster home for Jessica immediately.

"I hope the foster family will take good care of her," Mariel said. She had seen the foster mother and father when they had come to pick up Jessica at the Department of Social Services. They had both had kind faces.

"I'll check up on it," Jake said. "I'll be in touch with you."

Mariel managed a weak smile. "Do you suppose they'll find someone to adopt her right away?"

"They'll have to wait until they're sure they can't locate her parents," Jake reminded her.

"If you hear that they're going to let her be adopted, will you let me know?"

"Of course. Any chance you'd want her?"

"If they'd let a single mother adopt her, I'd certainly think about it."

"You know what, Mariel? You think too much."

She got into the car. "Goodbye, Jake. I hope everything goes well with you," she said, in a tone that was too formal by far.

"How can it?" he said, exasperated. "You know how I feel about you."

"I wish you wouldn't try to make me feel guilty," she whispered around the lump in her throat.

"All right," he said.

He shoved his hands down in the pockets of his water-stained red-and-black jacket and stared at her intently, as if that alone would make her stay.

Mariel tried again to picture him in the city, but he looked even more rugged and rough-hewn here, amid the buildings of the town, than he had in the woods.

She concentrated on putting the key into the ignition and starting the car's engine. When she eased out of the parking space, Jake stood back. She managed a brief smile that he didn't return. He watched her until she reached the corner and turned it. She wondered how long he would stand there.

As for her, she was on her way home, to her snug apartment, her friends and her life. Soon the town of Tellurian was behind her, no more than a dot on the map spread out on the seat next to her.

She never remembered what was between Tellurian and Pittsburgh. It flew by in a blur, less real to her than the castle and the time she had spent there.

When she reached home, Jake's message was waiting on her answering machine.

"Mariel, I miss you. When you decide to come back, I'll be here."

She erased the message. Jake was out of her life. Christmas was over. The magic was gone.

Chapter Fourteen

After a lackluster New Year's Eve spent at a boring party, and an equally uninspiring New Year's Day, during which she tried in vain to find something interesting to watch on television, Mariel tried to resume her former life. She spent too many hours sitting at her word processor, elevating the act of staring at her notes on Christmas folklore to a fine art. Writing about the mistletoe shooters seemed impossible; her hastily scribbled jottings made little sense, and her actual memory of the men and boys who had come calling at the castle on Christmas night was vague.

She certainly had no trouble recalling the hours before their appearance, when she and Jake had made love so joyously in the chamber off the gallery. It was easy to picture the glow in his eyes, and the answering passion that had made her urge him closer and closer, until their bodies blended into one. She remembered every moment as if it had been distilled down to its basic elements, clear and crystalline in her memory.

One Saturday in mid-February, with an air of determination, she sat down at her keyboard and typed *The Mistletoe Shooters* at the top of her computer screen. But, as always when she thought about their interlude in the castle, she found herself adrift in visions of making love with Jake. She wondered if Jake found that happening to him, too.

Not that she would ever ask him. He had called a few times, reporting that Jessica was thriving with her foster family, but Mariel had been pointedly unresponsive. When he left messages on her answering machine, she ignored them.

It was just as well that their connection had been broken, and yet sometimes, when she sat down to her solitary dinner, or when she spotted another tall, rugged, broad-shouldered man in a crowd, she felt a sudden, sharp pain in her heart. She had never dreamed that she was capable of missing someone so much.

But she'd better stop mooning over him. Right now she was supposed to be working, not thinking about Jake.

"Mariel, are you home?" called a voice outside her front door. It was Ellie, her friend and neighbor from down the hall.

"Come in, Ellie, the door's unlocked," she called back.

She heard the latch open and close, followed by footsteps clicking smartly down the hall. In a few seconds Ellie appeared in the doorway to her office.

"I brought you a cup of coffee." Ellie deposited a foam cup from the pancake restaurant around the corner onto Mariel's desk.

"Nice," Mariel said, managing a quick smile of thanks.

"It's a bribe to make you come shopping with me," Ellie said brightly. "We can take advantage of all these President's Day sales." Ellie folded herself onto the futon across from Mariel's desk and flipped her dark hair back from her face. She waited expectantly.

Mariel shook her head. "I don't think so, Ellie. Thanks for asking, but—" She gestured helplessly at the array of papers surrounding her. "Too much work to do. You can see what a mess this is."

"Crazy you. It's the weekend, and you should get out. Are you sure you won't change your mind?"

"I appreciate the coffee. It was sweet of you. Why don't you stay for a while and visit?"

"No, if I can't convince you to come along with me, I'll be on my way. I've had my eye on a lacy teddy since Christmas, and I'm hoping it'll be marked down."

Mariel tried to show interest. "Is it that black one that opens down the front? The one we admired in the window of our favorite boutique?"

"That's it, all right. If I buy it, Leo is in for a sexy night tonight. Did I tell you that we've decided to have a baby?"

"No. No, Ellie, you didn't, but I'm happy for you," Mariel said.

Ellie lifted her eyebrows. "You don't *look* happy, sourpuss. What's the matter? Ever since you wrecked your car in that backwater section of Virginia, you've seemed…well, one step removed from what's going on around you."

"It was difficult," Mariel said.

"I know, I know. Spending Christmas in a cave and a run-down old castle sounds awful, especially since it was with some rustic who probably doesn't even speak standard English," Ellie said, "and finding a baby under such strange circumstances must have been *too* awful for words."

"Oh, but Jake wasn't—" Mariel began, but Ellie wasn't in the mood to let her finish.

"Have they found the baby's parents?"

"I don't believe so," Mariel said quietly, inspecting her fingernails.

"Odd. I can't imagine how a baby could have ended up in the woods. Well, like I said, I'd better go before all the bargains are gone." Ellie stood up and tossed her own empty cup into the wastebasket. "What are you working on that's so important?"

Mariel sighed. "I'm hoping to finish writing down some of the stories I picked up in Virginia. A university press is interested in publishing the final manuscript."

"Great. I can't wait to see what you've been up to for all these years," Ellie said. She blew Mariel a kiss before disappearing out the door.

After Ellie had gone, Mariel stared at her empty computer screen for a while. She shuffled her notes. She pulled a loose hangnail off her thumb. The phone rang, but she ignored it. It was probably Ellie again, wanting her to change her mind about going shopping. She didn't intend to, mostly because she couldn't bear to be around Ellie and her happiness these days—Ellie couldn't stop talking about her wonderful husband and her perfect marriage, and now Mariel might as well steel herself to hear Ellie run on and on about the baby she was planning to have.

A *baby*. And after Ellie gave birth and Mariel went to visit, bearing gifts, if would only remind Mariel of Jessica. And Jake, of course.

Of course. After all, what *didn't* remind her of Jake? Somehow, over the past month and a half, Mariel had managed to relate everything in her life to him. She couldn't eat without thinking about the time she had fed him the apple in the cave, when his lips had brushed her fingers. She couldn't sleep without wishing he was curled around her, his legs warming hers. She couldn't do anything, because all she could think about was Jake.

She stood up and wrapped her arms around herself, suddenly chilled. She and Jake had really had something together—and now neither of them had anything. In the face of adversity, in the space of a few short days, they had somehow managed to build a loving, caring relationship—and she had walked away from it.

She was thirty years old. In her life, she had learned that love wasn't easy to find. You couldn't manufacture it, and you couldn't buy it. Love was a gift. And, when it had been given to her, she had been unable to accept it. She must be the all-time fool, the consummate idiot.

She did what she should have done a long time ago. She marched into her bedroom and raked an armful of clothes off the rod in the closet. She pulled a suitcase from the closet shelf and chucked the clothes into it. She scooped underwear from a dresser drawer, cosmetics from the bathroom shelf. It was enough—it was all she would need for her trip to Tellurian.

Because she was going to Jake, now, today, and she wouldn't look back. There would be no more sitting down and eating a lonely dinner for one in her silent apartment. No more daydreaming at work; she'd call on Monday and request an indefinite leave of absence. No more waking up at night and thinking she heard Jessica crying.

Come to think of it, she thought she heard a baby crying even now. She lugged her suitcase into the hall and stopped to listen for a moment, because it was such a faint sound. Finally, she realized that the noise was coming from the street.

She went to the window and adjusted the blinds so that she could look down from her second-floor apartment into the parking lot. The lot was full, but she made out an unfamiliar pickup truck parked in a visitor's parking space.

Snow had begun to fall, making it hard to see what was going on. She didn't see anyone—until a man carrying a baby walked around the pickup.

The man was tall, and he was wearing a navy wool jacket over faded blue jeans and work boots. He was concentrating on the baby, jiggling it in his arms, his head bent down as if he were speaking to it in a low tone. Mariel's heart stopped beating in her chest.

It couldn't be. But it was.

Mariel flew to the door and tore it open, rushing out on the landing as Jake Travis entered the downstairs vestibule and stomped the snow off his boots. She stared at him down the open stairwell until he instinctively looked up. Jessica looked up, too, her mouth open, her eyes wide. She emitted a small hiccup.

"Jake! What—what are you doing here?" Mariel gasped, unbelievingly. Just when she had been going to go to him, *he* had come to *her*.

"I brought a visitor," he said, turning Jessica so that Mariel could see her better.

"But— How? Why?"

He grinned at her, his eyes merry. "Why not?"

"How did you get here?" Her voice was strangled in her throat.

"In my new pickup. Aren't you going to invite us in? It's cold down here."

"I'm sorry," Mariel said as Jake hurried up the stairs, the baby round-eyed with wonder in his arms. Almost afraid to look at them for fear they would vanish, Mariel led the way into her apartment.

When she turned around, she realized that Jake was taller than she remembered, and she had almost forgotten about the bicuspid that overlapped the adjoining tooth.

He glanced at the white walls of her apartment, with their carefully chosen and nicely framed art prints, at the fireplace with its brass screen, at the gleaming hardwood floors. "Nice place," he said briefly, eyeing her suitcase by the door.

"You got a new jacket," Mariel said, momentarily flustered.

"I figured the other one was past saving after I fell in a moat," he said.

"I can't get used to the way you look in this one," Mariel said.

"You'll have to," he said. He hadn't stopped smiling.

Mariel suddenly remembered her manners. "I'll hang your jacket for you," she said.

"Here, you'd better take Jessica. I can manage the jacket." And then Mariel was holding Jessica in her arms again, was pressing her hot cheek against Jessica's cool one, was inhaling the scent of her soft, sweet baby skin. Memories flooded back, memories of her happiness, and she was overcome by a sense of loss.

Jake found the hall closet and hung his coat inside. He wore a red turtleneck under a blue chambray shirt, and he looked wonderful.

"I'd bet Jessica is ready for a diaper change," he said.

"Your turn or mine?" Mariel said through a blur of tears, but she laughed with Jake.

She hadn't noticed the diaper bag when he had first come in.

"This time I have all the necessary equipment. Flubbies," he said, digging deep in the bag and producing a disposable diaper with a flourish. "Something called a puddle pad. And a pacifier. Great little gadget, a pacifier. We should have had one in that cave. It works like a plug. Sure wish they'd make one for the other end of babies. Now, that would be something."

Mariel ignored this. "Jessica has grown so much." She marveled as she laid the baby on the couch. She unzipped Jessica's warm suit and felt the little arms and legs. She couldn't believe that the child was actually lying in front of her, waiting for a diaper change.

"And she eats a lot," Jake said. "She eats cereal now, don't you Jessica?"

For an answer, Jessica blew bubbles.

"I brought a bed for her. She'd probably like a nap," Jake said after Mariel had changed the baby's diaper.

Mariel had all kinds of questions, but they had to wait until Jake went back to the pickup and brought in a portable crib, which they set up in Mariel's tiny office.

Jake spared a quick look at the papers spread over the top of her desk. "Doing lots of work, it looks like," he said.

"Let's go into the living room," Mariel said. "I need to know—I need to know all kinds of things, Jake."

She led him into the living room, conscious of him close behind her. When they sat on the couch, he said, "I saw your suitcase in the hall. Are you going away or coming back?"

She might as well tell him she was planning to drive to Tellurian, that in fifteen minutes more she would have been on the road.

"I was—"

"Because if you're planning to go away for the weekend, you might as well forget it. I have some things to say to you, and I'm going to say them."

"I was—"

"I tried to let you know that I was coming to Pittsburgh this weekend, but you never returned my calls. Now that I'm here, you're going to hear me out, whether you like it or not."

"But I was—"

"Why didn't you call me back?"

Mariel gave up. He had no intention of listening to her—yet. So, first things first. She'd listen. She'd answer questions. And she figured that while she was at it, she might as well be honest.

"I wanted to call you more than once. But it seemed—futile. I thought it would make it all the harder to hear about Jessica and about your life and—well, I was trying to protect myself," she said, hoping he appreciated her candor.

"They haven't found Jessica's parents yet, Mariel. There are no clues, no leads. No one reported a child missing, and no one was seen in that remote area around the time that we found her," Jake said.

"How do you happen to have her?"

"I go to see her every day at her foster parents' house. Sometimes they let me baby-sit. They don't mind if I borrow her for a day or two. But they're going to have to give her up."

"Oh, that's too bad. Jessica seems so happy and well adjusted," Mariel said.

"I'm worried that Social Services won't be able to place her in a home that's nearly as good. I thought—" He stopped talking.

"What, Jake?" she asked gently.

He turned to look at her, golden flecks swimming up from the depth of those deep brown eyes.

"You're coming home with me. We're going to adopt Jessica. We're going to get married."

She felt a bubble of laughter in her throat. The timing couldn't be better. She was already packed.

"I don't want to hear all your reasons why we can't get married. We *can*," he said in a rush.

"I was already—"

"I love you. You love me. We both love the baby. You can't deny it," he said.

Deep within her, Mariel felt a wellspring of love, and hope, and joy. He loved her. She loved him. They both loved Jessica. It was all so simple, so elemental.

"Will you, Mariel? Will you marry me?" As if from a great distance, Mariel watched him reach for her hands, saw him capture them both in his, saw him lean forward and kiss her on the lips. But she didn't feel it. She didn't feel a thing.

"I—I—" she stammered, because even though she had dreamed of such a moment, her dreams hadn't prepared her for the reality of sitting across from Jake Travis and hearing him speak the words.

"I'll always love you, Mariel. When you drove away from Tellurian, I felt like my life was over. I don't want to go on without you. We're a good team. We were happy together with Jessica. So we're going to get married," he finished.

"I was already packed," she managed to say. "I was coming to see you. I was going to leave in a matter of minutes."

He stared at her, then threw his head back and laughed. "Why didn't you tell me?" he asked.

"You didn't give me a chance," she retorted.

"I've got it all planned. You can work on those Christmas legends in Tellurian in my big house, where there's a room that will make a wonderful office for you. We're going to stay in that house, Mariel. It's time to settle down. I can't wait for you to see it. There are four bedrooms, and lots of bathrooms, and a kitchen that I designed myself. And closets, lots of closets. And a large bed that's too big for me. Oh, and a nook off the master bedroom that will make a perfect nursery."

"I don't believe this is happening," Mariel said, her mind reeling. "I don't believe you're saying all these things."

"What do you want? Shall I go down on my knees to propose?"

"No, you don't have to do that," she said, but before the words were out of her mouth, Jake was on one knee in front of her.

"My lady, my love, will you do me the honor of marrying me?"

"Oh, Jake, get up. This feels so ridiculous."

"I'm not getting up until you tell me your answer," he said firmly.

For a split second, she wondered how she could help loving this man. How could she not want to recapture the magic she had found at Christmas and hold it close to her heart all the rest of their lives?

"This might help." Jake fumbled in his pocket and pulled out a sprig of mistletoe. Mariel looked blank. She knew what it was, of course, but what was it doing in Jake's pocket in the middle of February?

"Before I tossed my old jacket in the trash, I checked the pockets, and I found this. I kept it as a memento of

Christmas, the best Christmas of my life, because I found you and Jessica,'' he said.

"But why did you bring it now?" she asked.

"To help us recapture the magic," he said, standing up and pulling her with him. He held the mistletoe over their heads. "How's it working?"

"Kiss me, and I'll tell you," she said, lifting her lips to his.

He did kiss her, slowly and thoroughly, but she didn't tell him anything—at least not with words—until much, much later.

Epilogue

Tellurian, Virginia
The Next Christmas...

"Where do you want to drape this garland?" Jake asked, holding up the strand of evergreen boughs and studying it critically.

"How about on the banister?"

"Let's go see how it looks," Jake said. He paused to restrain the two little hands that were reaching toward the bulbs on the Christmas tree. "No, Jessica."

"Give me a heave up," Mariel said, waving at him.

He clasped her hand and pulled. "Up you go," he said, and, once on her feet, she slid an arm around his waist. "Feeling okay?" Jake asked her.

"Wonderful," Mariel said, smiling up at him fondly.

He patted her protruding stomach. "Can't have our little mother overexerting."

"I'm only five months pregnant."

"Since we think you conceived over the Fourth of July weekend, this baby's going to be a real firecracker."

"Have you ever noticed how holidays play a big part in our love story?" Mariel asked, pressing a hand to the small of her back as Jake measured the garland against the banister.

"Yes, and if we're lucky, maybe the Easter bunny will bring the new baby right after our adoption of Jessica is final." Jake adjusted the garland. "How does this look?"

"Terrific. Leave the garland on the stairs, and I'll tie it on with big red bows. I love the way you refinished the banister, by the way. You exactly matched the shade of the stain we put on the floor."

"I had good decorating advice from my wife," he said, swinging around the newel post and planting a kiss on her lips.

"Dadadada," said Jessica, crawling over to tug at the hem of Jake's jeans, unwilling to be ignored.

Jake bent down and swung her into his arms. "Leave the red ribbon on the steps, and I'll tie the garland on myself later," he told Mariel. "I don't want to take any chances that you might trip on the stairs."

"I walk up and down the stairs every day," Mariel protested. Her new office, where she worked while Jessica napped in a crib with her name carved into the headboard in a cheery yellow-papered nursery, was at the head of the stairs, right next to the master bathroom.

"That's different. Say, isn't it time for me to see those things you've been knitting lately? Why don't you hang our stockings by the chimney with care?" he suggested.

She smiled at him and lifted her eyebrows. "In hopes that Saint Nicholas soon will be there?"

"Hey, Mariel, you don't have to convince me. Santa Claus is real. Last year I finally got a couple of Christmas presents I'd always wanted—you and this little Christmas angel," he said, nuzzling Jessica's neck.

Mariel opened a drawer in the table beside the rocking

chair that Jake had lovingly refinished for her, and she took out a tissue-wrapped package.

"Have I ever told you about looking at the tapestry on the wall of the castle right before we left in the Jeep?" she asked.

"No. Did it look better up close than it did from far away?"

"I thought the tapestries were pretty," she protested.

"I was blinded by your beauty, I guess, because I didn't notice them at all."

Mariel crumpled the tissue paper and threw it at him. "Anyway," she said, moving cumbersomely toward the mantel, "I took a good look, and I saw the unicorn part, and the knights-jousting-in-the-meadow part, and there was one other part that I almost missed. It was something I've never seen in any other tapestry."

"Don't be so mysterious, Mariel. What are you trying to say?"

She kept her head turned as she affixed the biggest stocking, Jake's, to the mantel. "In the last tapestry, the one that was closest to the shadowy corner, there was a depiction of a round little man with a long white beard. He was riding in a sleigh pulled by reindeer," she said carefully.

"This was in a medieval tapestry?" Jake said skeptically.

"I don't know that it was an authentically *old* medieval tapestry, but yes, there he was, looking exactly like the man from the Magic Minimart, looking exactly like—"

"Like Santa Claus," Jake finished for her.

Mariel finished tacking her stocking to the mantel and began to hang Jessica's smaller one. "Exactly," she said.

"I've always wondered about the fact that the castle was

supposed to be owned by a guy named Mr. Nicholas. And I've never heard from him, even though I left my name and address and offered to pay for the food we ate. Mariel, why are you hanging five stockings?''

"For our family," she said carefully, turning so that he could see her figure profiled against the flames in the fireplace.

"Our family consists of you, me, Jessica, and the new baby. That's four people, which equals four stockings," he said.

She slanted a sly look out of the corners of her eyes. "Don't you realize that I'm gaining more weight than most expectant mothers at five months? Don't you know what I'm trying to tell you?"

Jake stared. His gaze dropped to her abdomen, which strained against her perky maternity top.

"Twins?" he said, as if he couldn't believe it. "Are we going to have twins?"

She walked up to where he stood in the archway between foyer and living room, a mistletoe ball suspended above his head. She put her arms around him, including Jessica in their embrace. "Twins," she confirmed, leaning over her stomach to kiss him on the cheek.

"But that's…that's…"

"The very best kind of magic," she said, and she kissed him again.

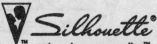

Where love comes alive™

From first love to forever, these love stories are
for today's woman with traditional values.

A highly passionate, emotionally powerful
and always provocative read.

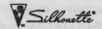

SPECIAL EDITION™

Emotional, compelling stories that capture the
intensity of living, loving and creating a family in
today's world.

INTIMATE MOMENTS™

A roller-coaster read that delivers romantic thrills
in a world of suspense, adventure and more.